Seven Rode Together

JOHN E. CRAMER
Author of No Man's A Mountain

Seven Rode Together

JOHN E. CRAMER

Author of No Man's A Mountain

Mayhaven Publishing

Mayhaven Publishing
P O Box 557
Mahomet, IL 61853
USA

All rights reserved.
No part of this book may be reproduced or transmitted in any form or by any means without written permission from the publisher,
except for the inclusion of brief quotations in a review.
Cover Design by Loren Kirkwood
Copyright © 2002 John E. Cramer

First Edition—First Printing 2002
1 2 3 4 5 6 7 8 9 10
ISBN 1-878044-92-3
Library of Congress Number: 2002 141565
Printed in Canada

For Cheryl, Denise and Tracy

Also by John E. Cramer

No Man's A Mountain

"...injustice will raise its head in the best of all possible worlds, but tyranny we can conquer. Evil will invade some men's hearts, intolerance will twist some men's minds, but decency is a far more common human attribute and it can be made to prevail in our daily lives."

Bernard Baruch

—John E. Cramer—

The seven who rode together that day were brave men. They would be remembered by everyone in the Valley as the "Last Posse From River Bend." These were the seven who rode together:

Mort Kane, owner of the Circle-K. and expert with a rifle.

Thorn Masters, a Texan, an adventurer, especially quick with the lip—and quicker with a .45.

Charlie Kio, Kiowa Indian and a blood brother of Thorn Masters since they were youngsters—equally handy with the .45.

Jeb Hofstader, ramrod at the Circle-K and a long-time friend of Mort whose loyalty could never be questioned.

Chad Youngman, U.S. Marshal, who wore the badge with a keen sense of duty and responsibility.

Jeremiah Dundee, veteran of the Civil War and a latecomer to the Circle-K.

Seth Longlittle, former bounty hunter and gunfighter, a deputy under Chad Youngman.

Chapter 1

The sun was hanging low over the foothills to the west as the two riders made their way along the trail just below the treeline. The lead rider, Thorn Masters, wearing buckskins and a Texas-size Stetson, astride a blazed-face roan, reined up and surveyed the trail ahead. Standing in the stirrups, Thorn pointed to where the trail dropped out of view behind a knoll and reappeared down the mountainside leading to the river. "That's what we've been lookin' for," he said. And then he added, "Tell me what else you see, Kio."

Kio, a scout for the U.S. Cavalry in earlier years, gazed toward the horizon, "The trail leads up toward the timber line on the other side. I'd say we've found the crossing we've been looking for."

"Yeah, and do you know what's on the other side? Oklahoma Territory!"

Kio nodded. "But we got a long way ahead before we get to Amarillo. A good night's sleep and some food in my belly would make me much easier to ride with."

—John E. Cramer—

"Fair enough! And right down below is a good place to bed down."

An hour later, they had supper on the campfire, coffee brewing, and had surveyed the river crossing they'd be making come morning. "What do you think, Kio? Will we be swimming before we reach the west bank, once we hit the current? We could enter upstream about a quarter of a mile, but the bank on the other side is straight up." He glanced at the horses. "Why the hell didn't you strip those saddles when you got the saddle bags and bed rolls? Could be you ain't got used to usin' a saddle yet?"

Kio ignored Thorn's comments. "Guess I'll take a look up river."

Thorn poured another cup of coffee, remembering when he'd first come across Kio—some thirty years ago—the same year Texas was admitted to the Union. A band of Mexican marauders raided a small band of Kiowas camped along the Red River, killing all of the inhabitants except a young squaw and her young brave.

Gil Kneeland and a half dozen cowhands from the Bar-K found Kio and the little brave's mother hunkered down along the river's edge. Thorn's Uncle Gilbert brought them back to the ranch. A year after the war began, Thorn's father, a young Virginia farmer, was killed. His mother, Rachel Lynn, sold out lock, stock and barrel, and with a few personal belongings returned to Texas with Thorn to live with her brother. From that day on Thorn and Kio considered themselves blood brothers.

Thorn sat before the fire as darkness closed in around the campsite. He didn't know what Kio could make out at this time of night, but he knew better than to question his friend's judgement.

—Seven Rode Together—

There were just too many times when Kio's instincts had saved his tired—

Thorn's thoughts were interrupted at the sound of footsteps coming down the trail. In the next instant, two men stepped quickly into the opening. The young man held a Winchester pointed directly at Thorn's stomach. Using the barrel as a pointer, he motioned Thorn to move away from the fire.

"You two lookin' for somebody?" Thorn asked. "Whoever you're lookin' for ain't here."

"He is now!" Kio said as he stepped out in the open behind the old man. The boy dropped his Winchester and slowly raised his hands above his head. The old man raised his arms much faster.

"We wasn't aimin' to do you no harm, Mister. Honest. See for yourself. That Winchester ain't even loaded."

"But mine is!" Kio drawled as he stepped up behind them and relieved them of their sidearms.

"He's right," the old man began, "We wasn't aimin' to hurt nobody. We're just lookin' for somethin' to eat. We ain't et nothin' for three days."

The boy nodded. "When we saw the smoke from your campfire, we thought we'd come on in and ask you to stake us to some grub—"

"You sure as hell got a curious way of askin'," Thorn cut in. "What were your plans if Kio hadn't got the drop on you?"

"See," the old man said to the kid, "You damn near got us both killed."

Kio, who'd picked up the Winchester, checked the chamber and let out a whoop. "Well, I'll be damned. This rifle ain't loaded."

Walking around from behind the old man and the kid, he

—John E. Cramer—

handed the rifle to Thorn. "You two can put your hands down. Ain't nobody holdin' a gun on you now."

The old man extended his hand. "I'm Jeremiah Dundee. Sit down, boy."

The Union Army uniforms they were wearing got Thorn's attention. "You two still in the Army, or ain't you had time to buy any new outfits?"

"We was mustered out a couple of months ago after President Hayes decided the Reconstruction Period in the South was over. All the Federal troops were pulled out. My twenty-year hitch was over and Tommy only had a couple of weeks left on his enlistment. We didn't have no place special to go, so we just headed further West."

"Why west?" Thorn asked.

For one thing neither of us ain't never been west of the Mississippi. And since my company Commander invited me to come see him if ever I needed anything, I thought I'd take him up on his offer and see if he was of the same mind."

"What about the kid?" Kio asked. "He got the same invite?"

"Not exactly, but I figured the Colonel won't have no problem findin' work for both of us. He owns the biggest cattle ranch in Kansas."

"That so?" Thorn asked. "Just where's this ranch located?"

The old man was more interested in the kettle of stew hanging over the fire than he was in their conversation. "It ain't too far from a place called River Band." He bared a toothless grin. "I think I could do a better job jawin' with you fellers if you're aimin' to let us have a man's helpin' of that stew while we're still healthy enough to enjoy it."

—Seven Rode Together—

Thorn eyed the old man for a moment and then he slipped Kio a quick wink. "Well, Kio, do you think these two Yankees, after they get their strength back, might want to try again to bushwack a couple of Jeb Stuart's finest?"

Before Kio could reply, the old man, quick to grab the irony of Thorn's question, answered in kind. "That ain't gonna happen, 'cause these two Yankees learned a long while back that you never bite the hand that feeds ya."

The boy chimed in. "And that ain't all this Yankee has learned. You're never gonna get a free meal from a couple of strangers wearin' buckskins when you try it with unloaded rifles. My name's Tommy Trinity," he said. It was a firm and friendly handshake.

"Now that we've cleared the air as to who the hell is who," Jeremiah exploded, "Let's eat. I'm hungry enough to eat a plow horse, harness and all."

An hour later the full moon slipped behind a cloud and everyone seemed content to relax and listen to the night creatures with the sound of the river always in the background. Jeremiah pulled out a tobacco pouch, filled a black-stem pipe and lit it.

It was Thorn who broke the silence. "How did you fellas figure on gettin' to Kansas with no supplies?"

"We had enough supplies to last us a couple of weeks when we left Little Rock. But just about sundown, one helluva storm hit us. It was lightnin' and rainin' so hard, you couldn't see the trail more than a few feet ahead. Anyway, a lightnin' strike hit a tree right behind us. It spooked the horses. The pack mule, with all our supplies, yanked the lead rope loose, reared up, and damned if he didn't just disappear. We figured he was headin' back to Little Rock."

—John E. Cramer—

He paused and took a long draw on his pipe before he added, "We was hopin' we'd find another tradin' post to get more supplies, but we ain't seen nothin' the past three days. Nothin' 'til we saw the smoke from your campfire."

"When we ride out in the morning, you and the kid can come along. There's a tradin' post up-river about a day's ride. It's owned by a fellow named Dutch. His wife, Bertha, and their six kids run the store. That's a square shooter. He came to the tradin' post two, maybe three, four years ago after he lost his spread up near River Bend.

"River Bend!" Jeremiah interrupted. "The Colonel's ranch is around there somewheres. You headin' for Kansas, too?"

"Nope. Me and Kio are headin' back home—back to Amarillo, Texas. And if the good Lord's willin' and the creek don't rise, come fall we might be pushin' cattle again."

"Right now I'm sayin' that if we all don't get some sleep, we ain't goin' to make it to the Turtle Creek Tradin' Post by sundown tomorrow."

Jeremiah and Tommy stood up, stretched and headed up the bank to find a place to bed down.

Kio and Thorn headed in the opposite direction. When they reached their bed rolls, Thorn turned to Kio. "You thinkin' what I'm thinkin'?" Kio nodded. Both spread their bed rolls, pulled off their boots, slipped their .45's from their holsters, and pulled their blankets up over their chests.

The night passed without incident, except for Kio's frequent trips to relieve himself.

"Some people can't hold their liquor," Thorn grumbled. "but you can't hold just three or four cups of coffee."

—Seven Rode Together—

By late afternoon the next day, they had come down out of the mountains and picked up the trail away from the river. They were about a mile or so from their destination when they pulled up to watch four riders headed from the southwest and riding hell-bent-for-leather toward the trading post. Three of the riders went inside. A fourth, a bearded, beady-eyed, swarthy character remained outside with the horses. The animals were heaving and sweaty.

Thorn reined his horse to the right of the four tied to the hitchrail. Kio went left. Both dismounted, secured their horses and stepped up on the boardwalk, sandwiching their quarry in between them. "You comin' or goin', Mister?" Kio asked the man.

Before he could answer, the barrel of Thorn's .45 came down on the man's head. Kio caught the limp body and lowered it gently to the boardwalk. "Keep an eye on him, Jeremiah," he said.

Inside, three men at the bar, all wearing sombreros, turned quickly to see Thorn and Kio standing in the doorway. A balding, bespectacled bartender stood in front of the open cash drawer. Two men standing in the middle of the room reached for their guns. Two shots were fired and both men pitched forward, sprawling on the floor. The third man, wearing a patch over his right eye, froze with his right hand hovering over the butt of his gun. For a few seconds, he sized up the two strangers in the doorway.

"Make up your mind," Thorn said. "Either use it or take it out real slow and put it on the bar." Once the gun was placed on the bar, Thorn added: "Now on the floor, belly down." The shifty-eyed bandit dropped to his knees.

Thorn holstered his .45 and walked to the bar where Kio joined him. "You can come up from under the bar now, Barkeep. The shootin's over."

—John E. Cramer—

Slowly, wide-eyed and his glasses dangling from one ear, he stood, looking first at the three bodies on the floor and then at the two strangers at the bar.

"Now that we're back in business," Thorn began, "We'll have two glasses and a bottle of your best whisky—after you put that cash back where it belongs—"

"Make that four glasses" Jeremiah yelled as he and Tommy burst through the doorway. Ignoring the three bodies, they bellied up to the bar.

"What about our friend outside that you're supposed to be keepin' an eye on?" Thorn asked.

"He ain't goin' nowhere. Tommy and me got him hog-tied and tethered, and he ain't twitched a muscle since you pole-axed him."

Before Thorn could reply, the door to the back room swung open. A man dressed in a business suit and holding a shotgun stepped through. Before they had time to react, a voice behind them ordered, "Put your hands on the bar," followed by the clicking of the hammer on a .45. "Now, with your left hand, all of you, unbuckle your gun belts and let 'em drop." After the last gunbelt hit the floor, they heard, "Now turn around."

Standing behind them were two men, one wearing a U.S. Marshal's badge and the other Thorn recognized. "Well, Dutch, how long do we have to stand here like a couple of skinned rabbits hung out to air?"

"It's alright, Marshal, that's Thorn Masters from the Bar-K ranch and the other one wearing buckskin is Charlie Kio, that's Thorn's short version of Kiowa. Now, the other two I don't know, but, if they're with those two, they're clean."

—Seven Rode Together—

The Marshal holstered his gun. "Now, that the reunion is over," he began, "maybe somebody can tell me what the hell happened here?"

Before either of them could speak, Dutch interrupted. "I almost forgot, this is U.S. Marshal Jacob Q. Devlan. If you get to know him well enough, he might let you call him Jake."

"The one outside," the Marshal began anew, "One of yours? Or theirs?"

The balding bartender related in anxious starts and stops, how he was in the storeroom to replenish supplies for the bar when three men, now lying on the floor in front of him, were waiting at the bar. "The shorter one, as you can see, is wearing an eye patch. He ordered me to empty the cash drawer into a saddle bag. The next thing I knew, while I was at the cash drawer, two men dressed in buckskin stepped in and I heard gunfire. I dived under the bar and didn't stand up until I heard someone ordering the three on the floor to put their guns on the bar." Sweat ran down his face.

When he finished, the Marshal stepped closer to the three lying face down on the floor and nudged the one nearest him with the toe of his boot. "Alright, on your feet."

"I'm afraid you're wastin' your time on these two," Thorn said. "Old shifty eyes, who's been playin' possum all this time, is the only healthy one left. As I recall," he added, "the last time he was standin', he was havin' trouble gettin' his gun out."

The man staggered to his feet. He had a crooked grin on his face as his black eyes took the measure of Thorn. Then, reaching down, he picked up his sombrero and set it on the back of his head.

One look at the man standing before him and the Marshal began shaking his head. "You're either the fastest man with a gun

—John E. Cramer—

this side of the Rio Grande or the luckiest man alive. Friends, this is Buck Farley. He's wanted by every lawman in both the Oklahoma and New Mexico Territories and for all I know, he might be wanted in Kansas and the State of Texas, too." He paused, staring at Farley's right hand. "Let's have a look at that hand." Farley, who never took his eyes off Thorn, raised his hand, palm up, toward the Marshal. The fingers were swollen twice their normal size and a fresh knife wound cut across the base of the forefinger to the heel of his hand.

The Marshal continued his explanation on the gunman who was now his prisoner. "He's got to know every gun slinger and hired gun in the country. We've always managed to get those who ride with him, but this'll be a red letter day for everyone in the territory, because until we can clean out his kind, the Oklahoma Territory ain't got a snowball's chance in hell ever gettin' Statehood."

Dutch, who had been looking at the bodies of the other two lying on the floor, called out, "Jake! Over here and take a look. Now, these two I know from my days in Kansas—near a town called River Bend. They're the Koehler brothers, Trout and Sam."

"You sure about that?"

"I'd never forget those two. I'd know 'em anywhere."

"That accounts for those inside," the Marshal said. "Have any idea who that hombre is that they got hog-tied outside? When we get 'em back to Powderville, I'll see if we've got any paper or wanted posters on 'em."

"You ain't thinkin' about takin' all four of 'em to Powderville by yourself, are you, Jake?"

"Why not? You're forgettin' there's two that ain't gonna cause any trouble."

—Seven Rode Together—

"Well, if I was you I'd want a square meal and a night's sleep before I started. You can bed down at my place and the two prisoners who are still healthy can be locked in the supply shed behind the Trading Post. How's that strike you? We might even be able to swap a few stories." Dutch paused. "I've been meanin' to ask you, what the hell are you doin' out here in the first place?"

"I've been trackin' those four since they tried to hold up the Powderville Bank two days ago. They didn't get any money but they killed the cashier and damn near killed Luke Tabor's oldest boy when he tried to stop 'em. You might know him. He's the one that always carries that Bowie knife his grandpa carried fightin' Mexicans down in Texas. One of the holdup men was kneelin' in front of the safe the cashier had opened. He must have tried to ward off the kid's knife, missed a grab at his arm and grabbed the blade instead. Luke told me the guy was wearin' an eye patch, I knew it had to be Farley. So, I guess you might say Luke saved Thorn Master's life."

Dutch smiled. "Maybe so," he said, "but I wouldn't want to bet on it. It could be Luke saved Farley's life."

They locked up the prisoners, ate a home-cooked meal, accepting the hospitality of Dutch and his wife. Missus Van Huss had excused herself and gone to bed. After she had left the room, Jeremiah was first to open the evening's conversation. "Dutch, I've been wantin' to ask you about River Bend ever since we got here, but with all that's happened, there wasn't a lot of time. Thorn tells me that at one time you worked a spread outside that town. That's where me and Tommy are headin'. Not bein' familiar with these parts, what's the best way of gettin' there?"

"Just keep followin' the river upstream to Copper's Corner

—John E. Cramer—

and head due west across the flat land and you'll come to River Bend. You could just keep followin' the river but it'll take two, maybe three more days." He paused, and then as an after thought, "You know folks in River Bend?"

Jeremiah nodded, "I served with him durin' the war—name's Burkhalter, Felix Burkhalter." Dutch's back stiffened. He sat quietly while Jeremiah rambled on. "—he was my commanding officer—told me to come and see him—offered me a job on his ranch."

"When did you last hear from him?" Dutch asked.

"Not since the war ended—"

"Well, then, you might be in for a surprise. He may not have a job to offer. Friends of mine have been keepin' me posted on what's been happenin' in River Bend since your commanding officer, judgin' from the uniforms you're wearin, had to be a Blue-Belly, cheated me and a lot of other ranchers in the valley out of our homes usin' his crooked land deals—bribin', blackmailin' and threatenin' all the honest folks in the valley."

"That don't sound nothin' like the Colonel Burkhalter I rode with durin' the war." Jeremiah protested.

Conversations among the others in the room stopped. After a moment of uneasy silence, Jeremiah, mulling over what he'd just heard, but still needing to know more, continued, "You were sayin' I might be surprised, and the Colonel might not have a job to offer. You sure about that?"

Dutch nodded his head. "That is, unless the governor gives him a pardon. And that ain't likely since he's gonna be tried for murder. Right now he's the guest of the town. He's in jail waitin' for his trial to begin sometime next month."

—Seven Rode Together—

"Next month?" the Marshal questioned. "Why's it taken so long? Anybody in Oklahoma Territory charged with murder and found guilty in Judge Sam Barton's court in Powderville would be meetin' his maker the next day. He might wait a day or so to carry out the hangin' if he thought it would attract a larger crowd."

Thorn, who had been sitting quietly on the far side of the room, gave Kio a nudge. "You wonderin' what I'm wonderin'?" Kio nodded.

"You got a question, Thorn?" Dutch asked.

"Well—ah—yeah, I gotta question. Kio and me were just wonderin'. Who's this Colonel 'sposed to have killed?"

"A feller named Kane, Steve Kane. He owned the Circle-K Ranch. Actually, his place bordered mine until Burkhalter put me out of the ranchin' business. Steve left a couple of months before I did. When the war was over, I got mustered out before him. Anyway, I never saw him again. When I got back, the Sheriff, another upstandin' citizen on Burkhalter's payroll, met me at my place and served me with foreclosure papers, claimin' I hadn't been makin' my mortgage payments. Martha and the kids had already been evicted and they was stayin' with Alec and Mary Johnson in River Bend. Alec owns River Bend's only general store. We moved here just about the time the war was over."

When he heard the name "Kane", and while Dutch rambled on, Kio muttered, "You thinkin' what I'm thinkin'?"

Thorn nodded. "This Steve Kane. Did he have a brother named 'Josh' livin' in Kentucky?"

"If he did, he never told me."

"Did he ever say what outfit he was joinin' up with?"

"Now, that he did tell me." Dutch replied. He was aimin' to

— John E. Cramer —

join with Captain Jeb Stuart who was under Brigadier-General Joe Johnston's Command."

Before Thorn or Kio could say a word, the Marshal interrupted, "If you folks are gonna fight the war again, I'm turnin' in." He pointed at Thorn and Kio. "And the rest of us better turn in." Looking directly at Thorn and Kio, he added, "Especially you two!"

"What's so special about us?" Kio asked. "Do you know somethin' we don't? Don't keep us in suspense, Jake. Or don't I know you well enough to call you 'Jake'"

Jake's face lit up and he broke into a broad smile. "Settle down, Kio. You're actin' as jumpy as a preacher in a bawdy house. Since you and Thorn are headed for Amarillo and Powderville is on the way, I figured you two could help me ride herd on those two we got locked in the supply shed—"

"How 'bout those two blue-bellies?" Kio asked. "They ain't aimin' on settlin' down here, you know."

"Now, hold it. Hold it, just a damn minute," Jake warned. "Jeremiah and the kid are headin' for River Bend. So, come mornin' they'll be headin' north. We'll be headin' west—"

"Then it ain't got nothin' to do with that little fracas Kio and me got into a couple a summers back in the Longhorn Bar?" Thorn asked. "Those three saddle tramps were the sorriest losers in a poker game we've ever met. And, that ain't all. Kio and I paid our part for bustin' up the place—"

"No," Jake began. "But you can be damned sure, now that you mention it, I'll check with the owner before I hand over any reward money—"

"Reward money?" Thorn blurted. "You mean?"

—Seven Rode Together—

"Exactly," Jake replied. Jeremiah and Tommy, who had been about to head for their bed rolls when the Marshal announced he was ready to turn in, suddenly became more interested in what was about to be disclosed, than getting a good night's sleep.

"There's a five-thousand dollar reward on Buck Farley—dead or alive. The others I'll check on when we get to Powderville."

Thorn let loose with a loud whistle and slapped Kio on the back. "That's more money than we're goin' to get on our next cattle drive. That's more than twelve-hundred bucks apiece."

Jeremiah looked puzzled. "Me and Tommy, we didn't have nothin' to do with the shootin' or capturin'."

"What's that got to do with anything?" Thorn asked. "We were ridin' together. Besides, both of you will have enough money to buy yourselves some first class duds when you get to River Bend—"

"Might have enough left over," Kio chimed in, "to treat yourselves to a good meal, a hot bath, a night on the town. And who knows what else? Jake will get in touch with the Sheriff at River Bend. You'll be able to pick up your reward money there."

Dutch and the Marshal were already headed upstairs. Jeremiah and Tommy headed for the barn. Thorn and Kio decided they'd like to bed down closer to the supply shed where they could keep an eye on their money. They selected a grassy plot under a giant oak tree and spread their bed rolls.

They both stretched out, arms folded behind their heads, and gazed at the blanket of stars overhead, with just a sliver of the moon peeping from behind a cloud. A slight, cooling breeze rustled the leaves overhead and from somewhere behind them an owl made

—John E. Cramer—

his presence known. Thorn broke the night-time spell. "Kio."

"Yeah."

"You sleepin'?"

"Nope, just thinkin'. Mostly about that Colonel your friend Dutch was talkin' about. He must have a mean streak in him a mile wide when he's appropriatin' property. Sounds like the one who was leadin' that band of Yankee cutthroats your Ma told us about when your Pa was killed. They made off with all the livestock and then stole everything in the house that wasn't nailed down, even that picture of the Shenandoah River scene your Pa painted."

"Guess we'll never know." Thorn replied. "Looks like these past two years have been a bust. At least I got to see the old home place again. I remember Ma sayin', when she found out I wanted to make this trip to find the men who killed my Pa. 'Even if you was to find out who killed your Pa, it won't change anything. What's done is done, and what will be, will be.'" Thorn's voice trailed off and for the next several minutes only the rustle of leaves disturbed the quiet.

Kio broke the silence. "There's one thing we found out tonight we'd never known about if Dutch hadn't got started on that Burkhalter feller the way he did and mentioned the name 'Kane'. At least Steve made it through the war. I remember his brother Josh got it in the third raid we carried out tryin' to befuddle those damn Yankees on the Manassas plain."

"You know what I'm thinkin'?" Thorn began.

"I know exactly what's on your mind. We need to make a trip to River Bend to see this Yankee Colonel who's accused of killin' Steve Kane, one of Stuart's finest. Right?"

"Right!"

—Seven Rode Together—

By sunup the next morning, the Turtle Creek Trading Post was a beehive of activity. The Marshal wasted no time getting the bodies of the Trout brothers tied down across their saddles and both Farley and the fourth member of the gang secured on their horses. He mounted his horse, and looking back at the others standing in front of the Trading Post he yelled, "You comin' or are you gonna talk Dutch's ear off? I'd like to make it to Powderville before sundown." He watched as Thorn and Kio shook hands with Dutch.

"When we get to River Bend, Dutch, we'll be sure to look up your friend at the general store and let him know you and your Missus are doin' fine."

They turned and headed for their horses just as Jeremiah and the kid stepped out of the Trading Post. As Thorn and Kio mounted up, Jeremiah said, "We been talkin' it over. And if what your friend told us last night about the Colonel bein' in jail waitin' trial is true, Tom and me were wonderin' if we could ride along with you?"

"Fine with me," Thorn replied. "Only we're headed for Amarillo."

"But you did say your uncle would be headin' up a cattle drive and you'd be headin' toward River Bend."

"That's right," Thorn grinned. "Now, don't tell me you two want to sign on for a cattle drive."

"Maybe they're thinkin' we'll keep all that reward money," Kio said.

"Hells-fire," Jeremiah fumed. "We ain't worried about no reward money. Me and Tom were hopin' we might land a job. True, we ain't never been on any cattle drive but we're both ready to learn."

—John E. Cramer—

"What do you think, Kio?" Thorn asked. "If they can't herd cows, maybe Old Bonaparte could use them with the chuck wagon."

"They won't be doin' anything at the Bar-K if they don't get some different duds in Powderville."

"And we won't be gettin' to Powderville before next week," the Marshal bellowed, "if we don't get movin'!"

It was a few shades before sundown when they reached the outskirts of Powderville. With Marshal Devlan in the lead, and Thorn and Kio bringing up the rear, they moved slowly down the main street. The few residents standing on the boardwalks on either side took a quick look at the small caravan and disappeared inside the business establishments for a moment. They reappeared with more spectators. As the riders passed the courthouse, a stocky built man wearing a dark suit, a white broad-rimmed hat and smoking a big black cigar, fell in step with the Marshal's horse. When the Marshal dismounted at the hitchrail in front of the jail, hauling the two prisoners down from their horses and hustling them up on the boardwalk and into the jail, the man followed.

Thorn and the others trailed behind. When they reached the door, they paused to look back at the gallows with four hangman's nooses nearly built. As they stepped inside they heard the stocky-built man with the big cigar questioning the Marshal.

"What happened to the two that you got draped across their saddles?" Before the Marshal could reply, he added, "I told you to bring 'em back alive!"

"How'd you know I'd be bringin' 'em back at all?"

"You've never failed me before."

"Well," the Marshal drawled, "I might have failed you this

time if it wasn't for those men behind you. When I reached the Turtle Creek Tradin Post, they already had 'em disarmed and hogtied."

Thorn and Kio had managed to slip behind Jeremiah and Tom and reset their Stetsons a notch or two lower on their foreheads. "Gentlemen," the Marshal continued, "this here's Judge Sam Barton. He's the only law in the whole damn territory."

The judge, straining to get a better view of Thorn and Kio, rubbed his hand across his chin. "Don't I know you two?" Before either could reply, he nodded his head as if answering his own question. "Now I remember. A little more than a year ago. I remember you were wearin' buckskin when you helped wreck the Longhorn Bar." Satisfied he was right, he said, "I never forget a face. Now, I'd like to hear your version of what the Marshal just told me. And it better be good or I just might have to charge all of you with murder."

"That won't be necessary, Judge," the Marshal said. "I got sworn statements from two witnesses both signed by the bartender and the owner of the Tradin' Post."

"Then I suppose you'll be tellin 'me next that they ought to be paid the reward money?"

"That's the way I figure it," the Marshal replied.

"I'll have to think on that 'til morning", he said. "Get the undertaker over here to take care of those two outside. And keep a close eye on those two you got locked up back there." And looking directly at Thorn, he added, "And you two. Don't leave town. We'll be havin' a trial for these two the day after tomorrow and I'll be expecting all of you to testify." He turned and headed for the door. "And Marshal, I'll need to talk to you first thing tomorrow morning."

—John E. Cramer—

"You heard what the Judge said. While I'm takin' care of these prisoners, why don't you boys head on over to the hotel and I'll meet you there for supper. You can get your horses stabled for the night. Don't worry about payin' anybody. Tell 'em I'll take care of it. I'll take it out of your reward money."

"If there is any," Kio mumbled as they headed for the door. "Wouldn't surprise me none if the old fart didn't come up with some trumped-up charge just so he wouldn't have to pay us that reward money."

He was still mumbling as they moved outside, slipped the reins from the hitchrail, mounted and the four of them rode down the street past the only blacksmith shop in Powderville to the livery stable at the end of the street. "See that they get proper feedin' and a good rubdown, Pedro," Thorn said. They all dismounted and yanked their saddle bags.

"Why is it?" Kio asked, "that every Mexican boy you see is always a "Pedro?"

"Take a breath, Kio!" Thorn cut in. Turning to Jeremiah who was grinning from ear to ear, he added, "Why don't you and Tom head on over to the hotel and make sure we have a place to bed down for the night. And grab those saddle bags and take 'em along with you." Nodding toward Kio, he added, "Me and Big Chief Windbag got some unfinished business over at the Longhorn Saloon."

"What kind of unfinished business?" Kio asked as they headed through the swinging doors.

"I figured we both could use a couple drinks to wash down the trail dust before supper."

The bartender had just finished pouring their second round

—Seven Rode Together—

when two lean, cowpokes stepped up along-side Thorn. He noticed they didn't appear to be as interested in having a shot of whiskey as they were in the poker-playing patrons seated at the tables around the room. He watched them scanning the room, curious about their clean-shaven faces and the outfits they wore—a few cuts above what an ordinary cowhand could afford. He was satisfied his hunches were correct when the taller of the pair leaned across the bar and asked, in a voice loud enough for Thorn to hear, "Seen anybody lately dressed in Yankee uniforms? One's wearin' long sideburns and a white beard and his partner is a slender kid about your size?"

The bartender shook his head, "Nope." he said, "ain't seen nobody fits that description. And I've been behind this bar since we opened this mornin'." He paused and then asked, "friends of yours?"

"You could say that," was the reply.

Thorn toyed with his glass, bending slightly forward as if he were contemplating something. Without taking his eyes from the glass, he said, "Somethin' tells me those two dudes may have some unfriendly business."

Kio mumbled, "They're headed this way. It's either them or us."

Thorn eased his chair back and stood up. "Evenin' gents. You two lookin' for a little action?"

They stopped a step or two from the table as Kio got to his feet. "Nothin' like a friendly poker game to take a man's mind off his troubles."

Before Thorn or Kio could speak, the Marshal came through the swinging doors, looked around the room and spotting Thorn, he headed toward their table. "Well, now," Thorn said as he broke into a broad smile, "here's the Marshal. Maybe he'd like to join us."

"Some other time," the taller dude said. They turned abruptly, brushed by the Marshal and disappeared through the swinging doors.

"Where the hell are they headed in such a big hurry?" the Marshal asked.

"Maybe they don't like playin' poker with the law." Thorn grinned. "Sit down, Marshal, I'll buy you a drink. That is, if Kio can afford it."

Ignoring Thorn's invitation, Devlan said, "I've got a hunch those two are workin' for one of those private detective agencies, like Pinkerton, who sell their services to anybody to track down outlaws they'd like put away. They have a problem in this territory where there's a damn good chance some of those they're huntin' might put them away."

"They didn't appear to be overly friendly," Kio said. Stifling a yawn, he added. "Best we be headin' over to the hotel, Marshal. Me and Thorn ain't had supper yet."

"Don't forget," the Marshal cautioned. "Tomorrow morning, nine o'clock. You boys be in my office. I should have the authority by then to issue a bank draft so you boys can pick up that reward money at the Powderville Bank."

They watched the Marshal until he disappeared through the swinging doors. "You thinkin' what I'm thinkin'?"

Kio nodded. "We'd better find out what Jeremiah and the kid have done to cause those two buzzards to come lookin' for 'em."

"That's part of it," Thorn agreed. They began moving toward the entrance. "We'd better be watchin' our backs once we get past those swingin' doors. Those two shifty-eyed dudes seemed

—Seven Rode Together—

mighty interested in talkin' to us until the Marshal arrived."

Once outside they headed down the boardwalk toward the Rock Creek Hotel. Just as they reached the alley that led to the rear of the Longhorn Saloon, two men stepped into the darkness.

At the Powderville saloon, further down the street, Thorn and Kio stepped quickly into the alley and watched as the men mounted their horses and headed west out of town.

"Now where do you think they're headed?" Thorn asked.

"Wherever they're headed," Kio replied, "they didn't seem to be in any hurry."

Thorn agreed, and before they'd taken a dozen steps, he said, "Maybe we'll be watchin' our backs all the way to Amarillo."

Jeremiah met them as they entered the hotel. "What kept you so long?" he asked. "That must have been a powerful lot of business you had to take care of at the Longhorn."

"Where's the kid?" Thorn asked.

"I sent him over to the Longhorn to see what was keepin' you. We'd gone ahead and et but we're a might short on cash."

"You won't be after tomorrow morning."

"Hey, there you are!" Tom came running across the street. Ignoring both Thorn and Kio, he took Jeremiah by the arm and pulled him aside. For several minutes he talked close to Jeremiah's face, with his back to Thorn and Kio.

Kio was eyeing them both with more than casual interest.

Jeremiah turned to Thorn, "Maybe I just ain't as hungry as I thought I was—"

"Is that a fact?" Thorn said. "Seems you lost your appetite awful quick. It wouldn't be because of a couple of dudes that the kid spotted at the Longhorn, now, would it?" Thorn continued.

—John E. Cramer—

"Let's go eat. And you can start worryin' again tomorrow when we hit the trail for Amarillo. The two men the kid saw at the Longhorn rode out of town. They were headin' west."

By the time the four of them had finished supper and returned to the hotel, Jeremiah, having already witnessed a demonstration of the professional use of .45's back at the Trading Post by both Thorn and Kio, decided, if they met those dudes on the trail again, their chance for survival had improved. "Before we turn in, Tom and I want to clear the air about those two he spotted tonight in the Longhorn. We wasn't exactly truthful about how we lost our pack mule and our supplies back there in the Ozarks. There wasn't any storm or thunderin' or lightnin' that spooked that mule, but there was one helluva shootout with some hombres that tried to bushwack us on the trail. It was two of them that Tom spotted tonight at the Longhorn. We'd stopped along the trail to give our horses a breather when we spotted a small waterfall and a mountain stream off the trail about twenty yards. We grabbed our canteens and rifles and headed up the slope for water and were headed back when we spotted them. They spotted us about the same time and opened fire. The kid and me dived behind the rocks and returned fire. It was kind of a Mexican stand-off for a couple of hours. We winged one of 'em. And those two, the ones Tom saw tonight, must have decided they wasn't gonna smoke us out. They rode out of there takin' our mule and all our supplies with 'em." He paused, looking first at Thorn and then at Kio. "And that's the God's truth."

"And you got no idea who they were or why they opened fire?" Kio asked.

Jeremiah shook his head.

"Looks like you must have had somethin' they wanted,"

—Seven Rode Together—

Thorn said. "And they must not have found it in the supplies that mule was totin' or they wouldn't still be tailin' you."

Although Thorn was thinking Jeremiah wasn't telling the whole story, he decided to wait to pursue it. "Well, gentlemen, we've all got an appointment with the judge in the morning. I suggest we all turn in and take advantage of a good night's sleep in a bed."

"Not a bad idea," Kio agreed. "We're gonna be spendin' five more nights on the trail before we git to Amarillo."

After the others had left the room and Thorn had turned in, he began to mull over all that happened since Jeremiah and the kid had joined up with them. He always returned to the same question. Outside of murder or a bank robbery, he thought, what could Jeremiah and a kid done that those two dudes were after? He reasoned it would have to be something mighty personal since they weren't soliciting any help from the law. Of course, it could be that lawmen, especially in the Oklahoma Territory, didn't take too kindly to bounty hunters.

The next morning, both Jeremiah and the kid came out of the town's only general store wearing some new outfits from top to bottom. Kio looked them over. "You two look more like humans again in those civilian duds. It's a good thing you decided to get rid of those Yankee outfits, at least now those cowhands at the Bar-K won't begin shootin' at you when we ride in." They urged their horses into a gallop.

By noon the following day, they were well on their way to Amarillo. Each of them twelve hundred dollars richer because of the reward money doled out to them without a hitch by the teller at the Powderville Bank.

The five days on the trail proved to be uneventful, but on

—John E. Cramer—

the sixth day, they arrived at the metal arch at the beginning of the quarter-mile lane leading up to the ranch house that notified all that passed under they had reached the Bar-K Ranch. Thorn pulled forward in the saddle. "Grazing land," he noted.

They rode past the bunk house, and up a lane toward a vine-covered veranda that stretched the width of a two-story house.

His thoughts were interrupted by Kio, "Nothin's changed since we left a year ago. What do you say we take a closer look?"

Nudging their horses out of a walk and into an easy canter, they pulled up to the hitchrail. Before they could dismount, the front door flew open and running down the stone walk toward them was a young woman wearing a Buckskin skirt followed by a woman with slightly graying hair. Behind them strode a tall, muscular man with a gray handlebar mustache and a black Stetson pushed back on his head. "Before you squeeze each other to death, come in the house!" Jeremiah and Tom were still in their saddles. The tall man noticed. "If you're waiting for an invitation, you might be sittin' there the rest of the day." He held the door open. Jeremiah and Tom quit their saddles and hustled up the walk. Shaking hands with them as they paused at the door, he said, "Welcome to the Bar-K, gentlemen. I'm Gil Kneeland. You boys arrived just in time. We were just gettin' ready to sit down to dinner. And you all better eat all you can handle because beginning tomorrow morning we're all going to be real busy around here. We got about three weeks left to round up about three-thousand head of cattle and head 'em north to Wichita."

"Can't we enjoy our dinner before you start planning the next cattle drive?" Martha Kneeland asked. "For goodness sake, Gil, the boys just got home. Let 'em enjoy it awhile before you start talking business. And, maybe, if you stopped talking, they just

—Seven Rode Together—

might have a few stories they'd want to share with us."

Following dinner, the ladies retired to the living room while the men ambled outside. They seated themselves under a giant Sycamore. Jeremiah filled his pipe and striking a match, he lit Gil's cigar before lighting up himself. "Me and Tom are mighty grateful to you, Mister Kneeland, for takin' us on. We ain't had any experience herdin' cattle. But we'll do our damnedest to earn our keep."

"Well, like I said," Gil replied, "we got three or four weeks to get things lined up. That'll give you enough time to get acquainted with my foreman and the rest of my boys. They're the best bunch of cowhands in the State of Texas."

"So where's Donovan now?" Thorn asked.

"He and a couple of the boys rode into town this morning. They had some business to take care of. Mike's going to check the telegraph office to find out if we got any messages from Mort Kane. He's the owner of the Circle-K. We cut a deal earlier this year to hold the herd over a week or so on his range to get 'em in shape for marketing before we take 'em on in to Wichita, a two or three day trip from River Bend. And we wanted to get a confirmation from him that the deal's still on."

"Seems to me you settled that when you made the deal."

"We did. But about two weeks ago he wired me that something had come up, but he'd confirm our deal in plenty of time for any arrangements I'd want to make. He didn't elaborate on what had come up that would make him pass up a chance to make some real money. But," he added, "it'll work out. I'm not going to lose any sleep over it. Now, what about your trip back east? Did you find out anything more than what you already know about your Pa's killer?"

—John E. Cramer—

Thorn, intent on what Gil was saying, looked toward the bunkhouse, avoiding Gil's steady gaze. He said nothing for several moments. "No! But I'm glad I made the trip. I did what I had to do."

"I know how you feel, Thorn, but after all—"

"No. No. You don't know a damn thing about how I feel."

"Well, maybe not," Gil agreed. "No more than I could understand why you were so all fired up to join the Confederacy. I knew most of those in Texas felt it was their duty. But I was like your Pa. Ben never had a slave. Didn't believe in it. He just wanted to be let alone. Let them that believed in ownin' slaves do what they believed they had to do. When the shootin' started, him and the rest of those Virginia folks were smack-dab in the middle of it. Ben, like some of the other farmers in that neck-of-the-woods, were hopin' they could just sit-it-out. But it didn't happen that way. Those cowardly, cutthroat renegades killed Ben and stole everything they could lay their hands on. It's a miracle you and Martha weren't killed."

For several quiet moments, Thorn, like a man in a trance, sat perfectly still, staring out over the vast range. He was remembering that day and the face he'd sworn never to forget. It belonged to the Union officer who was shouting orders to the others to round up the livestock, when his Pa stepped out onto the porch. His Pa never cleared the front steps before the officer fired. He was dead before his body hit the ground.

"You're right, Uncle Gil. But there's a man out there, somewhere, some place, that may one day wish he'd killed that scrawny kid when he had the chance." He stood up. "Let's ride into town. I'll buy you a drink. I got a hunch you're gonna hear from that Circle-K owner, Mort Kane."

Chapter 2

It was a hot, sultry August afternoon in River Bend with the temperature hovering a notch above the 100-degree mark on the over-sized thermometer displayed for public viewing outside the entrance of the newspaper office, across the street from the courthouse. Inside, the editor-publisher of *The Valley View*, Clancy O'Riley, sat at his desk cluttered with stacks of latest editions, books, documents and assorted notes he'd scribbled over the past several days. He had just returned from the courthouse where he had spent the day covering the opening of the murder trial of one of River Bend's oldest, and up until three weeks ago, most respected and honored citizens—Colonel Felix Burkhalter.

O'Riley, a lock of red hair hanging over his forehead, pushed his high-back leather swivel chair away from his desk, and with his feet on the desk, locked his hands behind his head and gazed out the window toward the townspeople who were still gathered in small groups in front of the courthouse. He was thinking about the day's events which had ended with the announcement by

—John E. Cramer—

Judge Ely Storm that "this court will stand in recess until Monday morning at ten o'clock." Immediately, the courtroom was a din of conversation as the spectators crowded together and moved in unison toward the entrance. O'Riley remained seated until all had departed. He was hoping he might get the opportunity to question some of those who had more at stake in the outcome of the trial than merely personal curiosity. It seemed to him the defense attorney got all the unsolicited support he needed from Judge Storm in selecting the jury to hear this case.

"This just might be a trial," O'Riley mused, "where the prosecution may find themselves battling a stacked deck, if the final outcome depends on Judge Storm's rulings."

Whatever the outcome, he thought, things will never be the same in River Bend. The killing of Steve Kane, the original owner of the Circle-K Ranch had occurred three years before. And although not everyone in the valley appeared to be satisfied with the Colonel's explanation, the incident was quickly laid to rest when the sheriff supported the Colonel's claim that Kane had been rustling cattle belonging to the Colonel. There were those in the valley also who needed no evidence. The fact that Kane had served in the Confederate Army was enough to satisfy them. It was no secret that Colonel Burkhalter had made enemies in the valley. There were ranchers forced into financial deals with him and found themselves unable to pay off loans when they came due. Yet, there were many more who were beholden to the Colonel for his vision to make a trading post of forty years ago into a prosperous and still-growing town of River Bend. He was one of the first to settle in the valley when Kansas was still a territory and had continued, because of his wealth and influence, to become the town's best known benefactor.

—Seven Rode Together—

Both before and after the war, the Colonel attracted professional people from the East to come to River Bend by promising financial help to get them relocated. In fact, Clancy remembered, it was the Colonel he'd met during the war when he was a fledgling reporter for the *Boston Review*, who had offered to help him start his own newspaper in River Bend. "This war won't last forever," the Colonel had said. "You should be thinking about owning your own newspaper. You'll never make any money working for the other fellow."

"You got somebody in mind?" O'Riley had asked. "Who's planning on selling a newspaper?"

"Who said anything about buying a newspaper? I'm talking about starting your own. You look to me like the kind of a man who has what it takes to start his own business. In fact, I got just the place in mind where an intelligent, enterprising fellow like you would fit in just fine."

"And where might that be?" Clancy had asked.

"Why, my town, of course. River Bend, Kansas. It's a growing community that could certainly use a newspaper. A good one, of course," he'd emphasized.

"Well, now, Colonel, you make it sound mighty interesting. But at the moment I'm a wee bit short of greenbacks to finance such a venture. And when this war is over—"

"When this war is over," the Colonel interrupted, "and you are seriously considering this opportunity, you let me know. I'll personally see you get the financing you need to put you in business."

And for the first time since their conversation had begun, Clancy realized the Colonel was dead serious about getting a newspaper in River Bend.

—John E. Cramer—

His thoughts were interrupted when he heard, "Clancy! Clancy! Where you hidin'?" That voice belonged to Jeb Hofstader, the ramrod at the Circle-K Ranch. A fiery, leathery-faced, bandy-legged cowhand who seemed always to have an opinion on anything that ever happened in the valley.

Before Clancy could remove his feet from the desk, Jeb was coming through the office door. "Hold it. Stop right there," Clancy said calmly. "Now, take a deep breath and slow down. You look like you're about to pop a blood vessel. Why all the yelling? Pull up a chair and let's hear what you're so all fired up about."

"You call yourself a newspaper man. Why ain't you over at the Silver Dollar listenin' to what common folks are sayin about what went on at the courthouse this afternoon? There ain't one person on that jury that's not beholden to old man Burkhalter for somethin' or other from the first day they set foot in River Bend 'cept maybe for Bert Tolliver, and I ain't too sure about him."

"What's this have to do with all your yellin'?" Clancy asked. "Why would I be interested in what they're doing at the Silver Dollar?"

"For one thing there's two strangers willin' to bet five dollars to one that the Colonel ain't goin' to be found guilty of nothin'. And there ain't nobody in their right mind that's gonna give them that kind of odds, lessen they know somethin' more than what happened in that courtroom this afternoon."

Clancy nodded. "Well, Jeb, I could use a wee bit of Irish whiskey right now. So, let's mosey over to the Silver Dollar and I'll let you buy this time."

"Me buy?" Jeb snorted. "I can't remember anytime when you ever bought anybody a drink. Anyways, I'm headin' out to the

—Seven Rode Together—

Circle-K after I check at the telegraph office for Mort to see if we've got any word yet from Gil Kneeland. Mort's needin' to know if he's plannin' to hold his herd at the Circle-K on his cattle drive he's headin' up down around Amarillo this fall."

Still smiling, Clancy watched as Jeb stomped out of his office. He paused at the door and looking back over his shoulder, "Mort wanted me to tell ya, if you can, drop out to the ranch Sunday, he'd like to talk to you."

Once Jeb had disappeared outside, Clancy turned back to his desk and plopped down in the swivel chair. "Mort Kane," he muttered, wondering why he didn't show up at the courthouse today. He, more than anyone else in the valley, should be the most interested in this trial. After all, he's the one who came to River Bend three years ago, almost a year after Steve Kane was killed, to inherit his uncle's ranch. Matter of fact, Clancy remembered, Steve's killing had been settled and forgotten by most everyone in River Bend after the Colonel explained that Steve had been caught red-handed stealing some of the Colonel's prime steers. The matter had been old news until Mort Kane and his young son, Joey arrived in River Bend. Mort, he recalled, seemed nearly obsessed with Steve's death once he learned Steve had been killed by the Colonel's son, Duane. The Colonel's foreman, Jim Arkus, and Sheriff Taylor had gone to the Circle-K to make an arrest.

Since the first day he arrived in River Bend and discovered the Circle-K ranch house had been burned to the ground, that lanky, broad-shouldered Kentuckian had been a thorn in the Colonel's side and Clancy's number one topic for the newspaper.

Mort Kane had arrived in River Bend as a stranger, so most everyone in the valley thought of him as an outsider. This was a nat-

—John E. Cramer—

ural reaction for some because his Uncle Steve had been a cavalry soldier in the Confederate Army. Ranchers and some of the townspeople took a wait-and-see period before they made up their minds toward the man who had inherited the Circle-K. Probably the only person in the valley who embraced Mort's friendship from the start was Jeb Hofstader. After his first encounter with Mort, Jeb knew he'd met the one person who might question Col. Burkhalter's motives, and his influence and power over everyone in the valley.

"Here's the way I see it," Jeb declared, "The Colonel's the biggest rancher in these parts because he's helped most of the business people get started. He even hand picks the sheriff, the mayor, and is closer than two yolks in an eggshell with the governor, but it don't give him the right to do anything he dang well pleases. Why nobody else is hardly entitled to an opinion lessen it's his—like he's a king—ya see? And he expects everybody to kowtow to his opinion about what's good for all of us, don't ya see? Now Mort figures different. He figures the Colonel's sovereignty in this here valley ends where Mort's nose begins—don't ya see?"

Jeb's early observations, Clancy now realized, had become a prophecy of things to come. Many of the town's leading citizens had paid the ultimate price. And the Colonel, although still a person to be reckoned with, would learn his fate at the end of the trial that had begun on this day.

"It remains to be seen what the future holds for the Colonel, his son, Paul, who wants to become a doctor, and Nora. Despite the hostile situation between Mort and her father, I'm pretty sure she's fallen for Mort. I hear he knows how she feels, and pretty much feels the same, but any thoughts about a future for Mort and Nora are on hold, and that could be t—it's a damn, sad situation."

—Seven Rode Together—

There was little doubt in Clancy's mind that the Colonel might be guilty of a good many things, but he seriously doubted the Colonel could ever be found guilty of killing anyone. If there was one thing he wasn't, it was a gun fighter. However, his oldest son, Duane, had proved he was probably the fastest man in the territory with a six-gun until a couple of weeks ago, when he was killed in a gun fight with Mort Kane, who never carried a gun but who could shoot the eye out of a squirrel at a hundred yards with a Winchester. The versions of how that gunfight occurred depended on the person telling the story. There were no witnesses since the Koehler brothers, Sam and Trout, who had supposedly been there when it happened, jumped bail and left town.

Following that shootout on the Circle-K alongside the river, the Koehler brothers had high-tailed it back to River Bend. They told Sheriff Taylor that Mort had ambushed Duane. "Shot him in the back," Trout reported, "after we spotted him branding some of the Colonel's yearlings." But Clancy also heard what the Koehler brothers failed to tell was that during the fire fight, Duane had shot Mort's son, Joey. Clancy remembered when the sheriff brought Mort and Doc Milburn into town in Doc's rig. Doc had been at the Circle-K to attend to Joey wound. The Sheriff wasted little time getting Mort in jail and notifying the Colonel that he had the man who'd shot his son. What happened inside the jail from then until sunrise the next morning, only Mort, Taylor and a bounty hunter named Seth Longlittle know.

The one thing Clancy and the other townspeople knew was that after a lynching mob formed in the street outside the jail, the biggest gun battle River Bend ever saw broke out after someone in the mob opened fire on those inside. Those waiting for a lynching

— John E. Cramer —

began diving for cover when Mort opened fire with a Winchester. Nobody knew where he got it.

When morning came so did the U.S. Marshal from Wichita, Clint Thurgold, and the damndest, biggest posse Clancy had seen for a long time. He remembered it didn't take long for Thurgold to round up the ring-leaders, including Sheriff Taylor, the Colonel and the Koehler brothers.

In the weeks following the "Shoot-Out at the River Bend Jail," as Clancy had headlined his story, other information had surfaced. It pretty much tied the Colonel into the killing of Steve Kane three years before.

Clancy's job hadn't been easy trying to separate fact from fiction. But there was one thing his thirty years experience in the newspaper business had taught him. There was much more to the story than the fight between Colonel Burkhalter and Mort Kane.

Chapter 3

The morning sun was peeking over the foothills burning off a hazy morning mist hanging low over the fields surrounding the Circle-K. A slight breeze rustled the branches of the giant sycamores lining the north side of the ranch house. Inside, Mort and Jeb were finishing breakfast.

"Like I was sayin'," Jeb was saying, "it ain't hardly likely that Colonel Burkhalter is goin' to get what ought to be comin' to him if Judge Storm and that jury has anything to do about it. Even that old tightwad, Clancy O'Riley, didn't seem one bit interested when I told him about those two strangers at the Silver Dollar that was tryin' to get folks to put up money that the Colonel wouldn't be found guilty. There weren't no takers."

Mort sat quietly listening to Jeb's views as to what transpired on the first day of the trial, but he was thinking about Nora Burkhalter and her brother, Paul. She had ignored the Colonel's orders to stay away from the Circle-K. Over the past three years, they had become more than close friends, and she had been like a mother to Joey, who'd never known his own mother. Mort had kept pictures and told Joey about her, except to tell him that his mother had left them for a river-boat gambler.

"You ain't been listenin' to a single word I've been sayin'." Jeb said, shoving his chair back from the table. "I'm tryin' to tell you that the Colonel's not gonna serve one day in jail when all this legal mumbo-jumbo is over. If you think about it, old Judge Storm didn't waste any time a'tall settin' bail for him and those no good Koehler brothers, even after the Marshal told him that they oughta be locked up until the trial." He paused long enough to see that Mort still wasn't going to respond, and then began again. "If you're worryin' about Joey, we both know he's gonna be just fine. You recollect Doc Milburn sayin' he'd be good as new in a few weeks. Course he's been wearin' that sling Nora fixed up for him. But it ain't slowed him down very much. Matter o' fact, he's been pesterin' me for the past few days to go fishin' with him."

"Does he ever ask you about Nora?" Mort asked.

"Don't sell that boy short, Mort. He's hurtin' same as you. Same as me. Same as all of us about what's happened. And, truth known, Nora and her brother, Paul, are both tryin' to figure out why all this had to happen like it did."

"Yeah, Jeb, you're probably right. But I can't help thinkin' if we'd never come to River Bend, the Colonel wouldn't be in the fix he's in and Nora and Paul wouldn't be—"

"Wouldn't be what?" Jeb cut in. "I was wonderin' when you'd get around to figurin' you was responsible for old man Burkhalter's problems. You know better than anybody that he had his own problems long before you arrived." He paused long enough to light his pipe and mumbled, "Seems I smoke more matches than

—Seven Rode Together—

I do tobacky. 'Member when you first laid eyes on this place? I do. There weren't nothin' here 'cept the chimney and that old heatin' stove. And we found out who done it. Then a year ago we lost our whole crop of wheat when the Colonel had your field set afire. All this happenin' 'cause you wouldn't sell the Circle-K to that old buzzard. And that ain't all. That gunslinger son of his, Duane, would of killed you a long time ago if he could have caught you when there wasn't any witnesses, whether you was wearin' a gun or not."

Mort knew what Jeb said was true. He also knew it was less than a month ago that he and Joey surprised Duane and the Koehler brothers while they were branding Burkhalter cattle with Circle-K irons in an effort to convince other ranchers in the valley that Mort was a cattle thief. Only this time Mort was armed with a Winchester repeating rifle. During the short-lived fight, Joey was shot, and he'd killed Duane—

Mort's thoughts were interrupted by Jeb. "I plumb forgot to tell you, I wired Gil Kneeland down there in Amarillo that we were lookin' forward to seein' him when he comes through River Bend on his cattle drive." He paused, trying to recall the second thing that he was going to tell Mort.

Before he could remember, someone from outside yelled, "What's a feller have to do to get a cup of coffee around here?"

"That's it," Jeb said, "Clancy O'Riley! I told him you'd like to see him today, but I didn't invite him for breakfast."

The door opened and Clancy stepped inside. "Top of the mornin' to you." Glancing at Jeb, he added, "I can tell by lookin' at you, Mort, that you didn't know I'd be callin' on you. I might of known Jeb didn't have a memory any longer than his thumb. I told him yesterday that I'd be acceptin' your invitation to ride out and

—John E. Cramer—

visit a spell this morning."

"Why you old coot," Jeb cut in, "we wasn't expectin' you to be ridin' out here before civilized folks finished eatin' breakfast. Wouldn't surprise me none if you went over to the Silver Dollar after I left your office yesterday and stayed 'til they closed and got such a snootful of that Irish whiskey your missus locked you out of the house—"

"If you can be quiet for a spell," Clancy said, "I came all the way out here to talk to Mort."

"Pipe down Jeb. Pull up a chair, Clancy. What's on your mind?"

"You were right about those two strangers trying to hustle some bets on the outcome of the trial. And they may know something we don't. I figure you were right about that too. But there's one thing more I learned last night. Those two have been hired by the Colonel and are beddin' down at the Burkhalter Ranch. One thing sure, they're not just a couple of ordinary, run-of-the-mill cowhands."

Jeb leaned back. "I told you so."

"They were dressed better than any cowhand I ever saw, and the hardware they wore wasn't the kind you'd see on cowhands to shoot rattlesnakes or turn a stampede. I'm guessing they're guns for hire!"

"You don't 'spose," Jeb blurted out, "that the Colonel's fixin' to get even with Mort by havin' a couple a hired guns go after him?"

Mort listened to Clancy's story without so much as raising an eyebrow.

Jeb sat up straight, "You see, Mort, that's the one thing I told you the first time I laid eyes on you and seen you wasn't totin'

—Seven Rode Together—

a gun. A man in these parts has got to learn how to use a gun if 'n he wants to stay alive. Now there's these two gun slingers that the Colonel has up and hired and I'd be—"

"Duane Burkhalter carried a gun, and now he's dead, Jeb. I'm still not convinced I need to be carryin' a gun. Duane made the mistake of not being able to choose the time or the place."

Jeb nodded. "You're right about that, Mort. But you're forgettin' something. If what Clancy is tellin' you is true, and those two hombres the Colonel's hired are hired guns, they're not goin' to wait around to have witnesses, and they ain't gonna be particular about how or when they're gonna be killin' you. The best advice from now on is that you'd better be watchin' your back."

Clancy didn't take his eyes off Mort. Jeb's was a fair appraisal of what Mort was up against. "Jeb's right, Mort. He's not right often but he's right about this. One thing that doesn't figure, though. Everyone in the valley knows you don't wear a gun, yet, some are getting up a campaign to run you for sheriff."

Mort shook his head. "A waste of time, O'Riley. Who knows about it besides you?"

Looking like he'd been caught red-handed dealing from the bottom of the deck, O'Riley avoided Mort's steady gaze.

Jeb chuckled. "If you're listenin' real close, Mort, you can hear his brains rattlin' around in that empty head o' his tryin' to think of somethin' to say."

"Well, actually," Clancy began, "there is going to be an election."

"That don't sound to me like folks are stampedin' to get Mort elected. If what you've been tellin' us about those two hired guns workin' for the Colonel is true, then they oughta be thinkin'

—John E. Cramer—

about hirin' somebody like Wyatt Earp over there in Tombstone."

"I'd agree with that," Mort said.

Clancy, thankful the conversation had gotten back on track, asked Mort, "Maybe not Wyatt Earp, but it would take somebody who's handy with a gun. I'm not sayin' he'd have to be too quick to use it, but people knowing he could handle himself in any situation would command respect. You know what I mean? I mean, look what happened with Duane Burkhalter. You took things into your own hands when you had to. I don't believe that story spread around about you rustling cattle."

"You reported it."

O'Riley looked away.

"I know exactly what you mean. Matter of fact, now that we seem to be serious about this, I might have a candidate for the job. I'm not sayin that he'd take the job, understand?"

Mort had their attention. Even Jeb suddenly became more interested in listening than talking, but Mort changed the subject.

"I had Jeb ask you to come by today because I got a letter the other day from Dutch Van Huss. And I thought you'd be interested. There's maybe even a story for *The Valley View*—"

"Sure," Clancy said, "I remember Dutch. He had a houseful of kids, didn't he? I really felt sorry for Dutch the day the Colonel called the mortgage on his place. He sold him out, lock, stock and barrel. I never did hear where he went when he left River Bend."

"He left Kansas. Went across the border into Indian Territory. He's runnin' a tradin' post near the Arkansas River."

"That's the story you have in mind?"

"I heard the Koehler brothers wound up at Dutch's Trading Post set on relieving Dutch of some of his money. But, instead they

—Seven Rode Together—

got themselves killed."

"Killed?" Clancy blurted. "You mean Dutch killed 'em?"

"No. Not Dutch." Mort said. "The fellow who did may be a candidate for the sheriff's job. His name is Thorn Masters. He works for Gil Kneeland. Gil owns the Bar-K ranch down near Amarillo. I met Masters a couple of years back when Kneeland held his herd over on Circle-K grazin' land before pushin' on to Wichita. He's plannin' on doing the same thing this fall."

"So, what about this Masters fellow?" O'Riley was anxious to know more. "Is he a gunfighter?"

"Nope," Mort said. "Not a professional, if that's what you mean. Thorn caught the Koehler brothers and a third partner by surprise. He hadn't even pulled his gun. The Koehler brothers both drew on him and he killed them both. Their partner decided not to go for his gun."

"Masters could be what River Bend needs," O'Riley agreed.

"We're gonna need something. And after what happened in that courtroom yesterday, I'm not sure the Colonel's ever going to see the inside of a jail cell."

"We'll see," Mort said. "We'll see."

"That we will," Clancy agreed. He stood up and looked at his watch. "I best be getting back. I still got a paper to put out. I'll keep it in mind, Mort, about this Masters fellow. I think I'll spring it on the members of the Town Council." He walked to the door. "We've been missing you and Joey at church the last three Sundays."

Jeb answered. "We got a lotta things that need doin' right here at the Circle-K, me and Mort."

—John E. Cramer—

"No," Mort began calmly. "You won't be seein' us this Sunday or any Sunday." He was thinking about Les Finfrock and Doc Milburn, killed three weeks earlier. It was his best guess Clancy hadn't seen the Burkhalters in church for the past three weeks, either. He wanted to ask but instead he added, "You'll most likely see Joey. He stayed the night at Ebert Youngman's place. Joey and Ebert's boys went fishin' yesterday over around Settler's Creek, and me or Jeb will be pickin' him up after church tomorrow."

"That's right," Jeb said, "I forgot—"

For the next few minutes, Mort stood looking out the window watching Clancy get in his buggy. He watched until the buggy topped a slight rise and disappeared. He was remembering his shoot-out with Duane Burkhalter and the following fire fight at the River Bend jail.

Jeb started to break the silence but decided now was not the time to ask Mort anything. Without saying a word, he got up from the table, grabbed his hat from the peg near the door and slipped out.

Mort remembered when he and Joey arrived in the valley. He knew nothing about how his uncle had died. In his first meeting with Les Finfrock, Recorder of Deeds for the valley, Mort learned his uncle had been killed in a shootout. It was Finfrock who also told him that the Colonel was interested in buying the Circle-K. However, Finfrock had hedged, Mort thought, when he'd asked who'd killed his Uncle Steve. Instead, Finfrock had told him, "If you want to know about that, ask Sheriff Taylor. That's his department. The word is that he was shot when he was caught stealing the Colonel's cattle."

From the beginning, Mort was convinced Finfrock, Doc

—Seven Rode Together—

Milburn and most everyone in River Bend knew much more than they were willing to disclose. Everyone he talked with was beholden to the Colonel, except for the one man who'd been his uncle's closest friend, Jeb Hofstader. It was Jeb who had named Duane Burkhalter as the man who had killed his Uncle Steve, adding, "and Steve was no cattle rustler!" But he had been a member of Jeb Stuart's Cavalry. That didn't make him too popular with most folks in the valley. That ain't to say Steve didn't make friends. But the Colonel sure as hell wasn't one of 'em and he could make life miserable for anyone who was." It was then that Mort knew he would never rest until justice was served. But he never counted on becoming a trusted friend to the Colonel's youngest son, Paul, or that he would fall in love with the Colonel's only daughter, Nora.

Nora, especially Nora, he thought. There were so many things about Steve's death and even the death of Nora's mother, Emily, that she would learn before the Colonel's trial was over.

Mort couldn't know how much either Nora or Paul knew about all the sordid events leading up to his uncle's death. And all, including the murder of her mother, were the result of the Colonel's driving ambition to acquire the Circle-K and rid the valley of yet another Reb, Steve Kane.

One thing was certain, everyone in River Bend and in the valley knew Mort Kane had killed Duane Burkhalter. Some, no doubt, believed the Koehler's story that Mort had ambushed Duane and shot him in the back while the three of them were inspecting Burkhalter cattle that carried blotched Circle-K brands. Few of them had not heard the true account of Duane's death. Nor had they heard that Joey had been shot. The plan, he was certain, had been concocted by the Colonel to get rid of Mort for good.

—John E. Cramer—

Although he'd never told Nora he loved her, she knew. She also knew Mort and her father could never be friends.

And now, Mort thought, how could any woman love a man who had killed her brother and would be the prosecutor's witness in the upcoming murder trial of her father?

For the first time since coming to River Bend, Mort was wishing he'd never inherited his uncle's ranch because Mort knew the agony and despair his actions had brought to both Paul and Nora Burkhalter. Nothing he could say or do would ever change that.

Chapter 4

Only a few of River Bend's dedicated church goers, this Sunday morning, were going directly inside. They chose, instead, to linger in the churchyard, visiting with those gathered together in small groups, discussing the main topic of the day: the trial of Colonel Burkhalter. Most were not so concerned about the outcome of the trial as they were in the events of the past several years that had led to the fateful gun battle at the River Bend jail.

"Sheriff Taylor should never allowed that to happen." Fred Findley, owner of the town's livery stable, ventured. "If he'd had any guts, he'd broke up that mob that was hell bent on a hangin."

A man standing next to him added. "The way I heard it he got locked up in his own jail. I'd like to know why the Colonel was so anxious to break Kane out of jail in the first place. He sure as hell wasn't goin' nowhere."

"You're forgettin'," someone countered, "it was Kane who killed the Colonel's son. I was there when Sam Koehler told him it was Kane who done it. Sam and his brother, Trout, saw the whole

—John E. Cramer—

thing—" The man continued. "Too bad they decided to leave town right after they posted bail. Makes it kind of hard to verify the facts. Anyway, if Kane shot Duane in the back, like they say he did, then who shot Kane's son? Mort sure didn't do it. Makes a feller kinda wonder who shot at who first."

Before anyone else could speak, someone whispered, "Here comes the Colonel now." As if it had been rehearsed, suddenly the talking stopped as the Colonel, followed by Nora and Paul, came up the walk leading to the entrance of the church.

The Colonel moved slowly up the walk a step ahead of Paul and Nora and stopped momentarily to pass the time of day before speaking to the ladies. He touched the rim of his white Stetson and greeted the men with a firm handshake. The Reverend Frank Cordier, formerly of Boston, had come to River Bend at the urging of the Colonel's wife, Emily. And as an added incentive 'to spread the Gospel and do God's work', The Colonel had promised he would make certain that a church and a home would be waiting for them when they arrived. "River Bend is a friendly, law abiding town," the Colonel had said. "And Emily and I are certain both you and the missus would feel right at home in River Bend in no time at all."

Now, as they approached the church doors, The Reverend extended his hand. "It's good to see you again, Felix. We've missed you the past few weeks." And, shaking hands with Paul and Nora, he smiled broadly. "Paul, so good to see you. You still planning to become the first doctor in the Burkhalter family?" Paul nodded. "And Nora may be returning to Boston with me to continue her music career."

Nora spoke quickly "We won't be leaving until the first of the year."

—Seven Rode Together—

Before the Reverend could reply, Chad Youngman, who had bell-ringing duty, began tugging at the rope inside the foyer of the church, signaling to all who had not yet entered that the morning's service was about to begin. The churchyard emptied quickly. The Reverend lingered at the door. He noticed two young boys standing at the far end of the path. He motioned for them to come in, "Joey Kane and Steve Youngman. Come join us. Maybe Chad and I can join you on that fishin' trip you're planning. You know the *big* catfish never start biting until after church is over."

"I didn't hear the bell," Joey said, entering the church.

"Me neither," Steve echoed.

"We'll just have to make sure Chad rings it louder next time." The Reverend smiled and added, "But if you're still of a mind to go fishing this afternoon, my offer still stands."

The congregation opened the service with a vigorous rendition of *Onward Christian Soldiers*. Steve and Joey, seated in the front pew, sang louder than most. They were thinking so hard about the fishing trip, they remained standing after the others were seated. When the Reverend opened the Bible and began to speak, the audience tittered and they dropped to the seat, both stealing sidelong glances at one another.

The Reverend continued, "Two younger members of our congregation and I talked briefly about what I have selected for the topic of this morning's sermon." He paused for a moment.

Joey nudged Steve with his elbow. "He's talkin' about us," he whispered.

Without turning his head, Steve whispered, "Wonder who told him? Chad?"

Joey nodded.

—John E. Cramer—

The Reverend, suppressing a smile, continued. "I should like to read now the topic for this morning's sermon taken from Matthew, Chapter Four, verses eighteen through twenty." He glanced quickly in the direction of Joey and Steve and began to read. "And Jesus, walking by the Sea of Galilee, saw two brethren, Simon called Peter, and Andrew, his brother, casting a net into the sea, for they were fishers. And he said unto them, 'follow me, and I will make you fishers of men.' And they straightway left their nets and followed him."

He closed his sermon exactly thirty minutes later, with the words, "Our Heavenly Father, we pray this morning for the families who mourn the loss of their loved ones, Milton Milburn, Leslie Finfrock and Duane Burkhalter. We pray thou will be with them during these darkest hours of their sorrow and grief both now and in the days to come. And we pray that thou will bestow upon those who in the days ahead will be judged, and upon those who will sit in judgment, the teachings of our Lord, Jesus Christ. Amen."

Outside the church, Jeb watched for Joey from the seat of the buckboard as the congregation poured out of the church into the bright sunlight. He watched as Nora Burkhalter emerged with the Colonel and her brother, Paul. Jeb watched as Joey spotted Nora standing at the foot of the steps.

Nora broke into a smile and motioned for Joey. She began talking. Joey, listening, kept nodding his head. Jeb saw her bend down and kiss Joey on the cheek, carefully slipping an envelope into his pocket, and together they walked toward Jeb's buckboard.

"Where's Pa?" Joey asked as he climbed up on the springboard seat alongside Jeb.

Jeb tipped his hat. "Morning Miss Burkhalter. He had some

chores to tend to," he muttered to Joey.

"Good morning Jeb." Nora caught Joey's eye and patted her pocket."

"Giddiup!" Jeb called to the team, and they headed out of town toward the Circle-K.

Neither spoke for the first mile or two. Finally, Jeb broke the silence. "Saw you talkin' to Miss Nora when you came outa church."

Joey nodded.

"What was it she gave you?" Jeb asked, without taking his eyes off the road.

"I ain't supposed to tell," Joey replied.

"Oh. Well, then," Jeb stammered. "I sure wouldn't want you to tell anything you ain't supposed to tell." He waited for awhile, thinking Joey might change his mind. When Joey remained silent, it didn't seem natural. Jeb knew from past man-to-man talks that when Joey wasn't talking or asking questions, he had something bothering him. "You're mighty quiet. What's on your mind? Forget about me askin' about what you and Miss Nora was sayin'—"

"That wasn't nothin', Jeb. But what about hearin' other folks talkin' and they don't know you're hearin' 'em. Would that be somethin' you wouldn't want to tell?"

Jeb screwed up his face and rubbed his fingers through his whiskers as he always did when Joey asked questions that might be better answered by Mort. "That's goin' to take a heap of thinkin' on my part especially since the folks you're hearin' don't know you're hearin' 'em. Now, if a feller was to hear folks talkin' about killin' somebody or robbin' a bank, he'd be needin' to tell the sheriff. But if what he's hearin' when folks are just gossipin' about other folks,

— John E. Cramer —

then, don't ya see, you're liable to stir up a heap o' trouble for some folks when you ain't sure what you heard was just gossip' 'stead of the truth?"

"But they wasn't talkin' about other folks. They was talkin' about me and Pa."

"You and your Pa?" Jeb echoed. "Well, now, that's a horse of a different color. What in thunder could they be sayin' about you and your Pa?"

"Last night I heard Mister Ebert talkin' to his wife sayin' he was sorry for me and Pa 'cause I didn't have no Ma." Joey hesitated for a moment. "Do you think the Colonel will ever let Miss Nora marry Pa after all this trouble between us and the Burkhalters?"

Jeb wanted to say that he probably had the answer to his question in the envelope he was carryin' home to give to Mort. Instead, he replied, "I sure can't answer that. That's up to your Pa and Miss Nora."

A few minutes later they turned into the lane leading up to the Circle-K ranch house. Spotting two horses tied to the hitchrail, Joey pointed. "Look, Jeb, Pa's got company!"

"Sure 'nough looks that way," Jeb agreed. Pulling the team to a halt, he sat staring at the two horses. "Well, what ya know. Looks like Mort's company are ridin' horses carrying the brand of the U.S. Cavalry. And more to himself than to Joey, he added. "I wonder who in thunder they might be. And what business they got with Mort?"

He snapped the reins and the team continued on toward the barn. They stopped just outside the stable and Jeb hopped down. "Let's get these horses unhitched and watered, Joey, and then, you can get 'um settled. I'm goin' to check some gear I got stowed in the bunkhouse."

—Seven Rode Together—

Inside the bunkhouse, Jeb lifted the shotgun from its resting place above the door, stepped outside and watched as Joey led the team into the barn. Once Joey was out of sight, Jeb made a bee-line to the rear door of the house. Gently, he eased the door open. From the front room, he could hear Mort talking. "I'd like to hear more about how Dutch and his family are getting along with their new life. It ain't always easy to pull up stakes and start all over in a new place. Joey and I found that out when we came here from Kentucky."

Jeb pressed himself against the wall, listening and watching.

Mort crossed the room to look out the window. "Joey and Jeb should be gettin' home any time now. If you ain't in any big hurry, we'd be proud to have you stick around and have dinner with us."

Before the visitors could reply, Joey burst through the back door and saw Jeb motion for him to be quiet.

"Where's everybody?" Then noticing the shotgun cradled in Jeb's arm, he added. "What are you doin' with a gun?"

"Joey!" Mort yelled from the front room. "Come on in here and meet these folks. Bring Jeb along with you." Before Jeb could react, Mort added. "Jeb, you can clean that shotgun another time."

"Joey," Mort began as they stepped into the room, "I'd like you to meet these two gentlemen." As Jeb appeared, he added, "And this is my partner here on the Circle-K, Jeb Hofstader."

"We're all partners," Joey added, eager to set the record straight.

"Well, partners," Mort smiled. "I'd like you both to meet Jeremiah Dundee and Tom Trinity. They came up from Amarillo where they've been staying with Gil Kneeland. Matter of fact, Jeb, they got some good news for us. Kneeland will be bringin' his cat-

—John E. Cramer—

tle drive up from Amarillo and they'll be here sometime in the next three weeks or so—"

"They should be headin' 'em out about now," Jeremiah cut in. "Since me and Tommy were headed this way on business, Kneeland wanted us to drop by and let you folks know he plans to hold the herd here on the Circle-K range for a week or so before takin' 'em on in to Wichita."

"What kinda business you got here in River Bend?" Jeb asked, and as an after thought, "not that it's any of my business."

"They're plannin' on gettin' some work at our neighbor's ranch," Mort interjected. "They were tellin' me they stayed the night at Dutch Van Huss' Turtle Creek Tradin' Post. They both got mustered out of the army about a year ago and headed this way when they met Thorn Masters and Kio on the trail. Matter a fact, just before you two arrived, Jeremiah was tellin' me that's how they ended up at Gil Kneeland's Bar-K ranch. They were plannin' on comin' along with Kneeland's cattle drive, but Jeremiah tells me they heard some disturbin' news about his former Commandin' officer and decided to come on ahead. That's when Gil asked him to drop by the Circle-K."

Jeb, who wasn't quite certain as to what his reaction was supposed to be, waited.

"Jeremiah was about to tell me his news when you and Joey arrived."

Jeb nodded. "About his Commanding Officer?"

"Colonel Felix Burkhalter," Jeremiah filled in. "Dutch Van Huss was tellin' us he's about to go on trial for murdering this Steve Kane fella. We didn't know he was Mort's uncle."

"You been to see the Colonel?" Jeb asked.

—Seven Rode Together—

"No. Since we promised Mister Kneeland to deliver his message to Mort, Tom and me decided to stop here on our way."

"We appreciate that, too," Mort said. "And I can appreciate the loyalty you have for your former Commanding Officer. It's a quality in a man anyone can admire, to trust him and believe in his ability to lead them 'to hell and back,' as the saying goes. In fact, Steve also spoke highly of his Commanding Officer, Jeb Stewart. And, of course, loyalty to someone you believe in and respect is not limited to men who serve in war, it's also an admirable trait for anyone to have for, say, a close and trusted friend, or loyalty a son may have for his mother or father and, of course, the loyalty a nephew may feel toward an uncle when he learns that uncle was shot down in cold blood."

Mort had not taken his eyes off Jeremiah. Likewise, Tom Trinity sat, never taking his eyes off Mort, nodding in apparent agreement with almost everything Mort said about loyalty.

Jeremiah cleared his throat. "Reckon we ought to be on our way. We thank you for your kind invite to stay on for dinner but since the Colonel don't know we're comin', Tom and me ought to be gettin' on."

"Suit yourself," Mort said.

"Ah, folks in River Bend told us the Colonel's trial begins tomorrow."

"Officially, it's already started." Mort said.

"We might see you there."

"You might."

They watched as Jeremiah and Tom walked their horses past the bunk house and into an easy lope until they disappeared behind the row of sycamores.

Chapter 5

It was after they'd finished Sunday dinner that Mort announced his plans for the afternoon. "Jeb, me and Joey are goin' to ride up to that old line shack of Holt Jasper's place and have a look around. I got a feelin' Kneeland might be able to make use of it since he'll be holdin' his herd on our range."

Jeb, clearing the last of the dinner dishes from the table, appeared in the doorway. "If you ask me, there's somethin' else we could make good use of around here and it ain't got nothin' to do with no line shack, either! Jeb spread his arms, displaying the dish water he had slopped over his shirt and his pants. "Look at me," he began, "washin' dishes and rattlin' around in a kitchen ain't no kind of work a man oughta be doin'."

Mort laughed. "You're right, Jeb, anybody who's as sloppy as you are in a kitchen really could use an apron."

"Apron!" Jeb blurted. "You know dang well I ain't talkin' about me gettin' no apron. I'm sayin' that while you're thinkin' about takin' on a couple more cowhands come spring, you oughta

—Seven Rode Together—

be thinkin' about hirin' somebody to do the cookin' and cleanin' around here—somebody kinda like a mother to Joey. You know what I'm thinkin'—"

The smile disappeared from Mort's face. "I know what you're thinking." He eyed Jeb for a moment and got up from the table. "Joey, get a move on if you're goin' with me," he said, and disappeared outside.

Jeb stepped to the door and watched him heading toward the barn. "Me and my big mouth," he muttered.

By the time they reached the line shack, it was the middle of the afternoon. They dismounted and headed up the dusty path. As they reached the door, a single shot rang out shattering the window. In one motion, Mort opened the door, shoved Joey ahead of him and dived inside. "Stay down, Joey! Stay down!" he yelled.

After a few moments, Mort eased up to look out the broken window. A rider, bent low over his horse, topped the small rise down the trail and disappeared. He turned back to Joey still crouched on the floor. "Looks like our welcoming committee decided to head out, Joey."

"Who'd wanna be shootin' at us, Pa?"

Mort was wondering the same thing. "Whoever it was, he was either a lousy shot or he was just tryin' to scare us."

Joey looked at Mort. "He might a scared me a little. But, he didn't scare you, did he, Pa?"

"Not enough to keep us from headin' down to the pond and seein' if we can't hook us a few catfish for dinner tonight."

Awhile later they had selected a spot along the bank of the

—John E. Cramer—

pond behind the line shack and were watching their bobbers a few feet off shore. Joey reached into his hip pocket and pulled out a wrinkled and slightly soiled envelope and handed it to Mort. "Miss Nora gave me this to give to you this morning right after church."

Mort looked at the envelope and then put it in his own pocket. "I'll save it for later," he said.

"Pa, the preacher was askin' folks to pray for the families of those who'd been killed, Doc Milburn, Mister Finfrock and Duane Burkhalter, but he never did mention Uncle Steve."

Mort kept looking at his cork bobbing as a breeze caused a small wrinkle on the surface of the pond. "I suppose," he began, "he was talkin' about those who were killed more recently than Steve."

"But ain't we Uncle Steve's family? Anyway, I done some prayin' for Missus Milburn and Missus Finfrock but I sure couldn't do much prayin' for somebody who got killed tryin' to kill us. I just couldn't do it, Pa. All I could think about was that Duane Burkhalter killed Major and shot me—" He wiped away the tears with the back of his hand when he mentioned Major. "Even though he was a dog, he was part of our family, wasn't he, Pa?"

"Yes, he was, Joey."

Before more could be said, Joey's cork disappeared under the surface of the water. "You gotta bite, Joey! Now, don't let him get away."

Mort was thankful the strike captured Joey's attention. He was distracted, too, thinking about what Jeb had said about the need for a woman at the Circle-K to look after things.

"Look, Pa, that ain't no catfish!" Joey had snagged a large soft-shell turtle and was having trouble trying to pull him ashore.

—Seven Rode Together—

Suddenly, the line snapped and the turtle slipped below the surface of the water. "Just ain't a good day, Pa."

"Jeb," Joey yelled as he ran toward the barn. "I caught the biggest old soft-shell turtle you'd ever want to see while me and Pa was fishin'—and we got shot at, too!"

"Now I ain't cleanin' no turtle. That's where I draw the line. If you two are thinkin' about eatin' turtle for supper, you or your Pa are gonna have to do the cleanin'."

"Don't worry, Jeb." Mort grinned. "He got away."

"Well, I ain't about to clean a danged old turtle for nobody. And what's this about gettin' shot at? Dang! I knew I should of gone along with you. I'm here, cookin' and cleanin' and you're out there—no one hurt, it seems."

"No one. I'll tell you about it later, Jeb."

That evening, after Joey had gone to bed, Mort poured another cup of coffee and sat down at the table. "About the mystery man who took a shot at us up at the line shack—only got a glimpse of his backside. He was riding a bay—"

Jeb began shaking his head. "Mort, I've been tellin' you since the day we both layed eyes on each other, I can't say who the shooter might be, but you and I both know damn well who's givin' the orders. There ain't but one person in the whole state of Kansas who'd like to see you dead—that's old man Burkhalter."

"You're right, Jeb." In the three years since he'd owned the Circle-K, there had been at least a half dozen attempts to send him

—John E. Cramer—

to the Promised Land. Although most every rancher in the valley, and most of the people in River Bend, knew the Colonel was responsible, no one had ever seen him threaten anyone with a gun.

"And the Colonel ain't goin' to be found guilty of killin' Steve, either! Anybody who's still alive and might know what a underhanded, connivin', low down shiftless skunk he is ain't goin' to be tellin' it to no judge. And them that could are dead! Even if there was a live witness, and I ain't sayin' there is, and they found the Colonel guilty of anything, the governor would up and pardon him before he ever got to the jail."

"Sounds to me like you've got it all figured out," Mort said. "You're forgetting what Doc Milburn told me that night before he was killed by that mob tryin' to break me out of jail—before the Marshal arrived. Doc wrote a letter tellin' the whole story about Steve's murder. And everybody knows that mob was all fired up by the Colonel—"

Jeb nodded. "You're right about that, Mort. But the Colonel ain't bein' tried for gettin' a bunch of cowhands liquored up and stormin' the jail. He's bein' tried for killin' your Uncle Steve. We ain't goin' to settle it tonight. Best we wait and see what the jury thinks." He stood up, stretched his arms over his head and began rubbing the kinks out of his neck. "Reckon I'll turn in."

The moment Jeb left the room, Mort opened the envelope Joey had delivered to him and began to read. Jeb reappeared in the doorway. "You can tell me what she had to say in the morning," he said. "Just remember what I told you about us needin' a woman around here to help look after things. She wouldn't have to be hired help, you know."

"Good night, Jeb!" Mort waited, listening to Jeb's hasty

—Seven Rode Together—

retreat down the hallway, then unfolded the letter and began to read: "Dear Mort, We need to talk about our future if we still have one together. Paul says he's returning to Boston to complete his medical studies after the trial. He wants me to go with him no matter what happens to father. I love you, Nora"

Mort folded the letter and for the next few minutes he sat quietly staring at the floor. He hadn't purposely avoided either Nora or Paul these past few weeks since the shootout at the jail. On the other hand, he hadn't made any effort to contact them, believing they might not want to continue a friendship with the man who'd killed their brother.

He understood how they might feel. His Uncle Steve's death haunted Mort. The Circle-K had given Joey and him the opportunity to begin a new life and to leave behind the bitter-sweet memories of the 60-acre dirt farm in Kentucky.

The trial, the note from Nora, old memories—all swirling around in his head. Knowing he wouldn't be able to sleep, he stood up, walked to the door and slipped outside.

There was a full moon and a refreshing southerly breeze rustled the leaves of two sturdy oak trees as he made his way to the hammock stretched between them. Folding his arms behind his head, he gazed at the stars. It was a quiet, peaceful night that allowed a man to sort things out. Mort knew, however, from past nights, the light of day erased all the starlight solutions. He also knew he could never change the events of the past, and no amount of thinking or hoping could change future events if they were destined to happen. No matter, he thought, nights like this were comforting to the soul.

Mort was about Joey's age when his Pa, Josh Kane, and his brother Steve, left home to join the Army of the Confederacy as a

—John E. Cramer—

member of Jeb Stewart's Cavalry. His ma was a strict, Bible-reading Christian fundamentalist. She believed man was put on this earth to serve God and to live his life strictly as set down in the Ten Commandments. There were no exceptions. "God has His ways of punishing those who do not obey his Commandments," she'd told Mort a hundred times. "You must know them and live by them," was her frequent reminder. It was a point of confusion for Mort. "What if Pa kills somebody," he'd asked. "Does that mean he ain't goin' to heaven?"

To avoid a direct answer, she would reply with a question. "What does the Fifth Commandment say?"

He remembered when word came that his Pa had been killed. His first thoughts were that although his Pa wasn't ever comin' home like he'd promised, the Yankee that killed him was goin' straight to hell. But he couldn't help thinkin' that if anyone had to be killed, he wished the Yankee had been instead of his Pa. But he never asked his ma how she felt about it.

Not long before the news came about his Pa, Mort had committed an act that, at the time, was so bad he would be meeting that Yankee down under—

It was the summer of 1863 that Mort experienced his first love. Her name was Ellen Lyndon. Her older sister, Lilly, was married and lived in Louisville. The Lyndon family owned the farm about a mile north of the Kane's. And although Rube Lyndon and Josh Kane were neighborly, they didn't agree on the war. It was Rube's considered opinion that Josh, in his words, "was plumb out of his mind for joining up with the Confederates, especially since Governor Magoffin had declared Kentucky's neutrality."

Mort remembered the last time he had talked to his Pa.

—Seven Rode Together—

"Son, I need you to promise to look after this place and take good care of your ma while I'm gone."

It was the following Sunday, Mort remembered, that he and Ellen met at their secret hideaway, a hunters' cabin along the bank of Simon's Creek. She had come to tell him that her Pa had warned her not to see or talk to him ever again. Instead, her Pa's words served only to strengthen their love for one another. Unlike their previous meetings, when embraces and kisses were standard only for greetings and departures, separated by earnest discussions about the future, their kisses became more intense and their embraces grew bolder. When they left the cabin that afternoon, they knew what it was like to lay in one another's arms and touch where they had never touched before. When they left that afternoon, they were no longer virgins.

It was that same year Rube Lyndon was killed when he was thrown from his horse. His neck had been broken from the fall. Missus Lyndon had not shared her husband's feelings concerning Mort and Ellen's affection for one another and when Mort volunteered to help with the farm work, she was grateful. In the Spring of '65, Mort and Ellen were married and Mort continued to work both farms. He had now made promises he was struggling to keep. He had promised his Pa to take good care of his Ma, and he had promises, on his wedding day, to take care of Ellen. Both were impossible to do. Ellen and his Ma could not get along. Things got worse each passing day. Ellen was finding reasons to make frequent visits to Louisville to visit her sister. Mort hoped, after Joey was born, the constant feuding between Ellen and his Ma would stop. It was not to be. And when Ellen's mother passed away, the Lyndon farm was sold and Ellen and her sister divided the inheritance.

—John E. Cramer—

Provided now with the means to escape the life she had grown to hate, Ellen issued her final ultimatum. "Mort, I cannot endure another day of your ma's holier-than-thou attitude toward me. She hates me Mort. There's got to be a better life for me and I intend to find it."

"What about Joey?" Mort had asked. "He's not yet a year old. If we could only—"

"I never wanted a baby in the first place," she said. "Besides, you have your mother. She knows to take care of a baby. She's been reminding me of that since the day he was born."

Mort tried to persuade her to stay, but in the end he failed. She left them the same day. Mort's Ma passed away five years later. He had fulfilled the promise to his Pa, and the day he learned he'd inherited the Circle-K, he made another promise—to begin a new life for himself and Joey.

A lone coyote's mournful howl interrupted Mort's thoughts. For some time he continued to gaze at the stars.

Chapter 6

It was the shank of the afternoon when Jeremiah Dundee and Tom Trinity reached the Burkhalter estate. They stayed in their saddles for several minutes, looking at the well-groomed lawn and rock gardens inside the white, stone fence. The roof above the veranda was supported by four glistening white pillars. They dismounted and walked through the gate up the brick walk toward the front door. Before they reached the steps of the veranda, the door opened and out stepped the Colonel.

"You men looking for someone?" he asked.

"Yes sir," Jeremiah replied and gave the Colonel a snappy salute. "Thought you might recognize me, Colonel. The name's Jeremiah Dundee. I served as your Clerk in B-Company of the 24th Regiment during the war. This here's my side-kick, Tom Trinity."

Eyeing them for a moment, the Colonel flashed a broad smile and extended his hand. "Oh, yes," he began, "Sergeant Dundee and," he paused, "Trinity? Trinity—"

"Tom Trinity, sir. I didn't serve in Company B. In fact, I

joined up just before the end and served until President Hayes decided we were no longer needed."

"I see. Well, won't you gentlemen step up here on the veranda and join me?"

After they were seated, the Colonel began again. "Now what brings you all the way out here in Kansas to see me."

Jeremiah was beginning to wonder if perhaps the Colonel might not be able to remember an invitation he'd extended after all these years. He was beginning to have second thoughts when the Colonel, smiling more broadly than ever now, began nodding his head. "Now I recall. Well, Sergeant Dundee, it certainly took you a long time to take me up on my offer."

"It certainly did, Sir. You see, I stayed on after the war and wound up servin' in the South during the Reconstruction Period—that's where I met up with Tom. We both knocked around a couple of years then decided to see what was on the west side of the Mississippi. Once we got to Fort Smith we decided to come on to Kansas and find out if you was still of a mind to do some hirin'."

He kept an eye on the Colonel, hoping for some sign that might indicate what his former Commander was thinking. The Colonel smiled, but revealed nothing.

"That's just about the jist of things," Jeremiah added. "I didn't have anything much back in Indiana that needed my attention."

"And how about you, Trinity?" the Colonel asked. "Where do you call home?"

"Kentucky, Sir. At least, that's where I grew up."

"Wouldn't you want to be going home after your hitch in the Army?"

Jeremiah spoke up, remembering Tom, for whatever reason,

—Seven Rode Together—

was reluctant to admit he never knew his parents. "Actually," Jeremiah began, "Tom never knew—"

"What I was gettin' into when I joined up with the Army." Tom said. "I was raised by the nuns in an orphanage outside Louisville. When I left there I joined up."

The Colonel seemed to take a genuine liking for this broad shouldered, young man with piercing blue eyes who looked directly into his as he spoke. "You must have been pretty young to be joining the Army," he said soberly.

Tom nodded. "You might say that. If it hadn't been for Jeremiah here, I might have cut and run before my hitch was up."

"I wouldn't be at all surprised," the Colonel said. "I'm sure I'll be able to come up with something that can keep both of you busy earning your pay around here." And looking at Tom, he added, "I might even make a cattleman out of you before it's over."

Jeremiah thought the Colonel sure wasn't actin' like he was about to go on trial tomorrow for killin' a man.

"I've got some business in River Bend tomorrow morning, fellas, but as of now, you can consider yourselves on the Burkhalter payroll. After supper, I'll introduce you to my foreman. He'll get you lined out. I suppose you know, if you stopped in River Bend on your way out here, I'm to appear in court tomorrow morning. I've been accused of killing a neighbor of mine who was planning to run off with my wife and a considerable amount of Burkhalter cash. That was three years ago. At that time, I wasn't accused of anything. In fact, the whole ugly affair had been forgotten until the man's nephew, Mort Kane, came to town. He'd inherited the Circle-K. His spread borders mine. In fact," he continued, "that same Mort Kane killed my son, when the Koehler brothers caught

—John E. Cramer—

Kane redhanded trying to put the Circle-K brand on Burkhalter cattle. There was a gun fight and Duane was shot—"

Tom and Jeremiah exchanged quick glances, both looking at the other to say something. The man they'd talked with earlier that day hadn't seemed like the sort of person who would be stealin' cattle from his neighbors or killin' someone. They both remembered the Koehler brothers. Why if it hadn't been for Thorn Masters and his friend, Kio, they might not be sitting here right now.

Jeremiah was about to break the uneasy silence when the door opened and Nora stepped out on the veranda. "Oh, there you are. We were wondering where you'd gone. I didn't realize you had company."

"Nora, I'd like you to meet Jeremiah Dundee, who was my Company Clerk during the war."

Jeremiah tipped his hat. Tom removed his hat before the Colonel introduced him. "His friend is Tom Trinity. He also served his country in the Cavalry during the war."

"I'm proud to make your acquaintance, ma'am."

Nora smiled. "Are you just passing through?"

Jeremiah smiled. "Oh, no, ma'am. We're stayin'—"

"They're both now working for the ranch, Nora."

"It seems you gentlemen arrived at the right time. Elinda has the dinner on the table."

"Oh, no, ma'am, Jeremiah and me don't want to impose on you. We'll just have a look around."

"Nonsense," Nora said. Jeremiah shrugged his shoulders, nodded for Tom to follow.

"You gentlemen can wash up and I'll tell Elinda to set two more places at the table."

—Seven Rode Together—

The Colonel broke the few minutes of silence after all were seated at the table. "When I first came to this valley, River Bend was nothing more than a trading post. I claimed most of this land and I've had to fight to keep it. Kansas was just a territory then, and life wasn't easy, but it was just the beginning for all of us. There are only a few of us left that first improved this land, raised our families, and made this valley what it is today."

"I doubt our guests are seriously interested in hearing about your exploits as a young man." Nora interrupted. "Mister Tinley, you seem awfully young to have been in the war."

"Oh, no, ma'am, I wasn't in the war. Like I told the Colonel earlier, I joined the army *after* the war."

Elinda came into the room. "Excuse me, Colonel. Mister Parker would like to speak with you. He says it's urgent."

"Thank you, Elinda. If you'll excuse me, I'll find out what's so urgent the foreman feels can't wait until after we've finished our dinner."

The moment he saw Parker waiting in the foyer, the Colonel nodded toward the door and they both stepped outside closing the door behind them. "I figured you had company when I saw the horses tied out front, but you told me to check with you when I got back from River Bend—"

"Yes. Yes. What about Paul? Did you see him?"

The foreman nodded. "Just like you told me. When he didn't leave with you and Nora after church, I watched him go into the Mary Belle Cafe. When he left about two hours later, he walked over to Fred Findley's Livery Stable, rented a rig and drove to Bert Tolliver's place. He was there until late afternoon. He came back to town, returned the rig and checked in at the hotel."

—John E. Cramer—

"How do you know he checked in?"

"After he didn't come out and it was gettin' close to sundown, I checked the lobby and then walked over to the registration desk. I asked if Paul Burkhalter had checked in. The clerk said he had, and wanted to know if I wanted his room number. I waited awhile and then left."

"Good," the Colonel patted Parker's shoulder. "Now, about those two inside. The older one, Jeremiah Dundee, was my Company Clerk during the war and the younger one is his friend, Tom Trinity. They rode in late this afternoon looking for work and I hired them."

Parker nodded. "I understand."

"Good," the Colonel smiled, "I'll be bringing them out later to meet you and the others. You might want to caution the men to save their usual initiation for new hands until later."

The others were still seated at the table when the Colonel returned. "I'm sorry to have kept you waiting." Noticing the first table had been cleared, he added, "I guess you weren't waiting after all."

Nora addressed the situation. "I didn't know how long you would be gone. I knew you wouldn't mind if we went ahead. I told Elinda we would wait to have our dessert together but neither Mister Dundee nor Mister Trinity felt they needed dessert," Nora explained.

"Well, in that case," the Colonel said, "I believe I'll take our new hired hands out to see where they'll be bedding down tonight. And then, Nora, you and I can discuss our plans for tomorrow—

—Seven Rode Together—

that is, if you can wait to speak with me."

Parker was waiting for them as they approached the chow hall. "The boys are all in here, Colonel. I'll see to it our new hands find a place to bed down tonight."

"Good. Then I'll see you two tomorrow. You might want to tag along with Parker and the others. They'll be going into town with me. If not, take the day off and rest awhile. Good night."

The Colonel turned quickly and headed toward the house. The moment he entered, he walked directly to the living room where Nora was waiting. "Sorry to have kept you waiting," he said. He wanted to ask her why Paul had been avoiding him since he returned home, but he wanted to bide his time. Instead, he asked, "What do you think of the two new men?" Leaning back in his chair, he lit a cigar. "The older one, Mister Dundee, he was probably the best Company Clerk in the whole Union Army. And the younger one, Trinity, he's a fine looking lad, looks you straight in the eye when he talks—he'll make a good cattleman—"

"You don't really want to know what I think about your new hired hands," she interrupted, a slight edge in her voice. "How can you sit there and talk about hired hands when tomorrow you're to stand trial for killing a man? I know you too well, Father. Why do you keep pretending as though tomorrow is just another day? And why are you and Paul avoiding one another? And where is Paul?"

"Whoa! One question at a time. That's better. Now, about your brother. We met him this morning at church. In fact, we ate lunch together afterward, if you'll recall." He lowered his voice, and leaned forward. "You know Paul and I have never seemed to agree on anything. He never showed any interest in ranching as I'd hoped." He quickly added, "That's fine. Medicine is an honorable

—John E. Cramer—

profession. Now with Duane and your mother both gone, you're the only one I have left."

"What about Mother? Paul says she never went to Boston."

"Now, Nora, with Duane and your mother both gone, and Paul soon off to school, you're the only one I have left."

"And what about Mother? Where is she? Paul said only that she never went to Boston—"

"Paul doesn't know what has happened to your mother."

"What do you mean? Did mother go to Boston, or didn't she?"

"Nora, Nora. That was years ago. I've told you what happened."

"But you never answer any questions, Father."

The Colonel wanted to say, ask Mort Kane. Ask him about your mother, but he didn't. He didn't say anything more at all. Nora stared into the fireplace.

Chapter 7

The main street in River Bend was crowded with buggies, carriages, rigs and cowhands on horseback before the trial of Colonel Felix Burkhalter was scheduled to begin. Many people living in River Bend had taken up vigil earlier that morning on the spacious lawn in front of the courthouse. Those who arrived first were standing on the steps to insure their chances of getting a seat inside.

From his office window across the street from the courthouse Clancy O'Riley was observing the scene. For several minutes, he stood watching the crowd grow larger. "Looks like everybody in Kansas decided to gather in River Bend today," he mused. He was about to return to his desk when he spotted a familiar figure having some difficulty crossing the street. He watched as the short, overweight man, dressed in a dark suit and wearing a derby hat, finally reached the safety of the boardwalk. A moment later, Mayor Jasper Dexhorn, still trying to catch his breath, opened the door and burst into the office.

"Well, Mayor," O'Riley greeted, "what brings you out and

—John E. Cramer—

about so early in the morning?"

"Do you see what's happening out there? Where are all these people coming from?"

Clancy shrugged and extended his hands palms up. "What would you expect? It's not every day one of the most prominent men in the whole state is accused of killing somebody. And, besides," he grinned, "it's bound to be good for business."

"That's what I'd expect you to say. And after all the Colonel has done for this town." The Mayor pointed a finger a few inches from Clancy's nose. "Or have you forgotten that?"

"No, I haven't forgotten," Clancy said. "That was nearly ten years ago and I've paid back every penny I borrowed. But that's not why you came busting in here all lathered up." He motioned for Dexhorn to sit, pulled open the bottom drawer of his desk, took out two glasses and a bottle of Irish whiskey. He poured three-fingers in one glass and handed it across the desk to the sweating Mayor. "Drink this. It'll settle your nerves. This occasion calls for a toast." he said, and raised his glass. "Here's to all the good folks in the valley," and with a nod and a quick wink, he added. "and that includes those on today's jury, the recipients of the Colonel's generosity. And may the Good Lord watch over those who have incurred his wrath."

For a moment, Dexhorn hesitated, then downed his drink in one quip. Placing his glass on the desk, he said, "That was a helluva toast, Clancy O'Riley. I didn't like the insinuation."

"I noticed you drank to it."

"I've never turned down a drink of Irish whiskey. Especially, when you're buying."

Both men turned to the rapping on the window by Dave

—Seven Rode Together—

Shelley, president of the bank. Clancy raised his glass and motioned toward the door.

The moment Shelley moved, a couple of curious cowhands, cupping their hands over their eyes, peered through the window. Clancy, flashing a quick mechanical smile, waved at them. They backed away from the window and joined others headed for the courthouse.

Shelley hurried into Clancy's office. "I'm glad I found you both here together. I think we're in trouble. Both of you were at our last town meeting when we decided to close all the bars in town during the court proceedings and," he paused to catch his breath, "and—and—"

Before Shelley could explain, Dexhorn asked. "What kind of trouble? We deputized a dozen of the town's leading citizens to help Deputy Cravens enforce the law."

"I know that," Shelley agreed. "But I just came from the Frontier Hotel and I saw Mort Kane and Jeb Hofstader talkin' to a couple of strangers."

"Strangers?" Dexhorn blurted. "Hell's fire, man, half the people in town this morning are strangers!"

"If you'd kindly shut up for a minute, Mayor, and let me explain! When I saw them shakin' hands all around, I just walked over and introduced myself and ask them if they were here for the trial. And before they could answer, Jeb Hofstader wanted to know if I was a self-appointed welcomin' committee or was I just used to stickin' my nose into other people's private conversations?"

"Well." Clancy asked, "Which was it?"

Ignoring Clancy's cynicism, Shelley continued, "Anyway, Kane introduced me to the two strangers. He said they were from

—John E. Cramer—

down Amarillo way and they were bringin' a cattle drive through here from the Bar-K Ranch. Said the cattle would probably be arrivin' the day after tomorrow. Him and his partner—he called Kio—just came on into River Bend to see Kane. They'll be holdin' their herd on Circle-K range for a few days. And when they arrive, I don't have to tell you, those cowhands after eatin' dust all the way from Texas won't be wantin' to wait around for the Silver Dollar or any others to open. Most likely they'll reopen them if they're closed."

"Nothing to worry about," Dexhorn chimed in. "The Town Council gave Cravens strict orders to post a man on roads east and west of town to collect all fire arms from everybody comin' into town. And I never saw anybody wearin' a gun this morning when I came over here to talk to Clancy."

"Well, you never saw those two at the Frontier Hotel. They didn't look to me to be just ordinary cowhands. And the way they both dressed, with those .45's strapped down, anybody could tell they weren't wearin' them to shoot at rabbits or rattlesnakes—"

"Well, now, Shelley," Clancy began, "You're on the Town Council. Why didn't you just speak up and tell 'em they'd have to check their hardware with you? At least, you might have asked why they didn't check 'em at the post when they rode in."

"That I did. And the man who seemed to be the spokesman for him and his Indian partner told me, 'That'll be the day when I check my gun before I ride into any town where a man like Bart Taylor is the Sheriff.'"

"Why didn't you explain to him," Clancy persisted, "that Taylor was no longer sheriff and probably was now awaiting his own trial for murder in some Missouri jail?" Shelley was aware of Taylor's background. His tenure ended rather abruptly when a bounty hunter came to River Bend on the night of the gun battle between the Colonel's organized vigilante committee and Mort Kane who was being held inside the jail.

"I didn't believe that any explanation was necessary."

"What was this fellow's name who was giving you all this trouble?"

"He called himself Thorn Masters. Said Gil Kneeland, the owner of the Bar-K was his uncle and that his partner worked on the Bar-K. Said he's taking Kneeland's place on this drive."

"Thorn Masters!" Clancy said. "That's the man I was telling you about at the last council meeting. He's the one Mort Kane suggested we hire to take Taylor's place."

"What makes you think he'd take the job? Besides, he's not from Kansas."

"Neither was Taylor. But the Colonel recommended him. Maybe he wouldn't want the job." Clancy shrugged. "But how can we know if we don't ask him? If he's as handy with a .45 as you seem to think, he might just be the man for the job. Who knows? He might be River Bend's Wyatt Earp."

"This is a matter we'd best talk first with the Colonel," Dexhorn volunteered. "Especially, since you saw him talking with Mort Kane. It appears he must be on good terms with Kane as he's doin' business with him. Anyway, this fellow Masters is already workin' for the Bar-K as the trail boss in charge of that herd gettin' to Wichita or Kansas City, wherever they're headed."

Shelley readily agreed.

"Suit yourself," Clancy said, still playing the part of the devil's advocate and enjoying every minute. "But the Colonel just might not be around after the trial. And then again, like you've

—John E. Cramer—

pointed out, Masters might not want the job anyway. He'd probably want more money than we could afford to pay him. A man with his credentials won't come cheap. It's whatever you decide to do. Course, we should see what the others think."

Shelley and Dexhorn exchanged glances and then looked at Clancy. "You don't really believe the Colonel is going to be found guilty of killing a man, do you?" Dexhorn asked.

Before Clancy could reply, their attention was drawn to the outside where they heard a cheer from those gathered on the boardwalks. Moments later they spotted the Colonel, flanked on either side by his cowhands, and with more than a dozen Burkhalter riders trailing behind.

They watched as the crowd melted away allowing the Colonel and the Burkhalter cowhands to gain access to the block-long hitchrail in front of the courthouse. The same courtesy was afforded the Colonel and his men as they moved up the front steps. They watched as the doors opened and the Colonel and his men, .45's in their holsters, moved slowly into the courthouse.

Clancy, glancing first at Shelley and then the Mayor, threw up his arms. "So much for the Council's temporary on hardware before entering our fair city."

As the Mayor and the banker turned away and headed toward the office door, Clancy couldn't resist asking one parting question. "You won't forget about checking with the rest of the Council to see what they think about hiring Masters as the new sheriff?" The door closed behind them before he'd finished.

Clancy returned to his desk and poured himself another drink. This just might be a red-letter day in River Bend, he thought. The Colonel has his way in court but finds he's lost his way in the

—Seven Rode Together—

selection of the next sheriff. If someone were to stir things up a bit, the good people of River Bend might decide they'd like their next sheriff to be elected and not appointed. An editorial might be a lot more persuasive, he mused, if we can convince an honest candidate to make a run for the job.

He set the drink on the desk. "I'll be back for you," he said, "after I can convince a certain young man that law enforcement can be an honorable profession if the people have a chance to hire him."

Chapter 8

Paul Burkhalter was watching the crowd from his second floor window in the Frontier Hotel when the Colonel and his parade of ranch hands passed by on their way to the courthouse. Moments later, he saw Nora cross the street and enter the hotel. He was still trying to decide. Should he tell her what he suspected had happened to their mother?

"Paul—Paul! Are you in there?"

Paul stepped quickly to the door and opened it. "What are you doing here? Why aren't you at the courthouse?"

For several moments they stood in the open doorway, locked in each other's arms. "What are we going to do, Paul?"

He wanted to console her. "Don't you worry, Nora. Everything will be alright." The words sounded hollow, without meaning.

"I'm sorry, Paul," she said, "but these past few weeks have been a horrible nightmare."

"I know," Paul began. He was wishing he hadn't told her

—Seven Rode Together—

that their mother did not go to Boston. If only he had gone with her the day she left instead of waiting all those months before deciding to join her. He remembered the day she left. She had confided in him and Nora. "I just need to be with my friends and family I left behind when your father and I came here to make our home. It was a hard life, but we were happy. And when you children came along, I knew I had made the right decision to come here with your father. In those days life was not easy, but your father had a grandiose plan that one day this valley and River Bend would somehow become his, and he would make it the most prosperous place in the entire territory. Then, after the war was over and he returned home, he seemed to have the money, the influence and the prestige that attends wealth. He did become one of the largest land owners in the state of Kansas. But he was no longer the man I had married. And I knew then you children and I were no longer as important to him as his desire to acquire more wealth and more power. I am deserting my family but I need to get away from here to have time to think. I pray that you will one day understand and will forgive me for any hurt my going away will cause."

As if she had been reading her brother's mind, Nora said, "It's probably best that mother isn't here. And after all this is over, we can hope everything will be different, but until then, all we have is hope. Perhaps then we all can get on with our lives."

"Does that include Mort Kane?"

"Oh, yes, Paul. Nothing can change that." She was smiling.

"Mort is the main reason I haven't left this valley. I love him, Paul. And I know he loves me."

"Aren't you forgetting something? Our father is being tried for the murder of Mort's Uncle Steve."

—John E. Cramer—

"I haven't forgotten. And I'm hoping and praying Mort and I and Joey will be allowed to live our lives and find happiness, regardless of what happens today."

Paul put his head in his hands. "I know what's been done, cannot be undone, Nora. I wish I had your resolve. I'm afraid to look at the future. I'll know after the trial is over and I've heard what the Colonel has to say—when he's sworn to tell the truth—"

When O'Riley reached the Frontier Hotel, he reached in his vest pocket and pulled out his watch. He glanced around the lobby hoping to catch a glimpse of Mort and Jeb. He wanted to see his choice for River Bend's next sheriff, Thorn Masters, and his sidekick, Kio. He spotted Mort and Jeb and the two cowhands from the Bar-K. Another man was with them. He recognized him as the U.S. Marshal, the lawman from Wichita he'd interviewed following the shootout at the River Bend jail. He slipped his watch back into his vest and walked across the room. He'd already decided he wasn't going to intrude with the same damn-fool question Shelley had asked. Anyone, he thought, with an ounce of brains, would know they were here for the trial. But before he could ask any question, the Marshal spotted him.

"Well, gentlemen, it seems the press has arrived to join us." He turned toward O'Riley and shook his hand. "You've arrived just in time. I'm sure you're acquainted with Mort Kane and Jeb Hofstader. These other two gentlemen are from Texas, Thorn Masters and his friend Kio. And now that we have dispensed with the formalities, I suppose you'll want to know if we're here for the trial. At least that was what your bank president, Mister Shelley,

—Seven Rode Together—

wanted to know."

"I figured as much," O'Riley replied. "And that was before I heard it from the bank president himself."

"Well, in that case," the Marshal smiled, "you may want to meet four of my newest deputies. They've all been duly sworn in and in the absence of your town's acting sheriff, we're going to do what he has apparently overlooked. Spectators don't carry firearms into the courtroom." He paused long enough to catch O'Riley's side-long glance at the other four, three carrying .45's and Mort, a Winchester rifle. "As I said, they're all legal and they're my deputies. And, now, gentlemen, we'll get back to the business at hand. O'Riley, if you'd care to accompany us, feel free to do so. We may be in need of an extra hand to tote those gunbelts back to the sheriff's office. Let's go." And with that, they all headed for the front door, the Marshal leading the way.

Those seated in the lounge watched as they filed past. The two most interested spectators, Paul and Nora Burkhalter were departing just in time to see them. She started to follow Mort. Paul grabbed her arm. "Not now," he said.

"But that was Mort and Jeb."

"And a U.S. Marshal. I met him three weeks ago at the River Bend jail. It appears they have business at the courthouse that won't wait."

The crowd was still waiting outside the courthouse when they arrived. Those waiting on the steps were quick to step aside when they spotted a U.S. Marshal heading their direction. The Marshal pounded on the door when he discovered it was locked.

"The doors will be opened at nine forty-five," a voice from the inside called.

—John E. Cramer—

"This is U.S. Marshal Thurgold. Open up!" They waited for a moment, then the door opened slowly, and River Bend's acting sheriff, Oscar Cravens, poked his head out. "It *is* you," he said as Thurgold shoved him aside and stepped inside. "What're they doing with you, Clint?" Cravens wanted to know, looking at the newly-appointed deputies.

Ignoring his question, the Marshal ordered. "Close the door and come with us, Cravens."

On either side of the lobby there were stairs leading to the balcony of the courtroom. Two large swinging doors separated the lobby from the courtroom on the lower level. The Marshal stepped quietly ahead of the others to the swinging doors. He pushed them open, giving him full view of the Burkhalter cowhands seated in the first row, directly behind the railing that separated the public from the participants in the court proceedings. Motioning to his deputies to cover him from the balcony, he told Cravens to follow him. Before the Colonel or any of his men could turn around, the Marshal ordered. "All of you men on your feet!"

"What the hell is going on?" the Colonel demanded, turning to face the Marshal.

The Marshal moved quickly down the aisle where he took up a position in front of them. "Now, all of you unbuckle your gunbelts and drop them on the seat behind you."

"Wait a minute!" the Colonel said and stepped out into the aisle. All of his men stood quietly, each with his gun hand resting on the butt of his .45. "I demand an explanation of what you think you're doing, busting in here giving orders?"

Without taking his eyes off the Colonel's men, the Marshal said quietly, "I'm enforcing the law, Colonel. And this badge I'm

—Seven Rode Together—

wearing says I have all the authority I need. I suggest you take your seat at the table."

Before he finished his explanation, he noticed the Colonel's foreman and two other cowhands as they gripped the butt of their guns. "Before you get any ideas, I suggest you might want to take a look at the balcony above you."

Every man, including the Colonel, saw the Marshal's back-up: Thorn Masters, Kio, Jeb, and Mort Kane had taken up positions across the width of the balcony. All except Mort had drawn their guns. He stood on the far side, a Winchester cradled in his arm. And as if on cue, the quiet of the courtroom was shattered by the sounds of three .45's being cocked, and the sound of a shell being pumped into the chamber of the Winchester. "Now, very slowly," the Marshal ordered.

The gunbelts began hitting the floor, and the Colonel took his seat at the table next to his wide-eyed attorney.

"Now, all of you, except the Colonel," Thurgold ordered, "move out toward those doors you came in." And turning to Cravens, he added, "Collect those gunbelts and come with me. These men are all under arrest for not checking their guns when they came into town."

As the Colonel's men, flanked by Craven and the Marshal's deputies, moved down the middle of the street, someone in the crowd yelled, "Those are the men who rode in with the Colonel this morning!"

"They don't look so high and mighty when they're walkin'!" another yelled.

An inebriated cowhand leaned against the wall at the Silver Dollar Saloon, talking to a plump lady in a satin dress. "They forget the Colonel? Did you see the Colonel?" When she failed to reply, he muttered to himself, "Either I missed him or the trial's over and the Colonel's waitin' at the courthouse to make another speech."

Nora and Paul, coming out of the Frontier Hotel just as the group of arrested cowhands passed by, knew the trial wasn't over. They were more interested in the men guarding them.

"Look," Nora said. "There's Mort and Jeb, and those are Father's ranch hands! Where are they taking them?"

"They're heading toward the jail."

"Why?"

The crowd filled in behind the deputies, obscuring Nora's view. She had wanted to talk to Mort ever since he and Jeb returned to the Circle-K following the incident at the River Bend jail nearly three weeks ago. Although she had not spoken to Mort, Jeb had told her the truth about what happened that day.

Mort had explained it was the Colonel's plan to use the cattle as evidence to support his claim that Mort was a cattle rustler. During the gunfight that ensued, Joey was shot and Mort had killed Duane. The Koehler brothers lit out for River Bend when the first shot was fired.

Mort brought Joey back to the Circle-K, dressed the wound as best he could, and hightailed it to River Bend to fetch Doc Milburn. While Mort was getting Doc out of town, the Koehler brothers were at Sheriff Taylor's office telling Taylor and the Colonel that Duane had been ambushed and shot in the back by Mort Kane. Doc Milburn arrived back at the ranch and Doc was working over Joey when the Colonel, Sheriff Taylor, Deputy Cravens and the Koehler brothers rode up. The Colonel demanded

—Seven Rode Together—

that Mort come out with his hands up or they'd come in after him. "And this was the best part," Jeb had told her. "When Mort told 'em he weren't comin' out and nobody was comin' in, the Colonel started up the walk with the others keepin' their distance. Mort didn't say a word. He just took a bead on the Colonel's white Stetson with his Winchester and blew it clean off his head. They huddled together for a short spell like a bunch of old maids at a quiltin' party, and then the Colonel must've decided he was gonna need a better back up than what he brung with him, yelled back that if Mort didn't turn hisself in before sundown, they'd be back."

"Well," Jeb explained. "Mort figured they'd not be wastin' any time with a shoot-out when they could burn us out. They knew Joey was gonna be alright. Mort decided to turn himself in but he wanted the Marshal brought in from Wichita to be sure he had a fair trial."

She had stayed the night with Joey and the next morning, surprisingly, Mort and Jeb came home. It was then she learned Doc Milburn had been killed during a shooting at the River Bend jail, and the Marshal had arrived to make a wholesale arrest of those attempting to break Mort out of jail, including the Colonel. She hadn't talked with Mort since that morning.

Her thoughts were brought back to the present when she heard Paul saying, "Have you decided to find out why Mort and Jeb are taking the Colonel's ranch hands to jail, or should we start heading toward the courthouse?"

"I believe I'll do both," she said, "but not in that order."

When they reached the courthouse, only a few were gathered outside. Once inside, they were directed to find seats in the balcony since the first floor had filled to capacity. They reached

—John E. Cramer—

their seats in time to hear the bailiff's announcement, "All rise." Moments later, Judge Storm arrived and seated himself at the bench.

Chapter 9

Jonathan Styche, the district attorney, was well aware the case he was about to try was the most important in his young career. If he succeeded in convincing the jury that Colonel Felix Burkhalter was guilty of murdering Steve Kane, it would be a big step in furthering his ambition of one day becoming the state's youngest governor. Another thing he knew, convincing a jury of a man's guilt without an eyewitness is nearly always next to impossible.

In the few weeks he'd been gathering evidence and researching the case, he'd learned that if the circumstances leading up to the killing were as the Colonel had described them, he surely would be found "Not Guilty." The Colonel in his sworn deposition had testified that he and the others had surprised Kane when he was in the act of rustling Burkhalter cattle. They had engaged in a gun battle during which the Colonel suffered a shoulder wound and Steve Kane was killed. The Colonel could not identify the other men who were with Kane because they fled the area when the shooting started. He identified the men with him that day as Sheriff

—John E. Cramer—

Taylor; the Koehler brothers, Sam and Trout; his foreman—Jim Arkus, and the Colonel's son, Duane.

The Colonel testified that Sheriff Taylor was in charge of the assault. The motive was sufficient to uphold the Colonel's testimony. Cattle rustling was a crime worthy of a hanging penalty for the perpetrator. However, Styche also learned that Sheriff Taylor, supported by the Colonel in his bid for the office, was later found to be a convicted killer wanted by the authorities in Missouri. He was now serving a life sentence at Fort Leavenworth.

Jim Arkus had been killed in a cattle stampede a year after the shooting and the Koehler brothers, Sam and Trout, Styche had just discovered, were killed while attempting to hold up the Turtle Creek Trading Post in Oklahoma Territory, owned by a former resident of River Bend, Dutch Van Huss. Dutch had written: "If it wasn't for a couple of Texans, I wouldn't be writing this letter."

The Koehler brothers were the last of the witnesses that could support the Colonel's testimony. One thing the Colonel had not revealed in his deposition was the name of the man who fired the fatal bullet. Styche also knew that the Colonel would have to be put on the stand for cross examination. That would allow him to ask the questions. Styche was confident he had the right questions, and he was equally confident of what the Colonel's answers would be. He reasoned his best strategy would have to be to surprise and confuse. He'd begin his questioning by lobbing a few soft questions in the beginning, and perhaps the Colonel would be more inclined to embellish his story. One thing Styche knew, the Colonel did not know was there were two witnesses for the prosecution whose testimony would not identify him as the actual shooter but it sure as hell would tear a man-sized hole in his account of the reason why,

—Seven Rode Together—

and the place where, the gunfight occurred. The one thing Styche could not determine would be the judge's ruling on a defense challenge.

The Colonel's attorney, C. Jefferson Harrison, over six feet, with a deep voice, was clearly the most impressive man in the arena.

Early witnesses testified to the weather, their contact with the Colonel, or the victim in the hours before the incident. Most, it turned out, had seen little or nothing. It was nearly noon and several people took a piece of fruit or a slice of bread from their pockets and began to nibble.

Mister Styche walked across the front of the courtroom and in front of the Colonel a time or two and then stopped directly in front of the witness. After a few preliminary questions, he got to the meat of the problem.

"You say that you and the others came across Steve Kane and his men branding Burkhalter yearlings with the Circle-K brand."

"Correct!"

"Be more specific and tell us exactly where this confrontation occurred."

"We spotted them on the Burkhalter range a couple miles south of the bend in the river near Burkes Crossing."

"I see. Now would you tell us in more detail what happened after you, Sheriff Taylor and the others spotted them? Did you begin firing?"

"Not at first."

"Did the sheriff order them to throw down their weapons?"

"I'm certain he did."

—John E. Cramer—

"How far away were you and the others when you first saw them?"

"A couple of hundred yards. That's when we recognized who they were and—"

"How many were there helping Kane with the branding?"

"Ah—"

"How did you happen to be out there?"

The Colonel looked toward Judge Storm who was quick to admonish Styche. "Give the witness time to reply before asking your next question."

Styche nodded and turned back to the Colonel. "One thing you forgot to mention in your earlier testimony," he began, "when did you first suspect Steve Kane was stealing your cattle?"

"It was about a month earlier that my foreman, Jim Arkus, told me he'd seen them from a distance, but they didn't see him. They were moving some Burkhalter cattle across the river to the Circle-K Ranch."

"And your foreman, he made no attempt to stop them?"

"He was alone. He thought it best to report it to me."

"But from that distance, he could identify Steve Kane?"

"Yes. That's what he told me."

"Did you report this to the Sheriff?"

"Yes. We rode in and Arkus told Taylor."

"Why do you suppose the Sheriff didn't ride out to the Circle-K and make an arrest?"

"Sheriff Taylor decided it best to catch them red-handed and then make an arrest."

"I see," Styche said, and turning toward the judge, he added, "That's all for now, Your Honor. But if it pleases the court,

—Seven Rode Together—

I would like to recall this witness later."

Judge Storm acknowledged his request with a nod, and added, "Call your next witness."

"I would like to call U.S. Marshal Clint Thurgold to the stand."

Immediately, Harrison leaned toward the Colonel and whispered, "Why would he want the Marshal to testify?"

The Colonel shook his head. "I don't know. But we'll soon find out."

Clint Thurgold, nearly as tall as Harrison, his dark hair streaked with gray, strode across the courtroom and settled himself in the witness chair. Without turning his head, his keen blue eyes swept the courtroom coming to rest on the Colonel and his attorney. The Colonel was the first to look away.

Styche, placing his thin, left hand on the railing in front of the witness box, looked first at the Colonel and then at Thurgold, he asked: "Do you know the defendant, Colonel Felix Burkhalter?"

"I guess everyone in the State of Kansas knows the Colonel."

"Do you know him personally?"

"You might say that. I've talked with him on several occasions in the past ten years."

"What were the occasions?"

Before Thurgold could answer, Harrison was on his feet. "Objection! We all know my client and the Marshal know each other. We're here today to learn the truth about an incident that occurred three years ago. I fail to see how social visits between my client and the Marshal have any bearing on this case!"

"We will learn the truth," Styche said. "And perhaps, if

—John E. Cramer—

Mister Harrison can refrain from jumping to conclusions, we will get to the truth much sooner."

"Overruled!" Judge Storm shouted. "Let's get on with it!"

Styche nodded. "Were these visits with the Colonel social?"

"I doubt whether a father who comes to my jail to bail his son out could be described as social calls. If that's what such meetings are called, then the Colonel and I had three of them within three months, ten years ago. On two occasions, I had cause to arrest Duane Burkhalter for disturbing the peace. The third time, he was arrested for killing a man during a disputed poker game. Witnesses testified it was a fair fight and that the dead man drew first, but I had cause to arrest him when he began challenging every man in the place to a gunfight. On each occasion, the Colonel came to Wichita."

"And your most recent meeting with the Colonel?"

"That was three weeks ago when I came to River Bend after learning the Colonel and a dozen others were attempting to break Mort Kane out of jail. It was believed their aim was a hanging. Kane had been accused of the shooting death of Duane Burkhalter. On that occasion I arrested the Colonel and the others who called themselves a 'vigilante committee'."

"Objection!" Harrison interrupted. "When does the witness intend to present the evidence that is supposed to connect my client with the death of Steve Kane?"

Before the judge could rule, Styche returned to his table, opened his brief case and removed an envelope and a well-used journal. He returned to the bench and gave them to Thurgold.

"This is the evidence, Your Honor. I ask that the witness be allowed to explain how he came to acquire them."

—Seven Rode Together—

Looking first at Harrison, Judge Storm ordered, "Sit down, Counselor, you're overruled!" And turning to Thurgold, he added, "And how did you acquire these?"

"As I was about to explain before the interruption, after my men rounded up the Colonel and his self-proclaimed vigilantes and locked them up, Mort Kane gave me this letter. Doc Milburn had addressed it to me. Kane said Doc wrote it during the gunfight with the Colonel and the others. It wasn't until later, when the shooting was over that he realized Doc was dead. He'd taken a stray bullet about an hour before me and my men rode into town." He cast a glance toward Harrison, anticipating another objection. "When the shooting stopped, Kane found Doc slumped over the sheriff's desk in the corner of the office. The envelope he still held in his hand was addressed to me. It had my name scribbled on it."

"Objection! Your Honor. You can't allow something scribbled on a piece of paper by a dying man to be admissible evidence—"

"I'll be the one to determine that!" Judge Storm interrupted. "This court is adjourned for a thirty minute recess!" And looking at Harrison and Styche, he added. "Come with me. We'll settle this matter in my chambers."

Once inside his office, Judge Storm seated himself at his desk, placing the envelope on top, and fixed his gaze on Harrison.

"You realize that you have just challenged the honesty and integrity of a United States Marshal, and as a United States Marshal, Clint Thurgold is a member of this court."

"I meant no disrespect, Your Honor," Harrison replied. "I was not challenging the Marshal's integrity, only the evidence he was about to present." He paused and then carefully choosing his

—John E. Cramer—

words he offered, "A letter written by a dying man with no corroborating witnesses could hardly be admissible evidence. My client, Your Honor, is not an ordinary cowhand. A half dozen witnesses testified this morning to the Colonel's generosity, his integrity and his vision that have made River Bend what it is today. It was the Colonel who has always been the leader in getting things done in this town: the schoolhouse, the church, and someday, soon, we'll have a railroad which can only add to the prosperity of River Bend. There's not a person in River Bend or in the whole valley, for that matter, who hasn't profited from his generosity and vision. He has been the one man responsible for persuading business and professional people from back East to come to River Bend. And they've all contributed to the growth and prosperity that folks enjoy today. And that's not—"

"That's enough," the Judge cut in. "You can save your summation for the jury. I called this recess to settle any doubts you might have as to the admissibility of this letter as evidence. We're all aware of the Colonel's generosity and his financial contributions to our community." Judge Storm also knew the Colonel had been well rewarded for his generosity. Many in the valley had learned he could be as ruthless as he was generous when they had something he wanted. He opened the envelope and removed the letter. Holding it up for all to see, he explained, "this letter is merely a brief note Doc wrote after he'd been wounded. It includes a confession of a man who knows he's not long for this world. It begins with this introduction." He began to read: "I have told Mort Kane the truth about his uncle's death. I wish I'd had the guts to tell him the story the day he arrived to inherit his uncle's ranch. Steve Kane was not a cattle thief. He was not killed on the range. He was killed at his

—Seven Rode Together—

ranch. The complete account of that day was told to me by Emily Burkhalter before she died in my office. The Colonel himself heard, but made no attempt to interfere. Later I wrote her story in my journal. The journal is locked in my office safe."

The Judge slipped the letter back into the envelope and held up the journal. "This includes dates, names and places, gentlemen. The Colonel did not kill Steve Kane. Duane Burkhalter did. The Colonel found out Emily was not going to Boston alone. Steve Kane was going with her. When the Colonel arrived at the Circle-K, Steve Kane, with a Winchester in his hands, stepped outside. Duane shot him. Emily, who had stepped out behind him, believing the Colonel had fired the fatal shot, picked up the Winchester and shot the Colonel in the shoulder. Duane, thinking she would fire again, shot her. The Colonel brought her to my office. She told me the whole sordid story before she died. Afterward, the Colonel warned Doc that if he didn't want the whole town to learn about his unethical activities in Boston, he would let it be known that he had prescribed a needed rest for Emily away from her family and the ranch. He never knew where the Colonel buried his wife's body until three weeks ago when Mort Kane asked him if he knew who was buried in a hidden grave on the Burkhalter estate. And that, to me, seems to be the reason for the Colonel's trumped-up charge against Mort Kane. He thought Kane had found out his family secret."

Judge Storm looked at both the attorneys. "That's the gist of the whole story Doc spelled out in greater detail in this journal. Up until now, only the three of us and the Marshal know what's in this journal. Mort Kane now knows that Emily Burkhalter is buried in the Colonel's hidden grave. The Colonel's children, Paul and Nora,

—John E. Cramer—

do not know that she is dead, or where their mother is buried, except they do know she never reached Boston."

Judge Storm pushed the journal toward the front of his desk and leaned forward. "Well, gentlemen, it's your call. I could rule either way on this matter. Personally, I'm inclined to let the jury decide. I believe both of you know what the outcome would be. The Colonel is on trial accused of the murder of Steve Kane. Nothing more. On the other hand, many in this valley believe the Colonel's accusations that both Steve Kane and now his nephew, Mort, are cattle thieves. There never were any charges or any evidence, for that matter, except those made by the Colonel. Clearly, he had taken the law into his own hands to cover up the real reason behind Steve Kane's killing and his attempt to frame Mort. For too long, the Colonel has been given free rein in this valley because he has, indeed, been the sole benefactor. No one will deny that. However, Kansas is no longer a territory where a man's fate is decided by his dexterity with a six-gun. We are trying to change that brand of justice with laws enforced by the courts. We're not there yet, and I doubt I'll ever live to see the day when carrying a gun is against the law. Of course, there is one exception, and that was demonstrated earlier today when Marshal Thurgold enforced a city ordinance that guns are not allowed in the courtroom. But do either of you really believe those cowhands, all of them from the Colonel's ranch, would have surrendered their guns peaceably if the Marshal had not had the backup he wisely decided he'd need to enforce the ordinance?"

He leaned back, and for a few moments fixed his gaze on Harrison. "One word from your client and the matter would have been settled. For far too long, the Colonel has assumed that because

—Seven Rode Together—

of his position, his actions are not to be judged. And that's why, gentlemen, I am ruling the evidence contained in Doctor Milburn's journal is admissible. We'll let the jury decide this case. If you have any objections, let's hear 'em now. If not, however the jury decides, the people of this valley are going to hear the truth as Doc Milburn wrote it. I figure we owe him that. The public will make a final judgment and let's hope the Colonel gets the message. He's no longer above the law. Some will realize his accusations and paranoia concerning the Kanes were made because of his own personal vendetta, and not because he was seeking justice for unlawful acts." Neither Harrison nor Styche, who had entered the chambers eager for the chance to present their views, had any further comments.

Rising from his chair, Judge Storm declared the recess over. "I expect to wrap up this case before sundown!"

Styche returned to the courtroom knowing his chances of convincing a jury the Colonel was guilty of the murder of Steve Kane were no longer a possibility. Harrison now was satisfied the Colonel would not be found guilty of murder, still having serious doubts that his client had leveled with him about what actually happened three years ago.

He made known his feelings and what he had learned during the past thirty minutes the moment he sat down next to the Colonel. "I've got good news and "

"That's great!" the Colonel exploded. "The Judge ruled in our favor. I knew anything Doc Milburn scribbled on a piece of paper wouldn't be admissible as evidence in any court, let alone any court presided over by Judge Storm—"

"Let me finish before you begin your celebration, Colonel. The Judge did not rule in our favor, and Milburn's scribbled note,

—John E. Cramer—

as you describe it, was not the only evidence Milburn left behind. He also kept a journal. He paused, and in an even tone, asked, "What really happened in Doc's office three years ago when you brought your wife in to be treated for a gunshot wound?"

The Colonel sat stone faced, staring at Harrison in disbelief. Suddenly, like a fighter who comes to after what should have been a knock-out blow, the Colonel regained his composure. "So, what it boils down to is my word against what Doc wrote in his journal. I don't know what Doc wrote. But everyone knows Doc prescribed a trip back East to visit old friends." He paused, anticipating a response from Harrison. "Put me back on the stand and I'll straighten out this whole thing."

"Everything?" Harrison asked. "You haven't heard everything yet. According to Milburn, you didn't kill Steve Kane—Duane did. He also says Duane shot Emily and she died in his office."

"That's a damn lie! There never was anyone killed that day at the Circle-K Ranch. Kane was killed when we caught him stealin' our cattle. And who in hell is ever goin' to believe that Duane shot his own mother? From where I sit it's a Mexican stand-off. I got no witnesses to support my testimony and they got no witnesses to back up the concocted lies Doc wrote in his journal."

"That may not be the case. My hunch is that Styche has a viable witness, one Doc mentioned in the note he wrote before he died. And if you'll take my advice, if he calls Mort Kane to testify, we should—"

"That won't be necessary," the Colonel cut in. "It's still his word against mine no matter what he says. And who do you think the jury is goin' to believe—me or a transplanted Kentuckian!"

—Seven Rode Together—

When they heard the pounding of the Judge's gavel, they both looked toward the bench. "If the defense has finished their discussion, this court will come to order!" Turning toward Styche and Marshal Thurgold, seated on the opposite side of the room, he added, "You may proceed with your witness's testimony."

For the next couple of hours, Thurgold's testimony included all entries in Doc's journal that had been reviewed by Styche, Harrison and Judge Storm during their thirty minute recess.

Against his better judgment, Harrison gave in to the Colonel's repeated demands that he take the stand to refute the evidence presented in Doc Milburn's journal. Their whispering debate ended when they heard Styche saying, "I now call Colonel Burkhalter to take the stand."

The moment the Colonel was seated, Styche began, "I know you're well aware of the penalty for perjury. I ask you now if there is any part of your previous testimony that you would like to change, having heard the testimony given by U.S. Marshal Thurgold. I must warn you that before you answer, the prosecution has a witness ready to testify under oath that Doc Milburn confessed Duane had killed your wife. She was buried on your ranch in a grave located on a grassy shelf in a shallow ravine located only a few miles east of your home. He is also willing to testify that he has seen the grave, well out of public view, marked only by a small white cross. Now, I ask you again, is there any part of your previous testimony that you would like to amend?"

The Colonel glanced first at Harrison, who now sat quietly. He shifted his gaze from Harrison to those seated in the balcony, and for the first time since the proceedings began, he saw both Paul and Nora. He watched as they both stood up and moved toward the

— John E. Cramer —

aisle without looking back. For a few fleeting moments, there was absolute silence, broken finally by an elderly lady who found it needful to clear her throat.

As he turned back to face his tormentor, the Colonel heard Styche ask. "Will you tell the court where your wife has been for the past three years?"

When the Colonel did not reply, Judge Storm leaned over and in a slow even voice, he directed, "Answer the question!"

"She's in Europe. She's visiting friends."

"No more questions." Styche said abruptly, walking quickly back to his table.

"The witness may step down," the Judge directed.

Within the next hour, both Harrison and Styche completed their final summations and were seated awaiting Judge Storm's final remarks to the jurors. "You may now retire and begin your deliberations, remembering the accused is charged only with the murder of Steve Kane."

Immediately the jury foreman stood up and motioned to the others to come closer. For the next few minutes, one by one he polled the other jurors. And having solicited a unanimous decision, he turned toward the bench. "No need to retire," he said. "We've reached a verdict."

Judge Storm asked the defendant to rise and face the jury.

"You've reached a verdict?"

"Yes, Your Honor. We, the jury, find the defendant not guilty of the murder of Steve Kane."

"Case closed! The defendant is free to go! This court is adjourned!" He rapped his gavel and left the courtroom, disappearing through the door leading to his chambers.

—Seven Rode Together—

The spectators cleared the courthouse, spilling out onto the grass and the streets. There were no loud outbursts or demonstrations, only the low drone of conversation among those who had witnessed the events of the day.

Both Styche and Harrison began clearing their tables of papers and documents and stuffing them into their satchels. Styche was thinking he might have to wait a long time before he'd have another case like this one—the kind he'd hoped would give him a leg up on his ambition to become the youngest Governor in the State of Kansas.

Across the room, Harrison stood looking down at the Colonel, who remained seated. He was thinking how ironic this case had turned out. It wasn't his years of courtroom experience in Boston that won this case today. In fact, it was testimony from the prosecution that won the case for him. Laying his hand on the Colonel's shoulder, he said, "You didn't need me to come all the way to win today. When I get back to Boston, I'll see your retainer is returned."

The Colonel sat quietly long after Harrison and the others had left the courtroom. He was still seeing the faces of Nora and Paul as they looked down on him from the balcony. He sat there alone, his teeth clenched, recalling memories that had haunted him since the morning, three years ago, when Emily had left the ranch for the last time. Doc Milburn had prescribed a cure for her loneliness—a trip to Boston and a prolonged visit with friends and family. But she would not have gone alone. He had learned from his friends at the River Bend Bank that she had withdrawn her savings. And before leaving the ranch, she had cleaned out the wall safe in his office. And he was also aware that Steve Kane, who had become

—John E. Cramer—

a close confidant of Emily over the years, had sold off most of his stock. When he and the others went to the Circle-K that morning, there was no intent to kill anyone. He aimed to have Taylor arrest Kane on a trumped-up charge of cattle thieving. He would take Emily back home, and everything would be alright. When Emily picked up Kane's rifle after Duane had killed Steve, she hadn't aimed at any of them, she just pulled the trigger. The bullet struck the Colonel in the shoulder. The gunfighter instinct in Duane fired before Emily could get off another round.

And what had begun as a simple maneuver to arrest Kane and bring Emily home, turned out to be a disaster. And when Mort Kane inherited the Circle-K, the same scenario began to repeat itself, only this time it was his daughter, Nora, whose friendliness with a Kane turned into a love affair.

Because of the Kanes, the Colonel believed, he had lost his wife, a son, and perhaps both Paul and Nora. He leaned forward rubbing his hands through his hair, and in words scarcely above a whisper he made a final vow, "If it takes all I own, all the money I have, even if it destroys me, I swear, from this day on, my reason for living will be for the day that I rid this valley of another Kane. So help me, God!"

Chapter 10

The four temporary deputies were waiting at the jail when Marshal Thurgold arrived. "Well, gentlemen," he began, "it appears I won't be needin' your services any longer. I'm much obliged for your help." Turning to Mort, he extended his hand. "I doubt the Colonel will be accusing you any time soon of stealing cattle." After shaking hands with Jeb, he thanked Thorn and Kio for their help. "From what the Mayor was telling me on my way over here from the courthouse, Mister Masters, you just might be the next Sheriff in this town. He tells me they're planning a special election in the next week or so and the only candidate for the job right now is Oscar Cravens."

"I'm afraid, if they're looking for an opponent for Deputy Cravens," Thorn grinned, "they'd best keep lookin'. There's not enough money in Kansas to hire this Texas cowboy. Kio and me will be headin' for your neck of the woods, Marshal, in a week or two. We'll be bringin' a herd of Texas cattle to Wichita."

"When you get there," the Marshal replied, "look me up and

—John E. Cramer—

I'll buy you a drink. That goes for all of you."

When the four of them stepped outside, they saw Deputy Cravens and the Colonel coming across the street toward the sheriff's office. Mort turned to Masters and Kio. "If you two need a place to bed down tonight," Mort invited, "You're welcome at the Circle-K."

"Thanks," Thorn grinned. "But Kio and me are hankerin' to see what kind of poker players they raise in Kansas. No need to wait up for us."

As they mounted up, they watched as the Colonel and Cravens entered the sheriff's office. "Reckon the Colonel's fixin' to collect his cowhands," Jeb said. "This sure ain't been one of his best days."

They headed west out of town, passed the Silver Dollar Saloon, the Mary Belle Cafe, Alec Johnson's General Store and the Livery Stable, to the fork leading off to the northwest toward the Circle-K Ranch. They spurred their horses into an easy lope and rode in silence.

Jeb's conscience had begun to cause him no little amount of discomfort knowing that within the next thirty minutes, Mort was going to find out what he'd done without first talking it over with him. In the nearly four years he'd known Mort, they'd always leveled with each other on matters they each had a stake in. He'd been aimin' to tell him for the past couple of days, but he reasoned Mort had enough on his mind without giving him something else to chew on. Besides, he was almost sure, given the same situation, Mort would have seen things the same way, and would have made the same decision. All the same, Jeb knew the moment of truth was only about five miles away.

—Seven Rode Together—

Jeb was right about one thing. Since his shootout with the Colonel's self-proclaimed posse at the River Bend jail, Mort knew Paul and Nora Burkhalter, especially Nora, were going to learn the whole truth about the Colonel's dirty secrets. Could he ever hope, in view of all that happened, that his love for Nora and his friendship with Paul could continue. A man can ask why, but the answer's always the same: What's done is done. Nothing or nobody can change that. And right now, he knew he had to look after Joey.

"You're a funny feller, Mort. It's never easy to know what you're thinkin'. I can tell you right now, you'd better be thinkin' about that skunk who still calls hisself a 'Colonel.' He's figurin' on gettin' even. Don't you ever forget it. One thing I ain't been able to figure out. Why does old man Burkhalter keep callin' hisself a Colonel when he knows damn well he ain't been a Colonel since the day he left the Army. Now, your Uncle Steve was a Major, but all the time I knowed him, he never once called hisself Major Kane. Steve probably saw more action in one week than Burkhalter did during all the time he spent in the Army. Truth known, he probably spent his whole hitch so far behind the fightin'—he probably never heard the shootin'."

By the time Jeb finished his appraisal of the Colonel's war experience, they'd turned into the quarter-mile lane that led to the Circle-K ranch house. "There's somethin' I've been meanin' to tell you, Mort. I know you'd most likely done the same thing I done if—" Before he could finish, they both spotted Joey who came running to greet them as they pulled up to the hitchrail. "Pa! Pa! Look at me! Do you see anything I've been wearin' that I ain't now?" Joey raised his arm above his head. "I don't need to be wearin' a sling no more."

—John E. Cramer—

"What do you think of that, Jeb? Our partner will be back doin' his chores with two arms. First thing we know, he'll be wantin' to go fishin'."

"That's not all, Pa. We got company!"

"Company?"

"That's what I was wantin' to tell you, Mort." Jeb cut in. "but we got to talkin' about other things."

They were half way up the brick walk when the door opened and Doc Milburn's widow, Blanche Milburn, stepped out onto the front porch. She didn't wait for them to come to her. She hurried down the steps, put her arms around Mort and kissed him on the cheek. "You'll never know how much Amanda and I appreciate your kind offer. I know you told me I could stay as long as needed before accepting your offer as permanent. We both knew what our answer would be the moment we stepped through the front door." Tears welled in her eyes, "I know Milt, God rest his soul, is looking down, and he, too, is thanking you."

"Now wait a minute," Mort looked back at Jeb. "It's you and Amanda who are doing us a favor. We're the one's need to be counting our blessings. I know Jeb is thanking you since he's relieved of his cooking duties. And Joey and I are thankful that he's relieved, too. So it's not hard to see who got the best of the deal." As he finished talking, Joey, who was bursting with excitement, bounded up the steps to the doorway as Amanda Milburn, a beautiful young lady in her teens, stepped outside.

"This is Amanda, Pa. Ain't she pretty? She's going to live with us."

"Welcome to the Circle-K, Amanda. Our home is your home for as long as you and your mother can put up with us. You'll

—Seven Rode Together—

have to get used to our partner, too. Jeb! Where'd he go? He was here a moment ago."

"Said he was goin' to take care of the horses, Pa. He said he had chores that needed tendin' to."

Amanda, who watched as her Mother and Mort came up the steps to the porch, finally found the chance to respond to Mort's welcome. "Mother and I both are grateful. We're happy to be here. Joey has spent most of the day showing me around the ranch."

"She wants to ride up to the cabin, Pa." Joey added. "When do you think would be a good time?"

"Amanda," Missus Milburn suggested, "why don't you and Joey find Jeb and see if you can help him with his chores. I'm sure he'd appreciate a little help."

As quickly as they disappeared around the corner of the house, Missus Milburn turned to Mort. "You have a visitor, Mort. She's waiting in the parlor. And, I believe I'll try out that hammock between those giant oak trees. I've been thinking about it ever since we arrived this morning."

"A visitor," Mort said to himself. "Could it be—" He stepped into the foyer and before he reached the parlor, Nora emerged. For a moment, they stood a few steps apart. Without a word spoken, they moved toward one another and into each other's arms. "Oh, Mort," Nora whispered, "What am I going to do? First Mother, then Duane. My own Father a liar—"

Gently, he slipped his arm around her shoulder and together they moved to the large, leather sofa in front of the fireplace. He wanted to tell her how much he loved her, and that they'd find a way to put all of it behind them. Instead, he pulled her closer toward him and suddenly heard himself saying, "I'm not very good

—*John E. Cramer*—

with words, Nora, but I'd do anything to make you happy. Things happened that we had no control over." For several moments they sat quietly looking at one another. "I guess what I'm trying to say, I never expected to feel this way again about any woman. And knowing you were the Colonel's daughter, I was determined not to care for you. Another place, another time, maybe under different circumstances—"

"You'd ask me to marry you," Nora said, knowing what he was wanting to say and certain he'd never get around to saying it. "That's what you were going to say, isn't it?"

Mort nodded. "I was comin' to that. But I don't think the Colonel would be too pleased to have me as a son-in-law."

"I know you'd have the blessing from a brother-in-law. Paul likes you. He always has. Neither Paul nor I blame you for anything that's happened. I believe you know that. We both know he can't stay here. Paul would never have returned from Boston if Mother had been there." She paused. Her eyes filled with tears. "In fact, Paul is leaving the day after tomorrow and he wants me to go with him."

"Are you going?"

"Oh, Mort," she cried. "I can't stay here. Not with everything that's happened. Hasn't there been enough killing? It's never going to stop so long as Father and you stay in this valley. And what about Joey?"

"Joey?"

"Yes. Father won't rest until you're dead and buried. And you must know by now that he knows ways and has the means to destroy his enemies. Do you want Joey to grow up without a father?"

—Seven Rode Together—

"Of course not. And that's not goin' to happen!"

"Oh, Mort, you're impossible! Look what happened to your Uncle Steve."

"I'm not my Uncle Steve," Mort said evenly.

"Then you don't intend to leave?"

"I can't."

"Can't, or won't?"

"When and if I leave the Circle-K, Nora, it will be because I want to, not because the Colonel wants me to. And if, as you say, he wants me dead, there's no place I can go that he can't find me. He doesn't need to do the killing. Like you said, he has the means."

"I'd hoped you loved me enough to marry me and the three of us could begin a new life together."

"I do love you, Nora. And I do want to marry you. Joey loves you, too. And, I do want to begin a new life together—"

"But not enough to leave this god-forsaken valley to start a new life. It doesn't have to be in Boston. East, West, North or South. Any place but here."

Mort knew what she wanted to hear, and he knew she meant what she said. She may have her heart set on Boston, but if he decided to resettle in Montana Territory or Texas, she'd be satisfied.

When he didn't reply, Nora pulled back. "I guess I should have known you wouldn't be leaving no matter how much I tried to convince you. When I arrived and saw Doc Milburn's wife and her daughter, Amanda—I knew you'd already made up your mind."

"It may be part of the reason, but it's not what you think. A few days ago Alec Johnson told me that Dave Shelley had foreclosed on the Milburn home. No doubt he was following the Colonel's instructions. I asked Blanche Milburn and her daughter if they'd like to make their home at the Circle-K until they could decide what they wanted to do. Missus Milburn said she'd accept my offer if I would allow her to look after the cleanin' and the cookin'. And I believe Jeb and I have other friends in the valley who just might be needin' a helping hand if the Colonel decides to make them a target. As far as Missus Milburn and her daughter are concerned, I figured I owed Doc that much."

"You're quite a man, Mort Kane. That's why I fell in love with you. And I'm never giving up on you, no matter where I am. It's getting late and I'm not going home. I doubt there are any rooms left at the Frontier Hotel. I could perhaps impose on Paul whose been staying there since he arrived in River Bend. He brought me out here in a rented rig, I'll need a ride into town. Any suggestions?"

"Only one. And we both know what that is. And before morning, I might be able to convince you that today's problems ain't never goin' to last forever—you'll see."

Chapter 11

It was nearly sundown by the time the Colonel arrived home after bailing out his men from the River Bend jail. He was met at the door by his housekeeper, Elinda.

"So good to have you home, Colonel. This house can be a mighty lonely place when nobody's around."

"Paul and Nora, they're not here?"

"No sir. No one is here but me. Will you be having dinner?"

"I believe not, Elinda, but you can bring me a cup of coffee, and if you still have any of that delicious blueberry pie you served last night, I'll settle for that this evening. I'll be in the library."

He walked into the library and sat down in the large, leather swivel chair at his desk. Elinda was right, he thought, this place can be lonely when you know there's no one here. He stared at the pictures of Emily, Nora, Paul and Duane on his desk. They'd all be here tonight if it were not for Steve and Mort Kane, he thought. He was still reviewing the events of the past four years and recalling the mistakes in judgment by underestimating Mort Kane's ability to

—John E. Cramer—

strike back. He was still wondering how a dirt farmer from Kentucky had managed to battle him to a standstill when Elinda came in with his coffee and pie.

"Elinda," he began, "You've been wanting, for a long time, to visit your sister in St. Louis. Would you still like to see her?"

"Oh, yes, I'd like that very much. But what would you do with no one to cook and do the housework?"

"Now, don't you worry about that. I can manage for awhile. And, Elinda, when Wade Parker arrives, tell him I'm in the library."

By the time his foreman arrived, the Colonel had reviewed his finances and re-read several letters from his associates in the state capitol and from supporters for the expansion of Kansas railways linking the cities not yet served by rail transportation to eastern markets. The Colonel had invested heavily following the end of the war, hoping to influence the decision makers to build a line connecting River Bend to the midwest and eastern markets. He was gambling that if he could succeed in providing rail transportation for River Bend and the ranchers in the valley, he would regain the confidence and respect he may have lost during the trial. The beauty of it all was that he would never have to use one dollar of the profits he earned from the ranch. His plans for Mort Kane and the Circle-K he'd put on hold, at least for awhile. There was no hurry. There would be no more contrived schemes that would backfire. The key for the elimination of the one man he despised the most in this world, he reasoned, is patience and planning. When he told Dave Shelley to foreclose on Doc Milburn's home, that was a mistake. It didn't fit the new Colonel Burkhalter. That can be remedied, he thought, I'll talk with Blanche Milburn tomorrow and apologize for Shelley's unwarranted action. "Felix," he said to himself, "you need to remember one thing if you ever hope to even the score with Kane without becoming implicated. Forget about your anger and concentrate on getting even. The end itself will justify the means." Who knows, he mused, I may be asked to say a few kind words over the graves of the newly deceased when the time comes.

"You talkin' to yourself now?" Parker asked as he entered the library.

"Just thinking out loud," he smiled. "Have a seat. We've got things to talk over. Care for a drink?"

Parker shook his head. "Nope. Just had a couple of snorts with the boys back at the bunkhouse. Seems they're doin' a little celebrating because of the way the trial turned out today. 'Course we all had a pretty good idea before it began that no jury in River Bend was goin' to find you guilty."

The Colonel nodded. "Just let 'em know they can do all the celebrating they want tonight. But remind them that ends it. Tomorrow's a new day. We made one mistake today that won't be repeated. Breaking the law won't wear well from here on out at the Burkhalter ranch."

"You mean like wearin' guns in the courthouse?"

"You failed to check them with Deputy Cravens when we rode in."

"Cravens?" Parker grinned. "When he saw you, he just waved us on through."

"I wasn't wearin' a gun."

"Why in hell didn't he say somethin'? If he was supposed to be collectin' gunbelts, where was he when those two Texans rode into town? They sure as hell weren't pointin' fingers at us when they rousted us out of the courthouse."

—John E. Cramer—

The Colonel nodded in agreement. "You're right about Cravens. But we've got more important things to talk about. Besides, they'll be holdin' an election in River Bend soon, and it's not likely Cravens will be our next sheriff. Seems that some of the members of the Town Council would like to persuade Thorn Masters to quit punchin' cattle and settle down here in River Bend. And if they're successful, it would be an unexpected help in my plans I have for disposing of Mort Kane permanently."

"But what if Masters don't hanker to become a lawman?"

"No matter. What I'm planning for Kane may take a little time. But when it does, you can bet your share of the gold from that train heist during the war that neither I nor any of our men will ever be suspected of having anything to do with it."

Parker's eyes lit up. "This don't sound like somethin' that's goin' to happen overnight."

"Exactly."

"Well, then, what you got in mind?"

"All in due time," the Colonel said evenly. "But it won't be some cock-eyed story accusing Kane of stealin' cattle. And you're right. It's not goin' to happen overnight. But I can be a very patient man. First things first. And tonight I need to know if you've got anything to tell me about our two new cowhands, Dundee and Trinity."

"Like you told me," Parker began, "I gave 'em enough to do to keep 'em busy all day. Sent 'em over to the north range, the other side of Arrow Canyon, to look for any newborns or yearlings not carryin' the Burkhalter brand. Told 'em to round 'em up and herd them and the cows back to the holdin' pasture. They rode in while me and the rest of the boys were eatin' supper. I ain't had time to

—Seven Rode Together—

talk to 'em, but you oughta know, Colonel, we're goin' to be short four cowhands, includin' Luke Keltner, come mornin'."

"What do you mean, short?"

"I mean come mornin' they'll be seein' you for the pay they got comin'. And you and I both know Keltner will be wantin' to talk to you about more than just back pay."

The Colonel leaned back in his swivel chair. "I see" he said finally. "Got any idea what his plans are?"

"He didn't say and I didn't ask. All four of them cornered me outside the chow hall after supper. Just said they're leavin' the outfit in the morning. Keltner knew I was headin' up to see you. After the others had gone back to the bunkhouse and I started up here, he caught up with me. Said to tell you he was expectin' to get all his back pay. He said both you and me would know what he meant by 'all'."

He *did* know what Keltner meant. A year before the war ended, the Colonel had gotten wind of a shipment of gold from Texas to the Confederacy to help finance the war. The Colonel seized upon the information to devise a plan that, if successful, could compensate him far beyond his army pay. His plan went off without a hitch, but besides the Colonel, only three members of his raiders had survived: Jim Arkus, Wade Parker and Luke Keltner. Jim Arkus had been killed in a cattle stampede while Foreman at the Colonel's Ranch. Wade Parker was his current foreman and had worked for him since the war. He wondered what Keltner had in mind. The two hundred thousand dollars in gold, the amount the Colonel had reported stolen, was to be divided four ways. The Colonel had convinced the others, to avoid capture, they would have to wait until he could convert the gold into currency. The

—John E. Cramer—

Colonel secretly emerged with one-hundred thousand dollars as his share of the gold, but he also devised a plan to make him the custodian for the others' shares. For their security, he gave each of them deeds to a portion of the Burkhalter Estate, and each one would be a partner in the Burkhalter Ranch until they could safely convert the gold and go their own way. In the meantime, they would be paid wages and share in the profits from the ranch. When the time came, he'd said, each would exchange their deeds for their share of the gold. The Colonel was still thinking about what to do about Keltner when he heard Parker ask. "Do you think Keltner can cause us problems we can't handle?"

"No!" The Colonel shook his head. "It's not Keltner I'm worried about. Right now, I'm more concerned about Jeremiah Dundee. As Company Clerk he was privy to all the activities of the troops under my command. I know he kept official records, but it's quite possible he kept a diary of his own. If he did, the two men I hired to ambush him on his way here say there was no sign of documents or a diary in the gear his pack mule was carryin!"

"I can't see how you've got anything to be concerned about, Colonel. If they was thinkin' about causin' us any trouble, they'd not come all the way out here to work for you."

"You may be right," the Colonel agreed. "But there's no statute of limitations on what we did. We could still face a court martial."

"Ain't you forgettin' somethin', Colonel?"

"Such as?"

"For one thing that young side-kick of Dundee's, Tom Trinity. It ain't unlikely that if Dundee kept a record of us during the war, he may have shared a few stories with him, and Dundee

—Seven Rode Together—

has more than a train robbery to talk about."

The Colonel began nodding his head in agreement the moment Parker mentioned Tom Trinity. "Like I said, you could be right. On the other hand, Jeremiah didn't seem to recall you, and they rode in here with nothing but bedrolls and saddle bags. There was nothing of interest in those saddle bags, so, let's not be lookin' for trouble behind every tree. A man who keeps runnin' scared is most likely to make stupid mistakes. Meanwhile, so far as they're concerned, we just keep our eyes and ears open."

"You're the boss," Parker said. "And you're right about a man runnin' scared. He's the guy who wakes up in the night, thinks he hears somethin' and shoots himself in the foot."

"Exactly. There are ways to make your worst enemy run scared. All you need are two hired guns who can work behind enemy lines, so to speak." He was thinking of his arrangement with Buck Farley. His hired guns worked for him. His clients were never known by them. Farley's headquarters in Indian Territory across the southern Kansas border, was a safe haven. The two hired guns, who'd taken pot shots at Mort and Joey a week before the Colonel's trial, for instance, weren't paid to kill anybody. They were just meant to get Mort's attention. After a few more such treatments, Mort would begin to run scared. The hired guns collect their pay from Buck Farley. There was no contact with the Colonel.

That was one reason why the Colonel was quick to reply when Parker asked, "What do you aim to do about Keltner?"

"There's nothing I can do except pay him off."

"Just like that? What if he won't settle for less than one-third, since Arkus ain't ever goin' to see his share?"

"I'll give it to him." The Colonel said nothing about his

arrangement with Farley, no matter what he gave Keltner for his share, he'd never live long enough to spend it.

"You might tell him not to spend it all in one place," Parker grinned. "I've been meaning to ask you, Colonel, about Paul and Nora. They plannin' to stay with you?"

"They won't be staying."

"I knew Paul's gettin' his schoolin' back East and plannin' to become a doctor. But Nora? Isn't she kinda sweet on Mort Kane? I thought maybe that she'd be stayin'."

"Wrong on both counts!" the Colonel snapped. "No daughter of mine will ever marry a man who killed her brother!"

"Well, I just thought—"

"You thought wrong!" the Colonel barked. "You know, Parker, a man can be pushed just so far before he either cracks or decides to stay the course. When I came out here, I was determined to succeed—make somethin' out of nothin'. Never once did I think about givin' up. Those were hard times. I saw some come and saw some go. They didn't have the guts to fight to keep what they had. Those who stayed, carved out empires of their own by fighting like hell to hang on to 'em."

"Steve Kane was that kind of man until he decided to sell land to dirt farmers. Land he'd shed blood to hang on to."

"On the other hand," those small ranchers have made a big difference in the growth of River Bend. Without them River Bend might still be an Indian Tradin' Post."

Oblivious to Parker's observation, the Colonel leaned back in his chair and stared into the fireplace. "So, you see Parker, I plan to stay the course. Steve and Mort Kane have cost me my wife, two sons and a daughter, but the battle is far from over."

—Seven Rode Together—

Parker nodded. "You can depend on me, Colonel."

"Well, then, I believe we've covered about everything." He stood up, slipped his arm around Parker's shoulder, "I'll walk you to the door. I believe I could use a little fresh air before I turn in."

Once outside, Parker headed for the bunkhouse and the Colonel sat down on the veranda. It was a starry night with just a light southern breeze rustling the leaves in the giant oak trees. The Colonel, once again alone with his thoughts, envisioned the future. In Tom Trinity, he liked what he saw. A young lad, alone in this world with no family. He could take care of himself. In some ways, the Colonel liked to think, he could be a mixture of the best qualities of both his sons. Like Paul, he displayed good manners, was soft spoken, showed respect, and had a determination to succeed in this world at whatever he set his mind to. Like Duane, he appeared to the Colonel to be one whose loyalty would never be in doubt once he was satisfied you'd earned it.

Why, the young Tom Trinity could be the recipient of his legacy, if he proved to be the son he no longer had. Neither Paul nor Nora would ever embrace the Colonel's world. He allowed himself, for the moment, the luxury to imagine what Tom Trinity could become. Supposing, he thought, I could, within the next few years, convince Tom that this is *his* home. And with the proper legal moves, he could even carry on the Burkhalter name. Tom Burkhalter, he thought, it seems to fit. The more he thought about it, the better he felt. It was good to have something to look forward to. They would need to know each other better. But he had a hunch Tom, given time to learn, would take to ranching like a duck to water.

The breeze picked up, a night owl let his presence be

—John E. Cramer—

known, and a mare whinnied from the corral. The Colonel leaned back, his hands behind his head, and watched the moon slip behind a cloud. Although he was well aware his plans for Tom could not happen overnight, the Colonel was a patient man. Who knows, he thought, one day I could be giving the Circle-K to him for a wedding present. Just thinking about the possibilities triggered a smile.

Chapter 12

Blanche Milburn greeted Mort when he came to the kitchen after completing his morning chores. "Good morning. My goodness, you certainly are up and about early this morning."

Mort smiled. "Looks like I'm not the only one who's up and about early. Jeb's gonna be disappointed that he won't have to be fixin' breakfast. We thought we'd need to get an early start this morning since I'll be takin' Nora in to River Bend. She and her brother, Paul, will be headin' back East today."

Missus Milburn nodded knowingly. "I'm sure it was a difficult decision for both of them—after all that's happened." She turned back toward the stove. "Miss Burkhalter came down earlier and helped get breakfast started. I think she went back upstairs to get her things together. She's a wonderful lady, Mort. I can only hope and pray that one day things will work out for you both."

After breakfast, Mort hitched the team to the buckboard and brought it around to the front gate. Nora said her goodbyes to Missus Milburn and Amanda on the front steps and hurried down

— John E. Cramer —

the walk toward the buckboard where Joey and Jeb were waiting.

"Sure hate to see you leavin' us, Miss Burkhalter. We're sure gonna miss you." Ignoring Jeb's outstretched hand, she leaned forward and kissed him on the cheek. Jeb stepped back, eyeing her for a moment as he rubbed his fingers over his whiskers. His grin broke into a broad smile. "Now, why'd you go and do that fer? I ain't gonna be washin' that side of my face 'til we meet again."

Joey was waiting patiently, fighting to keep back the tears. Nora knelt down beside him. She reached in her pocket and pulled out an envelope and handed it to him. "Now promise me you won't open this until supper time. And I'll promise to write you when I get to Boston and tell you about my trip. One day, Joey, we'll all be together again."

"Promise?"

"I promise."

He threw his arms about her neck and hugged her. "Me and Jeb will look after Pa," he whispered. "Reckon we'll be just fine so long as you'll be comin' back."

Nora slowly took his arms from around her neck and stood up. "I reckon you will, too," she said. She turned quickly and Mort helped her up into the spring seat. He spoke to the team and they headed down the lane to the road leading to River Bend.

Paul was waiting at the Overland Stage office when they arrived. He stepped out to the buckboard to help Nora. Mort reached behind the seat and lifted out her suitcase and followed them into the stage office. "Looks like you're the only ones leavin' River Bend this morning, Paul." They shook hands.

"I'm sorry things turned out the way they have, Mort."

Mort nodded.

—Seven Rode Together—

"I'll wait outside, Nora. The stage should be along any time now." Turning to Mort, he added. "Take care of yourself. And, Mort, I don't have to tell you—watch your back. I think we both know the Colonel's not going to forgive or forget."

"Nor am I." Mort said solemnly.

Paul picked up the luggage and disappeared outside. For a moment Mort and Nora were alone, wrapped in each other's arms. "Let's not say goodbye," she whispered.

Their goodbye kiss was interrupted when the stage rolled up in front of the office. They stepped outside into the morning sunlight.

"We're runnin' a little late, folks," the driver said as he finished storing the luggage atop the stage. "I'd like to get to the Beaverland Way Station at Freedom Ridge by noon. We'll have a layover there for dinner and a change of horses. We'll get a good start to Wichita come morning."

A few minutes later, the stage pulled out. Mort watched until the stage rounded the corner past Fred Finley's Livery Stable and headed north. He stepped from the boardwalk and headed across the dusty street to Alec Johnson's General Store. He was still thinking about Paul's warning and wondering how long it would really be before he would ever see Nora again. About one thing he was certain, he'd not have to wait long to hear from the Colonel . The next time, he thought, he won't have the element of surprise.

The moment he stepped through the door of River Bend's only general store, Alex was there to greet him. "By yimminy, Mort, it's good to see you!" He reached out and grabbed Mort's hand and continued to talk as he shook it. "I haven't seen you since before all the shooting at the jail and that's been a month ago, by

—John E. Cramer—

golly. Me and the Missus both was sorry to hear about Doc Milburn. He was one good man and a fine doctor, too. It was a fine thing you did for his Missus and Amanda. That Colonel, he's no good for anybody. Maybe now, he won't be so high and mighty anymore. That feller who owns the newspaper, Clancy O'Riley, says a lot of good things about you, by golly." He paused and looked under the counter and pulled out the day's newspaper. "It's all right in here, by golly." He offered it to Mort who made no move to reach for it.

"I'll take your word for it. Right now, I'm more interested in buyin' than readin'. He handed Alec the list Blanche Milburn had given him. "If you're more interested in sellin' than promotin' O'Riley's newspaper, I'd like you to fill this order. I'll be back later and pick it up."

"You betcha. I'll have it ready for you. I just thought you'd want to know about O'Riley's story—"

"And there's one thing you need to know, Alec. You can't believe all you read in the newspaper."

Alec picked up the list from the counter, mumbling to himself. "By golly, I'll not be the only one in River Bend who believes what he reads in this newspaper, I betcha."

Mort was still thinking about Paul's parting words of warning as he headed toward the Post Office. Missus Milburn was hoping to hear from some of her folks back East. Mort hoped he'd hear from Ellen's sister Lilly on the news around Louisville. It had been nearly a year since his wife's sister had written. "Mort! Mort Kane!" He turned and watched as Thorn Masters and Kio made their way across the street toward him. "We've been looking for you," Thorn said. "We just rode in from the Circle-K. The lady we

—Seven Rode Together—

talked with there said we'd find you in town."

"Looks like you found me, alright. What's on your mind? You decide to make a run for sheriff after all?"

"The day I run for sheriff in any town, that'll be the day the Rio Grande flows north and drains all the water out of the Gulf of Mexico." Thorn rubbed the back of his neck. "From what me and Kio have been hearin', there's some folks in this town who'd like to pin the sheriff's badge on you. Seems you're the first man in these parts who stood up to Burkhalter and lived to tell about it. 'Course there's the other side of the coin. There's some who don't believe they oughta be electin' a sheriff who don't wear a gun. But there was some who were arguin' that you was damned handy with a Winchester."

"And this is what you rode all the way out to the Circle-K to tell me?" Mort asked.

Thorn shook his head. "No, but you're the one who brought it up. What I wanted to tell you has to do with the cattle drive we're bringin' up from Texas. Got a telegram from Gil Kneeland this morning. Seems we won't be comin' through here as soon as we thought. Gil's plannin' on swingin' the herd east from Amarillo to avoid an ambush from Apaches crossin' that part of Indian Territory. The Apaches and some other border raiders have been raisin' hell with cattle drives in some of them mountain passes. Anyway, they'll be comin' up west of Powderville and crossing into Kansas a little west of Freedom Ridge. Me and Kio are headin' back that way today. We aim to do a little scoutin' along that route and join the drive before they reach the border."

"Sounds like you got your work cut out for you," Mort said. "Is Gil still willin' to let me join up with about fifteen hundred head

—John E. Cramer—

of Circle-K cows for the drive on into Wichita?"

"That's what he's figurin' on," Thorn nodded. "Pickin' up your cattle and a dozen more Circle-K cowhands to help pushing the herd the rest of the way."

"I might be able to do better than that," Mort said. "You say you and Kio are gonna be headin' for Freedom Ridge on your way back to join up with the drive?"

"Nothin' wrong with his hearin', is there Kio? That's exactly what I said. There's a Stage Way Station there. We figure on pickin' up our gear at the hotel, have a bite to eat and then head out. We'll get to the Way Station along toward sundown and if old Jake Frishee is still runnin' the place and ain't filled up, me and Kio will have one more night we won't have to cook or bed down under the stars. Does that answer your question?"

"I guess Missus Milburn and Jeb and Amanda could look after things at the Circle-K for a week or so." He was not forgetting Paul and Nora would be staying the night at the Way Station. "Alright. Here's what I got in mind. I gotta couple of things to tend to back at the ranch. Then I'll tag along with you and Kio and help bring the herd back to River Bend. You never can tell. You might run into Apaches. Like you say, an extra Winchester might come in handy."

"It takes you a helluva long time to answer a question," Thorn cut in. "We'll be lookin' for you tonight. Bring along a little extra cash. Me and the boys on the trail can always enjoy a friendly game of poker come nightfall. He broke into a broad smile. "Ain't that right, Kio?"

They hurried back across the street to the Frontier Hotel. Mort headed back to the general store. "Now, there's a pair any man

—Seven Rode Together—

would be proud to ride with."

Alex had already filled Mort's order and carried it out to the buckboard. "Ebert Youngman was here awhile ago, Mort. He was wondering if you'd stop by his place on your way home. Didn't say what kind of business. I yust listen, I don't ask questions. But he did say it was important. And when Ebert says something's important, by golly, he means yust that." Ebert Youngman's spread bordered the Circle-K on the south which also gave him access to the river. Ebert, like the Colonel and Steve Kane, were among the first settlers in the Valley. He'd always seen eye to eye with Steve, and later with Mort, where Colonel Burkhalter was concerned. Ebert and his wife, Jessie, had two fine looking sons, Steve and Chad. Chad was the older of the two by several years. He, like his Pa, was a fair hand with a six-gun. He rode with Marshal Thurgold the night the Colonel and his vigilantes had Mort pinned down in the gun battle at the River Bend jail. And though it was no secret, several of the single women in River Bend would like to get him to the altar. Chad's major aim was to one day make Amanda Milburn his leading lady.

Mort was still wondering what was so important that Ebert would want to see him today when he turned into the lane leading to the Youngman Ranch. Mort recalled seeing him the last time before the trial. Ebert was rejected by the Colonel's lawyer during the jury selection. It was no big surprise, Mort thought. Had Ebert been selected, it would have been a hung jury.

Ebert came out of the house when Mort pulled the mare to a halt at the hitching post. He met Mort with a firm handshake and motioned toward the shade of the front porch. "I figured we could talk better out here. It sounded urgent, but I've made my mind up.

—John E. Cramer—

Jessie thinks I'm making this decision because of her. I am, but I love her more than I do this ranch or anything in this world. Chad knows what I'm plannin' and he thinks it's the right thing. Haven't said anything to Steve." He stopped talking, his hands clenched together, his elbows resting on his knees. When he sat up he looked Mort squarely in the eye, his jaws tightened. "I'm fixin' to sell out, Mort, and move back to Philadelphia where most of Jessie's kinfolks live."

"It's hard to believe what I'm hearin'. You've been in this Valley a mighty long time—"

"It's for Jessie's sake, Mort. She needs doctorin' she can't get anywhere around here. Doc Milburn was lookin' after her but he's not around anymore. He warned us about her ailin' a couple years back. Said if she's to get better, she's goin' to have to find a specialist. For awhile after that she seemed to be gettin' better. Well, anyway, I've made up my mind, Mort. I know the Colonel would be the first to want to grab this ranch, given half a chance. So, now you know why I needed to talk to you. You're the only one in this Valley, besides the Colonel, who'd be able to buy this place. And before I'd sell to him, I'd sooner turn it back to the Indians. It's free and clear. There ain't no mortgage. Jessie and me went through some hard times a few years ago, but we never made any deals with the River Bend Bank like Holt Jaspers hated to make. The Colonel foreclosed on them soon as they missed a payment. That damn bank ought to be called the Burkhalter Bank. He's the one who makes all the decisions. Anyway, Mort, that's the way it is. You interested?"

"Sure, I'm interested—"

"Then it's done. We can take care of the details later. It'll be

—Seven Rode Together—

a few weeks before I'm ready to leave." He stood up and they shook hands.

"If you change your mind," Mort said. "We'll forget we had this conversation. And if there's anything I can do between now and then, just whistle."

Mort was still pondering all that happened since he left the Circle-K that morning. When he pulled up in front of his house, the front door flew open and out ran Joey waving the envelope Nora had given him, screaming at the top of his voice. "Pa! Pa! You'll never guess what Nora gave me. Never in a million years! You can't guess, can you, Pa?"

"'Fraid not, Joey. But it'd have to be mighty small to fit in an envelope."

Before Joey could explain, Amanda met them in the kitchen where Mort was putting a box of staples on the table. She was cuddling a German Shepherd pup in her arms. "He wasn't in that envelope, Pa," Joey whooped. "Nora gave him to Jeb to look after. He's the spittin' image of Major, Pa. You want to hold him, Pa?"

"Have you named him yet?"

Joey nodded. "I'd like to call him Sarge."

"Sarge, it is," Mort agreed. "Couldn't have thought of a better name, myself." He was about to tell Blanche he wouldn't be around for supper when Jeb came in.

"Chad Youngman just rode in, Mort. He says he needs to see you." And casting a quick glance at Amanda, he added, "Seein' as how you're busy admirin' that pup, I could ask Amanda if she'd go out and tell him he'll have to come in." He slipped Mort a wink as Amanda headed for the door. "That'll give her a chance to invite him for supper."

Chapter 13

When Jeb and Mort came out of the house, Amanda was busy explaining to Chad why he could wait until after supper before he went back home. Mort and Jeb waited a moment on the porch. It appeared to both of them that young Chad Youngman wasn't in that much of a hurry to talk to Mort. When he saw Mort and Jeb heading in his direction, he said something to Amanda.

"I was just asking Chad to stay for supper, but he says he's got to get home." She walked hurriedly past them and disappeared into the house.

"So, what's on your mind, Chad?" Mort asked.

"Pa said he heard you intended to meet that Texas cattle drive and help 'em with the drive to Wichita, and that you're plannin' on supplyin' a few hands to help after you add some of the Circle-K stock to take with 'em when they come through River Bend."

"Yeah," Mort nodded, "I believe I did say somethin' about that when I talked with your Pa."

—Seven Rode Together—

"Pa was wonderin' if maybe you'd be able to cut the same deal for some of the Lazy-Y cattle you and Gil Kneeland's gonna. get. He says he's willin' to supply some cowhands to help out."

"I don't see why not," Mort said.

"He said you were headin' out this afternoon to meet those Texas fellers at the Stage Way Station at Freedom Ridge. Pa says if you're needin' somebody to ride with, I could go."

"Wait a goll-dern minute!" Jeb exploded. "How come I ain't heard nothin' about this?"

"Well, now you know," Mort shrugged. "I just hadn't been able to tell you before. Seems to me you were so all fired up to get Chad here to stay for supper, I didn't get a chance to tell you anything."

"Don't matter," Jeb muttered. "You plannin' on my goin' along, ain't ya?"

"That I was," Mort grinned. "See if you can round up Luke McCambridge and let him know that I'd like for him and the others to keep an eye on the place 'til we get back. Tell him we'll be gone for a week or so." Before Mort had finished, Jeb was headed for the corral where Luke and some of the Circle-K cowhands were gathered to watch one of the men trying to break one of the four mustangs they'd recently brought in.

Turning to Chad, he said, "Tell Ebert we'll be back in a couple of weeks. If he can spare you, you're welcome to come along."

Mort headed for the house. He wanted to tell Missus Milburn and Joey they'd be heading out before supper. "We could be back sooner," he said.

"We'll do fine," Missus Milburn said. "Especially now that we've got Sarge to look after us. Right, Joey?"

—John E. Cramer—

"You're jokin' now, Missus Milburn. But you wait and see. He's gonna be just like Major. And he was the best, wasn't he, Pa?"

"Never saw one better," Mort said.

When Mort came out of the house, Jeb was waiting. He had saddled the palomino and his blazed-face roan with saddle bags and bedrolls. Chad was waiting for them at the fork in the road north of River Bend. "Thought I'd save us a little time," he said. "Pa said to tell you he appreciated your help."

"Well, then, let's move out," Mort replied. And the three of them headed east toward Freedom Ridge.

Nora and Paul sat quietly for the first several miles after the stage coach pulled out of River Bend. The morning sun was peeking over the foothills to the north, spreading across the flat land, lending light to the peace and tranquility. The road ahead stretched out into a wide curve at the base of the first step in the hills to the east. Finally, Nora turned from watching the landscape float. "Do you think we'll ever be back, Paul?"

Paul continued to gaze out of the window. Without turning to look at her, he said, "The way I'm feeling at this moment, I can't think of a single reason why I'd come back. The first time I left, I was dead set on studyin' medicine at Harvard University and looked forward to a practice in Boston. I may have returned for a visit, but never to live. Now, after all that's happened, I have nothing to come back to. How about you? You don't really believe Mort will ever give up his life here for life in the city, do you?"

"No. I don't believe he will. But it wouldn't have to be in a city. If we could be together, I'd be happy anywhere on earth."

—Seven Rode Together—

"Even in River Bend? On the Circle-K? He's never going to leave there, you know. I wouldn't be surprised if one day Mort Kane, not the Colonel, will be the wealthiest man in that area, but one most remembered as the quiet man whose honesty and integrity displaced the Colonel's grandiose schemes to gain wealth and power on the backs of others. Mort Kane leave the Circle-K and the Valley? Not a chance. And our father will go to his grave still plotting to pry him loose."

The stage coach began slowing down. Paul stuck his head out the window and yelled at the driver. "Why're we stopping?"

"Look ahead yonder!" the driver yelled back.

Paul saw where the road made a slight bend. The man he saw standing at the side of the road was carrying a rifle with saddle bags slung over his shoulder. While Paul watched, the man moved to a position in the middle of the road, frantically waving his arms over his head. "You stoppin'?" Paul asked.

"Pete's got him covered with a shotgun. Ain't likely he's plannin' any holdup!"

The stage rolled to a stop. "You can put that shotgun away!" he hollered. "All's I need is a ride to Wichita. I got money to pay for it," he added.

"What the hell you doin' way out here on foot?" Pete wanted to know.

"Some son-of-a-bitch shot my horse out from under me back up there a few miles." He pointed toward the foothills. "There wuz two of 'em. Had me pinned down 'til I winged one of 'em. Then they high-tailed toward the back country. Took me the past four hours to get here."

"Well, hand me that rifle and saddle bags and get inside,"

—John E. Cramer—

Pete ordered.

"You can have the damned rifle but I'll hang on to these saddle bags."

"Guess it won't hurt. We're only carryin' two passengers. I guess you can find room for 'em."

When the man stepped from in front of the stage and opened the door, Paul and Nora recognized him immediately. After he got in and seated himself opposite them with his saddle bags positioned between him and the side of the coach, he heaved a sigh of relief. The driver yelled at the horses. They heard the crack of a whip and the coach lurched forward.

"Mister Keltner," Nora said, surprised to see one of the Colonel's long-time employees hitching a ride on a stage coach. "What on earth are you doing way out here?"

Before he could answer, Paul was echoing Nora's question. "What are you doing out here? Where you headin'? I heard you say you were bushwhacked by two men?"

"I quit ridin' for the Colonel. Just decided I'd try somethin' different. So, I'm headin' back East. If those two gunslingers hadn't jumped me, I'd be a lot further along than I am now."

For the first time, Nora noticed blood on his right arm just below the shoulder. "Why you've been shot, Mister Keltner. Let me have a look at it."

"No need. It's just a flesh wound. It don't bother me none. I'll get it looked after when we get to the Way Station." He shifted his gaze from them and began looking out the window.

"We should be pullin' in there in a few hours," Paul volunteered. And more from curiosity than concern, he asked, "Recognize either of the two men who jumped you?"

—Seven Rode Together—

"Not really. One was wearing a black sombrero. The other one had a heavy black beard. Either would fit most of the population south of the Kansas border living in Indian territory. There's been an increase in border raids I've been hearin' about. Mostly they raid ranches and small settlements. They've been gettin' bolder recently. Stagin' hit and run attacks further north into Kansas. When they hit a place there generally ain't any witnesses left to tell about it. As if runnin' off stock and stealin' anything that's not nailed down ain't enough, I've heard tell of some raids where they carried off women and kids hopin' to get ransom money for 'em. They're really a mean bunch of bastards."

"You don't suppose they'd ever venture as far north as River Bend, do you?" Nora asked.

"I doubt it. All the ranchers there in the Valley, your Pa, Mort Kane and most of the others just got too many cowhands who know how to handle six-guns and rifles. They'd be more likely to hit the bank in River Bend, than takin' a chance of gettin' a lot of 'em killed. Least ways, that's the way I figure it."

It was late afternoon when they arrived at the Way Station. The driver and his partner climbed down from their seats. Pete opened the door. "Well, we made it, folks. And not too soon, either. From the looks of those dark clouds to the southwest, I'd say we're about to git one hell of a storm before mornin'." He offered Nora his hand. "Watch your step, lady. Don't worry about your baggage. Roy and me'll see to it."

She thanked him and the three of them walked to the front entrance of the Way Station and disappeared inside.

"Let's get these horses 'round back and unhitched." Roy said.

—John E. Cramer—

After they'd fed and secured the horses, they scanned the evening sky. "Ain't a star in sight," Pete observed. "Wouldn't surprise me none if we don't git a real gully-washer before the night's over."

Roy nodded. "You comin' with me or you plannin' on spendin' the night out here star gazin'? Let's slip in the back door. Maybe we can get an idea of what Jake's wife is fixin' to serve for supper."

Roy took the lead with Pete close on his heels. They moved down the hallway, past the doors on either side, each leading to bedrooms for the overnight passengers. They passed through the swingin' doors into the dining area with one long table on one side and Jake's make-shift bar on the other. Spotting Jake behind the bar, they started in his direction. They had taken a couple steps toward the bar when a voice from behind stopped them dead in their tracks. "Hold it right there! Now, real slow unbuckle your gun belts and let 'em drop!" They did as they were told. They stood stock still, listening to the gunman behind them give the orders. "Cisco! Take these two back to the storeroom with the others. Tell Booth if any of 'em makes a false move, he knows what to do. Bring Keltner back here with you. We'll see if his memory is workin' any better."

Pete and Roy, with the Mexican behind them, headed out of the room through the swinging doors leading to the storage area. After a few minutes, the Mexican came back with Keltner. One eye was nearly swollen shut and a gaping cut across the left side of his face was still bleeding. "You ready now to tell us where you ditched your saddle bags?" The gunman giving the orders asked. "Surely, gringo, your life is worth more than the fifty-thousand dollars in

—Seven Rode Together—

gold you carry. The next stage, she don't arrive 'til ten o'clock in the morning. If you're not ready to tell us what we want to know before sun-up, neither you nor these other gringos will be alive to see it." He flashed a smile and nodded toward Cisco. "Take him back with the others. Let 'em know that how long they stay alive depends on this gringo telling us what we want to know. Maybe then, he'll change—"

His orders were interrupted by the sound of horses. "Never mind him! Cover the door!"

He shoved Keltner toward the bar where Jake Frishee stood watching them. He was covered by a double-barrel, sawed-off shotgun held by the fourth gunman crouched down behind the bar.

When Thorn and Kio stepped through the doorway, they spotted Jake. Before either of them could make a move in Jake's direction, they felt the barrels of .45's jabbed against their backs. "One quick move and you're both dead!" The gunman punctuated his warning by a second jab with a .45. "Just drop the gunbelts and step over to the bar."

They were a few steps away from the bar when the leader of the quartet raised up, facing them with the double-barreled shotgun cradled in his arms.

"Well, look who's here, Kio." Thorn exploded. "It's the one-eyed gun slinger we met at the Tradin' Post." He felt the barrel of the .45 dig deeper into his back.

Buck Farley did not usually venture north of the Kansas border. His gang of cutthroats carried out the missions Farley and Colonel Burkhalter had agreed to. But with fifty-thousand dollars in gold at stake, Farley decided to take charge of this latest assignment to make sure his hired guns didn't get greedy. He smiled exposing a row of pearly white teeth. "Only this time," he said, "the tables, as you gringos say, are turned around. Now, this time, I give the orders."

"Hear that, Kio?" Thorn mocked. "He's learnin' to talk. How'd you break out of jail at Powderville? Crawl through a crack?"

Farley's smile disappeared and his black eyes narrowed. But only for a moment. "Cisco," he said, "take these two back with the others. We shall see just how funny this one can be when we torch thees place tomorrow morning."

"Don't do us any favors," Thorn replied.

A few minutes later, Thorn and Kio were shoved into the same room with Paul, Nora, the stagecoach drivers, Pete and Roy, and Keltner, who was propped up in a corner where Nora was tending to his battered face. Thorn was still wondering why Buck Farley would risk capture. "Does anyone know what's happening here? Buck Farley wouldn't be risking his neck to rob a Way Station."

Paul nodded. "We all know the answer to that question," he explained. "Apparently, Keltner has a good deal of money in his saddle bags. He's stashed them away somewhere around here when he got off the stage. We've been trying to convince him to tell that bunch of cutthroats where he hid those saddle bags."

Thorn shook his head. "Him tellin' them where they'll find them saddle bags ain't goin' to help us get out of here alive. Not if Buck Farley has his way. Someone's got to get out of here and get help."

"There's not a ranch or town within fifty miles of this place. Where would anyone go to get help?" Paul asked.

—Seven Rode Together—

"Mort Kane and his top hand on the Circle-K are plannin' on meetin' us here tonight. They're aimin' to help us on a cattle drive comin' up from Texas. We can't let 'em ride in here like we did and be ambushed. We've got to get someone out of here." Thorn looked around the room. His gaze stopped on the small windows near the top of the ceiling. "Those windows are too small for even Kio to get through."

"There's another way out of here but it's goin' to take a powerful lot of diggin'" Pete chimed in. "When the stage line built these Way Stations, they didn't waste a lot of time puttin' 'em together. This storage room ain't got any floorin' like the rest of the place. All we're standin' on in here is the ground with some thick burlap for a carpet."

Before he'd finished talking, Thorn was on his knees. "See if you can't find something to dig with besides our bare hands." A quick search by all of them produced a meat cleaver, a couple of thick-bladed knives, two short-handled shovels and a post hole auger. Thorn pulled the thick floor matting away and the digging began. A short time later they had tunneled an opening large enough that Kio managed to squeeze through. While those remaining inside replaced the dirt, Kio was on his way back-tracking the trail that led to River Bend. He was hoping Jeb and Mort had decided to follow the main trail.

His fears were put to rest. A short ride up the trail, he met them. He was even more pleased to learn that they had brought Chad Youngman with them. "We got trouble waitin' for us at the Way Station," Kio said, as he reined his horse alongside them.

"Trouble?" Mort asked. "What kind of trouble?"

"There's four gunslingers holdin' everybody at the Way

—John E. Cramer—

Station hostage. Two Mexicans and a couple others. One's Buck Farley. Thorn and me had a run-in with him at the Turtle Creek Tradin' Post in Indian Territory. Thorn and me were ambushed when we walked in. He's back there with the others—"

"Others?" Mort cut in. "What others? You mean the folks on the stage?"

Kio nodded. "They walked into the same ambush we did when the stage arrived from River Bend. Them, the stage driver and the fellow ridin' shotgun, and another passenger calls himself Keltner. He's been messed up pretty bad. Seems Farley and his boys believe Keltner's carryin' a sizeable amount of money. That seems to be their reason for stakin' out the Way Station. He ain't told 'em where the money's hid. Now, they're threaten' to burn down the Way Station if he ain't told 'em by sun up."

"The two passengers, a man and woman. They alright?" Mort asked.

"They were when I left 'em. But we'd better not waste anymore time gettin' 'em out of there."

"Looks like we got one thing goin' for us," Jeb said. "We got one more gun than they have." He nodded toward Chad. "He's a pretty fair hand with that pistol he's totin'."

"He'd better be," Kio said. "And we'd better get movin'. No tellin' what's happened since I left."

They pulled up a couple hundred yards before they reached the Way Station and dismounted. "We'd best move in on foot," Mort said. They quit the road leading up to the front entrance of the Way Station and circled around past the corral where Farley and his men had staked out their horses. Directly behind the rear entrance was a wood pile and beyond that an outhouse. Several scrubby oak

—Seven Rode Together—

trees lined the outer borders of the Way Station area.

The four of them surveyed the situation from among the trees. They could see the lights in the dining area of the building. Over head, storm clouds allowed only short periods for moonlight to filter through. "We'd better start decidin' how we aim to handle this situation," Jeb said. "It ain't gonna be too long 'til them clouds up yonder are gonna cut loose like a heifer pissin' on a flat rock." Lightning flashed far to the southwest, followed by the inevitable sound of thunder.

"Kio," Mort asked, "do you think we might move in and get a closer look to see if the situation has changed any since you left?"

Kio nodded. "Let's hope they ain't discovered they're missin' one of their prisoners."

"Chad, you secure these horses back here and keep an eye on the back. Jeb, get around front and cover it. Once Kio and me get a look at what's goin' on inside, we'll see if we can't wrap this up without gettin' any of their prisoners killed."

When they moved to within a few feet of the building, they could pick up the sound of the voices, punctuated by loud laughter. Kio risked a look inside. "Looks like I ain't been missed. I don't see Jake or his wife. The rest are playin' cards and drinkin' Jake's whiskey." He dropped down to the ground with Mort. "See for yourself." Before Mort could react to Kio's invitation, the loud talking and laughter stopped. Kio risked another look. He watched as one man Farley called "Booth" came out of the kitchen behind Jake and his wife. They were both carrying trays of food which they placed on the table. "Now, they got both Jake and his wife waitin' tables for 'em." He spoke in a voice slightly above a whisper. "Hold it! Booth is takin' both of them back toward the storeroom." Once again, he dropped down beside Mort. "All hell's gonna break loose in there when Booth takes a nose count."

"Let's wait until we're sure," Mort said. "Take another look."

"He's back. He's got Keltner and he's talkin' to Farley. Now him and Farley are headed toward the rear entrance. The other three are just talkin'. Looks like Keltner has decided to show Farley where he stashed those saddle bags."

"You check in with Jeb in the front," Mort said. "I'll see if I can warn Chad they're headin' out his way."

Mort reached the rear of the building just in time to see Farley shoving Keltner past the stacked pile of firewood. Keltner stumbled, and Farley never knew what hit him as Chad brought the barrel of his .45 crashing down on the outlaw's head. Farley dropped to his knees and was struggling to his feet when Mort, following Chad's lead, dropped him for good with the butt of his rifle.

"Looks like he ain't goin' anywhere," Chad grinned. "What about this guy?" he added. "Looks like he's been hammered pretty good."

They heard an exchange of gunfire coming from the front of the building. "Come with me. They ain't goin' nowhere," Mort said as he reached down and relieved Farley of his gun.

Together, they entered the rear door into the hallway leading past the storeroom when the door flew open and Thorn stepped out. Spotting Mort, he asked. "What kept you so long? Where's Kio?"

Before Mort could answer, the door at the end of the hallway leading to the dining area opened and the Mexican called Cisco appeared. Before he could get off a round, Chad fired. Cisco

—Seven Rode Together—

fell back, dead before he hit the floor. The next man stepped through the door and over his partner lying on the floor. Kio dropped him.

"Another late arrival?" Thorn whooped.

Jeb crashed through the front door and Mort breathed a sigh of relief. "These two in here learned the same lesson as this one. Nobody shoots straight when he's all liquored up!"

Before Jeb could get it all out, Nora emerged from the storeroom followed by Paul and the others.

"Mort! Oh, Mort! Thank God this nightmare's over." Nora threw her arms around his neck. Mort extended his other arm and clasped Paul's out-stretched hand.

"Looks like you can't get rid of us." Paul said.

"It could be we can't get rid of each other." Mort's reply was punctuated with a blinding flash of lightning, an ear-splitting sound of thunder and then the heavens opened up with a downpour.

"Somebody give me a hand!" Chad shouted, trying to make himself heard over the noisy conversations in the hallway. "There's two guys out back that's goin' to drown if we don't drag 'em inside!"

Jake Frishee and his wife, Mary, were the last to emerge from the storeroom into the crowded hallway. "We could sure use some help cleanin' up in here, too!" He pushed open the door to the dining area. The hallway quickly emptied.

"Come on, Nora," Paul said. "I believe Mort's got some cleaning up of his own." A moment later Chad and Jeb carried Buck Farley in from the outside. He'd not yet recovered from the blow to his head. They were followed by Kio and Thorn who were helping Keltner inside out of the rain. He was still groggy from the beating

—John E. Cramer—

Farley had given him when he refused to disclose the whereabouts of his saddle bags.

"Take 'em to the storeroom," Mort said. We'll see if we can revive 'em. Maybe between the two of 'em, we'll get some answers about these saddle bags of Keltner's."

While the others were trying to bring Farley and Keltner back to the talking stage, Chad slipped out the rear door. A few minutes later, he returned with the missing saddle bags. "Take a look at these, Mort. I stumbled over 'em when I came around to cover the back before the shootin' started. He must have been in a helluva hurry to hide 'em. One was stickin' out from under the pile of wood. I checked inside. There's enough money in there to retire on."

When Keltner was able to sit up, the first thing he saw were the opened saddle bags. "Those saddle bags are mine! What's in 'em belongs to me! That's what was owed me when I quit workin' for the Colonel. Part of it," he lied, "is money I been savin'."

Thorn let out a whistle. "Anybody punchin' cows ain't goin' to make that much money in ten life times."

Before Keltner could offer further explanation, Mort closed the saddle bags and handed them to Chad. "You and Jeb just avoided a trip to Texas and back. And Keltner, you'll have more time to think things over on your trip back to River Bend. Farley's makin' the same trip. We'll all be anxious to find out how he knew Keltner was carryin' this kind of money."

"Why don't me and Chad make sure these two ain't goin' anywhere, then we'll join you up front." Jeb said. "I heard Jake tellin' the other folks he's payin' for breakfast this mornin'."

Chapter 14

Jake Frishee was as good as his word. Before his overnight guests left the next morning, they all enjoyed a breakfast Jake described as "the finest he'd ever served." "Folks, this is the best eatin' you're ever going to find west of the Mississippi. I've been dishin' out food for a mighty long time, and I'm here to tell you, it's never going to get any better than this."

Every person seated at the table, after surviving the harrowing experience of the past twelve hours applauded. Jake held up his hands signaling he had something to add. "I need to explain why I can make that statement with complete assurance." Turning to look toward the kitchen, he added. "Mary, please come out here and let these people see a real cook."

When Mary Frishee emerged from the kitchen, he slipped his arm around her shoulder. "I want to introduce you to the best damn cook in the whole state of Kansas—my wife and my partner." This introduction triggered a second round of hand clapping and cheering. It was good to laugh again.

—John E. Cramer—

Nora and Mort were still smiling when the stage was ready to depart. After a goodbye kiss and an extra long embrace, she looked up at Mort. "Take good care of yourself, Mort. I need you all in one piece the day we get married."

An hour later, with the help of Kio and Thorn, Chad and Jeb were ready for their trip back to River Bend with their prisoners. They were strapped across their saddles. While Kio and Chad secured Farley and Keltner on their horses, Thorn, Mort and Jeb looked on. "If the people in River Bend are looking for someone to take Taylor's place, you're looking at him right there, " Thorn said, nodding toward Chad.

"I was settin' my sights a notch higher," Mort said. "When you get back, get in touch with U.S. Marshal Clint Thurgold. See if you can't convince him that River Bend needs a man to enforce the law that's not beholden to any man who votes. I think he'll get the picture."

"It won't hurt," Thorn added, "if you let him know the man most responsible for bringin' that one-eyed gun slinger and his three wanted cronies in is the guy you're about to ride with."

"How'd you know they're wanted?" Jeb asked.

"Just ridin' with old One-Eye ought to be reason enough. But if you want confirmation, get in touch with U.S. Marshal Jacob Quincy Devlon. He's the Marshal down in Indian Territory at Powderville."

"What makes you both so sure Chad would want the job?"

"I figure a young fella like Chad might be lookin' to get married one of these days," Mort said. "Besides, I really believe he's the right man for the job. And there's lots of people in River Bend who'll feel the same way once you tell Clancy O'Riley what

—Seven Rode Together—

happened here. I got confidence in you, Jeb. I know you won't spare any details when you're reportin' a story. And you might drop those saddle bags off with Judge Storm, just for safe keepin'."

"Guess that won't hurt none," Jeb agreed. "I'll be seein' you again in a couple of weeks."

Chapter 15

"Chad, you lead out. I'll bring up the rear with the three we got draped over their saddles. That way we'll keep these two yahoos twixt the two of us. And if either one of 'em gets any foolish notions before we get to River Bend, all's we'll have to deliver will be five slung over their saddles 'stead of three."

"Sounds fair enough to me," Chad agreed. "I figure we should be in River Bend in time for supper."

The sun was high overhead when they reached the bridge over the Little Jayhawk River. The storm had caused the river to raise over its banks. The water was only a few feet from flowing over the roadway. After surveying the situation, they decided to cross over before giving the horses a rest and a chance to drink. "I figure we could use a little break here," Jeb said.

"How about those two?" Chad asked. "S'pose they could use a drink and a chance to stretch their legs?"

"Keep an eye on him," Jeb said, nodding toward Farley. "I'll see to it that Keltner behaves himself."

—Seven Rode Together—

Chad filled the canteen and brought it back to where they had dismounted and were standing a few feet from the edge of the road. Keltner eased over where Jeb was standing and with his back to the others, he got Jeb's attention. "I can make it worth your while if you just cut me loose. Half of what's in those saddle bags would be enough for you to start your own ranch. And if you wanted to cut him in on it, you'd still have more money than you could spend."

"What's all the talkin' about over there?" Chad asked. "Don't tell me Keltner's tryin' to cut a deal with us."

"I kinda believe he's not too anxious to see his old boss so soon after he left." Jeb said. "Maybe none of that fifty-thousand dollars he had in them saddle bags came from the Colonel. If it did, I imagine somebody's gonna be wantin' to know just what Keltner had to do for that kind of money."

"Let's get goin'" Chad said. "I don't think Farley's enjoyin' all this speculation."

Farley, who seemed oblivious to their conversation, had edged a few feet closer to the water's edge since he'd gotten out of the saddle.

"You'd better have another swig on this canteen," Chad said. "We don't aim to be makin' another stop until we get to River Bend."

Farley eyed Chad for a moment and then turned back to look at the rushing waters of the swollen river about four feet below. "Don't even think about it!" Chad warned. "You'd be dead before you hit the water."

In the next few moments, as though the scenario that followed Chad's warning had been pre-arranged, a hawk circling overhead swooped down toward the water's surface. A few feet

—John E. Cramer—

above the rushing current, a shot was fired, the hawk dropped into the water emerging a few seconds later downstream. Farley turned just as Chad slipped his .45 back into its holster. Apparently satisfied his plan to escape by leaping into the water would not have a happy ending, he turned and headed for his horse.

Jeb, who'd been watching the action, turned and mounted up. "I'd say that boy's got what it takes to make a first-class lawman," he muttered to himself.

It was a couple of hours before sundown when Clancy O'Riley decided to call it a day. As he stepped out onto the boardwalk in front of his office, he saw several people along Main Street all watching the strange caravan passing the courthouse, led by Chad Youngman. Someone from in front of the Frontier Saloon yelled, "Look what's comin' down the street."

By the time they reached the front of the newspaper office a crowd of on-lookers on both sides of the dusty main street had gathered to watch. All seemed attracted to the three horses trailing Jeb carrying three men draped across their saddles.

Certain as to where the seven-horse caravan was headed, the more curious of the spectators moved along with it toward the sheriff's office at the end of Main Street. Clancy wasted no time in catching up with Jeb. "What the hell's goin' on, Jeb? Where'd all these dead bodies come from?"

"They ain't all dead. I'll be talkin' to ya," Jeb said, "soon as we git the two live bodies locked up. Tell ya what you could do for me if you wuz a mind to. Hustle over to Judge Storm's office and tell him he's gonna be needed down at the jail."

"What if he needs to know what for?"

"Tell him Mort Kane says he's gonna be needed to handle

—Seven Rode Together—

this situation. Specially all's that required by the law in matters such as these—"

"What kind of matters you talkin' about?"

"Hell's fire, Clancy! He don't need to know everything. Just tell him what I done told ya!"

Clancy shrugged, then turned and shouldered his way through the group of curious spectators toward the courthouse.

Cravens and two of his temporary deputies were waiting on the steps in front of the jail when Chad and Jeb, with Farley and Keltner ahead of them, started toward the jail. "Hold it!" Cravens ordered. "Where you takin' these men? And who are those men that you got tied to their saddles?"

"Where the hell does it look like we're takin' 'em," Chad said as he shoved Farley and Keltner ahead of him toward the door of the sheriff's office.

Cravens looked at the crowd and then back toward Chad and his two prisoners as they disappeared inside. He quickly gained his composure and in a voice loud enough for those across the street to hear, he ordered one of his deputies, "Get inside and see that the prisoners are locked up!" Turning to the second deputy, he ordered, "Get Ben Flowers to take these dead men down to his place! Show's over, folks!" And seeing Flowers coming down the boardwalk from his undertaker's establishment, he added, "Here's Ben now. Some of you men gave him a hand." He turned and headed back to the office door where Jeb was waiting.

"For a little bit there," Jeb drawled, "you were soundin' like a real sheriff."

Ignoring Jeb's comment, Craven went inside. Chad had locked up the prisoners and was waiting for Cravens. He tossed the

—John E. Cramer—

keys on the desk. "Got 'em locked up in separate cells, Sheriff."

"Now, 'sposin' you tell me who I got locked up and the names that go with those bodies you brought in."

"You might need to wait awhile for that," Jeb cut in. "Judge Storm will be comin' along any minute now."

"What's he got to do with all this? What's goin' on, anyway." And noticing for the first time, the saddle bags Jeb was carrying on his shoulder, he asked, "What have you got, there?"

"All in due time," Jeb said. Before Cravens had a chance to ask another question, Clancy and Judge Storm walked in.

"It wasn't easy," Clancy explained. But here he is."

We figured you'd best be in on all this," Jeb said as he shook the Judge's hand. "You know Chad Youngman. He's the one that brought 'em in."

"Well, that ain't all entirely so," Chad began. And for the next half hour, he held the Judge's interest in his description of what had happened at the Way Station. "So you see, Judge, with all this money Keltner was carryin' and with Farley's reputation, bein' wanted and all, we figured you oughta know what's goin' on, 'cause it sure as hell raises a lot of legal questions, and we figured you needed to be in on it from the start. And Mort Kane figured you'd be the right man to take charge of the fifty-thousand dollars until all this is straightened out."

"What fifty-thousand dollars?" Cravens asked. His gaze shifted from Jeb to Chad and around the office. "Where you got—" He paused as Jeb lifted the saddle bags from his shoulder.

"Now you know what's in these saddle bags, Cravens" Jeb said as he handed them to Judge Storm.

"I believe the sheriff's office should be takin' charge of that

—Seven Rode Together—

money, Judge. After all, I'm the one lookin' after the prisoners.

"You just keep right on looking after 'em," Judge Storm said. "You might want to find out from Farley the names of his friends. If he's reluctant to talk about it, go down to the undertakers office and get a look at 'em. Then, if you can remember all that, check your Wanted Posters. You just might find their pictures on three of 'em. Jeb, you and Chad come with me. I'll need you two to ride shotgun for me on the way back to my office. Craven, you might want to contact Colonel Burkhalter. Tell him one of his cowhands is in your custody. Ask him if he's missin' any money. And, oh yes, you might also tell him that Keltner's bein' held without bail. He'll find me in my chambers if he's interested in helping me find some answers."

The Judge, along with Jeb and Chad, disappeared out the door. Two deputies, who'd watched the whole proceeding from behind the desk, watched the door close, then turned toward Cravens. "You want me to ride out and tell the Colonel?" the smarter of the two asked.

"I'll take care of that!" Cravens squared up his hat and gave his gunbelt a tug. "You two just stay put and keep an eye on the prisoners. I'll be back before dark."

Colonel Burkhalter was feeling especially cheerful. He'd resigned himself to the fact he no longer had a family. If things work out, he thought, I think they're in for one helluva surprise. He smiled inwardly just thinking about the plans he had in mind for young Tom Trinity. In the few weeks since he'd arrived, the Colonel had observed how quickly the lad had taken to his new situation. A hard worker and a fast learner, the Colonel was certain he'd found a place he would call home. He saw in Tom Trinity all

—John E. Cramer—

the qualities he wished he might have seen in either Duane or Paul. Duane had been a hell-raiser and Paul was never meant to be a rancher—too much like his mother. She only tolerated this kind of life. Nora was not cut out for this kind of life either. And they both had chosen to seek out his enemies, Steve and Mort Kane, to find solace. Steve was dead, and it wouldn't be long until Mort wished he'd never left Kentucky. Things are going to get better. Much better, he thought.

Before Elinda left, she found her replacement, Ethyl Rhinegold, a better cook and certainly a much better companion. But the one thing that he was especially happy about this evening was what he was certain had already happened to Keltner. Anytime now he'd be hearing from one of Buck Farley's boys that Keltner had never gotten out of the county with the payoff he was carrying. And now there were only two left to share in that half-million dollars that had been destined for the Confederacy's war chest. And he knew Wade Parker might very well not be able to collect his share before the year was out. There were two things in life that gave Colonel Felix Burkhalter pleasure. The acquisition of wealth, in whatever form, was one of them. The other, the prospect that one day, maybe a year, maybe two or three, young Tom Trinity might agree to changing his name to Tom Burkhalter. Becoming his adopted son would be the best thing that could ever happen to an orphan raised by Catholic nuns in a Louisville shelter. His thoughts were interrupted when his newly acquired housekeeper tapped on the library's open door. "Come in, Ethyl, come in."

"There's someone who would like to see you. He's in the parlor. Sheriff Cravens. He says it's real important."

"Well, then, tell him to come on in, and Ethyl, this will only

—Seven Rode Together—

take a minute. Why don't you break out a bottle of that cognac and the chess set. Maybe I can get even tonight." She flashed a quick smile and left.

"You're not goin' to like what I got to tell you," Cravens began the moment he stepped in the room. The Colonel, who at this moment was in no mood for bad news of any kind, resented the interruption. He dropped his feet to the floor and leaned forward, looking Cravens squarely in the eye.

"Cravens, if you've come all the way out here to tell me one of my men has busted up the Silver Dollar again over a poker game or an argument over some bar maid, I'm going to kick your ass all the way back to River Bend. I've told you before, lock 'em up. I'll take care of the damage and take it out of their wages. Who was it this time?"

For several moments Cravens was speechless. He hadn't anticipated the Colonel's reaction, and was having second thoughts about telling him the truth. Right now he was wishing that he'd sent one of the deputies.

"It's one of your men in the lock up. But I didn't put him there. I mean I didn't bring him in. It's Luke Keltner. And he didn't bust up any saloon—"

"Keltner! He left yesterday morning—headed for somewhere back East. He's not workin' here anymore—" He paused. Suddenly, Cravens' news got his attention. "You say Keltner is locked up but you didn't bring him in? Well, then, who the hell brought him in, and from where?"

"Chad Youngman and Jeb Hofstader brought him in. Seems Keltner got into some trouble at the Way Station at Freedom Ridge. And he was carryin' saddle bags filled with one helluva lot of money. They brought in another fella. Calls himself Buck Farley." Cravens kept a sharp eye on the Colonel, bracing himself for another outburst. The Colonel seemed no longer in a shouting mood. Instead he got quiet. Too quiet, thought Cravens. "They also brought in three of Farley's men, only they were draped over their saddles."

"You tellin' me that Hofstader and Chad Youngman killed three of Farley's men and then brought them back to River Bend all the way from Freedom Ridge?"

"I'm not sure about that. But Jeb did mention that Mort Kane was with 'em when they got to the Way Station. Buck Farley and the other three had taken it over. Farley was tryin' to get Keltner to tell him where he'd stashed the money. So, accordin' to Jeb, Farley had to know Keltner was totin' fifty-thousand dollars. Anyway, there was a shootout. Keltner wouldn't say how he happened to have fifty-thousand dollars, and Farley was wanted by the law, so they just packed 'em all up and brought 'em back to River Bend."

"What happened to the money? You got it locked up at the jail?"

Cravens shook his head. "Judge Storm's lookin' after it."

"Judge Storm! How the hell did he get involved in all this? Was he at the jail when Hofstader and Youngman brought 'em in?"

"Chad Youngman brought 'em in. Jeb showed up a little later with Judge Storm. That's the one thing I rode out here to tell you. The Judge said that if you were thinkin' about bailin' Keltner outta jail, you'd have to talk to him. Since Keltner worked for you, he thinks you might shed some light on how he got hold of that much money. And says he's also curious as to how a wanted man from south of the border would know Keltner was haulin' that

—Seven Rode Together—

much money around with him."

The Colonel sat quietly, staring first at the floor and then over Craven's head to somewhere in the far side of the room. His mind was cluttered with questions, but none Cravens could answer. In fact, at the moment, he was far more concerned about the questions Judge Storm would be asking him. How could he possibly come up with the right answers? What had Keltner told him? And Farley? How could he explain why Keltner was carrying that much money? Two things were certain. If he expected Farley to be available for any future jobs, he couldn't stay locked up. And Keltner? What if he were to decide to save his neck by telling the real story behind why he was paid that kind of money when he quit the ranch? He was still thinking about his meeting with Judge Storm when he heard Cravens saying, "Well, Colonel, maybe I should be heading back unless, of course, there's more we need to talk about."

The Colonel began shaking his head. "No. There's nothing more. Not tonight, anyway."

Cravens nearly backed out of the room. "If there's anything more, I'll drop by in the morning before I see Judge Storm. I'd like to see Keltner. Maybe he can tell me where he got fifty-thousand dollars after he quit his job here at the ranch. You say you got 'em in separate cells?"

"Yeah. Separate cells."

"Across from each other?"

"No. I got Keltner in the cell nearest the door. We put Farley in the last cell. I ain't worried about Keltner. But, Farley? He's a different story. You can tell by lookin' at him that he's one mean son-of-a-bitch!" Cravens paused at the door. "If there's anything I can do, you can count on me."

—John E. Cramer—

The Colonel nodded. There were plenty of things that needed to be done, but Cravens wasn't the man he would depend on to do any of them. The major concern of the Colonel was the best way he could make certain Keltner would not betray them. Besides himself, Keltner and his foreman, Wade Parker, were the only three living who had taken part in the train heist. The Colonel was aware that the statute of limitations for criminal acts while in uniform would never expire. Perhaps, he thought, Parker may have some ideas of his own. If not, he would have to do the job Farley had bungled—eliminate Keltner.

Chapter 16

The news of the capture of one of the most notorious outlaws in the Southwest quickly became the major topic for discussion among the citizens of River Bend and throughout the valley. Those who'd been in River Bend the day before had watched the procession led by Chad Youngman move down dusty Main Street to the sheriff's office. They drew their own conclusions without benefit of any explanation. Jeb Hofstader helped to bring them in, but it was Chad Youngman who killed three of Farley's gang and then brought Farley in alive. There was also much speculation as to why Luke Keltner had been locked up. Anyone telling the story added his version by beginning, "The way I heard it—" And with each story told, the exploits of Chad Youngman grew larger.

The story appearing the next day in the *Valley View* put to rest in the minds of some that there were others besides Youngman who took part in Farley's capture and the killing of the other three. But there were those who seemed still to prefer that it was Youngman, alone, who was responsible for the shootout at the Way

—John E. Cramer—

Station at Freedom Ridge. And it was Youngman whose name was bandied around as the favorite candidate for sheriff in the upcoming election.

A week later, Mort returned to the Circle-K with the news that the cattle drive would be arriving in two or three more days. "They'll be holdin' the herd here for a few days." he told Jeb. "That'll give us and Ebert Youngman time to round up what cattle we're plannin' on takin' north with Kneeland's herd. Me and most of the men here at the Circle-K will be goin' with 'em. It's goin' to be up to you, Jeb, to look after things around here."

Although Jeb was counting on making the trip north, the way Mort put it left little room for further discussion. Instead, he proceeded to fill him in on what had been happening in River Bend concerning the appointment of a U.S. Marshal. "Judge Storm is leanin' toward havin' a Marshal take over the law enforcement in these parts. But it wouldn't hurt none if you had a talk with him. And we're still holdin' Farley and Keltner in jail without bail 'til we find out more about where that money came from and how Farley knowed about it. And knowin' Judge Storm, it ain't likely that neither of 'em are goin' anywhere 'til he finds out."

"He's a stubborn cuss," Mort agreed. "And, I don't doubt for one minute he'll do just what he says he'll do. Course he's got the law on his side. Matter of fact, he is the law in these parts."

"He's the kind of feller I wouldn't want to tangle with in a rough and tumble fight," Jeb said. "Ever notice the size of his arms and them broad shoulders? Before he took up bein' a judge, he and his Pa owned a blacksmith shop back East. I was talkin' with O'Riley durin' the Colonel's trial and he says when the Judge was about twenty years old, a knuckle buster came to town advertisin'

—Seven Rode Together—

he'd give any man a thousand dollars that could stay in the ring with him for four rounds. Accordin' to Clancy, Ely, folks back there called him Ely, figured that a thousand dollars would git him an education at one of them lawyer's schools. Clancy says it was the bloodiest, bare-knuckle fight you'd ever want to see. Although, Ely was gettin' his licks in, he got floored three times, but he never stayed down. Countin' each knock-down as a round, the fight already had lasted most of an hour. And most of the town that had turned out to watch it wuz yellin', 'Eeee-Leee! Eeeee-Leeee!' Clancy says the old, bare-knuckle fighter and the guy in his corner were gettin' plenty worried with the fourth round comin' up. They stood to lose a thousand dollars if he couldn't hit Ely hard enough to keep him down. After about a half hour in that fourth round, their faces were so cut up and swelled up, you couldn't recognize either one. They were in the center of the ring, Clancy says, and Ely cut loose with one of his round-house, blacksmith, haymakers that knocked the guy clean across the ring and he dropped to his knees. Clancy says the crowd went wild. You could of heard 'em all over town."

"Well, what happened?" Mort asked. "Did they call it a knockdown if the guy was just on his knees?"

"Ely's a Judge, ain't he? And he couldn't make the money to pay for gettin' educated by shoein' horses."

Later that afternoon, Mort was still thinking about Jeb's blow-by-blow description of the Judge's bare-knuckle fight, when he and the Judge sat down to talk.

"I believe River Bend will soon have the services of a United States Marshal," Judge Storm began. "And it looks like Chad youngman will get the job. That is, if he's willing. And Jeb assures me he's available. He's over twenty-one and a citizen of

—John E. Cramer—

these United States. I've contacted the Justice Department in Washington and received the necessary papers he'll need to sign when he's sworn in. I thought I'd get your opinion on Youngman's qualifications since, as I understand it, you've known him and his family for some time. And from my observations, I'd say you're a pretty good judge of a man's integrity and character. And, from what Jeb tells me," he paused and eyed Mort for a moment, "Jeb has a way of embellishing his eye-witness accounts of what happened when he gets wound up. Did Youngman actually, single-handedly, capture Farley during that melee at the Way Station?"

"That he did." Mort said. "When Farley came out the back entrance of the Way Station, Chad dropped him with the barrel of his .45. And that's not all. He also saved my hide when the one called Cisco came in the back room with his gun in his hand. Chad got off a round that dropped him in his tracks. Later, Chad located the saddle bags that Keltner had hidden out back. I'd say that Chad Youngman can handle himself very well in tight situations."

Judge Storm nodded. He leaned back in his chair and rubbed his chin thoughtfully. "Got any ideas where Keltner might have gotten fifty-thousand dollars? The Colonel tells me he paid him what he had coming in wages when he quit his job a couple of weeks back. And that was just a month's wages. He says he doesn't have any idea where Keltner got that much money."

"It's a cinch he didn't win it in a poker game. No, I don't have any idea." Mort said. "Do you believe the Colonel's tellin' you the truth?"

"I've given that some thought. But if Keltner was paid that kind of money by the Colonel, then what's the Colonel trying to hide? The thing that bothers me the most," he added, "how do you

—Seven Rode Together—

suppose Buck Farley knew Keltner was carrying that much money?" Before Mort had a chance to speculate, the Judge added, "You knew, of course, that Keltner was ambushed by a couple of men who shot his horse? Keltner hailed the stage about ten miles from the Way Station. He was carrying his rifle and his saddle bags, according to the men driving the stage. And Keltner says the Mexican, Cisco, and one of the other two that was killed at the Way Station, were the two who tried to waylay him and shot his horse. Does that give you any ideas?"

Mort hesitated. And for a moment they sat eyeing one another across the Judge's desk. "There are a lot of ifs," he said. "If the Colonel did give him the money, and if Keltner doesn't want to own up to it, they both may have the same reason for not wanting to tell. But, there's even a bigger if. If that's true, either the Colonel or Keltner would have had to let Buck Farley in on it, and, I doubt it would have been Keltner!"

"Exactly!" The Judge thought a moment. "There's one other possibility. If a fourth party knew about the transaction between the Colonel and Keltner unbeknownst to either Keltner or the Colonel, he could have passed on the message to Farley."

"And that ain't likely," Mort said. "My best judgment tells me there is no fourth party."

"Then, what are you saying? I can't keep Keltner locked up forever. And, as far as I know, there's no law that puts a limit on how much money he can carry with him. I have serious doubts that any of them will give us the full story voluntarily."

"I don't know about the law. But there's one thing I do know. If the Colonel did give Keltner the fifty-thousand dollars, they both knew the reason. And now Keltner should know the

—John E. Cramer—

Colonel aimed to get it back, with Farley's help, and he'd wind up a dead man. You and I both know the Colonel can stand to lose fifty thousand dollars. But if there's a connection between the Colonel and Farley, he can't risk Keltner's decision to save his own neck by telling what he knows about their mutual secret."

"We'll have to wait and see," the Judge said. "Meanwhile, we'll see if I can't hurry up this U.S. Marshal appointment for Youngman. I'm not comfortable knowing Cravens is beholden to the Colonel for the job he holds." He stood up and reached out for Mort's hand. "I want to thank you for coming in to see me. I think we both see eye-to-eye on this matter. Give my regards to Blanche Milburn and Amanda. I'm sure they appreciate your help, Mort. It was a fine thing you did for them."

"I can tell you one thing," Mort smiled. "She's a very brave woman and is deserving of any help I could give. Besides all that, we're all eatin' a whole lot better since she arrived." He turned to leave. "There is one other thing I wanted to ask you."

"Fire away."

"Did folks ever call you, Eeee Leee?" Without waiting for a reply, he disappeared, closing the door behind him. The Judge shook his head. "I'll have to have a talk with that red-haired Irishman."

Mort left the building with a smile on his face, wishing he'd waited long enough to catch the Judge's reaction. He slipped the reins from the hitchrail and was about to mount up when he heard someone call his name. "Mort Kane! Wait up a minute!"

It was then that he saw Chad Youngman darting between a couple of buggies. "I guess you've heard the news. I'm on my way to see Judge Storm. Guess you've already talked to him. He told me

—Seven Rode Together—

he wanted to talk with you about me gettin' the marshal's job. Said you're one of the few men in River Bend whose opinions he valued. That's what you were seein' him about, wasn't it?"

Mort nodded. "What's your Pa think about it?

"He didn't take to it much at first. But with Ma not feelin' so well and them plannin' on sellin' out and goin' back East, he knew I liked it out here, even though I ain't such great shakes as a rancher, and he's needin' all the money he can get hold of not knowin' just what it's gonna take when they get back East."

"How about your brother? He goin' or stayin'?"

"He's goin' with 'em."

He shook hands with Mort and turned to leave. "I almost forgot. Pa said if I saw you in town to tell you he'd like to see you."

"Did he say what for?"

"He said to tell you Colonel Burkhalter seems to be wantin' his spread awful bad. He's offerin' Pa nearly three times what Pa says the place is worth. The Colonel's also offerin' him top dollar for his whole herd. Pa's runnin' about six thousand cattle. Most of 'em, he was plannin' on joinin' up with that Texas cattle drive. Said he and Ma would be able to start East sooner if he'd sell his herd with the place."

"Is that what he's aimin' to do?"

"No, I don't believe so. He said before he made up his mind, he'd have to talk to you. That's all he said."

"Well, congratulations," Mort said. He turned and headed the palomino out of town. "Could be Ebert's havin' second thoughts about takin' me up on my offer," he thought. "Why's the Colonel offerin' that kind of money to buy Ebert's place," he wondered. Though he figured he knew the reason why.

Chapter 17

Since his meeting with Judge Storm, Colonel Burkhalter was convinced the Judge was not buying his explanation of where Keltner might have gotten fifty-thousand dollars. He had suggested perhaps Farley and Keltner may have known each other in the past. "They could have been members of Quantrill's Raiders, or Farley may have headed up his own band of raiders during the war, and somehow Keltner decided to cut out on his own with more than his share of the loot—fifty-thousand dollars more."

"Possible, but not likely." Judge Storm had replied. "Anyway," he'd added, "I aim to find out before he ever gets out of jail. I can't order a man hung for carrying fifty-thousand dollars and not wanting to explain where he got it. But, Farley, now, that's a different story. He's wanted for murder in three states and the Oklahoma Territory. It's possible we could convince him he might escape the hangman's rope if he decides to tell us how he knew Keltner was carrying that much money. Faced with a choice," Judge Storm had said with a smile, "He just might figure he's got

—Seven Rode Together—

nothing to lose." He had eyed the Colonel. "Wouldn't you agree, Mister Burkhalter?"

One other bit of news the Judge announced during their visit had convinced the Colonel his plan to break Farley and Keltner out of jail would need to be expedited. As the Colonel was preparing to leave, Judge Storm had seemed to take a good deal of pleasure in letting him know Chad Youngman was soon to become a U.S. Marshal. "He'll be replacing the current sheriff right here in River Bend. He'll be a most welcome relief from the kind of lawman we've had in the past several years. Wouldn't you agree, Mister Burkhalter?"

The Colonel, responsible for getting Bart Taylor elected, felt obligated to agree, but added, "Let's hope he's not too young and inexperienced to handle the job."

The fact that the Judge had told him, "Youngman will be taking over by the end of next week," had made him decide the jail break would need to happen before Cravens lost his job.

That evening, following his talk with Judge Storm, the Colonel decided on his plan of action. It would be a simple wartime maneuver, a diversionary tactic, and would require only a couple of men to pull it off. The one person who had as much at stake as he did if either Farley or Keltner decided to talk was Wade Parker. The two of them and one other unsuspecting recruit could do the job. The Colonel was satisfied that Parker would have little, if anything, to object to when he learned what he had planned for Keltner. Two can keep a secret better than three, he smiled when he thought about the next step. And somewhere down the line, it will be said that one can keep a secret better than two.

The fifty-thousand dollar loss will have to be written off. He

—John E. Cramer—

was certain Parker would agree. Especially now that the remaining two-hundred thousand would be split between them. And with that kind of money, Parker was not going to be satisfied punching cattle. Knowing that, the Colonel was not in the least bit surprised at Parker's reaction when he talked with him about his plans to break Keltner and Farley out of jail. "Deal me in," he smiled while he stared the Colonel in the eye. "It's something got to be done." His smile disappeared but he kept staring at the Colonel. "But this is my last caper with you givin' the orders. I don't know why you'd want to keep a cutthroat like Buck Farley alive after the break. And I don't wanna know. I don't know either what you've got planned for Keltner. I reckon that's between you and him. But I ain't Keltner."

"What the hell's got into you!" the Colonel snapped. "I hadn't intended to tell you until later. But since you appear to be about to tell me something I don't want to hear, you may as well know what my plans are for you in this Valley. I made an offer to Ebert Youngman the other day to buy his spread. He wants to sell out and take his ailing wife back East. It's an offer he can't resist. I'm paying him way above the market value, not for just the house and a few hundred acres. My offer included his forty-thousand acres and all the livestock he owns right down to the last heifer." He leaned forward and returned Parker's steady gaze. "I want to show you just how much I value our friendship. I'm ready to sign it all over to you. Consider it a bonus and a partial payment for all you've done for me ever since the day we started riding together." He leaned back in his chair. Parker's expression never changed. He sat there stone-faced still eyeing the Colonel.

"And the remaining two-hundred thousand dollars from the heist?"

—Seven Rode Together—

The Colonel nodded. "That, too."

"You keep the ranch, Colonel. I'm not lookin' for any bonus or partial payment. And I'm not fixin' to spend the rest of my life starin' at the rear ends of a bunch of dirty, stinkin' cows. So, all I'm gonna need from you, once we've taken care of our business at the county jail, is half of that two-hundred thousand dollars. All paper. Nobody, besides me, is gonna know where I'm headed or when I'm gonna git there. Not even you, Colonel. Especially you."

The Colonel leaned back and for the first time since they set down to talk, he shifted his eyes from Parker's steady gaze. "I'm truly sorry you feel this way. You know, of course, you're tossing away a chance of a lifetime to make more money than you ever knew existed. It's not going to be too many years until the railroad I've been pushing for will become a reality. There'll be no more long cattle drives. More businesses will be coming to River Bend. The kind a man of means can buy into. Yes sir, Wade, you're missing an opportunity that never comes along but once in a lifetime." He paused, drew a deep breath and added, "But if your mind's made up—" He shrugged, closing out their conversation.

"My mind's made up. And that's the way I want it." Parker stood up and started to leave. "There's one more thing I'd like to get your opinion on, Parker."

"Sure."

"He's only been with us a couple of months, but do you think that young Tom Trinity might make me a good foreman?"

"I can tell you this. He's the first up in the mornings and ready to go to work. And there ain't no job he hasn't mastered. I'd say right now he's better'n some we got. He must of come from good stock. I like him. Looks you in the eye when you're talkin' to him. Since he's been here, any spare time he has, he's practicin' his ropin', learnin' how to use a six-gun, and he ain't afraid to tackle any assignment. A couple of days back, he even crawled on one of those mustangs the boys brought in and tried his hand at bronc bustin'. He busted his ass two or three times but he stayed with that bronc until a couple of the boys convinced him he didn't have to master it all in one ride."

Long after Parker left, the Colonel was more than satisfied his first impressions were correct. "I'll give him a year or two and if he's of a mind, I'll make Tom Trinity an offer that he'll not want to turn down." he mused. The way the Colonel had it figured seemed obvious enough. A kid who never knew his parents, raised in an orphanage, cut loose on his own to join the Army, and apparently workin' to make his own place in this world, reminded him of the kind of kid anybody could be proud of. But right now the Colonel had more important things to occupy his mind. He had only a couple of days before the planned jail break. He would need to make a run on the bank to get Parker's share of the loot. Once he sees it's waiting for him, he thought Parker might have second thoughts about running. And if he does, he had one comforting thought—he can run but he can't hide.

Chapter 18

It was a few minutes past midnight and the folks in River Bend had settled in for the night except for the few cowhands from the Texas cattle drive. They were still trying to persuade the barkeep at the Silver Dollar Saloon to keep the place open for a couple more hours. Thorn Masters, who'd just won the last pot in the poker game pushed back from the table. "Alright, men, let's give the barkeep a break. Drink up and we'll all head back to camp. We got a big day tomorrow."

"Seems to me," one grumbled, "you had a big night."

"You'll get your chance to win it back once we get to Wichita."

The room was cleared in the next few minutes with Thorn and Kio bringing up the rear. When he reached the swinging door, the barkeep was a step behind. "Thanks for your help, Masters, I was beginnin' to think I was stuck here for the rest of the night."

"No need to thank me. We're headin' our herd toward Wichita come morning. And cowhands on a cattle drive nursin'

— John E. Cramer —

hangovers ain't much use to me. Down the street at the sheriff's office, Deputy Mule Hagen looked up from the chair behind his desk and listened to the sound of running horses as they passed the jail. He glanced at the clock. "Reckon that bunch closed the Silver Dolla'," he muttered. He stood up and after stretching his arms, he reached for a rifle on the rack behind him. He hesitated for a moment wondering if a midnight check was necessary. Deciding the night air might revive him, he left the office and headed down the street checking the doors of each business establishment he passed.

As he stepped down from the covered boardwalk into the street entrance to the alley between the Frontier Hotel and Harley Brineger's Dry Goods Store, he heard what sounded like a man clearing his throat. He stopped, and for a few minutes his eyes searched both sides of the alley for some sign of movement. Drawing his gun, he began to move cautiously toward the opposite end of the narrow passageway. A few feet from the end of the alley, he paused again. Satisfied no one was around, he holstered his gun and turned to head back to the street. The barrel of a .45 crashed down on his head. His knees buckled and he dropped to the ground. Wade Parker stooped down and relieved the deputy of his gun. He got a firm grip on the collar of the deputy's jacket and dragged him behind the Dry Goods Store where Brineger stored his crates and packing boxes. Looking down on the lifeless body of the deputy, Parker mused. "Ain't no wonder the town's wantin' a U.S. Marshal." With the toe of his boot, he rolled Hagen over, got the keys to the jail and headed toward the back entrance. Once inside, he unlocked Buck Farley's cell. Placing his finger to his lips and then pointing to Keltner's cell near the office, Farley moved quietly toward him. Parker nodded toward the rear door and Farley fol-

—Seven Rode Together—

lowed him outside. "Got a horse saddled and ready to ride," Parker began, "The Colonel's waitin' for you at the line shack on Settler's Creek. It's a couple of miles from where the fork on the road leading west is joined to the old wagon trail that heads south. He's got some travelin' money for you and needs to talk to you about some important business down the line aways."

"What kind of business?"

Parker shrugged. "All he said was, it's what you do best. Now git the hell outta here. We ain't got all night."

As Farley began to mount up, Parker slipped back inside the jail. He moved quietly between the rows of cells toward the door leading to the office. Passing Keltner's cell, he paused long enough to notice Keltner was sleeping, and continued on to the office. Spotting the pegs behind the sheriff's desk, he slipped off the only two gunbelts and returned to Keltner's cell. He unlocked the door and eased inside along side the bunk where Keltner was still sleeping. He shook him and quickly placed his hand over Keltner's mouth. Keltner sat up and swung his legs to the floor. "What're you doin' here?"

"What the hell does it look like," Parker whispered. "And keep your voice down. We wouldn't want to wake Farley." He nodded toward the back of the cell block. "Got your horse saddled and ready to ride. It's out back. Now, let's get goin'."

Keltner got quickly to his feet. "Lead the way. I'm right behind you." Outside, Keltner noticed the gunbelts Parker had slung over his shoulder. Before he could ask the obvious question, Parker explained. "Didn't know which one was yours so I brought 'em all." He pulled them from his shoulder. Keltner quickly grabbed his.

Parker ignored Keltner's question concerning the disposal

—John E. Cramer—

of the remaining two gunbelts. "We ain't got all night." he began.

"The Colonel knows you're goin' to need some travelin' money." He proceeded to give Keltner the same directions he'd given Farley earlier. "Colonel says he needs to know where you are once you git to where you're goin'. He'll see you get all that's yours soon as you let him know."

"How do I know he'll send it?" Keltner whined.

"For crissake, man! Why'd you think we're riskin' our necks to spring you outta jail? That deputy I slugged in the alley ain't goin' to be layin' there much longer. So you'd better get your butt in the saddle and get the hell outta here." Confident that Keltner wouldn't be taking his next bit of advice, he added. "If you don't need the ten thousand in travelin' money and you don't give a damn about ever gittin' the rest, forget about talkin' with the Colonel. Just git the hell on your way!"

Keltner quickly reined the horse around and walked him for the first few hundred feet down the narrow lane in back of the shops until he reached the road leading out of town. Parker watched until he disappeared. "He's not leavin' the territory until he talks with the Colonel," he muttered. Immediately deciding, that he, too, needed to be hittin' the trail. His night's work was completed, he thought. Now it was up to the Colonel.

When he reached the road leading out of town, he nudged his horse into an easy gallop and headed for the ranch. As his horse sloshed across a shallow ford in the river, he pulled the keys to the jail from his pocket and then threw them upstream.

The Colonel was waiting when Farley arrived at the line shack and met him as he dismounted. "This won't take long," he began. "Here's ten thousand dollars. It's the travelin' money I

—Seven Rode Together—

promised. It's money I had on hand at the ranch. Couldn't afford to raise too much curiosity by drawin' all of what you got comin' out of the bank. But if you're a mind to, you can collect the fifteen thousand I promised before you get back to Indian Country across the border. You got the ten I gave you just now. Keltner is carryin' the other five and five more, which means you'll be getting five thousand more than we agreed on in the first place."

"But Keltner, hees locked up."

"Not anymore he's not. Fact is, he'll be along any minute now, and he'll be carrying ten thousand dollars. It's up to you. I'm giving you a second chance to do what I hired you to do in the first place. Only this time I don't want any slip-ups, and I don't want any dead body found in these parts. Savvy?"

Farley nodded. A sardonic smile crept across his face. "You are one gringo I can do business with. I like that. Thees Mort Kane we talk about. I don't like heem. You let me know when you want to deal with heem. I'll be ready." He mounted up and with the smile plastered on his face, he added, "Adios Amigo. Do not worry about thees hombre who follows me. You will not see him again."

According to the Colonel's plan, a short while after he watched Farley ride down the trail leading toward the border, Keltner arrived. "Here's ten-thousand dollars," the Colonel said. "You can take it or leave it. It's what I had on hand at the ranch. I don't want to arouse any suspicions at the bank by suddenly drawing the fifty-thousand I owe you. I'll be making a purchase of some property soon. Then, I can draw what's needed to cover both the land deal and you. I'm doing you a favor," the Colonel added. "I paid you off once. It's not up to me to make sure you're going to be able to hang on to it, but I'm willing to see you get the full amount.

—John E. Cramer—

Just let me know where you'll be when you get settled. That's the best I can do. Take it or leave it."

Keltner eyed the Colonel for several minutes. "You know if you don't keep your word, I can still let the law in on our train heist during the war?"

The Colonel nodded. "And you know you'd get the same treatment I'd get. You helped with that heist, too."

"What's to stop you from shooting me in the back when I leave?"

"If that's what I had in mind," the Colonel countered, "I could have blown your head off when you came down the trail. Now I'm just about fed up with all your talk about killing."

Keltner toyed with the idea of asking the one question that could set him off, but figured instead it would be prudent, for the moment at least, to get out while he could. Still, he wondered, if the Colonel was afraid of what Farley might say, then why didn't he break him out of jail? Parker could have tailed him and killed him. Before he had fully made up his mind to ask that question, the Colonel interrupted his thoughts.

"If you're planning on me staying here the rest of the night while the Sheriff collects a posse to come hunting for you, you're going to be here alone. I'm heading back to the ranch unless, of course, you're thinking about shooting me in the back when I leave. In that case, I'll have to take my chances." He picked up his rifle and headed toward the door.

"Alright, Colonel, I'll be lettin' you know when I get settled."

"And you'll be hearing from me."

A few moments later, Keltner watched through the opened doorway as the Colonel mounted up and headed out.

Chapter 19

It was early morning at the Circle-K when Mort and Jeb finished breakfast. Mort was hoping Ebert Youngman had decided to join him on the cattle drive to Wichita. He figured that if he did, it would mean he'd decided not to sell out to the Colonel. Since Thorn Masters had told him they intended to get the drive started by first light the next morning, he would take the day to ride over to the Youngman ranch. "I'm thinkin' I'll get in touch with Ebert today, Jeb. You might check with Missus Milburn and see what she may be needin' in town."

"Come to think of it," Jeb said, "She was sayin' somethin' about wantin' to go into town one of these days to see if she couldn't find some material for Amanda. They're both lookin' forward to goin' to that shindig next month that's bein' held to celebrate River Bend bein' a town 'stead of just a tradin' post. They're plannin' on makin' a day of celebratin'. Wouldn't surprise me none if the Colonel ain't promotin' the whole affair just so he'll be able to make another of his long-winded speeches."

—John E. Cramer—

Mort was still smiling as he swung up in the saddle and headed the palomino toward the open road leading to the Youngman Ranch. Since the trial, the Colonel had been keeping a low profile, Mort thought. Jeb may be right. The Colonel just might have something to offer that would polish up his image and help him regain the support of the citizens of River Bend and the ranchers in the Valley.

At mid-morning, Mort arrived at the Youngman Ranch. He was tying up the palomino at the hitchrail when Chad came out of the house. "If you're wantin' to talk to Ebert, Mort, you just missed him. He and Steve and the rest of the boys are roundin' up the cattle they aim to drive to Wichita with Thorn Masters' herd."

"That pretty much takes care of what I rode over to talk to him about." Mort said. "Where you headin?"

"Goin' into town. Judge Storm wants to make sure I'm still of a mind to accept the U.S. marshal's job in River Bend. I told him the other day I'd have to talk it over with Pa and the rest of the family."

"So what's your decision?"

"Looks like if Judge Storm's willing to make the appointment, I'll be the law in these parts. Pa and I talked it over before we told Steve and Ma about it. The whole family seems to think I'm the right man for the job. Ma insisted that Steve could go with her back East and Pa and me could stay here and run the ranch. 'Course I won't be doin' a whole lot of ranchin' if I get the marshal's job. But, Pa says he was ranchin' before Steve and me came along. Anyway, we aim to give it a try for a year. Maybe by then Ma will be recovered and we can decide what's the best for all of us. Pa never did want to sell out. He told me you'd made him a standin'

—Seven Rode Together—

offer if he did decide to sell."

Mort nodded. "I'm happy you're goin' to hang on. And there's a good chance your Ma might get to feelin' better and decide she wants to come back. Least I hope she does."

"You knew, of course, that Colonel Burkhalter also offered to buy the place? He offered Pa about three times more than Pa figured it was worth. Pa says anybody offerin' to pay that much for it must know somethin' he doesn't."

"Knowin' the Colonel and the way he operates," Mort agreed, "it wouldn't surprise me none if you or your Pa one day discover your ranch is sittin' on top of a gold mine."

"The way Pa feels about it, he'd probably just keep on ranchin'." Chad grinned. "Where you headin'?"

"I was thinkin' I might ride into town and see Judge Storm. I'd like to know if there's anything he's found out about those two jaspers you and Jeb brought in."

"Mind if I ride with you?"

"Best offer I've heard so far today," Mort said. He mounted up and reined the palomino away from the hitchrail. Chad dashed in the house. A few minutes later he joined Mort and they headed out toward River Bend. Ma said for you to tell Blanche Milburn she'll be over to see her before she goes back East. They've been close friends for a mighty long time."

When they passed the River Bend jail, they noticed several people gathered around the entrance to the sheriff's office. They continued down the main street. "Wonder what that's all about?" Chad said, as they tied up their horses and headed up the walk to the courthouse.

When they entered Judge Storm's chambers, Chad repeated

—John E. Cramer—

his question. "Looks like we should have had you on the job a day earlier," Judge Storm replied. "Seems Sheriff Cravens decided to take the night off and left one of his deputies to look after his prisoners. Both of them escaped last night. They found Deputy Hagen this morning in the alley behind his store. He had a lump on his head the size of a goose egg. Said he was checking on some disturbance behind the store when he was pistol whipped."

"Did he see the guy who dropped him?" Chad asked.

"See him? He never knew what hit him. Cravens dug up a posse and they rode out after Cravens discovered they'd broke jail when he got to his office this morning."

"How'd Cravens know which way they headed?" Chad asked.

The Judge shrugged his shoulders and threw up his hands. "I don't suppose he had any idea. O'Riley was in to see me this morning. He says Cravens deputized a half dozen men to form a posse. O'Riley says two of 'em weren't even wearing gunbelts. Truth known," the Judge continued, "Cravens is probably hoping he doesn't catch up with 'em. No doubt they most likely headed south and since nobody knows when they broke out, they could be half-way to Mexico by now. It's a safe bet they're no longer in Kansas. If they headed south they'd at least be in Indian territory. And if they headed west, they'd be in Colorado territory. One thing for sure, it's a reasonable guess they won't be back to claim the fifty-thousand dollars any time in the near future. I was hoping we might get Keltner to tell us how he happened to be carrying that much money so soon after he'd quit working for Colonel Burkhalter."

The Judge opened his desk drawer and pulled out a U.S. marshal's badge. "We've got our witness here for your swearin' in,

—Seven Rode Together—

Chad. And I don't know of a better time than right now to declare you the man to wear this badge. I'll leave it up to you. If you're needing a deputy, pick your man."

When they left the Judge's chambers, Chad confessed to Mort, "I may be getting into something a little over my head. What do you think, Mort?"

"I think you'll do just fine, Chad. There's one thing for sure. You won't be making a posse with men who don't wear gunbelts."

"Not unless he was somebody like yourself, who don't wear a gun but is handy with a Winchester." As they headed toward the sheriff's office, Chad asked. "Got anybody in mind for the deputy's job?"

"Nope, but if I think of someone, I'll let you know. There's one man I know who just might be able to help you out. You might get in touch with Clint Thurgold, the Marshal in Wichita. In fact," Mort added, "there is one man he and I both know who could be a likely candidate. His name is Seth Longlittle. He's the bounty hunter who tracked down our former sheriff, Bart Taylor. He rounded up a posse that helped Thurgold break up the Colonel's attempt to get me hung four years ago. In fact, as I recall, you, your brother Steve and your Pa were all members of that posse. That's one night I'll never forget."

"Sure, I remember Longlittle," Chad said. "But he might not want to settle for a deputy's pay. He probably makes more in reward money when he brings in somebody like Taylor than a deputy makes in a year. Besides there's no tellin' where he is. He covers a lot of territory."

Mort agreed. "But there's one thing I can do. I'll probably see Clint in a couple of weeks. He might know where Longlittle could be found. It ain't too far fetched for a bounty hunter to turn lawman. It's happened before."

Chad agreed. "It's worth a try. A fellow like Longlittle could probably make my job a lot easier. But I can't see a fellow with his reputation wanting to take a job as deputy when he might well be picked for a sheriff or a marshal most anywhere they needed one or the other."

They parted company when they pulled up in front of the jail. Chad moved through the crowd to the entrance where he issued his first order as a U.S. Marshal. Those on the outside began to mosey off toward other destinations and a few moments later those inside the office began coming outside. No longer were they discussing the jail break. Their talk now was about Ebert Youngman's oldest boy who was now wearing a badge.

Mort stayed in the saddle and watched until the area was nearly cleared of curious spectators. Chad soon appeared in the doorway, smiled at Mort, then disappeared inside.

Chapter 20

The first full rays of the morning sun were peeping over the eastern foothills and spreading across the valley. The autumn air was crisp and welcome to all of those tired of the August mornings that stifled the breathing and slowed the steps of early risers. Somewhere in the distance the cooing of mourning doves broke the stillness.

Inside the house on the Circle-K Ranch, everyone waited until Missus Milburn had completed setting the breakfast table. And as was the practice every morning, she and the other members of the family were seated and remained silent, heads bowed, until Mort completed the blessing. The topic for conversation on this morning was the cattle drive. Joey was hoping, by some miracle, he would be able to convince his Pa he was old enough to join the others in moving the herd to Wichita. "I'm not sayin' I'd be able to do all the hard ridin' that the men do. But there's got to be other jobs on a cattle drive I could handle. Jeb says he was herdin' cattle when he was even younger than me. Ain't that right, Jeb?"

"Come to think of it," Jeb began after stealing a glance at

—John E. Cramer—

Mort seated at the head of the table, "they wasn't long cattle drives like this one. In fact, now as I recollect, they was more like movin' cattle from one grazin' range to another. Besides, I'm gonna be needin' a heap more help here at the ranch than most other times. Ain't that what you figured, Mort?"

"That's what I figured," Mort said. "And don't forget, you got school you wouldn't want to miss for two or three weeks. And if Jeb ain't got enough work to keep you busy, I'm sure Missus Milburn will be needin' help now and again."

Their conversation was interrupted by someone knocking on the back door. Missus Milburn excused herself. "Go on with your breakfast. I'll see who that could be at this time of the morning." In a moment she returned. "There's a man at the door, Mister Kane. Says his name is Jeremiah Dundee and he's wanting to speak with you. Says it's real important."

"Tell him to come on in. See if he's had breakfast. If he ain't, just set another place."

When she returned, Mort had left the table and was giving Jeb some last minute instruction on some matters needing attention in River Bend. "Tell Dave Shelley at the bank I ain't gonna be needin' any loan after all. Ebert Youngman's not sellin' out."

"I'm sorry to be botherin' you at breakfast, Mister Kane, Jeremiah began. "But what I want to see you about is kinda personal."

"I'm headin' out. Come along. We'll talk on the way." Mort said as he joined Jeremiah and left the room.

Once outside, Jeremiah fell in step as they walked toward the stable. "I was hopin' you might need another hand to help out on this cattle drive. I could sure use the job. I believe I can stay in

—Seven Rode Together—

the saddle with the best of 'em. If not, I'm a pretty fair hand with the chuckwagon."

"Thought you and the boy were workin' for the Colonel."

"He is, but I ain't. That is, I was until last night." Jeremiah paused at the stable door while Mort continued to saddle the palomino.

"What happened last night?" Mort asked as he slipped on the saddle blanket. "Thought you and the Colonel went back a long way."

"We served in the same outfit, but him bein' a major at the time and me bein' a sergeant didn't make us bosom buddies. Toward the end of the war I was promoted to Sergeant Major and took over as Company Clerk. I was never sure if it was a promotion or a demotion."

Mort nodded, and reaching under the Palomino he grabbed the cinch belt and tightened it. He couldn't help thinking that Jeremiah wasn't too anxious to tell him what had happened last night that made him walk off the job. "What's all that got to do with what happened last night?"

Jeremiah hesitated. He watched as Mort secured his saddle bags and bedroll. "It's a kinda long story," he began. "And maybe, just maybe, I could be wrong about some things. But some things have been goin' on that don't seem normal—"

Mort led the palomino out of the stable with Jeremiah walking alongside. He still had the uneasy feeling Jeremiah might be having second thoughts about telling him the reason that caused him to make a quick decision to ride out leaving his saddle buddy, Tom Trinity, back at the Burkhalter estate. He tied the Palomino alongside Jeremiah's Blazed-face Sorrel. "Looks like you ain't

—John E. Cramer—

goin' to finish that story for quite a spell, Dundee. You'll have to finish it while we're riding out to where they're holdin' the herd. I'm goin' to hike up to the house and make sure Joey and the others know we're leavin'."

"You mean I got the job?"

"How else am I ever goin' to hear the rest of your story?"

Mort hurried up the walk. Jeremiah knew he was going to like working for his new boss. He recalled his first visit with Mort and found himself wishing he'd asked him for a job then. Everyone in the Valley and River Bend he'd talked to since he'd arrived had a good word for the lanky Kentuckian who had inherited his uncle's ranch. All, that is, except Colonel Burkhalter and some of his cowhands at the Burkhalter ranch. Jeremiah knew that in any showdown Mort might have with anyone, including the Colonel, Mort would be the one he'd ride with. He was still wishing Tom had joined him when he left the Burkhalter Ranch. He'd made up his mind to level with Mort about why he'd chosen not to work for the Colonel any longer when Mort came out of the house with Joey on one side and Jeb on the other. Joey cut loose with a shrill whistle, and as if he was waiting to be invited to join them, Sarge came racing toward them.

"Well, Mort, you should be convinced now," Jeb began as he reached down and patted Sarge who had taken a sitting position between him and Joey. "You got nothin' to worry about. There ain't anything that can happen that the three of us can't handle."

"He's right, Pa. Don't worry about a thing," Joey chimed in. He dropped down on one knee and wrapped an arm around Sarge's midsection.

Mort eased up into the saddle and for a few moments he sat

—Seven Rode Together—

looking at the three of them. "While I'm gone, Joey, you might get Jeb to give you a few pointers on how to handle a quarter-horse. Maybe you'll be able to pick up a few dollars in the calf ropin' and the barrel racin' contests at this year's Anniversary Celebration." He slipped Jeb a wink and reined the Palomino around and headed toward the lane leading to the road with Jeremiah close behind. They rode silently for the first quarter mile before Jeremiah opened the conversation with a question.

"Did you know the Colonel lost another foreman?"

"Nope. The Colonel never confides in me."

Jeremiah shook his head. "That was a damn fool question. But that's what happened. Wade Parker lit out right after breakfast. Heard some of the boys talkin' who usually hang around with him. They wasn't too sure why, either. One of 'em said Parker told him he was headin' for California to try his hand at somethin' besides punchin' cattle. Accordin' to what the boys were sayin', it don't pay to be a foreman at the Burkhalter Ranch. Jim Arkus was killed in a cattle stampede. Sam Keltner left awhile back and wound up in jail, at least until last night, when he managed to break out of jail along with that Mexican feller. Then Parker rode out this mornin'. Strange thing about that, he'd never slept in his bunk last night. Anyway, I was awake when he came in this mornin', picked up his belongin's, spent a little time at the house talkin' with the Colonel, and then lit out."

"Is that why you decided to check out, too?" Mort grinned. "Afraid the Colonel might give you the foreman's job?"

"I wasn't cut out to be a foreman. Besides, I'd made up my mind a week ago. I told the Colonel I'd be leavin' at the end of the month. Figured that if he was agreeable, I might just as well quit

—John E. Cramer—

with a month's pay in my pocket."

"How'd the Colonel take it? You quittin' so soon after you arrived?"

"Under different circumstances, I might have toughed it out awhile longer because of Tom. I sorta took him under my wing from years back when he joined up with our outfit. I guess I kinda got the idea he needed lookin' after. And I think he was lookin' for a friend. You know he was raised in an orphanage back in Kentucky?"

Mort shook his head. "Wonder why he decided to join the Army? The war was over by then."

"I dunno why he decided on the Army. Could be he wanted to just get away—be on his own. He's a really good kid. Tough as nails and pretty savvy about things. You know, the kind who catches on fast. The kind of kid that anybody would be glad to have around."

"Did you ask him to come along with you?"

"Yep. I talked to him. But I think he's lookin' for somethin' more than bouncin' around from one place to another. Fact is, it seems to me the Colonel has takin' a likin' to him. He and the Colonel spend a lot of time together. Fact is, he takes most of his evenin' meals up at the house. Maybe he's found a home. I'd feel better if he could've found some place like the Circle-K, for instance, where he'd be part of a regular family."

"A regular family." Mort echoed.

Jeremiah picked up on Mort's tone of voice and hastened to add, "Well, I understand you lost your wife. But then there's Missus Milburn and her daughter—"

"Well, the Colonel also has a housekeeper."

—Seven Rode Together—

"Not right now, he doesn't. I understand she's back East visitin' some kin folks. Anyway, she was just a housekeeper. I have a hunch that though Missus Milburn keeps house, she and her daughter are treated just like members of the family. I noticed this mornin' they were havin' breakfast with the rest of you."

"From all you've told me, you seem to have left out the reason you left like you did."

"Alright. I'll level with you, Mort. It's a feelin' I have deep down inside me. The kind you might get if you know somebody's watchin' you but you ain't sure why."

Mort nodded. "I think I know what you mean."

"There was a jailbreak last night. Keltner escaped. He had to have some help from the outside. Parker never slept in his bunk, packs up and leaves at the crack of dawn, but not until he visits the Colonel, who either couldn't sleep or else was also up all night. And, then, I find out that Jim Arkus died in a cattle stampede. That, may not have been just an accident, especially with a guy like Arkus who probably had been workin' cattle all his life—"

"I see what you're drivin' at." Mort acknowledged. "But maybe you're imagining things that are merely a matter of timing or coincidence. Things happen sometimes that defy explanation."

"But there's one thing I haven't told you. I know every one of those men, Arkus, Keltner and Parker. Served with 'em for years in the same Company the Major commanded."

"You mean the Colonel?"

Jeremiah shrugged. "He was a Major when I knew him. Maybe he got himself a promotion after he was mustered out." He paused, with a slight smile on his face, added. "Just a thought."

Mort was mulling over what Jeremiah had told him about

—John E. Cramer—

activities at the Burkhalter Ranch. What reason would the Colonel, or Parker, for that matter, have for breaking Luke Keltner or a gunfighter like Buck Farley, out of jail? It was obvious to Mort that Farley's only interest in Keltner during the fracas at the Freedom Ridge Way Station was the money Keltner was carrying in his saddle bags. The only reason they had for bringing Keltner in with Farley was to find out if the money was stolen. And according to Judge Storm there were no reports of any robberies, and the Colonel said, when Keltner left he had paid him only what he had coming. But the one question that neither he nor Judge Storm could answer was how Buck Farley would know Keltner was carrying that much money. The only logical answer would seem to be some of Farley's men engineered the jailbreak. But why would they bother with Keltner? The Judge had confiscated the fifty thousand dollars.

When they topped a ridge, they saw spread out below the two thousand head of cattle being rounded up, getting ready for the two weeks on the trail to Wichita. They both pulled up and surveyed the scene.

"Looks like we're ready to go to work." Mort said. "Guess we'll have to try to unravel this business about the jailbreak later."

"Are you sayin' I might have a job at the Circle-K when we get back?"

"That's what I'm sayin'. But we'd better get started on this first." With the touch of a spur, the palomino broke fast into a full gallop leaving Jeremiah sitting. In the next few minutes they were riding into the camp of Thorn Masters, the trail boss. He was the first to greet them.

"You're a little late for breakfast. But Charley's still got some hot coffee on the fire." He was talking to Mort and at the same

—Seven Rode Together—

time he was sizing up Jeremiah. "Well, what do ya know. I see you made this cattle drive after all. Where's your sidekick? I was thinkin' you two were goin' to work for the Colonel at the Double-B?"

"He's now workin' for the Circle-K. Says he'd like to eat a little dust on this cattle drive or help Charlie with his chores. But you're the boss."

"Tom decided to stay on with the Colonel," Jeremiah explained. "I heard Mort was takin' part in this drive so I signed on at the Circle-K. Besides, I ain't never been to Wichita."

"Well, you can give Charlie a hand. He's always sayin' he's over-worked. Later on we might break you in ridin' drag." He slipped Mort a wink. "You might get to Wichita a bit later than some of the rest of us, but you'll be enjoyin' that first bath more."

They each poured a cup of coffee. "Heard about the jail break in town last night, Mort. Sorry to hear Buck Farley is on the loose again. He's one mean hombre. He'd kill anybody over a warm glass of beer. I thought we'd seen the last of him when they locked him up in Powderville."

Before he'd finished talking, Jeremiah had finished his coffee, doused the remainder on the fire, and was helping Charlie get the chuckwagon loaded to move out. Some dark clouds were forming far to the southwest as they started moving the herd. Mort had joined up with Ebert Youngman and the others when Thorn caught up with them. "We need to keep 'em movin' if we aim to out-run this storm that's brewin' behind us," he yelled. "I'd like to make that box canyon before night in case that storm catches up with us."

Before they reached Wichita, Jeremiah had discovered that riding drag was the last place a man wanted to be on a cattle drive, especially on the dusty flatland. He discovered the bandanna he had

—John E. Cramer—

tied over his nose and mouth was the only thing that kept him from choking on the dust stirred up by two thousand head of cattle. Charlie and his chuckwagon kept moving along the side of the herd managing not to lag behind.

Two days short of the two weeks they figured, they arrived on the outskirts of Wichita. The men began serious negotiations with one another as to who would be left to hold the herd and who would be the first to ride the last few miles to Wichita for a hot bath and a night on the town. Since they were the three who had the cattle to be sold, Mort, Thorn, and Ebert were a cinch to be going.

"We're takin' Kio and Jeremiah, and ten of the rest of you men in town tonight. We'll most likely be holdin' the herd here tomorrow night. The rest can have a go at it then," Thorn announced after they'd finished eating. "So you'd better decide, if you haven't already, who's ridin' in with us tonight."

"There ain't no reason for any of us goin' into town tonight, boss," one lanky cowhand from Texas volunteered, "lessen you're plannin' on payin us off now."

"Reckon it's settled then," Thorn said. "But one thing you all need to remember when you do get into town. Wichita's got a U.S. Marshal that don't take too kindly to anybody raisin' hell and shootin' up his town. A few of you found that out last year."

That night Mort was the first to check into his room at the Cattleman's Hotel. After dinner he excused himself, telling the others, "If you gentlemen will save some of your celebrating 'til tomorrow night, I'll join you then. Tonight, I'm plumb tuckered out and ready for a good night's sleep." Actually, he had a letter to write and some thinking to do.

He heard from Nora the day before he'd left on the cattle

—Seven Rode Together—

drive. He reached into the saddle bag and pulled out her letter. He already had it all but memorized from the several times he'd read it. But after each reading, he was haunted by the same disturbing thoughts. After all that had happened since they first met, would she ever again return to the Valley. He took the letter from the envelope and began to read: "Dear Mort and Joey, I'm sitting here tonight in my room wishing you were with me. I can't help thinking what might have been, but I know one day my hopes and dreams for our future together will be realized. Although we are worlds apart right now, I know we will find a way to be together again. A real family, you and I and Joey. Oh, how I pray for that day to come.

"We are staying with Grandmother Thompson who insisted that Paul and I live with her. They have a lovely, spacious home not far from the ocean. Since Grandfather passed away, she's been living alone. I have told her about you and Joey, and that one day she will have a Great Grandson to spoil. My mother was their only child. Paul has enrolled at Harvard and is more certain than ever that medicine will be his life's work. He speaks of you often. We have told her so much about you and Joey that she said recently, 'I like your young man. I feel I already know him. You tell him for me that he and Joey should come to Boston. Our home is large enough for all of us, and for maybe a Great Granddaughter, too.' She says she can't understand why anyone would want to live so far away from civilization. Paul and I have tried to explain, without much success, that you and Joey love the beauty of the land and the life that ranching affords, the same as she loves Boston and the life it affords.

"How is Joey? By now I hope Sarge has helped fill the emptiness he felt when Major was killed. I remember so well how much he loved him. In his eyes there was no dog in the world as

—John E. Cramer—

great as his Major. I'm hoping one day he'll feel the same about Sarge. And Jeb? How is he doing? He certainly has less to be grumpy about since Blanche Milburn has relieved him of his cooking chores. She wrote me and told me how much she appreciated your thoughtfulness and kindness in giving her and Amanda an opportunity to share your home. She says she's treated like one of the family, and it is the first time since she lost Milt that she felt alive again, and full of hope. How I envy her!

"Well, I must close. Paul has just returned home and told me that dinner is about to be served. He says to give you his very best wishes and is looking forward to the day we can enjoy an evening together. Give my love to Joey and Jeb. I miss all of you so very much. And Mort, you know I shall always love you. I'm living for the day that we all will be together again. Please write as often as you can. All my love, Your Nora

"P.S. Neither Paul nor I have heard from Father. I pray for him, for I fear one day he will die a lonely man and no one will regret his passing."

Mort finished reading the letter, folded it and slipped it back into the envelope. For quite awhile he sat quietly wishing that somehow he could feel as optimistic about their future as he was convinced she felt. Somehow, he couldn't escape the feeling, after all that had happened since they first met, that perhaps she may now have the same feeling about living in the West that her grandmother had described. Boston? He could never see himself living there. One thing he knew for certain, neither she nor Paul would ever return to River Bend so long as the Colonel was alive. And the last time he saw the Colonel, he looked to be very much alive. Mort

—Seven Rode Together—

figured the Colonel would outlive everyone in the Valley, unless he met someone dead-set on sending him to his maker. Somehow, he couldn't visualize the Colonel ever facing down anyone.

For just a moment, Mort wondered if the Colonel was grooming young Tom Trinity to replace his late son, Duane, behind whose gun he could hide when faced with a life or death showdown. He quickly dismissed the thought. Right now, he should be thinking about his answer to Nora's letter, to make her believe he, too, was optimistic about their future together. There must be millions of people in this world who have had a 'Colonel Burkhalter' in their family to deal with. But right now, he was determined not to let the Colonel's demise become his obsession. Like Nora wrote, things have a way of working themselves out for the better. If there was one thing he'd learned, now was not the time to answer Nora's letter.

He was about ready to douse the light, slip off his boots and get some shut-eye, when someone pounded on his door. "Mort! You in there? It's Jeremiah. Lemme in!"

A couple of long strides and Mort opened the door. Jeremiah burst into the room. "Get your boots on and come with me. We got a bad situation on our hands down at the Traders' Saloon!"

"Calm down and tell me what you're so all-fired, steamed up about. And you don't have to yell, I'm standin' right here."

"Thorn and Kio are goin' to need our help. Grab your Winchester. We're gonna need it."

In a few minutes they were on the street with Jeremiah talking as they headed for the saloon. "We was at the bar, mindin' our own business. I noticed a couple of saddle tramps at the far end. They were pourin' whiskey down like it was free. They kept lookin' at us and gettin' louder by the minute. Seems they didn't cotton to Kio drinkin' at the bar. Thorn and Kio wasn't payin' no heed, but I seen Thorn in action and those two saddle-bums, if they don't back off, ain't goin' to see the light of day."

Across the street, the swinging doors of the Traders' Saloon swung open and a dozen or so cowhands suddenly emerged. Some kept moving. Others lingered outside to peer through the large plate glass windows on either side of the entrance.

As they stepped upon the boardwalk directly in front of the swinging doors, one lanky cowhand emerged clutching a half-empty bottle of whiskey in his hand. He had suddenly decided to finish it off outside. Seeing Mort headed toward the swinging doors, he warned. "I wouldn't be goin' in there Mister, if I was you. There's two loaded guys at the far end of the bar threatenin' to blow the hell out of that cowpuncher and his Indian friend on the other end. They already put a dent in the barkeep's head with a whiskey bottle when he tried to shut 'em up."

While he talked, Mort was getting his own look at the situation inside by peering over the top of the swinging doors from one side and then the other, making certain he wasn't spotted. Both drunks had moved out into the room from the corner of the bar, both with guns drawn, eyeing Thorn and Kio who seemed to be ignoring their threats.

Mort nodded toward the plate glass window to their left, behind the two trouble makers inside. "Slip down there, Jeremiah. Pick up that bench, and when I give you a nod see if you can't break that window." By the time Mort had finished, Jeremiah was on his way. He hoisted the bench and checked for Mort's nod.

In the split second after he nodded, Jeremiah sent one end

—Seven Rode Together—

of the bench crashing through the window. With his Winchester at the ready from his hip, Mort stepped through the swinging doors. The two rabble rousers whirled around at the sound of breaking glass. "Freeze! Right where you are." Mort yelled. "If you roll your eyes, you're both dead men!"

They were in no mood to risk a glance toward the swinging doors to see who had the drop on them. "All you need to do is just let loose of your guns." The guns hit the floor. The taller of the two risked a look, turning his head slowly around he saw Mort's Winchester pointed at his midsection. "Now turn around and kick those guns over here." They didn't hesitate, and Jeremiah who again appeared at Mort's side, stooped down and picked them up.

"Now, what you plan to do with 'em?" Thorn asked, slipping his .45 back into his holster as he came across the room to give Mort a slap on the back. "That's two I owe you, Mort. You saved my rear-end at the Way Station last month and it appears you done it again."

Kio and Jeremiah quickly stepped in and collared the two would-be shooters and slammed them down hard on chairs at the nearest card table. Jeremiah, who'd witnessed Thorn's dexterity with a gun at the Turtle Creek Trading Post a couple of months earlier, joined them. "One thing I can't figure, Thorn. How'd those two yah-hoos ever get the drop on you and Kio, anyways?"

Thorn eyed Jeremiah for a moment and broke into a broad smile. "Just a lousy judge of human nature I'd guess. Me and Kio thought they were all talk. Just a couple of thirsty cowhands makin' big talk. Besides, they wasn't talkin' about me, and I figured when Kio felt they was gettin' too personal, he'd let me know. At the end they was so liquored up, I'd bet a month's pay they couldn't have

—John E. Cramer—

found their butts with both hands, let alone pull a six-gun and point it in the right direction. But when the fat one pole-axed the barkeep with a whiskey bottle, we were watchin' where he was gonna fall behind the bar. That's when the whole thing got our attention. When we took a second look, they were wavin' those .45's in our direction. That's when the front window caved in."

Before Thorn finished his story, the barkeep was pulling himself up from behind the bar. At the same time, some of those who'd cleared the saloon earlier were drifting back inside. Thorn picked up again on his story. "You remember I was warnin' the men before we left camp about the U.S. Marshal here in Wichita who don't deal too kindly with them who try to shoot up his town."

Spotting Marshal Thurgold, who was shouldering his way past the onlookers coming toward them, Mort asked. "What was you sayin' about the U.S. Marshal in this town, Thorn?"

"I was just explainin' that he's a pretty hard-nosed bastard when dealin' with them who can't hold their liquor."

Just as he finished, he felt the large, meaty hand of Marshal Thurgold clamp down on his shoulder. "And that goes for those who throw benches through windows. I always require the trail boss of the cattle drive to ante up the money for any damage done by his men. But in this case, I'll make an exception. The trail boss pays only half of the cost. Those two who seem to have triggered this mess will have to come up with the rest."

"Fair enough," Thorn agreed. "The trail boss will ante up his half right now. He figures then the Marshal will have enough money to buy us all the round of drinks he promised us when we came to Wichita."

"Well, it's past closin' time for this establishment,"

—Seven Rode Together—

Thurgold began—

"No excuses." Thorn cut in. "This trail boss hates to think a man who's wearin' a U.S. marshal's badge would ever welch on a promise he makes."

"In that case, if it'll make the trail boss and the others happy, as quickly as we can get these two back to a cell where they can sleep it off, I'll make good my promise on buyin' those drinks. It'll give me a chance to talk to Mort about that jailbreak in River Bend."

A short time later they'd locked up the two men. They had both worked for Dave Linfield, owner of a ranch about four miles west of Wichita. Then Marshal Thurgold poured each of them a steaming cup of black coffee. "These ain't the kind of drinks you boys had in mind. But they'll have to do for tonight."

After they'd reviewed the events of the evening at the Traders' Saloon, Thurgold eased back in his swivel chair, opened a drawer, pulled out a wanted poster and slapped it down on his desk. All four of them, Jeremiah, Mort, Kio and Thorn readily recognized the face on the poster as Buck Farley. "Haven't heard anymore from the new Marshal in River Bend," Thurgold began. "But we're pretty sure Farley's headed back to his own stompin' ground in Oklahoma Territory. I've not heard who might have helped them break out, but we're sure Luke Keltner, who broke out with him, wouldn't be headed in the same direction. Judge Storm wired me that Keltner might be headed to Nebraska. Judge Storm says he's been told Keltner had some kinfolks there before the war. Nebraska was a Territory in those days."

"Why all the interest in Keltner?" Mort asked. "Outside of the fact he was carryin' all that money?"

—John E. Cramer—

"This ain't common knowledge, and I'm not sure I know all that's goin' on in Washington, but from what I understand, there's an investigation still goin' on into a train heist before the war ended. Those who pulled off that robbery made a clean getaway with a hell of a lot of money—all in gold. It was bein' sent to Jefferson Davis to help finance the Confederacy. According to my contacts, they're damned sure that heist was carried out by Union soldiers."

Mort leaned forward. "Wouldn't they know where all their troops were when it happened? Dundee, you were a company clerk for the Colonel's outfit. Didn't you keep records and file reports on your company's whereabouts?"

"Sure. We filed reports." Jeremiah said.

"How could they be sure Union soldiers pulled off the robbery?" Thorn chimed in. "Anybody might have found out the train was carryin' the gold. Hell, it could be the Rebs ridin' shotgun on a train carryin' that kinda money. Even if Union troops did do it, they could've been wearin' somethin' different than Army uniforms."

"Anything's possible," Thurgold said. "This train was carryin' Confederate troops and the regular train crew. The train was halted by trees felled across the tracks. Those who made off with the money made certain there was no one left alive to tell anything."

Mort leaned back and stretched. "This has been an interesting discussion, gentlemen, but it's goin' to have to continue without me. I'm headin' back to the hotel. We'll all be puttin' in a long, hard day's work tomorrow."

Jeremiah followed Mort's lead without making any explanation. They walked back to the hotel, both too worn out to talk. Jeremiah was occupied with what he'd learned about the train robbery. Mort was wishing he'd gotten a letter written to Nora.

Chapter 21

Jeb Hofstader stepped out of the River Bend Bank where he'd delivered Mort's message to Dave Shelley. He squinted up at the sun, checked his pocket-watch and decided there was still plenty of time before noon to check with River Bend's newly appointed U.S. Marshal. He was hoping Chad Youngman might have something new on the jailbreak. "Nothing more than most folks have read about in the *Valley View*. Course that was a couple days ago. If there's anything new, I've not heard about it."

Jeb stuck his head in the door and asked. "How come you're sittin' there when you oughta be out there trackin' those two prisoners I brung you?"

"Come on in, Jeb," Chad said. "I guess since Mort's left for Wichita, you don't have anything to keep you busy at the Circle-K. Truth is, I got back last night. I'm afraid those rascals are out of the state by now. We tried to pick up their trail figurin' they'd head south to the nearest border. They must have had a good six-hour lead before anyone knew they were gone. The deputy is still nursin'

—John E. Cramer—

a lump on his head as big as your fist. Says he never saw or heard anything."

"Got any idea who it was helped 'em escape?"

Chad shook his head. "Nope. But whoever it was knew his way around here."

"Why would you be thinkin' that?"

"For one thing, he stole two of Fred Findley's best saddle horses out of the Livery along with saddles and bridles. You know Fred lives above the stable and he sure as shootin' would've heard anyone takin' horses out, but Fred's never home on Friday nights. That's the one night a week he's over at his sister's place. Besides a good home-cooked meal, Fred and his brother-in-law set up playin' cut-throat cribbage."

Jeb screwed up his face and began rubbing his fingers through his beard. "I know that. He's always braggin' on Rose Mary's cookin'. But a stranger might just have been lucky that old Fred Finley wasn't home."

"Could be," Chad agreed. "But not likely."

"Well, I guess you got things pretty much figured out," Jeb finally admitted. "It don't seem likely it could've been one of Buck Farley's gang that busted them outta jail."

"Exactly." Chad said. "And that's not all. We picked up tracks. They wasn't made by any three riders travelin' together. One headed west at the fork about ten miles out of town, and there was two sets of tracks leadin' south toward Burkhalter's old line shack near Settler's Creek. But each had taken a different route to get there."

"Too bad you didn't have Thorn Masters' sidekick with you. I got a hunch Kio could've figured 'em out."

—Seven Rode Together—

"Possible." Chad agreed. "That one rider who continued west might well have been headin' toward the Burkhalter Ranch, too."

"Could be." Jeb agreed. He stood up, took a hitch on his gun belt and walked over to the door. "I'd better be headin' back to the ranch after I make a stop at the Post Office. Missus Milburn thinks she oughta be hearin' from some of her kinsfolk back East. I reckon Mort and your pa will be gettin' back from Wichita in a week or two. If you git any free time, drop by the Circle-K. I'm sure Amanda Milburn would like to see you—might even ask you to stay for supper."

A few minutes later Jeb was entering the Post Office when he bumped into Tom Trinity carrying a fistful of mail. "Hi there, young feller," Jeb said. "From the looks of all that mail you're totin', I'd say you gotta be the most popular man in River Bend."

"This mail belongs to the Colonel."

"I'd a thought a good lookin' feller like you would have a gal or two back home you'd be hearin' from. Jeremiah and Mort took off this mornin, bright and early, with the cattle drive to Wichita. Jeremiah was tellin' us he'd decided to quit the Burkhalter place. Anyway, he signed on with the Circle-K. I kinda think Mort was hopin' you might decide to join us over at the Circle-K one of these days."

"I thought about it. I don't know about Jeremiah's reason for makin' a change, and we both know there ain't no love lost between the Colonel and Mort. The way I figure it, that's between them. I've been knockin' around on my own since I can't remember when. I've really been lookin' for someplace permanent—some place to put some roots down."

—John E. Cramer—

Jeb nodded. "I sure can't argue with that. You think you've found what you've been lookin' for with the Colonel?"

"That's what I'm thinkin'. I got no beef with the Colonel. He's givin' me a chance to learn about ranchin' and the cattle business, and I'm drawin' good wages." He flashed a broad smile. "I got a nice place to live. Get three square meals a day, and I ain't spent a dime of my wages. I'm not a big drinker. Don't gamble, and got no hankerin' to bed down with whores."

"Maybe you missed your callin'," Jeb cut in. "Sounds like you got all the qualifications to make a good preacher."

Tom laughed. "You might be right. Until I was sixteen, I was raised by nuns, and spent a hitch in the Army. I learned to take care of myself. Probably, that's why I'm headin' across the street after our little talk and makin' a deposit of this month's wages. So you see, you wasn't too far wrong. It's just one gal I do get a letter from now and then. I've got some plans for the future and they don't include workin' for wages all my life."

"Well, I gotta be gettin' on," Jeb said as he clapped Tom on the shoulder. "Maybe we can get together again and swap a few stories. But there's one thing I've learned from this talkin'. I ain't never gonna tell nobody again that they've missed their callin'. But I'd like to tell you one thing before we have somebody out here tryin' to charge us rent for campin' on Post Office property. You'll have to get together with Mort. From what you've been sayin' I gotta notion you two would hit it off just fine. Knowin' Mort the way I do, I don't see it would make a damn bit of difference if you was to have dinner with us some night."

Tom nodded. "Maybe we can work something out," he said. "I'd have a chance to compare notes with Jeremiah, too."

—Seven Rode Together—

Once inside the bank, Tom paused long enough to sort through the mail. As always, it seldom included personal letters. He was aware of Paul and Nora, although their names were never mentioned in daily conversation, and it was only following the trial, the Colonel talked about Duane, "In some ways you remind me of Duane," he'd begun. "You're loyal and you learn quickly. But you're disciplined, and you're looking ahead to making a future for yourself, and for a wife and family. That's something Duane never was interested in."

It was during that discussion Tom told the Colonel that he planned to marry a girl he'd met in New Orleans.

"Are you wanting to make your monthly deposit, Mister Trinity. If you are, you're next."

She was a waitress. When she first came to the table where he and Jeremiah were seated, he was instantly captivated. She was, he thought, the most beautiful girl he'd ever seen. Her dark hair, smiling green eyes, and the way she seemed to glide across the room captured his complete attention. Later that same evening, after he and Jeremiah had finished eating, she passed by their table with a tray filled with food. Tom watched the bearded soldier extend his foot. Before Tom could react, she stumbled and the tray crashed to the floor. In an instant, Tom was out of his chair. "Let her clean it up, soldier. That's her job." Tom ignored the advice. The soldier tapped him on the shoulder. "Do I have to tell you agin? Or do I have to rub your nose in it?"

"Looks like you've bit off more than you're gonna be able to chew." Jeremiah suggested, standing behind the bearded soldier. By now, everyone in the room was watching. In the next instant he whirled and delivered a blow aimed at Tom's chin. It never found it's target. Tom stopped the punch when he grabbed the wrist a few inches from his face. "Now, mister, guess who's going to clean up this mess."

"What's all the trouble here?" It was the voice of the cafe owner. He'd watched from behind the bar.

Tom turned to the owner. "This gentleman you see on his knees has kindly consented to clean up the mess he caused when he tripped your beautiful, young waitress. With a little coaxing, he might agree to pay for the damage unless, of course, you'd rather notify his commanding officer."

The owner extended his hand. "I'd like you to meet the benefactor of your quick action, Miss Becky DeLaney. And, this is—"

"Tom Trinity, Miss. And this is Jeremiah Dundee."

During the next two months, Tom and Becky were together every possible hour. They went to church together on Sundays, had picnics, took long walks together, watched sunsets in the evenings and sunrises in the mornings. They talked about their pasts and made plans for the future. They discovered they were both orphans. "If you never knew your parents, how ever did you get your name, Tom Trinity?" she'd asked.

"I was found on the steps of the Trinity orphanage."

"Missus Tom Trinity," she'd said softly. "I like it. I like it just fine."

He'd told her he loved her the night before he was mustered out of the Army. He told her he would be back. When he arrived in River Bend, he used part of his reward money for the capture of Buck Farley to send her an engagement ring. Now Tom was dead

—Seven Rode Together—

set on saving enough money to have a place of their own ready when she arrived.

During one of their frequent talks, the Colonel said he was considering hiring a man and wife to share his home. "There's plenty of room in this house to live a good life and with all the privacy they would require," he'd said. "They'd even have plenty of room if they decided to have children. Matter of fact, if I was to find the right couple, they'd have the run of the house. Be more like a family. I'd even be willin' to hire a maid to help the wife with her housekeepin' chores. Course the right couple might be hard to find. I'd want the husband to hold down a responsible position—like a foreman or general manager who'd share with me the responsibilities of the day-by-day operations."

It sounded like an ideal arrangement to Tom, but he was beginning to have some reservations after Wade Parker quit and Jeremiah decided to throw in with Mort Kane and the Circle-K.

Anyway, he thought, as he placed the Colonel's mail in one of his saddle bags, I kinda got my mind set on havin' a place of my own the day I get married. He untied his horse and swung up in the saddle.

It was late afternoon when Tom headed west out of town. He noticed several people gathered in front of the marshal's office. He recognized Jeb Hofstader and Mort's son, Joey. At the edge of the crowd was the owner of the general store.

"What's all the commotion about?"

"I yust got here, but I was watching from my store when Jeb Hofstader and the boy rode into town. Jeb had a dead man across his horse."

Tom dismounted. Jeb was talking to the town's undertaker,

—John E. Cramer—

he walked over to him. "Understand you brought in a body, Jeb. Do you know who he is?"

"I oughta," Jeb said. "Me and Chad Youngman are the two fellas who brought him in a week ago. Luke Keltner. He did work for the Colonel. He broke jail with that Mexican gunslinger, Buck Farley."

"Where'd you find the body?"

"A couple of miles south. Joey and me were lookin' for a good place to wet a line when Joey spotted him half in and half out of the water on the other side of the creek."

"What do you suppose happened to him?"

"Wasn't hard to figure out when you find a body with two bullet holes in the back. Somebody bushwhacked him."

"What about Farley?"

"What about him?" Jeb snorted. "He's probably the one who done the bushwhackin'. If you figure on findin' *him*, you gotta long ride. He's probably in Mexico by now."

Tom had heard all he wanted to. As he was about to mount up, Jeb added. "You might want to tell the Colonel he might try doin' the decent thing and cough up the buryin' money for one of his hands."

The sun had set by the time Tom rode into the Double-B Ranch. He stripped his mount and turned him loose in the corral. A two-horse carriage was tied up near the front gate. He was wondering who might be visiting the Colonel as he crossed the veranda. The door opened and the Colonel and an older, graying gentleman, dressed in a dark business suit and carrying a brief case, emerged.

"Here he is now," the Colonel said. And turning toward his visitor, he added. "This is the young man I was telling you about.

—Seven Rode Together—

Tom, I'd like you to meet Lloyd Harrison. He's my attorney and an old and dear friend of mine."

"I've been hearing a lot of good things about you." Harrison said, extending his hand.

"I've been tellin' Lloyd you've taken to this cattle ranching like a duck to water."

"I've got a lot to learn, yet. But I figure I've got a good teacher. And if he don't give up on me, maybe in a few more years, I'll be able to earn my pay."

"What did I tell you, Lloyd? This boy is not only a quick learner, he's modest, too."

They watched as Harrison hurried down the stone path. Tom turned and followed the Colonel inside and placed the day's mail on the Colonel's desk.

"Have a seat and make yourself comfortable while I take a look at this mail. He picked up one envelope, opened it, gave it a quick read and laid it aside. "What's new in River Bend?"

"For one thing," Tom began, "they won't need to be lookin' for Luke Keltner any more."

"Turned himself in, did he?"

"No. He came in draped over Jeb Hofstader's saddle. Him and Mort Kane's boy, Joey, fished him out of Settlers Creek. Seems whoever shot him wanted to make sure he was dead. There were two bullet holes in his back. Jeb figures Buck Farley was the one who done the shootin'."

"Well, now that doesn't make a lot of sense. Why would Farley want to kill him when they both broke jail together? What did the new Marshal have to say about it?"

"Never talked to him."

—John E. Cramer—

The Colonel dropped the last letter on his desk. "I've been meaning to ask you if you've given any more thought about sending for the young lady you were telling me about?" Before Tom could reply, the Colonel continued. "If she's all you say she is, she just might attract one of those southern boys, and he might not keep her waiting. Stranger things have happened when a fellow waits too long."

"With some, maybe," Tom said. "But not with Becky."

"I've been thinking lately that you two might just be the couple I've been looking for. How do you think she'd react to coming out here and the two of you helping me run this place?"

"To tell you the truth, Colonel, and I don't mean to sound like I don't appreciate what you're offering to do for us, but I've been workin' for wages ever since I've been makin' my own way and so's Becky. The only reason I joined the Army was to be on my own. But even in the Army, there was always somebody tellin' me what to do and when to do it. Best thing the Army ever done for me was when they sent me to New Orleans where I met Becky." He looked at the Colonel. He sure wasn't wanting to talk himself out of a job, and what he was about to say, might give the Colonel the idea he didn't want to stay on at the Double-B.

"Go on, son, You were saying—"

"When we decided we'd get married, I promised her we'd have a place of our own. I've never owned anything of my own, except the clothes I'm wearing, in my whole life. It was Jeremiah who bought my horse when we mustered out of the Army. And when that horse pulled up lame on our way to River Bend, Thorn Master's uncle gave me a horse when we stopped over at the Bar-K. I offered to pay him with the reward money. Well, that Reward

—Seven Rode Together—

was more money than I'd had at any one time in my whole life." Tom continued. "What's more, it gave me a big start on savin' enough to get a place of our own. I'm hopin' to have enough when we get married to have our own place and work for myself. And that's the way I see it, sir. And I know Becky sees it the same way."

The Colonel liked what Tom was saying. It made him even more certain his first impressions of Tom were right. He was interested in persuading Tom that he and Becky could be together while he was working toward the day he would have enough saved to get his own place. "You did say you were going to have enough saved to have your own place?"

"That's about the size of it," Tom replied.

"Well, then, the whole matter is as good as settled. I believe you've said Becky was working in New Orleans."

Tom nodded. "She's savin' money, too. It's goin' to be *our* place."

"Well, since she's working in New Orleans already, and you're working way out here in Kansas, why wait a year, maybe two or more, to be together? You both might just as well be working for me. I figure I'd be paying her as much, maybe more, than she's making now. And at the risk of repeating myself, this is a big house." He paused and slipped Tom a quick wink. "And, it's up to you and Becky whether you would be needing two bedrooms or one."

Tom forced a little smile. "Well—that does make some sense. Let me think on it awhile. I'll need to find out if Becky would give it a try."

"When you write her," the Colonel suggested, "tell her, when the time comes you two are ready to get married, I'll personally see to it that you'll have the biggest wedding folks in these

—John E. Cramer—

parts have ever seen." He paused, studying Tom's reaction. "That'll be my wedding present."

That night Tom found it difficult to sleep. What the Colonel suggested meant he and Becky would be together real soon. But he was trying to understand why the Colonel would be wanting to make such an offer. He knew he had to be the least experienced cowhand the Colonel had working for him. He was reminded of one of Jeremiah's favorite expressions whenever something was offered him by someone or something that had happened that defied explanation, "You never ever look a gift horse in the mouth. Just accept it like you was entitled."

He suddenly felt the need to talk with Jeremiah. As his most trusted friend, he'd level with him. Jeb's invitation to visit the Circle-K seemed more important than when he accepted it.

The Colonel was finding it equally difficult to sleep. Long after Tom had left, he remained at his desk satisfied he'd set in motion a plan depriving both Paul and Nora from their inheritance. But of far greater concern, was the smoldering hatred of Mort Kane. The first step in fulfilling the vow he'd made, was in place. Now that he was on the loose, Buck Farley would see it through. There were important details to be decided before Farley could carry out the deed. Any plan to seek revenge against Mort Kane should require patience and time. He was satisfied he still had plenty of both. He also knew the blame had to fall on Farley or his cutthroats. There could not be the slightest suspicion he was involved. He could also have Farley eliminate any left connected to the train heist of so many years ago. Wade Parker, he was satisfied, would never return to the Valley unless he succumbed to a death wish. Accusations against the Colonel would make public his guilt as

—Seven Rode Together—

well as the part he played in Farley and Keltner's escape from the River Bend jail. The one person, he reasoned, who might have any proof connecting him with the heist, would be Company Clerk, Jeremiah Dundee.

Chapter 22

It had been two weeks since Mort and Jeremiah had returned from the cattle drive to Wichita. Thorn and Kio had been persuaded to stay over awhile as guests of the Circle-K after Jeb had told them, "You fellers deserve to do a little celebratin' yourselves before you head out for home. Ain't that right, Mort?"

"I've never known you ever to be wrong when it comes to celebratin' anything, Jeb."

Thorn looked at Kio, "You thinkin' what I'm thinkin'?"

Kio smiled, "Ain't I always?"

Thorn shrugged. "Looks like you got yourself a couple of boarders for a few days, Mort. It ain't the celebratin' me and Kio are thinkin' about. It's Missus Milburn's cookin', 'specially those apple pies we've been enjoyin' the last couple of days."

"Now that we've got that settled," Mort said, "I'm headin' into town." He was anxious to get the cash he'd received from the sale of cattle in Wichita deposited in the bank. He was equally anxious to mail the letter he'd written to Nora the night before.

—Seven Rode Together—

Knowing she was hoping he'd give up the ranch and move to Boston, he'd written that he'd never be able to do that. He had invested too much in the Circle-K to walk away from it for the uncertainty of what his future might be in Boston. In the half-dozen years since he became owner of his Uncle Steve's ranch, he'd more than tripled the original holdings in spite of the Colonel's efforts to force him out. He was certain the worst of the battles had been fought, and the Colonel's hold on the Valley and the people in River Bend had been broken. The trial had stripped the Colonel of much of his influence and popularity among the majority of the Valley's population. Mort was confident the worst was over, but he was also aware, as long as the Colonel lived in the Valley, he'd bear watching. More important, Mort had to let Nora know he was building a future for Joey and any other children who might come along. The same as his Pa had tried to do for him. Had it not been for the war, he would still be trying to eke out a living on that Kentucky dirt farm. Mort figured, with the land grants being awarded to build railroads, it wouldn't be too many years until River Bend would have access to Eastern markets—a big boon for ranchers like him. He could only hope Nora could understand his reasons for not wanting to sell the Circle-K.

As he headed down the boardwalk toward Fred Finley's Livery Stable, Mort noticed the banners stretched across the street advertising the celebration that would begin in two more days. Store fronts were decorated with flags. Signs announced events to be held during the three-day celebration. The street was filled with wagons and rigs belonging to itinerant vendors hoping to cash in on River Bend's celebration.

The Silver Dollar Saloon was doing a thriving business. He

—John E. Cramer—

caught a glimpse of Jeb and Jeremiah entering through the swinging doors. Stepping up his pace, he followed them inside.

The place was alive with cowhands and others getting a head-start on the festivities. Seeing Jeremiah and Jeb, he eased over and stepped between them. "I thought I'd find you here. Bartender, three whiskeys right here. You fellows don't mind if I buy you a round?"

Jeb clapped him on the shoulder, "Don't hurt my feelin's none. Why don't you make it a bottle and I'll grab us a table."

"A bottle!" Mort echoed. "You two aimin' to do any work tomorrow?"

"We just came from the Frontier Hotel. We told Thorn and Kio we'd be here. They oughta drag in by the time I can find a place to sit down."

Jeb spotted a table on the far side of the room and made a beeline toward it. They'd just sat down when Thorn and Kio came through the swinging doors and spotted them. "Be with you in a minute," Thorn yelled, and headed toward the bar. He appeared a few minutes later, a bottle in either hand. It was then that Mort spotted Tom Trinity. "I see you brought a friend along with you."

"Who? Him?" Thorn replied crooking his thumb in Trinity's direction. "Tom and me go back a long way."

Mort reached across the table and shook hands with Tom. "Good to see you again. Jeremiah was tellin' me you'd decided to stay on with Felix Burkhalter. Too bad," he added with a smile. "The Circle-K sure could use another hand now that we're steppin' up our cattle business. Have you heard from that Southern belle?"

Tom nodded. He was turnin' over what Mort had said about needin' another hand. He couldn't escape the feeling that these men

—Seven Rode Together—

were his real friends. Thorn and Kio were the ones who insisted him and Jeremiah collect the reward for bringing in Farley. And Mort seemed like the kind of guy you'd want in your corner. He watched him now as the others listened to Jeb's story of how he first met Mort. "Anyway, him and his boy, Joey, were gettin' ready to have supper. They was cookin' outside since there wasn't any house left." He paused long enough to relight his pipe and empty his glass of whiskey. "Colonel Burkhalter was wantin' to throw a scare into Mort thinkin' he'd be wantin' to sell out. First thing I asked him was what happened? He says to me, 'We had a fire.' Hell, that wasn't what I was askin'. I meant, did he know who done it? Then I ask him did he plan on sellin' the Circle-K. 'Nope,' he says. 'Me and Joey plan to be here for a long time.' I knew right then that I met the man Burkhalter wasn't goin' to be able to scare, like he'd done some others."

Mort frowned. "Jeb's a mighty good example of what happens to a man when he starts drinkin' on an empty stomach."

Ignoring Mort's remark and the laughter that followed, Jeb turned to look at Tom who hadn't touched his glass of whiskey. "Drink up, man, we never let good whiskey go to waste. 'Specially, when we're celebratin' River Bend's birthday."

"Or when somebody else is payin' for it," Thorn cut in.

Tom raised his glass and replied. "Here's to River Bend's birthday." He drank it down and poured another.

"Speakin' of the Colonel. You 'spose he'll be makin' any speeches durin' this celebration?" Jeb asked.

"I don't know," Tom said. "You can ask him yourself when he gets back from Topeka. He'll be back the last of the week."

For the next couple of hours, the story-telling and the laugh-

—John E. Cramer—

ter continued. Mort kept an eye on Tom. It was clear Tom was not a drinking man, but he'd been caught up in the celebrating mood of his friends seated around the table. When the bottles had been emptied, Jeb announced he and Jeremiah would be heading back to the Circle-K. "One thing about our boss," he began, "he ain't got no sympathy with the hired help come mornin'. He'll be gettin' me and Jeremiah up and around when the rooster crows."

By the time he'd finished, everyone was on their feet. Mort pulled Thorn aside as the others moved on toward the swinging doors. "You and Kio might want to see that Tom gets home without fallin' out of the saddle. I have a feelin' he's not much of a drinker."

Thorn agreed. "Me and Kio will see he gets back in one piece. You ain't aimin' on gettin' Kio and me up with those damn roosters, are you?"

Mort shrugged. "Depends on whether you want to find out just how good Missus Milburn's breakfasts are. She don't keep it on the table for any late-comers."

A few minutes later, Kio and Thorn were heading out of town, one on either side of Tom. The cool night air worked its magic and before they reached the Double-B, Tom had regained some of his ability to set a horse at an easy gallop. But when they reached the ranch, his walking required some support. When he attempted to duck under the hitching rail in front of the house, he fell flat on his face.

"Well, he's home," Thorn said. "Do we leave him be or are we supposed to take him in and put him to bed?"

"I'll take care of his horse," Kio said. "You put him to bed." Without waiting to hear more from Thorn, Kio grabbed the reins of Tom's black and white piebald and headed toward the barn.

—Seven Rode Together—

Thorn helped Tom to his feet, but instead of heading toward the house, he headed for the pump. After the first dousing of well water, Thorn could see a quick improvement in Tom's ability to stand alone. After the second half-filled bucket had been emptied over Tom's head, he was not only able to make it under his own steam to the front entrance, he was beginning to talk enough to be understood. "Come on in."

"I'll come in for a minute," Thorn replied. "Always did want to see where a Colonel lived."

They entered the foyer and moved on in to the spacious living room. "Have a seat," Tom invited. "I'll see if I can rustle up some coffee."

Thorn's gaze swept the room and came to rest on the painting above the fireplace. He moved closer until he stood squarely in front of it. There was no doubt about the painting even without seeing the initials in the lower right-hand corner. It was a painting of the Shenandoah Valley, at the confluence of the Shenandoah and the Potomac Rivers. The painting had at one time hung over another fireplace in his home in Virginia. It had been painted by his father, Ben Masters.

He knew there was one man responsible for the theft of that painting, the Union officer in charge of the raiding party who'd killed his Pa. He hadn't yet seen Colonel Burkhalter, but the image of the man responsible for his Pa's death was one he'd never forget.

He was still looking at the painting when Tom returned with Kio and a tray of coffee in big mugs. "I see you're admirin' that painting," Tom said, as he set a tray on the table. "It's a beauty."

Thorn nodded. "Do you know how the Colonel happened to have it?"

—John E. Cramer—

"Nope. He's never said and I've never asked. If you're interested, I could ask the Colonel when he gets back."

"Don't bother," Thorn replied. "I wouldn't know one painting from another. I guess I was admiring it because it looked to me like the place would be good for fishing."

A few minutes later, Thorn and Kio were on their way. "Know what I'm thinkin', Kio?"

"If that Colonel's the one you're thinkin' he is, he won't be makin' many more speeches."

Glancing toward Kio, Thorn replied, "Damned if you ain't gettin' to be a regular mind reader, Kio."

Chapter 23

Colonel Burkhalter arrived home the night before the celebration was scheduled to begin. He seemed to be in exceptionally fine spirits when he found Tom seated in the living room reading the latest edition of the *Valley View*. Tom quickly laid the paper aside as he stood to greet the Colonel.

"Good to have you back, Colonel."

"It's good to be back. I see you're catching up on your reading. That's last week's newspaper. I guess Clancy likes to call it a special edition."

"I was checking the deadline for entering tomorrow's horse race. I see the winner collects a hundred-dollar prize. Kinda caught my eye. A hundred dollars would come in mighty handy right now."

"A hundred dollars would come in mighty handy any time. But if you're thinking you're going to win this horse race, you'd better think again."

Tom shrugged his shoulders. "I noticed Joey Kane and Steve Youngman are entered."

—John E. Cramer—

"And so are about twenty-five others, and they're not all boys. Anyway, I was counting on you to help some of the others to get the Town Hall ready for tomorrow night's dance."

"Sure, I'll be glad to lend a hand. By the way, I've been meanin' to tell you. Got a letter from Becky, and she's mighty anxious to come out here and not wait, like we first planned. I guess that's what got me to thinkin' about entering the race. That prize money would be more than enough to bring her out here."

"I wouldn't worry about that. Whenever she's ready to come, we'll see that she comes first-class. And, so far as you not ridin' in this horse race, I'm doin' you a favor. This is no Kentucky Derby. This race they're having tomorrow will have anywhere from twenty-five to thirty entries. They'll be racing on a route laid out over rough terrain that crosses the river twice. Only one of those crossings will be made at a fording place. And it's more like a twelve-mile race. The only flat land that allows the horses to go all out is the mile and a quarter at the start and about the same at the finish. And the men enterin' the race will be out to win any way they can. You can bet on it. Think you're ready for that kind of horse race?"

"Guess not," Tom replied. "Guess I'll just hang on to that five-dollar entry fee."

"Good," the Colonel smiled. "I'd like you to come along with me tomorrow when I open the festivities by announcing that River Bend, by next year at this time, will be havin' rail service from here to just about any place they want to go. And I'd like to introduce you, too, as my new foreman and partner at the Burkhalter Ranch." Before Tom had a chance to react, he added. "So, tomorrow you can send Becky a telegram and wire her the

—Seven Rode Together—

money to make that first-class trip out here."

"But I—"

"No need to thank me, son. You've earned it. This past year you've proved to me you can handle the job. And Becky, I'm sure, will add a whole new grace to this place."

Long after Tom had turned in for the night, he was worrying about his conversation with the Colonel. A foreman? That, he might handle. But a partner? If I'd gotten promotions that fast in the Army, he thought, I could've retired a general. But, he recalled, it's like Jeremiah always said, "Never look a gift horse in the mouth. Accept it. Just like you was entitled."

The Colonel, too, was finding it difficult to sleep, but wasn't reviewing his talk with Tom. Instead, he was concentrating on his two-day meeting with Buck Farley just across the border in New Mexico Territory. They'd gone over every detail of a plan that would, if there were no hitches, give him the revenge he'd been seeking against Mort Kane. It had helped in his negotiations that Farley had a score to settle with Kane who'd engineered his capture at the Way Station, but Farley was still pressing for a better deal. "I ain't snatchin' no keed and knockin' off hees old man without a guarantee I'm gonna see fifty-thousand dollars when the job's done," Farley demanded. "How the hell are you so damn sure Kane can even come up with thees kind of ransom money?"

"He's not going to have trouble raising fifty-thousand dollars," he'd tried to assure Farley. "His spread alone is worth two, maybe three times that amount. I know Kane. If that boy's life is at stake, he'd go through hell and high water to get him back even if

—John E. Cramer—

it means selling the Circle-K. And if it comes to that, he's not going to have any trouble selling. I'll guarantee that."

Farley wasn't buying. "You'll have to do better than thees," he'd challenged. "You forget that I know Kane, too. He ain't the kind that's gonna roll over and play dead even if he raises the ransom money and gets the boy back. He'll never quit 'til he tracks down everyone who does thees kidnapping."

"You make it clear in the ransom note. He's got to come alone. You get the money. You knock him off. It's up to you then what you do with the kid. If you think he could identify you or any of your men, get rid of him."

"You don't hear too good," Farley had countered. "We ain't dealin' with no peasant. A ransom note sayin' he's got to come alone don't convince me he'll be comin' alone." His dark eyes riveted on the Colonel's, and slowly his lips parted, displaying a row of snowy, white teeth surrounded by a heavy, black beard. "You forget, Colonel, you've had six years to take him out. Your son, ah, what's his name?"

"Duane."

"Si." His smile grew even broader. "Duane. A very fast man with a gun. He and the Koehler brothers didn't stop your Mister Kane. Three men couldn't take out thees man armed with a single rifle. The Koehler brothers rode with me. They tell me about thees Mort Kane." He had gotten the Colonel's attention. "Two rounds, that's all he needed. The horse—then Duane. Right between the eyes. And he has friends—more now than before. Thees man, you tell me, will be alone when he comes with the ransom money?"

"This is a different situation. Besides, if he doesn't come alone, who in River Bend will volunteer to come with him? The

—Seven Rode Together—

new marshal's got no jurisdiction in New Mexico Territory. Even if he decided to go along, the men who'd make up a posse in River Bend all have families. They wouldn't be sticking their necks out. They'd be ready to go home."

Before he'd completed his explanation, Farley had begun shaking his head. "You forget, Colonel. You say thees Mort Kane could be coming with a posse?" He held up a finger, shaking it from side to side in front of his face, and then tapping it against his temple. "Thees he would not do. A posse? No. He will come with two, maybe three or four men. Two of them I know from an unfortunate meeting I had with them at a Trading Post. Thees men and others will ride with Kane when he comes to bring the ransom."

"You'll be holed up in a box canyon with one trail leading in to the old miner's shack where you'll be holding the kid. A couple of men posted at the entrance could easily eliminate three, maybe four or five men, who might be with Kane."

The smile disappeared from Farley's face, his eyes narrowed to slits, and then slowly the smile returned to his whiskered face. "You are certainly the most forgetful one, Colonel. I am the one, not you, who will be taking thees risk. What risk? You laugh. I don't know, I say. But when I am dealing with men like your quiet man, Mort Kane, who will have friends like thees Thorn Masters and his friend Kio, and others who would not need to be asked to join him, I know there is a risk. They are not school boys, they are cunning, crafty men who find a way when there is no way to do the unexpected." Farley leaned forward like a lawyer who knows he's cinched his case. "You say I will be taking no risk. I say my guts tell me there is a great risk. So, Mister Colonel, I am sure you will be willing, without further convincing, to set my mind at ease by

—John E. Cramer—

agreeing to my terms for this undertaking—"

"You're wanting more money?"

"No."

"Well, then, what do you want?"

"You will accompany us after we grab thees kid."

"But he'd know. He'd recognize me!"

"Ah, you forget again, Colonel. It was you, not I, who suggested we get rid of thees kid. And if you are so anxious to rid yourself of thees enemy, Mort Kane, as you have said." He paused, spreading his arms, palms up. "It's such a small request, Colonel, and I would say to myself, the Colonel agrees to my terms. Now, I feel much better. He proves to me there is no risk. And I'm again a happy man. My guts no longer bother me. So, what do you say? Are we now in agreement?"

"But I'm expected to be a major sponsor at the dance that night. I would be missed. If the kid is snatched during the race as we plan, and I'm not around after the end of the race, Kane would immediately believe I, somehow, had a hand in his disappearance.

"Oh, then," Farley had replied. "We can forget about it. One day you may think of a better plan to fulfill thees vow you tell me you've made to rid yourself of thees man, Kane."

Now, on the eve of the kidnapping, the Colonel was beginning to have second thoughts. He sat at his desk wondering if his burning hatred of Mort Kane had caused him to agree too hastily to Farley's demands.

Farley had driven a hard bargain. He demanded the Colonel show up across the river where they'd be waiting to grab the boy

—Seven Rode Together—

on the day of the race. If he didn't, the boy would be released. "And maybe we just, how you say, slip-of-the-tongue, and the boy knows you are responsible for his inconvenience," Farley added.

The Colonel had become so determined to hasten his revenge that he quickly accepted Farley's additional demands with a handshake. He would still be able to make his welcoming speech at the park in the morning. With the race scheduled at two o'clock, he could make the night-time rendezvous in plenty of time.

Chapter 24

Joey Kane was up with the first light of morning. Jumping out of bed, he moved quickly to the window and scanned the sky. The sun peeking over the Eastern mountain range, the soft, billowy white clouds reflecting the first rays of the morning sun, assured him it would be a perfect day for a horse race. Without Mort's approval, he'd paid his five-dollar entry fee and was officially entered in the race. Remembering his pa's promise that he would be getting his decision at breakfast, he wasted no time getting dressed. While pulling on his boots, he could hear voices and smell the bacon, both eminating from Missus Milburn's kitchen. After pausing to sneak another look at the sky, he was in high spirits when he walked into the dining room to discover the table prepared for breakfast but neither Jeb nor his Pa were seated. He hurried past the table and into the kitchen where both Missus Milburn and Amanda were busy, Missus Milburn preparing breakfast and Amanda her picnic lunch for two to be auctioned off to the highest bidder at noon. The auction was one of the first scheduled

—Seven Rode Together—

activities of the day at the city park.

"Where's everybody?" Joey was quick to ask.

"Both Jeb and your pa are doing what they always do before breakfast, tending to the livestock and layin' out the day's work for the men." She turned and smiled, "but there won't be much work done today. Just about everyone on the Circle K will be going into town for the celebration." She turned to look out the window. "Here comes Jeb and your pa, now."

Joey met them at the door, and before either could say a word, he asked, "What do you think Pa? Do I get to ride in the race?"

"The first thing you've got to do is to get back in the house and get ready for breakfast. A man can't ride in a horse race on an empty stomach."

"You mean it, Pa? Even though I didn't ask you first, you don't mind me bein' in the race?"

"Son, not gettin' my permission almost cost you five-dollars. You'd better thank Jeb for convincin' me that you'll do what I tell you to do, if I let you ride."

"Anything you say, Pa. I'll do whatever you say."

"Let's not keep Blanche waitin' breakfast, but we'll have some talkin' to do before this thing's settled."

Once they were seated at the breakfast table and "amens" were voiced, following Missus Milburn's blessing, Mort announced, "Me and Jeremiah are goin' into town after Joey and me have an understandin' about a horse race. Jeb and Joey can help you and Amanda do what needs to be done to make ready for this picnic. They'll see you get there on time to hear the speech makin' in the park. I got some business to 'tend to, and I'm gonna drop by the post office and see if any of us has heard from anybody since I checked a week ago."

Joey made sure he was finished when Mort was ready to leave the table. Once outside, he hurried to catch up with Mort who was headed toward the corral. "I'm ready to listen to this understanding, Pa."

"Well, I'm not lettin' you ride the Palomino," Mort began, "but that Pinto we broke to the saddle this spring, you named Pepper, will do just fine. He'll go the distance, but you can't expect him to go all out for the full twelve miles. There're men in this race who'll do anything to win. You'll be smart to not attempt those two river crossings with a dozen riders or more. It won't hurt to lag behind a little. This race will most likely be won by somebody smart enough to let those who want to fight it out eliminate each other at those river crossings. Just remember, that last few miles is a stretch of flat land all the way to Main Street and the finish line. There, you can swing wide, and give that Pinto a chance to run. Just don't let yourself get boxed in."

"I understand, Pa," Joey said.

"Well, then, Jeremiah and I are headin' into River Bend. We'll meet you at the park. Make sure you give Missus Milburn and Amanda a hand."

The first couple of miles to River Bend they rode in silence, each to his own thoughts. When they came to the ford at Beaver Creek, Mort pulled up at the edge of the water, leaned forward on the saddle horn and eyed Jeremiah for a moment. "Ever since we got back from Wichita, Jeremiah, you've been acting mighty strange. You got somethin' eatin' on you? Thinkin' about quittin' the Circle K and movin' on?"

"No, I'm not thinkin' about movin' on, not just yet anyway."

"You worried about your friend, Tom stayin' on with the Colonel?"

Jeremiah nodded. "I've been givin' that considerable thought, but I reckon he's old enough to make up his own mind where he works and who he works for."

"That sounds fair enough," Mort readily agreed. "So what's there to worry about?"

"Remember that night when we first got to Wichita, U.S. Marshal Thurgold tellin' us about an investigation still goin' on?"

"I do remember that," Mort said. "Had to do with a train robbery durin' the war. That happened nearly twenty years ago. You thinkin' Colonel Burkhalter had somethin' to do with it?"

"Back then, I served as his company clerk. And that train heist happened in the spring of '63, the same time the Union's Mississippi River Campaign was goin' on. The Union Army carried out a seven-week siege of Vicksburg. We got orders from Regimental Headquarters nobody was to go in or come out a there. It was during those seven weeks Burkhalter and some men in the Company was given a special mission lastin' two or three days. That's the way it went in the Company Records. At the time, I figured the orders came from H.Q. After hearin' Marshal Thurgold's story, I reckon those orders might just as easily have been issued by Colonel Burkhalter hisself."

"Sounds like there's more speculation than proof that Burkhalter had anything to do with a train robbery. Did you ever find out what his mission was?"

—John E. Cramer—

Jeremiah shook his head. "No, and the first I heard was from Marshal Thurgold. Since I been here in River Bend, I've heard about the Colonel's hired hands—several from our Company. There was an Arkus, Parker and Keltner. And there was a fellow in our Company named Bert Pierson. He's workin' at the River Bend Bank."

Mort thought a moment and then asked, "And you remember all those names from twenty years ago?"

Jeremiah smiled. "You call muster and have mail-call as many times as I did durin' my hitch in the Army, you won't have much trouble rememberin' names. Faces maybe, but not names."

"I see—"

"Besides," Jeremiah continued. "If I couldn't remember 'em, I could always check Company Records."

"Company Records?"

Jeremiah nodded. "When the war ended, there was a mad rush by nearly every man in the Company to get out of the Army. Anyway, when I signed on for another hitch and was transferred to New Orleans, I was still carryin' 'em."

"You still have 'em?" Mort asked.

"Not any more."

"You turned 'em in when you quit the Army?"

"No. I wasn't a company clerk while I was stationed in New Orleans. And I'd been packin' them around with me since the war ended, so I got rid of 'em."

"You threw 'em away?"

"No, I didn't throw 'em away. Shortly before I got mustered out, I got this letter from a friend of mine. She sent along a clipping from the town paper tellin' how folks were collectin' stuff from the

—Seven Rode Together—

war for a display in some kind of a war museum. So, that's where the Company Records wound up, along with a few other things I figured I'd been haulin' around long enough."

"It appears to me," Mort began as they started to ford the creek, "you might want to talk to our new Marshal when we get to River Bend. He's no doubt got the same word on this train robbery as Marshal Thurgold had in Wichita. It sure couldn't hurt, and it just might help ease your mind."

Chapter 25

Chad Youngman's appointment of bounty-hunter Seth Longlittle as his deputy caused considerable debate among members of the Town Council. Mayor Dexhorn opposed Youngman's decision to fire Cravens. An editorial in the *Valley View* by Clancy O'Riley ended the opposition in the Town Council to Longlittle's appointment.

The editorial stated that Longlittle's appointment had the endorsement of Judge Storm. "Longlittle is a master in the use of the handgun and a crack shot with a rifle. The one man in the State of Kansas who may be his equal or better with a rifle is Mort Kane. Both men are strong advocates for strict enforcement of the laws. Longlittle's record as a bounty hunter shows his willingness to abide by the law and his cooperation with law enforcement agencies. He believes every man wanted by the law deserves a fair trial. His record shows his preference has been to bring wanted criminals back alive if they agree when confronted. Dead if they disagree. He has become thoroughly familiar with the terri-

—Seven Rode Together—

tory during his years of tracking wanted men. His motto, 'They can run but they can't hide!'"

The morning of the opening ceremonies of the three-day celebration to be held in the city park, Marshal Youngman was seated at his desk getting his first look at the Wanted Posters that had arrived in the day's mail. Seated across from him, sipping a cup of black coffee, with his feet propped up on the corner of the desk, was his newly appointed deputy, Seth Longlittle.

"Take a gander at this one," Youngman said, sliding one of the posters across the desk. "They've upped the ante on Buck Farley. Offering a ten-thousand dollar reward now, dead or alive, on old One-eyed Whiskers. If you was to bring him in now, you'd be gettin' a whole two hundred dollars for the month. Anybody else bringin' him in would collect enough money to keep drunk and disorderly for the next twenty years. You thinkin' about early retirement?"

"Not a chance," Seth grinned. "But if I was you, I'd be mighty uneasy 'cause I got my sights set on one day to be wearin' a U.S. marshal's badge." His grin disappeared. "If I was to catch up with him and bring him in, he's one son-of-a-bitch I'd pay just for the privilege of hangin' him myself."

"You'd pay to do what?" O'Riley asked as he appeared in the doorway. "Is this a private meetin' or could the editor of the best newspaper this side of the Mississippi pour himself a cup of coffee and join the discussion?"

"Help yourself to the coffee," Chad said. "Seth and me were just thinkin' about takin' a walk over to the park. I understand River Bend's self-appointed benefactor is gonna be makin' a surprise announcement."

"No need to bother about goin' to the park," Clancy replied. "Whatever the Colonel has to say, you can read about in the next edition of the *Valley View*."

"That's not the main attraction for me," Chad said. "I'm plannin' on one of those picnic lunches they'll be auctioning off."

"Anyone in particular?" Seth asked, thankful Clancy's interruption had lightened up the conversation.

"I'd guess everyone in the Valley could answer that question." Chad answered. "Anyone who outbids me will be subject to immediate arrest."

"Since I'm the one who's been selected to be the auctioneer," Clancy said, "I'll find out which basket Amanda Milburn brings and wipe my face with my handkerchief, whether it needs it or not." Clancy picked up the poster. "By the way, I just came from the lobby of the Frontier Hotel where they've been signing up late entries for this afternoon's race. The last four to sign up I didn't recognize as bein' from around here."

"I doubt you would," Chad said. "Looks to me like everybody in the state is in town today."

"Well, you may be right," Clancy agreed. "But the four I saw weren't your average lookin' cowhands. Matter of fact, they didn't look like cowhands at all. More like hired gun-slingers."

"Before the race starts this afternoon," Chad said, "I'll mosey over to the starting line and check 'em out. They shouldn't be too hard to spot if they look like hired guns, I think I'd be able to spot start the bidding after 'em, too."

"If Chad or me think they need any special attention," Seth chimed in, "we can probably think of some reason to lock start the

—Seven Rode Together—

bidding after 'em up before they start the race."

"Just thought you might like to know," Clancy said as he turned to leave. "I'll talk to you later."

When Mort and Jeremiah reached the outskirts of River Bend, the boardwalks on either side of Main Street were crowded with lookers and buyers. The store owners, it was easy to see, were doing a land-office business. And since Main Street would be the start and finish line for the afternoon's horse race, Fred Findley's Livery Stable, located on the last block of the street, became the best location in town to secure horses, carriages, wagons and buckboards for the day.

They reached the south side of the park when the sun had begun to sizzle. Seating themselves under a giant oak tree, they waited for the others to arrive.

"There they are now," Jeremiah said, pointing to the carriage with the pinto trailing behind. Joey was carrying Amanda's picnic lunch in a basket with a blue-ribbon bow attached. He headed for the table behind the speaker's platform to wait, along with the others, for the auction scheduled after the speech making.

Mort and Jeremiah helped Missus Milburn with the baskets of food she'd prepared for the rest of the family. After she'd spread a quilt on the ground and the places had been set, she sat down beside Mort. "I've never seen anyone so excited about a horse-race as Joey," she said. "He's never stopped talking since you and Jeremiah left home. All the way here from the ranch, he's been telling Jeb about his strategy for the race."

A few moments later, the trumpet player in the 14-piece

—John E. Cramer—

band seated at the back of the platform, stood up and sounded a few bars of the bugle call used by the Cavalry to signify the Charge. Immediately following, Mayor Jasper S. Dexhorn arose and took a position behind the lectern. "I want to take this opportunity," he began, "to welcome all of you to River Bend's birthday celebration! We have a schedule of events in the next two days that our Celebration Committee is certain all of you, men and women, boys and girls, are going to enjoy!" He paused to allow cheering and hand-clapping to subside before going on.

"I see the Colonel brought along your friend, Tom Trinity," Mort said. "Is he going to be making a speech, too?"

"I wouldn't know. Could be," Jeremiah replied and as Dexhorn raised his hands for quiet, he added, "Looks like we're about to find out."

"I'd like to take this opportunity to introduce to you our guests. The two people on my right are Missus Alec Johnson who's been busy the past couple of weeks in charge of the committee for the dance that will be held tomorrow night. Next to her is the publisher of River Bend's newspaper, the *Valley View*, Clancy O'Riley. He's consented to be the auctioneer for the young ladies picnic baskets for today's celebration. The proceeds from this sale will go to our school for the purchase of books for the library. Clancy asked me to announce that all you young men out there get ready to dig deep in your pockets when the bidding begins. Not only is the money going for a good cause, but you'll also enjoy the best picnic lunch you ever had, and the privilege of sharing it with some of the prettiest young women you've ever seen."

The last remark triggered a spontaneous shouting, whistling and arm waving that continued long after the Mayor began asking for quiet.

"This could be interesting when Amanda's basket is auctioned," Missus Milburn confided to Mort.

"Those who'll be doing the bidding won't know whose basket they're bidding on. That might prove to be a problem for our new Marshal."

"Why do you think Amanda put that blue ribbon on her basket?" Chad called from the crowd.

"In that case, it might cause Marshal Youngman a month's pay." Mort pointed to the table where the baskets had been placed. "There's got to be at least a dozen baskets with blue-ribbon bows."

The applause faded away and Dexhorn stepped back to the lectern. "The next person I'm about to introduce really needs no introduction."

Cupping both hands around his mouth, a lanky cowhand from Bert Tolliver's ranch yelled, "If he don't need no introduction, why the hell you fixin' to introduce him?"

This was followed by yet another outburst of more yelling, some scattered booing, catcalls and hand-clapping. Missus Milburn, nudging Mort with her elbow. "There was a time when Sheriff Taylor was around when that cowboy would be on his way out—feet first."

"I guess the new Marshal believes in free speech."

"Not only that," she added, "He's a U.S. Marshal not beholden to the Colonel for getting his appointment."

Ignoring the demonstration, Dexhorn continued. "I'd like to present to you one of River Bend's earliest settlers in this valley and one of it's biggest contributor's to the growth and prosperity of River Bend, Colonel Felix Burkhalter."

—John E. Cramer—

Before the Colonel took his place behind the lectern, the initial applause had quickly faded to scattered clapping. Without any noticeable reaction to the brief and scattered response to his introduction, he began. "Thank you, Mayor. I realize many of you are looking forward to the day's activities which will begin with the fund-raising auction. The money is to be used to buy much-needed books for our school library. And without benefit of bidding for an opportunity to enjoy a picnic lunch with one of these beautiful young ladies, I would like to present Mister O'Riley with my personal check for two-hundred dollars toward this very worthwhile and needed addition to the library. And now, I have a couple of announcements. The first will be, I believe, appreciated by all the people of River Bend and this valley. All that remains to be done on acquiring railroad service from River Bend to the markets in the East are some final meetings among representatives of the railroad, state officials, and representatives from several towns and cities in this part of the state. If all goes well, within the next three years the people in this valley will be privileged to travel from here to Kansas City, St. Louis and Chicago by rail. Shipping cattle and other freight by rail will eliminate long cattle drives and give us a faster and less expensive means of getting our crops to market."

The announcement was greeted with genuine applause from the large crowd gathered in the park.

"Which brings me to my second important but brief announcement. Because the first of several meetings I mentioned is to be held in the capitol two days from now, I must leave this afternoon. For those scheduled activities I'd hoped to attend, I'm turning over my commitments and responsibilities to my newest employee, Tom Trinity. He, I would like to add, has accepted the position as my

—Seven Rode Together—

personal assistant in the management of the affairs of the Double-B. Tom is a very talented, capable young man who has been with me for nearly a year. He served his country as a member of the Union Army during the Reconstruction Period after the War. And by next spring, Tom is hoping to send for his fiancee who now resides in New Orleans. But, whenever he does, the Double-B will host a first-class wedding celebration and invite everyone in River Bend and the Valley to attend. Tom, I know, hadn't expected me to make this announcement. He's a doer, not a talker, a virtue sadly lacking in most of us. We hope all of you enjoy the celebration."

A polite applause followed as the Colonel and Tom left the speaker's platform and disappeared into the crowd. "I can't help but wonder," Missus Milburn said, barely loud enough for Mort to hear, "if that young man knows what he may be letting himself in for."

Mort was having similar thoughts enforced by what Jeremiah had told him during their ride to River Bend that morning. There was something about Tom Trinity he liked. Perhaps the young man had heeded Jeremiah's advice, 'Never look a gift horse in the mouth, just accept it like you was entitled.'"

A short time later, following Clancy's pre-arranged signal, two people attending the day's opening activities were enjoying their picnic lunch in the shade of a blossoming apple tree away from the others in the park. "How in the world did you ever know which of those many baskets with blue ribbons was mine?" Amanda asked Chad the moment they were together.

Raising a fore-finger and tapping his forehead, Chad slipped her a quick wink. "Instinct. A small voice whispered in my ear, 'bid on this one and you'll be eating your picnic lunch with the one you'd like to spend the rest of your life with.'"

—John E. Cramer—

"It was a pretty expensive lunch. Did you notice who was bidding against you?"

"Wouldn't have mattered. I always listen to that 'small voice'."

"Then maybe you might be interested in knowing who it was that was raising your bids?"

"Someone behind me, but it wouldn't have made any difference." He tapped his forehead. "Remember, that small voice—"

"Did that small voice say you were bidding against your deputy, Seth Longlittle?"

"I should've known," Chad smiled. "He doesn't know it yet, but that last bid he made, costing me an extra ten dollars, is coming out of his next pay."

"You wouldn't."

"I could. But I won't. I figure I got a bargain."

For a few fleeting moments, they looked into each other's eyes. Their smiles grew bigger. They began laughing. "You should have seen your face when I told you it was Seth."

"Now, if you can stop laughing long enough to let me look inside the basket, I'd like to see what this expensive lunch looks like."

Following the auction of the picnic baskets, Thorn and Kio waited until the crowd around the speaker's platform thinned out before they moved closer. Thorn was wanting to talk with the new Marshal about the former Union Army officer, Colonel Felix Burkhalter. The painting he'd seen at the Double-B on the night he and Kio took Tom home and sobered him up, made him all but positive his vigil, after 17 years, was all but over. He needed to be sure the Colonel was the officer in command of a foraging patrol during the first years of the war. The officer who allowed his troops to run amuck, running off livestock and ransacking his home, stealing anything of value they could find. His father, Ben Masters, had chosen to remain neutral, even after Virginia seceded. He'd never owned a slave, nor did he intend to. His father had worked his land and his father before him, and it was his stoic decision that he could remain neutral and continue to work his land. He'd never been convinced slavery was the real reason the war had begun. This position did not keep him from being killed on the day the Union soldiers pillaged their home. Thorn remembered his father stepping out on the front porch that morning. When the Union soldiers arrived, the officer in charge, still mounted, pulled his side-arm and shot his Pa.

Although Thorn had vowed never to forget the face of that officer, seventeen years had blurred his memory. But the silent promise he'd made that day, he never forgot. And now fate had led him to the man who'd so cold-bloodedly ended his father's life. He wanted to be certain Colonel Burkhalter was the man. It was all he needed to end his vigil for vengeance. When the time came, Thorn knew he could never kill the man he'd searched for all these years without facing him. If a man was going to die, Thorn wanted him to know why. At least, Thorn believed, he will be getting a better chance to live than his father had.

Thorn was still mulling this over when he and Kio saw Seth Longlittle. He was heading straight toward them on his way back to the marshal's office. "Mister Longlittle."

"Would you be knowin' where I might find the Marshal?"

"He's over there." Seth pointed toward the picnic area behind the speaker's platform. "But I don't believe I'd be botherin' him right now. Unless, of course, your business is so urgent you can't wait until he gets back to the office. I'm headin' back to the office right now if you'd like to come along. The name's Seth Longlittle."

"Thorn Masters," Thorn said, extending his hand. "This fellow's my partner, Kio."

They headed for the marshal's office, talking as they went. "I've heard about you two," Seth said. "You're the two who brought a herd of cattle up from Amarillo and joined up with Mort Kane's herd for the cattle drive to Wichita. They don't come any better than Mort Kane. There ain't but one man in this whole damned valley who's locked horns with the Colonel and come out on top, except Kane."

When they reached the marshal's office, the boardwalks on either side of Main Street were crowded with spectators. The balconies on either side of the street were filled to capacity. Others who found their way to the roof tops were lined up like ducks in a shooting gallery, their legs dangling over the edges of the roofs—all awaiting the start of the much publicized race. The generosity of the merchants and store owners in River Bend had insured a large turn-out and guaranteed a record number of entries. Their collective contributions to the winner's purse totaled more than five hundred dollars.

"Looks like everybody's ready for the horse race," Seth said. "Which reminds me, the Marshal's lookin' for another judge to be posted at the first river crossing."

"Well, I see you rustled up another judge, Seth." And turning toward Thorn and Kio, he asked. "Now which one of these gentlemen has volunteered to help us out?" He shook hands with Thorn and Kio. "Good to see you two fellows again. I don't think 1 ever got the chance to thank you two, personally, for helpin' us bring in

—Seven Rode Together—

Buck Farley a few months ago."

"That's right," Thorn said. "And I see you had a little problem keepin' those hombres in jail."

"That happened before I was made Marshal. Now which of you two is going to help us out?"

"Kio could handle it," Thorn said. "But he's not used to workin' for free."

"It'll be the easiest ten bucks he's ever made. All we're wantin' him to do is to make sure there's no foul play when the riders ford the river. We've posted judges about every two miles along the route to make sure there's no cheatin'—whatever form it takes. A judge has the right to disqualify any rider who does."

"What do you think, Kio?" Thorn asked. "I'd like to talk with the Marshal about a little matter I'm needin' some help with."

"I'm your man, Marshal." Kio said. "When do I head out to this location, and how do I get there?"

"Chad looked at the clock behind his desk. The race will be starting about an hour from now. That'll give Seth plenty of time to ride out with you and get back in time to start the race."

"And when it's over," Seth chimed in, "Thorn and the Marshal will buy the steak dinners for us before the dance begins at the Frontier Hotel."

An hour later the entries for the twelve-mile race were lining up across the Main Street at the starting line. There were three rows—ten riders in each. Chad spotted the four riders that Clancy had talked about earlier in the day. To him they didn't look any more or any less like gun slingers than several others.

Seth reminded the riders of the rules of the race, fired a shot in the air and the race was underway.

Chapter 26

The Colonel and Tom, following their appearance at the city park, wasted no time in getting back to the Burkhalter Estate. They reined up in front of the house and the Colonel paused long enough to tell Tom, "Get one of the men to saddle up that blazed-face black stallion for me right away and come up to the house." The Colonel was well aware he had little time to waste if he was going to join up with the others.

By the time Tom returned to the house, the Colonel had changed clothes and packed his saddle bags, including his gunbelt and a colt .44 he hadn't worn for a good many years.

"Anything particular you'd like me to be doin' while you're gone, Colonel," Tom asked.

"They'll still be celebrating for the next couple of days in River Bend. If everything goes as planned, I should be back here by the middle of next week. I'm counting on you to keep an eye on things around here. We'll be hearin' from the Army in a couple of weeks. They'll be telling us when they want those horses delivered

—Seven Rode Together—

to Ft. Hayes. You'll be the one to see they get there. Right now, I need to be on my way. I got some hard ridin' ahead of me before sundown."

As he headed for the door, he glanced at the clock on the wall behind his desk. He wasn't lying, he did, indeed, have some hard riding ahead of him. Remembering his arrangement with Buck Farley, he knew Farley's participation in the kidnap scheme would end if he failed to show up at the first river crossing.

Kio was surveying the area trying to determine the best spot to be when the thirty riders made the crossing. On the opposite side of the river, where they would emerge from the water, the trail was straight away for the first hundred yards, then it curved around the base of a small foothill into a ravine, bordered on either side by steep slopes covered with rock and scrubby undergrowth. Kio discovered a foot path leading from the main trail to the top of the foothill. Tying his horse to a small shrub, he made his way on foot to the top of the ridge. From there he would have a clear view of the riders as they approached the river, continued around the trail, and entered the ravine. Satisfied he'd located the perfect spot for a judge to be, he hunkered down and awaited the arrival of the riders.

Minutes later, Kio spotted clouds of dust drifting skyward caused by the pounding hooves of thirty riders strung out along the trail. Approaching the river, the fastest among them were putting distance between them and the next group that followed. As they moved closer to the river's edge, Kio saw the final group bringing up the rear—only five riders. They were trailing the others by an eighth of a mile.

—John E. Cramer—

The first dozen riders splashed across the fording area without incident. The next group were not so tightly bunched, but had no trouble reaching the opposite shore. They were followed by a half dozen others who trailed each other across the river. The final five riders approaching the river seemed to Kio to be glued together. The rider of the pinto was flanked on either side by riders. The lead rider, directly in front of the pinto, appeared to be setting the pace for all of them, including the lone rider directly behind the pinto. He watched the five of them approaching the river's edge. The rider of the pinto was boxed in by the four others who seemed more intent on keeping the pinto boxed in than they were in winning the race. When they crossed the river, Kio recognized the rider on the pinto was Joey Kane! He was fighting to keep control of the reins. The men on either side had secured a grip on the bridle straps and were controlling the pinto's direction. After they crossed the river, all the horses stopped. Two men tied Joey's wrists to the saddle horn, remounted and continued on the trail.

Making certain he wouldn't be seen, Kio moved across the ridge, keeping an eye on the men below. Glancing back at the river he saw a lone rider on a black, blazed-face horse fording the river. He watched as the Colonel caught up with Joey and his captors and together they quit the trail and struck out southwest across the open prairie at a full gallop, Joey's pinto now being led by the rider in front. The Colonel followed a short distance behind. "There goes five contestants that won't finish this race," Kio mused. "The Colonel's headin' the wrong way to attend a meeting plannin' a railroad," and, he said to himself, "here's one judge who'd better make his mind up in a hurry. Either I trail Joey's captors or head back to River Bend for help."

—Seven Rode Together—

He stood up on the ridge. Already the riders were fast becoming mere specks moving across the flat land toward the range of mountains to the southwest. Reasoning Joey's life was in danger, he had to make the best choice. By the time he got back to town, informed the Marshal, Mort, Thorn and the others and returned to pick up the trail, Joey's captors would have more than an hour head start. During that time they will have reached the mountains. If it's as it appears to be, he thought, Joey's life could be in danger. 'Best he follow them, he decided, and find out where they hold up. With luck, he could high-tail it back to River Bend before morning, get help and return to their hideout. He was already on the trail across the prairie before he'd finished his reasoning.

An hour later he was entering the ghost town of Hollow Hill. The tracks continued past the town. He could still make out six riders, still heading southwest. Another hour's ride later, he pulled up and watched as the group entered into a box canyon. Kio took to the high ground. By riding the ridge, he watched the six riders below dismount when they reached the end of the canyon. They disappeared inside the mouth of a cave, protected on either side by huge boulders. Satisfied he'd tracked them to their hiding place, he watched as they pulled Joey from his saddle and hustled him inside the mine entrance. A few moments later, they'd stripped their horses of saddle gear and bedrolls, and were building a fire. At least he knew they were socked in for the night. It was three, maybe four hour's ride to River Bend. If I head back now, he determined, we can be back here in time to ruin their breakfast.

He watched the activity below long enough to determine that Buck Farley and two other men had met the four men and Colonel Burkhalter when they arrived. A few minutes later, he was

—John E. Cramer—

back on the trail high-tailing it to River Bend.

Later that night, after they had eaten and Farley had ordered two of his men to take the first watch at the entrance to the canyon, he motioned to the Colonel to follow him. "Come with me, Colonel, we got much to talk about." The Colonel hesitated, and noticing Joey Kane was nowhere to be seen, asked. "Where's the boy? You haven't already—"

"Killed him?" Farley completed the Colonel's question. "No. We don't kill the boy," he added, flashing a broad toothy smile. "We need him until we get the money. Your Mister Kane, he is no fool. Before he turn over the money, he must see the boy and know he's alive. After we get the money, then we kill him and the boy. Come with me." He turned abruptly and started walking up the slight incline toward the old mine-shack. The Colonel followed. The four men seated around the fire, each with his own bottle of Tequila supplied by Farley, were well on the way to getting roaring drunk before morning.

Once inside the mine-shack, Farley lighted a kerosene lamp setting on top of a dust-covered table in the middle of the room. He pulled up a rickety straight-back chair, pulled out a pint bottle of Tequila from his coat pocket and set it on the table. He motioned to the Colonel to be seated. He removed the cap on the bottle and glancing around the room, said, "This place could use a woman. Come, have a drink, Colonel. Then, we talk business, you and me."

The Colonel, knowing it would be to his advantage to comply, raised the bottle and after a gesture to signify a toast, took a short drink and handed the bottle to Farley. Following a few man-sized gulps, Farley set the bottle down in front of him and wiped his mouth with the back of his hand.

—Seven Rode Together—

"What kind of business do we need to discuss?" the Colonel asked.

"Tomorrow, the message will be delivered to Mister Kane. It will say, if he wish to see his boy alive again, he will have twenty-four hours to deliver fifty-thousand dollars to me. The note will say he must come alone to the empty town of Hollow Hill. There he will get final instructions where he must bring the money."

"You now trust him to come alone?"

"No. Your Mister Kane will not be alone. But it will make no difference to you and to me. It is best that only you and me know that. This canyon, they will know, has only one way to come in. The same way to come out. Mister Kane and the money, we will let come in. But him and the boy will not go out. That is what I plan. When he come in, he will tell us he needs to see the boy alive before he gives to us the money he brings. This, we agree to do. The boy will go to him and we will take the money and allow both of them to leave—"

"You aim to let 'em go!" the Colonel nearly shouted.

"No. They will not leave this canyon alive. Two of my men posted at the entrance will not miss, and both will be killed."

"Why wait? Why not get rid of them when we get the money?"

"Oh, Colonel," Farley said, shaking his head from side to side. "You think like a woman. Fifty-thousand dollars is not enough to be divided with six other hombres. You do not listen well what I say. Believe me when I say Kane will have others we will not see. This is big country. These mountains surrounding us have many ways to get to the ridge. All those ways with six men we cannot cover. They will see the man and the boy leave when we get the

—John E. Cramer—

money. My men, I have told, will get their money when we leave the canyon. The shots we hear will tell us the man Kane and his boy—"

"What will we be doing all this time? Sitting here in this shack toasting our good fortune?"

"Again, like a woman, you are impatient. You must first let me finish. We will be out of this canyon and these hombres I have brought with me—"

"How do we get out of here when the shooting starts?" The Colonel cut in.

"We will leave by the back door. We will leave with all the money. Only I know this tunnel. It leads away from the entrance of this mine to the west side of the mountain. Two horses I have staked out. We will be on our way when the shooting starts. You? You will be going back to River Bend. Me? No, I will be on my way, too."

The Colonel thought for a moment before he spoke. "You're forgetting one possibility. Supposing the four men you've hired decide not to shoot it out with the men who will be coming with Kane."

"Makes no difference," Farley shrugged. "We can still do as I've planned. Any more questions, Colonel?" After a few moments, Farley added, "In that case, I would say our meeting is over. Have another drink, Colonel, and we will all call it a night."

Chapter 27

The spectators who lined the roofs of the two-story buildings along River Bend's Main Street were the first to sight the leaders when they came into view a quarter-mile from the entry onto the Main Street. Those lining the street got their first look as the riders entered town from the East, three blocks from the Courthouse. The half-dozen riders who led the field came pounding down the Main Street to the roar of the spectators.

Mort and Jeb, along with Chad, Seth, Jeremiah and Thorn, had decided to watch the proceedings from the boardwalk in front of the marshal's office a block from the finish line. They watched as the leaders flashed by, followed by the largest group spread the width of the street, still going all out toward the Frontier Hotel and the finish line.

Jeb scratched his head. "Looks like Joey and Ebert Youngman's boy must be bringin' up the rear." he observed.

"I kinda figured they would be. But Joey was dead set on giving it a try."

—John E. Cramer—

"Anyway, they'll have somethin' to talk about for the next few days." Jeb said.

As they talked, the also-rans kept moving by, but at a much slower gait now that the winner had been determined. Jeb and Mort kept a lookout for the Pinto with Joey in the saddle until what appeared to be the last riders passed by in a walk amidst the spectators who'd flooded onto the street.

"Over yonder looks like Steve Youngman just gettin' off his horse." Turning toward the Marshal, Jeb asked, "Ain't that your brother?"

"It's him, alright," Chad grinned. "I wouldn't be surprised if his racin' days started and ended on the same day."

"Still don't see Joey," Mort said. "Didn't figure him to be crowdin' the leaders, but I was sure he'd finish on the same day. Looks like all them that started are all accounted for. Wouldn't you say, Jeb?"

"It's hard to say. But it wouldn't surprise me none that a few might have taken a bath in the river at that second crossin'. Why I wouldn't be a bit—"

"Any of you seen Kio since he got back from his judgin' duty?" Thorn interrupted. "I figured he'd be back long before the racin' was over."

"He probably came back and decided to watch the end of the race at the Frontier Hotel," Jeb said. "Me and Mort was wonderin' what happened to Joey seein' as how he wasn't amongst them that finished the race."

"Think I'll head over to the Frontier," Mort said. "Maybe I'll be able to spot Steve Youngman again and see if he knows anything about Joey."

—Seven Rode Together—

"Good idea," Thorn agreed. "Believe I'll join you. Maybe Kio's over there." Turning to Chad, he asked. "You comin', Marshal?"

"I'll see you fellas later. I've got a few personal matters I need to talk over with my deputy. I'll see you this evenin', Mort. I got an invite for dinner at your place tonight from Amanda. Then I'm escortin' her to the dance."

Mort, along with Thorn and Jeb, pushed through the crowd, headed for the hotel. Jeb spotted Steve Youngman. "There's Steve," he said to Mort as he pointed toward a small group standing in the street a few doors down from the hotel. "Looks like he's talkin' to his Pa and some other folks."

"Howdy, Ebert," Mort said as they joined them. "Looks like your boy got to the finish line. I'm wondering what happened to Joey. We haven't seen him since he started the race. Thought maybe Steve might know where he is."

"Steve!" Ebert yelled. "Mister Kane wants to talk with you about Joey."

"Howdy, Mister Kane," Steve said as he joined the group. "Me and Joey started together. We're in the last row of the line up. We got separated pretty soon after we got out of town. There was about five or six ridin' together for a spell. I got a few jumps ahead of the others, and I don't remember seein' him after I made the first crossin' at the river. Then, again, I was pretty busy watchin' where I was goin'."

"So, you didn't see him anymore after you crossed the river? Was he ridin' alone when you last saw him?"

"As I recollect, I looked back when I got a few jumps in the lead. Joey was kinda squeezed in the middle of four or five others.

—John E. Cramer—

Never saw no more of him after that."

"Don't 'spose his horse pulled up lame, do you?" Ebert asked. "Could be if he got so far back at the start, he just gave it up and headed home?"

"No, I don't think Joey would quit the race," Mort said. And for the first time since the race had ended, Mort began to grow uneasy that something more happened than a decision by Joey to give up on the race. "Come on, Jeb." he said. "Let's do a little back-trackin' along the race course. I'd like to check out those river crossings before we head back to the ranch." He glanced up at the sky. "We don't have much time before sundown to have a look." He doubted he'd find any trace of Joey on the trail. He knew Joey would never quit the race and head for home even if he was behind. There was always the chance he could have fallen off or lost control of the pinto when they hit the water at the last crossing. He knew it was a much deeper and more difficult crossing to make. Whatever the reason, Mort wanted to make use of the daylight left to have a look. Then, they could head home.

"Mind if I ride along?" Thorn asked, as Mort and Jeb turned to leave. "I haven't seen Kio since before the race started. Maybe somethin' happened to him."

"We're tied up over at the park," Mort said. "We'll meet you over there. Jeb, I haven't seen Jeremiah since we left the park. See if you can find him. Let him know where Thorn and me are goin'. And make sure Amanda and her mother get back to the ranch alright."

Mort and Thorn went to the fording place along the river. Once they'd crossed over to the opposite side, Mort reined up. "I'm not sure what I expect to find," he said, "but it don't figure that any-

—Seven Rode Together—

body who can set a horse would have any trouble at this crossing."

"And I'm still tryin' to figure out what happened to Kio after the last of the riders crossed over."

They continued on the trail around the base of the cliff and into the ravine. Thorn pulled up and standing in his stirrups, he looked back up the side of the ravine to the ridge, jutting out over the trail. Pointing toward the ridge, he said to Mort, "Now if I was lookin' for a full view of the crossing, that's where I'd want to be. And knowin' how Kio thinks, I'd bet that's where he was."

"Sounds reasonable," Mort said. "But that doesn't explain why he never returned to town after all the riders made the crossing and were on their way through this ravine."

"You're right about that," Thorn said. "Well, let's head on around to the high-water crossing while we got some daylight left. And if we don't find anything there, we can head on to your place." He paused, slipped Mort a wink. "I'll bet that's where we'll find him."

"And if we don't?" Mort asked.

"And if we don't, we got a problem to solve. And I'm beginnin' to think wherever we find Kio, we'll find Joey. Maybe Joey fell off at the next river crossing and Kio helped him get home."

"But why would Kio take him home instead of headin' back to town?"

The sun had already disappeared over the western mountain range when they reached the Circle-K. "Looks like you got company," Thorn said, noticing the two horses tied to the hitching rail. "That Roan belongs to the Marshal, and the other sure enough belongs to Kio."

They were met at the front door by Missus Milburn. "Oh,

—John E. Cramer—

Mort," she cried. "Something awful has happened to Joey!"

They moved quickly into the parlor where Kio had the attention of both Chad and Jeb. Before either of them was aware Mort and Thorn had entered the room, Amanda jumped up from the sofa, tears streaming down her cheeks, and threw her arms around Mort. "They've kidnapped Joey," she cried. "They've taken him to some awful place—"

Mort, his arms around Amanda, looked toward Jeb, anxious to hear some explanation. Gently, he pushed Amanda away. "Amanda, why don't you and your mom finish getting dinner, We'll talk later. Don't worry about Joey."

He caught Missus Milburn's attention and nodded toward the dining room. She slipped her arm around Amanda. "Everything's going to be alright, Amanda." she whispered.

After they'd left the room, he looked at Kio. "Alright. What's happened? What's this about Joey being kidnapped? Who'd want to kidnap him?" His heart had skipped a beat or two as he searched Kio's face.

Chad spoke up. "Kio just rode in not more than five minutes before you arrived. He says four men in today's race grabbed Joey at the first river crossing. Colonel Burkhalter joined the men after they'd grabbed Joey and rode off with 'em."

"You say Colonel Burkhalter was with 'em?"

"When they started to ford the river, four riders had Joey boxed in. They jumped off and grabbed the pinto's bridle. I was about to leave my spot atop the ridge when Burkhalter joined 'em. They mounted and rode off southwest."

"Then, where the hell you been all day?" Thorn chimed in. "Why didn't you hightail it back to River Bend and let us know?"

—Seven Rode Together—

"By the time I got back to town and back to the crossing, they'd have an hour's lead, maybe more. I figured they was most likely goin' to be holdin' Joey for a payoff. I decided it was better to tail 'em. I know where they're holdin' him, how many men they got, and how long it'll take to get there. They've camped for the night."

"You made the right choice," Mort said. "I believe we all agree. Let's talk about where they're holdin' Joey. We can better decide what we're up against."

A short time later they were gathered around the kitchen table when they heard some one ride in. A few seconds later, a rock crashed through the front room window. Jumping up from the table, Mort dashed to the window and looked out. The rider was already too far away to be recognized, even on a moonlit night. Mort picked up the rock. Attached to it was an envelope with a note inside.

"Looks like they're not wastin' any time." Chad said.

Mort read the note. "At least we know what they want," Mort said, and handed the note to Chad. "They're demanding fifty-thousand dollars for Joey's release. They're givin' me twenty-four hours to deliver the money if I want to see Joey alive."

"How're you supposed to know where you make the exchange?" Thorn asked.

Chad continued reading: "If you want to see yore kid alive, bring fifty-thousand dollars and come alone. Come to Hollow Hill by noon tomorrow. Check into the Sundown Hotel. Our man will meet you there and tell you when and where to deliver the money."

Jeb, shaking, shouted, "Where the hell's Hollow Hill."

Thorn put his hand on Jeb's shoulder. "Just across the border in New Mexico Territory."

Chad continued to read: "Come alone. Yore deadline is

—John E. Cramer—

noon tomorrow. Bring fifty-thousand dollars. Noon tomorrow. If you do not, the kid dies."

Chad folded the letter and handed it to Mort. "They ain't givin' you much time to raise fifty-thousand dollars and be in Hollow Hill by noon tomorrow. You goin' to be able to manage that, Mort?"

"I got no choice. It's a little after ten now. Anybody know how long it'll take to get from River Bend to Hollow Hill?"

Thorn, who'd been talking to Kio since he'd arrived, stuck a finger in the air to get Mort's attention. "Yeah, we know how long it'll take. Matter of fact, we know a helluva lot more than even the Colonel or those thievin' cutthroats think we know. Tell 'em what you've been tellin' me, Kio."

"When Thorn asked me earlier why I didn't come back to town after I'd seen what happened to Joey, I've been tryin' to explain. The way things turned out—"

"He made the right decision, alright," Thorn interrupted. "Tell 'em, Kio, what you told me."

"He will," Jeb snapped, "if you can quit talkin' long enough to let him."

"I made the right decision," Kio began anew. "It took me less than two hours to get to River Bend from Hollow Hill. The thing they don't know is I trailed them to where they're holdin' Joey. It's a box canyon west of Hollow Hill, about twenty miles south of the trail to Santa Fe. I followed the rim of the canyon to the end. There's an old abandoned mine and a couple of shacks on either side of the entrance. I saw four other men who were there when the Colonel and the four I'd been trailin' arrived."

No one spoke. Kio had their attention. "Thorn's always

—Seven Rode Together—

askin' me if I'm thinkin' what he's thinkin'. Well, I'm thinkin' we're goin' to get that boy out alive."

"Let's hear it," Mort was quick to reply.

"First, if you deliver that money, they're not gonna let Joey out alive. Colonel Burkhalter would make sure of that. Joey, so far as the Colonel knows, is the only one who could tell folks that he and Buck Farley were his captors."

"So, what's your plan?" Chad asked.

"They don't know we don't need directions to their hide-out." He paused and looked at Mort as he continued to speak. "The plan I have in mind is not without risk. Mort will be taking the greatest risk. If the Marshal and the rest of you agree, me and five others, Thorn, the Marshal, his deputy, Jeb and Jeremiah could leave within the next hour. We could be at their hide-out before daybreak. Me and Thorn will eliminate the men they got posted at the entrance to the canyon. I'll take Jeb and Seth with me. Thorn will take Chad and Jeremiah with him. And if we can take out these guards without gun-play, we'll not blow our element of surprise. That's the best thing we got goin' for us."

"I follow you so far," Chad said. "Once we dispose of those two guardin' the entrance, we've evened the odds. That's gonna leave Farley and the Colonel with four of Farley's men who'll be on hand when Mort arrives for the pay off. That leaves six of them and six of us. But Mort and Joey still have to get out of the canyon—"

"Now, I'm thinkin' what Kio's thinkin'," Thorn said. "We're gonna know they're there, but they ain't gonna know they got company. Right, Kio?"

Kio nodded. "When we take care of the guards at the

—John E. Cramer—

entrance, Thorn, Chad and Jeremiah will move down the rim of the canyon on the right to the mine entrance. You'll be able to move in closer to the floor of the canyon and take up your watch under cover of the boulders and rock formations. Jeb, Seth and me will take up positions on the other side. If we're lucky, we'll be able to watch the exchange down the barrels of our rifles. When the shooting starts depends on how Mort handles the exchange. He'll probably be dealin' with Farley."

"If the Colonel shows," Mort said, "it's a cinch they don't intend for Joey and me to get out of that canyon alive. But if I was a bettin' man, I'd bet he's goin' to want to stay out of sight. If he does show himself—"

"I'll have him in my sights," Thorn cut in. "And if the others show and Joey and Mort ain't in our line of fire, we might just be able to start the fireworks early. Kio can draw a bead on Farley, and the rest of you can pick your target for the first round. I got the feelin' that if the Colonel and Farley go down, those other hombres will be ready to throw down."

"And if they don't," Jeb said, "Mort and Joey might be the first ones they'll be shootin' at."

"Could be." Thorn agreed. "But I got a feelin' if there's any still standin', they'll either be reachin' for the sky or gettin' the hell out of the line of fire. Kio and I ain't gonna miss our targets. And as fast as the rest of you can pump those Winchesters, the rest of 'em ain't gonna make it to cover."

"Well, gentlemen," Mort began, "we could discuss the possibilities the rest of the night and never know what surprises they may have for me and Joey. There are a couple of things I do know. I intend to meet their deadline and with your help and the

—Seven Rode Together—

element of surprise on our side, I believe we'll pull it off. It's late. We might all get a chance for a little shut-eye before time to head out."

"There's one thing more," Thorn said, "How does Mort get hold of fifty-thousand dollars and still keep this operation secret until it's completed?"

"I gotta idea. There's one place in River Bend," Chad said, "where Mort can get that kind of money and still keep his meetin' in Hollow Hill at noon. And if things go as we're plannin', we'll be bringin' that ransom money back with Joey." Lookin at Mort, to added, "I believe our friend, Judge Storm has exactly that amount in his office safe. We turned it over to him after our little fracas at the Way Station. What do you think, Mort?"

Mort nodded. "Since you'll be gone before I can see him, it might not hurt if I had a letter from the U.S. Marshal that he's endorsing the request."

"Well, then," Chad said, "that's all settled." Looking at Kio, he added. "When do you figure we ought to be ridin' out of here? We can pick up Seth at my office on the way."

"There's one more thing," Jeb said. "How do you plan to explain your absence if some of the good people of River Bend drop by tomorrow morning and you and Seth ain't there?"

"That's easy," Chad grinned. "I'll stick a sign in the window sayin' 'Gone fishin' with Jeb Hofstader!'"

Chapter 28

It was two-thirty that same morning when the six of them pulled up about a mile from the narrow entrance into the box canyon. It was Kio who pointed out that it would be wise to split up to avoid riding straight toward the entrance where they could be spotted by the lookouts. Maintaining their distance from the entrance to the canyon, they fanned out into a wide arc and approached the entrance on both sides. Kio, and those with him, came in from the South. Thorn and the others from the North.

The trail along the mountain side extended the length of the canyon, some two hundred yards from the rim. From there Kio left the others with the horses and continued on foot. The rocky slope with protruding ledges and boulders left Kio to figure out the safest way to the rim of the canyon.

As he eased his way around a large boulder, Kio got his first look at the guard who'd taken up a position on a rock shelf that offered a full view of the canyon floor. He sat on the shelf, his legs crossed, leaning back against the boulder with his rifle at arm's

—Seven Rode Together—

length beside him. Reaching down, Kio picked up a fist-sized rock and tossed it over the guard's head. It landed on the shelf and rolled over the side. The guard leaped to his feet looking at the spot where the rock had landed. In a couple of quick steps, Kio was behind him. As the guard turned around, Kio cold-cocked him with the butt of his rifle. Awhile later, dragging the limp body behind him, Kio joined the others where they waited with the horses. "Hog tie this guy, Jeb, and put a gag on him. We'll pick him up on our way out if we have the time."

"How do you think Thorn and the others are makin' out on the other side?" Seth asked.

"Haven't heard any shootin'" Kio said. "Wouldn't surprise me none if Thorn's already got another one of these hombres wrapped up just like this one." And scanning the sky, he added, "We better move along. I'd guess we don't have more than a half hour before daylight."

When they reached the end of the canyon, they followed Kio single-file up the rocky slope to the rim. Using the boulders for cover, they maneuvered down the inside wall of the canyon, each staking out his cover, giving him a clear view of the mine entrance. They spotted the shack below them, located about fifty yards from the mine entrance on a gentle slope that lead up to the front door. Kio offered to slip down and take a closer look.

"You'd better make it quick," Jeb said. "If that sun pops up and you're still down there, there ain't nothin' but open space 'tween them and these boulders."

Jeb and Seth watched as Kio made his way down the rocky slope, darting from one boulder to the next on a zig-zag course until he reached the rear of the shack. Looking into the first window, he

—John E. Cramer—

immediately dropped to his knees and crawled slowly to the corner. Another quick look and he disappeared.

Moments later, Jeb spotted one of the gang heading up the path to the shack. Catching Longlittle's attention, he pointed down the path to the mine entrance. After a minute, that to Jeb was an eternity, the hombre under the sombrero appeared, heading back down the path. They both watched as he disappeared inside the mine.

Before they had a chance to speculate, they saw Kio moving back along the same zig-zag course he'd taken on his way down. "We got problems," he said as squatted between the two boulders. "Get Seth over here."

Seth negotiated the space between the two boulders in record time. "What're they pow-wowin' about down there?"

"Seems the Colonel's changed his mind. Now, *he* wants to do the exchange instead of Farley. The messenger they sent up to the shack told the hombre guardin' the boy—"

"You mean Joey's in the shack?" Jeb cut in. "Did ya' see him?"

"They got him laced to a chair. If the Colonel has his way, him and Mort ain't got much of a future once Farley gets his slimy hands on the money Mort's deliverin'."

"Well, then," Jeb snapped, "we'd best be gettin' him outta there, and pronto!"

"Now, don't be gettin' all lathered up," Longlittle said. "Let's hear what Kio's got to say."

"From what I heard down there, seems the Colonel ain't satisfied just gettin' the money and knowin' they ain't gettin' outta this canyon alive. He's gotta tell 'em they ain't." Kio paused, shook his

—Seven Rode Together—

head, and added. "He sure must have more hate for Mort Kane than the devil hisself allows."

"So, let's git started," Jeb said.

"Hofstader," Longlittle said, "You're beginnin' to git on my nerves. Kio's beginnin' to sound like a man who's got an idea how we're gonna surprise the Colonel. You do have an idea, don't you, Kio?"

Shifting his weight, Kio cautioned: "We all gotta hand in this. And we'll pull it off because we got the same thing goin' for us that's got us this far. The element of surprise. Now, let's see what you think about this. That messenger explained to the hombre guardin' Joey that there'd be no shootin' until they got the money and Mort and the boy are leavin'. When the Colonel wants Joey brought down from the shack, he'll give the hombre in the shack a signal to join 'em. But, Seth is gonna be the one who'll be bringin' Joey down to 'em."

"And how do I handle that?" Seth asked.

For one thing, the hombre guardin' Joey is just about your size. You and Jeb are going to make certain you relieve him of his sombrero, his jacket with the silver trim, and his drawers. He's left-handed, same as you, Seth. Wears his holster strapped down. Since they ain't expectin' anything, you can take your time gettin' there. Jeb, you'll be in close enough to cover 'em, but, you're gonna have lots of help. One more thing, Seth, this guy you're replacin' carries a rifle. Got that?"

Longlittle nodded. "When's the fireworks gonna begin?"

"Seth, I figure you've been there before. I figure you're gonna know the answer when the time comes."

"And what are you gonna be doin' all this time me and Jeb

—John E. Cramer—

are walkin' into a fire-fight and tryin' to keep the boy from gettin' shot?"

"And, where's this lots a help comin' from?" Jeb asked, struggling to make his voice sound conversational.

"Well, if we're gonna pull this off and stay alive, the right hand's gotta know what the left hand's doin'. Thorn and the others across the canyon need to know what we know about Joey and the Colonel's plans. Mort will be arrivin' pretty close to noon. That gives us plenty of time to get ready. I'm fixin' to circle back the way we came, and unless one of those guys we took care of earlier today at the entrance has found a way to communicate our arrival, I'm not gonna have any problem gettin' over there." He pointed to the north side of the canyon. "And they're gonna know what we're plannin'."

"Make damn sure you let 'em know the fella bringin' Joey out from the shack ain't no friend of Buck Farley or the Colonel." Seth added.

"We'll be movin' in as close as we can." Kio continued. "There'll be five of them and five of us. And the way I figure it, you, Chad and Thorn will be gettin' off three rounds to their one. Just let Joey know that when the shootin' begins, for him to grab a handful of the canyon floor and hang on 'til it's over."

"There's just one more thing," Longlittle said. "There's a chance, and it's gonna be kinda thin, the Marshal's gonna want to take Farley and the Colonel back to River Bend alive."

Kio nodded. "That's fine with me. But you might have a hard time convincin' Thorn."

"Let's git on with it," Jeb said. "And we'll be seein' you again around noon."

—Seven Rode Together—

Shortly after noon that day, Mort reined up the Palomino at the entrance of the box canyon. For several minutes, his keen eyes scanned the rocky walls and scrubby undergrowth inside the canyon. Looking down the rocky trail that wound around boulders on the canyon floor, he realized it would take only a few men to hold off an army. A few hundred yards ahead, the trail bent sharply to the left where he got his first glimpse of the entrance to the old worked-out mine. He spotted the shacks on either side of the entrance, just as Kio had described. There was no one in sight, but he knew he was being watched and wondered where Jeb, Chad and the others had found cover. In front of the shack on the left, Mort spotted Joey's pinto and six other horses tied to the hitchrail. In front of him was the opening to the mine. A wide rock ledge extended over it.

"That's far enough, Kane!" It was the Colonel who stepped into full view on the right side of the boulder. A moment later, Buck Farley made his appearance on the left. As they both moved toward Mort, four of Farley's men, rifles aimed at Mort, stepped from the cover of the rock formation onto the rock ledge above the entrance. A fifth man followed behind Farley as he and the Colonel approached the palomino.

"Did you bring the money?" Farley asked.

"Where's my boy?" Mort said, knowing they could blow him out of the saddle anytime, but confident the four standing above the entrance on the rock ledge were already in the sights of four Winchesters.

"You'll see him in due time," the Colonel said. And turning toward the hombre who'd followed them from the entrance, he ordered, "Grab that bridle. And you, Kane, stay where you are!

—John E. Cramer—

When we get that kid of yours down here, you're going to know that I believe in an eye for an eye."

Mort's expression never changed. The Colonel retreated a step from Mort's steady gaze, and turning quickly away, yelled at Farley. "Tell him to get the kid down here." Farley pulled out his .45 and fired a shot in the air. Mort shifted his gaze toward the shack on his left and watched as Joey appeared, followed by the hombre in the sombrero with a rifle cradled in his arms. As they came close Mort knew that wherever his back-up was, they'd be looking for him to make the first move. He never got the chance. The hombre trailing Joey yelled, "Mort!" shoved Joey to the ground, and tossed his rifle in Mort's direction. In the same motion, Longlittle drew his .45 and in the split second before he got off a shot, Farley fired. Both men dropped to the ground. The Colonel turned to escape to the mine entrance. At the same moment Farley's men atop the rock ledge, without getting off a single round, toppled from the ledge to the ground, their rifles hitting the ground with them. All hell had broken loose.

The Colonel, who'd retreated to the cave, never made it. Thorn followed him in his sights until he was a step from safety and then dropped him with a single shot. He fell among those who moments before had tumbled from the ledge. The hombre who was holding the bridle of Mort's palomino was getting up from the ground after Mort had pole-axed him with his rifle butt. Mort had quit the saddle and was helping Joey to his feet when Jeb, yelling like an Apache on the warpath, came running down the trail from the shack. The rest of the River Bend posse left their cover on the right with Chad in the lead and Thorn bringing up the rear.

Seeing Seth on the ground, Chad dropped down beside him.

—Seven Rode Together—

"We got a man down over here! Somebody give me a hand with him! Somebody give me a hand with him!" Mort and Jeb helped Joey to his feet. "You gonna make it, Joey?" Mort asked.

Jeb nodded. "He's fine," he said. "Nary a scratch."

Before Jeb finished, Mort was heading toward where the Colonel had dropped. As he passed Buck Farley's body, he raised his head, a twisted grin on his face. "Kane," he whispered. "I told him you wouldn't come alone. Did you bring the money?"

"Didn't figure we needed to," Mort said. Before he finished, Farley's head dropped face down in the dust, blood running from his mouth. Mort turned and headed toward the Colonel when he noticed Thorn heading in the same direction. One look at the Colonel lying face down convinced Mort the nightmare was really over. He and Thorn both stood a moment looking down at the Colonel's outstretched body. "It's too bad," Thorn said, barely above a whisper, "I wanted him to know who I was before I killed him."

"Why?" Mort asked.

Without replying Thorn turned quickly and together they headed back toward the others. Jeremiah watched Thorn and Mort turn away from where the Colonel had fallen.

"Look out!" Jeremiah yelled. "He's got a rifle!"

In the same instant, both of them dropped to the ground. Thorn rolled over once and came up with his .45 in hand and fired. The rifle in the Colonel's hand fired harmlessly in the air. Without a word, Thorn got to his feet and started toward the others who had witnessed his expertise with a .45. Only one among them knew that a single shot had put to rest Thorn's vigil of 18 years. Kio met Thorn as he joined them, but he knew now was not the time to say what was in his heart.

—John E. Cramer—

After checking his deputy's wound, Chad reported. "He's one lucky feller, but he's gonna have one helluva headache. That shot Farley got off just greased his skull." He pulled a red bandanna from around his neck and wrapped the wound. "This is gonna have to do." he said, "'til we get you back home."

"Hey, Marshal!" Jeb yelled. "We got three of these cutthroats that's still breathin'. One yonder." He pointed to the one put out of action by the butt of Mort's rifle. "We got two hogtied at the openin' to the canyon unless Thorn didn't do the same kind of work on the one he took out as Kio did on his'n. How about these here who wasn't so lucky? Do we leave 'em for the coyotes or drape 'em over their saddles and take 'em with us?"

"We'll be loadin' up all of 'em." Chad replied. "Most of 'em got to be wanted for somethin' if they was ridin' with Farley. And he's worth a thousand dollars dead or alive. I believe Seth's eligible to collect the reward. He don't know it yet, but I recollect firin' him just before we left River Bend. And seein' as how he done a good job today, I figure I might hire him back once he collects his reward."

"You all heard the Marshal," Jeb hollered. "Let's get them that can't set a horse draped over a saddle, and those who can ride tied to the saddle horn."

An hour later, a strange looking caravan left the box canyon with the Marshal, Mort and Joey in the lead, and the others bringing up the rear.

Chapter 29

Clancy O'Riley had spent the night sleeping on the cot in his office when he was awakened by the sound of someone pounding on the door. He sat up, rubbed his eyes and tried to focus in the general direction of the front door.

The pounding, for the moment, had stopped, and he was about to lie down when it began again. "Don't be knockin' my door down, he yelled. I'll be with you in a moment."

When he opened the door, Jeb Hofstader shouldered his way in. "What kept you so long?" He looked at Clancy who was still rubbing the kinks out of the back of his neck.

"Why in the name of all that's holy, would you be knockin' my door down at this time of the morning?"

"What a damn fool question," Jeb snorted. "I know what time it is. It's time for them who ain't been out drinkin' and carousin' around all night to be up and ready to go to work."

Clancy waved his arms in disgust and motioned for Jeb to have a seat. "So, what have you got to tell me that couldn't wait for

—John E. Cramer—

civilized hours?"

"You won't be talkin' like that once you hear what I got to tell ya. If it wasn't for me keepin' my eyes peeled for news you can put in that gossipy rag you call a newspaper, folks around here wouldn't have no notion of what's goin' on. In fact, after all the news I bring ya, you oughta be payin' me wages."

Ignoring Jeb's usual tirade, Clancy dropped down in his chair, propped his feet up on the corner of his desk, pulled the desk drawer open and asked, "Want a whiskey?" He poured himself a shot. "So now I'm listening. And it better be good or I"m callin' Marshal Youngman and have you arrested for disturbing the peace."

"You wouldn't be sayin' that if you knew where I've been the last three days."

"When I went to see the Marshal a couple of days ago, it said he'd gone fishin'. I figured it was with you. So that's it. You caught a big ole catfish."

"No! That ain't it!" Jeb sputtered. "If you'd keep from askin' those damn fool questions, you just might think that what I'm tryin' to tell ya might be worth talkin' with Marshal Youngman about. You might even want to reward me by buyin' my breakfast over at the Mary Belle Cafe."

"Will you stop beating around the bush and tell me what you got on your mind besides eggs."

"I suppose you did know Joey Kane never finished that horse race. Well, we located him."

"That's it?"

"That's it alright. We also found them who done the kidnappin'."

—Seven Rode Together—

"Kidnapping?" Clancy swung his legs down off the desk and stuffed the bottle of whiskey in the drawer. "Mort Kane's boy was kidnapped?"

Jeb nodded. "That's right. We just got back a little while ago. Got two of 'em locked up. And the other eight we brought in wasn't feelin' well enough to ride so we brung 'em slung over their saddles—"

"Dead?"

"Well, they'd better be. We got the undertaker down at the marshal's office now fixin' to take care of 'em. We already sent a man out to the Double-B to fetch Tom Trinity. And they're fixin' to send a telegram to Paul and Nora Burkhalter notifyin' 'em that the Colonel's deceased."

"Colonel Burkhalter? Dead?"

"Yep. Him and Buck Farley and six of Farley's gang ain't with us anymore."

Clancy's feet hit the floor and he was up and heading toward the door when Jeb finished. "Why didn't you say so without all that hem-hawing around?" Clancy said as he slammed the door.

"How about that breakfast?" Jeb yelled after him. "He ain't gonna find anyone at the marshal's office," he muttered. "We already took care of all that had to be done for."

After Clancy left the office, Jeb decided he'd wait until later to ride out to the Circle-K. And if he waited until after eight o'clock, he could pick up the mail. He spotted the cot where Clancy had been sleeping. He walked over, pulled off his boots and laid down. "Clancy ain't gonna be needin' this cot for awhile," he mused. "Maybe, when he gets back, it'll be time for breakfast at the Mary Belle.

—John E. Cramer—

"It was mid-morning when Jeb was awakened by Clancy. "You aimin' to sleep all day?" he asked as Jeb sat up.

"What time is it?"

"It's time for any fella who's been in the saddle for the most of three days to go back to the Circle-K and grab some real shut-eye."

"Who you been talkin' to?" Jeb asked, pullin' on his boots. "When I left to come on over here, Chad said they'd tie up the loose ends."

"That they did. They'd gone over to the Mary Belle about the time it opened this morning. Chad filled me in on where you'd been and what you'd been doin'. That must have been one hell of a gun-fight."

"Where's everybody now? Mort and Joey, they go home?"

"Yes, except for Chad and Seth. Seth's a vet, but he's been doing some doctoring and he thought he ought to change that bandanna for some clean wrapping."

"How 'bout Jeremiah? He go with Mort?"

"He was going to the Colonel's place to let Trinity know what happened to his boss. Want some coffee?"

"Did anyone send a telegram to Paul and Nora?"

"The Marshal. They'll be inheriting the Colonel's holdings, I suppose."

Jeb was thinking about what Clancy had said about Nora and Paul inheritin' the Colonel's estate when he stopped to get the mail. Mort had never confided in him much when it came to Nora, but he knew one thing was certain, if those two were ever to get

—Seven Rode Together—

together, which would be the best thing ever happened to them and Joey, Nora would have to be willing to make the Circle-K her home. It was a lead-pipe cinch Mort would never give up the ranch to take up housekeeping in Boston.

When Jeremiah tied up to the hitchrail in front of the Colonel's estate, Tom stepped out onto the veranda. "What brings you out so early in the morning? I was hoping to see you. Come on inside and I'll give you the best news I've had since mustering out of the Army."

Tom chattered on as they entered the house and sat down at the dining-room table. "Have a seat. I'll rustle up some coffee."

He disappeared into the kitchen. Jeremiah was beginning to have second thoughts after seeing Tom in such high spirits.

He came in with the coffee and some bread and butter. "This should tide us over." He sat down across from Jeremiah. "Now, you remember Becky. Well, she's gonna be here next Saturday. We figure we'll need a few days to make all the arrangements."

"But I thought," Jeremiah began, "You were plannin' on first savin' enough money to buy your own place before you got married."

"We were, but things changed. The Colonel made me an offer I can't refuse. He's makin' me his assistant. It will take me some time to know all I need to know, but he says he'll pay me wages while I'm learnin'. And that's not all. He's going to pay Becky, too. She'll look after the housekeeping. Not by herself, mind you, but she'll be able to hire someone to help her. And, we'll

— John E. Cramer —

be livin' here. Right in this big, old house. When we used to talk about what our plans were once we got out of the Army, I never in a million years would have thought Becky and I would be able to live in this kind of place. Colonel says to treat it just like our home. Becky and me will be able to save money and then, who knows, maybe we can buy our own place. Well, now," he concluded. "You got some news?"

Jeremiah remained silent.

"If you're here to see the Colonel, you're out of luck. He's gone to a meeting at the state capitol and won't be back 'til next weekend. Is that why you're here? To see the Colonel?"

"Not exactly."

"Then what? You figure on givin' up ranchin' and your job at the Circle-K? Thinkin' about goin' back to Indiana?"

"No. But maybe it wouldn't be a bad idea. Thar ain't no easy way to say this, Tom, but the Colonel's been killed in a shoot-out in New Mexico Territory."

Someone knocked loudly at the front door.

"Sit tight. Sounds like I got more company."

Jeremiah could here the voices from the entry hall.

"We just got back from town. We got some real bad news you ain't gonna believe."

"Come on in," Jeremiah heard Tom say.

The graying cowhand followed Tom into the dining room, three other hands trailing behind.

"What's he doin' here?" one of them asked.

"The Colonel's dead," another nearly shouted.

"Hold it!" Tom said. "One at a time. The Colonel's in Topeka. Left three days ago. Won't be back 'til Saturday. Who told

—Seven Rode Together—

you all he was dead?"

The men looked at one another and at Jeremiah. "Nobody told us. We saw him. All three of us stayed the night in River Bend. This morning we was eatin' breakfast at the Mary Belle when the waiter asked did we know that Marshal Youngman and his posse, early this mornin', brought in the Colonel, Buck Farley and eight members of his gang. All dead, but two of the gang."

"And the Colonel and Farley? Both dead? Where did all this happen? The waiter tell you?"

"No. While we was talkin', the Marshal, Mort Kane and those two cowhands from Texas—" he pointed to Jeremiah, "and him, came in."

"Jeremiah?"

"That's right. I was fixin' to tell you when they came in. We was lookin' for them that grabbed Mort Kane's boy durin' the horse race Saturday. Tracked 'em all the way to New Mexico Territory. Farley and his gang of cutthoats, along with the Colonel, was holed up in a box canyon 'bout thirty miles west of the border. We had a little trouble convincin' them that the kidnappin' was agin the law. After the shootin' was over, two of the gang was the only one's left that could set a horse."

"What about the boy?"

"He's alright. Roughed him up a bit. Nothin' serious."

Tom was visibly shaken. For several minutes, he stood quietly looking at the floor. Slowly he raised his head and gazed steadily at the cowhands. "You say you saw him?"

"We went back over to the undertakers. He had 'em all laid out in the back room. Then we lit out for home, knowin' you'd be the one who'd be makin' the decisions around here now. Anything

—John E. Cramer—

we can do to help out, just whistle." He tipped his hat and the three cowhands left the room.

Tom sat down across the table from Jeremiah. Finally, he looked up. "Looks like there won't be a wedding for a spell. Least not anyway soon. The first thing I have to do is to let Nora and Paul know what's happened."

"The Marshal's already sent them a telegram."

"Well, I figure they'll be needin' to hear from me, too. And I need to write Becky."

"Now, Tom, I wouldn't be too hasty about that. I gotta strong feelin' that everything is goin' to turn out just fine for you and Becky. This ain't the end of the world, ya know. It might even be they'd like you to stay on here and run the place for 'em. You got the moxie to run this place, that's for sure. And they ain't goin' to mind makin' a profit off a spread like this and not even raisin' a finger. If you was to run into any problems, I know another feller besides me who'd be the first to give you a hand. That's the kind of feller Mort Kane is. 'Course I'm not sayin' that you'd run into any problems you can't handle. Well, I best be gettin' back."

Together they walked outside into the bright sunlight. They spotted one of the cowhands coming toward them. "Been talkin' to the rest of the boys," he began, "they're just wonderin' if we'll still be needin' to round up that herd of horses we been breakin' for the saddle—"

"Nothin's changed," Tom said. "We don't make promises we can't keep."

"You're the boss. We'll start roundin' 'em up at first light tomorrow."

Jeremiah reined his horse away from the hitchrail with a

—Seven Rode Together—

smile on his face. He couldn't help wonderin' what a best man is expected to do. A light, southwest breeze pushed a dust-devil across the dry ground toward the corral. Tom watched until Jeremiah disappeared over a slight rise, turned and headed back to the veranda, recalling what Jeremiah had said on many occasions: "Never look a gift horse in the mouth."

Chapter 30

Jeremiah was beginning to have second thoughts concerning the advice he'd always given Tom. If he got Becky out here and then Paul and Nora Burkhalter was to decide they'd rather sell the ranch, what happened to Tom's plans? There was one thing for sure, he was gonna have the answer to that question by next week.

He stripped the roan of the bridle and saddle, slapped her on the rump and turned her loose in the corral. He started across the barn lot and spotted Mort sitting with Chad and Kio in the shade of the front porch. "You almost missed your supper. The others are inside. There's a place set for you. When you're finished eatin' we'd like to hear about your trip to the Burkhalter ranch."

The next morning, Mort rolled out of bed at first light. He dressed hurriedly and went downstairs. Missus Milburn was sitting at the kitchen table nursing a cup of coffee. "Good morning. I didn't expect anyone to be up this early."

—Seven Rode Together—

Mort watched as she poured his coffee. "No one else been down this morning?"

She shook her head. "No. Did you expect there'd be?"

"Thorn said last night they'd be startin' back to Texas this mornin'. I didn't want them to leave without thankin' them for all their help in getting Joey back. Since I have some business needs tendin' to in River Bend, I thought I'd ride along with 'em. When they come down, tell 'em to grab a cup of coffee and meet me on the front porch."

Mort had just settled in, when Jeb appeared. "What's up Mort? It's pretty early to start talkin' about next springs cattle drive, ain't it?"

"Nothin' like that, Jeb."

Thorn and Kio appeared too, carrying cups of hot coffee and hand pie.

Mort was awful quiet, Jeb thought. He sat down beside him. "I ain't knowed you all these years without bein' able to tell right off when you got somethin' botherin' you. So you ought to lay'er on the line."

"One thing I've been wonderin' since our shoot-out with the Colonel," he said. "Did you and the Colonel know each other before you came to River Bend, Thorn?"

Thorn stiffened. "Why're you askin'?"

"If you think it's none of my business—I got the feelin' back in that box canyon when you dropped the Colonel that you had satisfied a personal score."

"It's over with. I don't mind explainin'. It's the damn pic-

—John E. Cramer—

ture over his fireplace. My pa painted that, even had his initials on it. I recognized it right away. It stuck in my crawl."

"You plannin' on takin' it with you when you leave?"

"That's right."

"Supposin' young Tom Trinity doesn't agree?"

"Like I said, I'm takin' the paintin' with me."

"Don't suppose you'll have any objection if me and Jeremiah tagged along, would you?"

"It's a free country."

The sun was still climbing when the five of them walked their horses across the open area between the corral and the stone fence surrounding the Burkhalter mansion. They reined up at the hitchrail outside the bunkhouse. "Looks like the place is deserted," Mort said. He threw a leg over the saddle-horn and slid to the ground. Before the others could follow, a cowhand, wearing a beat-up, sweat-stained Stetson stepped out on the terrace.

"Who ya lookin' fer?" he hollered.

"We came to see Tom Trinity," Thorn called back.

"If you're needin' to talk to the Boss, he's up at the house." Looking them over he spotted Jeremiah. "Thought we got rid of you the other day."

"Yeah, ya did. But I come back to see Tom this mornin' and brought these fellers along with me." Looking back at the others he added, "This here's—"

"Name's Ezra Rhodes," he cut in. "Friends call me Dusty. If you've brought the Marshal and his deputy along, you'd have the whole posse that brung in the Colonel and those dead outlaws yes-

—Seven Rode Together—

terday. What's your business with the Boss?"

No one had noticed that Tom had come out of the house and was striding toward them. He was within earshot of Dusty's question before Jeremiah had time to answer. "That's alright, Dusty. These are friends of mine. You go ahead and send that wire to Ft. Hayes. Let the Commander know he'll have his horses on the date we agreed on."

"If you say so, Boss. I'll see ya later." He loped off toward the corral.

"Well, why're we standin' around here? Come on over to the house."

Once inside, Tom invited them to have a seat in the spacious parlor, complete with fireplace and Ben Masters' painting above the mantle. "Now, what's on your mind? I have a hunch I might already know why some of you are here. It's not just a social call, I guess." He fixed his gaze on Thorn. Since you and Kio brought me home that night, I've been thinkin' about it. Are you any kin to the artist who painted that scene there?"

They all looked at the painting and at Thorn.

Thorn got up and walked closer to the painting. "He was my pa."

"Another hunch tells me you're here to reclaim it. It's a beautiful painting. I've admired it from the first time I laid eyes on it. I got no idea how the Colonel came by it. But I do know, from the short time I spent in the Union Army, the veterans collected some valuable items. They called 'em trophies." Keeping his eyes on Thorn, he asked, "How'm I doin' so far?"

Returning his steady gaze, Thorn replied, "I'll let you know when I hear your bottom line."

—John E. Cramer—

"Fair enough. If I was in your shoes, and under the same circumstances, I'd make damn sure that paintin' left here when I did."

Mort, feeling a need to change the subject, asked, "Have any of you heard from Paul or Nora?"

Tom nodded and took a seat in a side chair. "I kinda thought you'd be askin' about them, Mister Kane. Haven't heard from them directly, but Judge Storm tells me they should be here by the middle of next week. They asked him to see the Colonel gets a Christian burial in the town cemetery. I guess the Judge must have been a close friend of the Burkhalters."

"What makes you think that?"

"For one thing, the Judge said they wanted the Colonel to be buried in the family plot with their brother, Duane."

"Sounds like a natural request," Mort said.

"That's not all the Judge had to say. He told me that when they get here, they'll be wantin' to have their mother's remains removed from the ranch and buried in the family plot alongside the Colonel and their brother." He paused. "I've been here for over a year, and I've never seen any grave-site on the ranch. Sounds like they're not aimin' to keep this property."

"I wouldn't be too sure about that. It seems natural enough, they'd want the whole family buried together."

You been here awhile, Mister Kane. "Do you know where she's buried?"

When Mort seemed to ignore his last remark, Tom added: "Anyway, for whatever reason, the Judge also said Nora and Paul would want to be here for the reading of the will."

"Sounds to me like a routine request. After all, they're the next of kin."

—Seven Rode Together—

"You're right about that. But why would the Colonel be tellin' Judge Storm he'd made some changes in his will since he'd lost his wife and his son?"

"Did the Judge tell you that?"

Tom nodded.

"So far as I know, the Colonel and Judge Storm were good friends. The Colonel probably figured the Judge would be the person he could confide in on matters like this."

"That's just it. The Judge doesn't have the new will. He says it's here in the Colonel's safe."

"He's probably right." Mort said. "No doubt you'll be findin' out once they arrive. I sure wouldn't lose any sleep over it. And if they do decide to sell the ranch, and the new owner doesn't have a place for you, I'm always lookin' for experienced hands at the Circle-K. But if I were you, I wouldn't be doin' and speculatin' 'til all the cards are dealt."

"I appreciate your offer, Mister Kane. But if I do come callin', you might have to be hirin' two extra hands. Becky and me will be gettin' married—"

"Tom, you can stop callin' me Mister. And I know we've got plenty of people who'd help you plan that weddin'. And now, I think I'll just take the advice I gave you and quit speculatin', but there could be a couple of weddings at the Circle-K before we're finished."

When the five of them headed for town, Jeremiah took a position alongside Mort. "Look's like Tom's found another friend in this valley he didn't know he had. Could be, you might have found out that you and Tom think a lot alike. Did he ever mention

—John E. Cramer—

the Colonel?"

Mort nodded. "His name was mentioned, but only in regard to what Judge Storm told him about Paul and Nora comin' back to take care of business. Nothin' hostile about our trackin' him down. Anyway, I'm satisfied he holds no grudges. Seems to me he's got his head on straight. I think he's more concerned about not havin' a job when his Becky gets here." Mort hesitated, as if saving the best for last. "It's a good possibility you two might be workin' for the same outfit again."

When they reached River Bend, they reined up in front of the Frontier Hotel. Thorn explained: Me and Kio figure on waitin' 'til mornin' to head home. We both feel we'd like to get a full night's sleep since we were up most of the night at the Circle-K. Meanwhile, I've got to find some way to get this painting ready to travel. So, I guess this is where we part company. Could be we might be seein' you again at next year's cattle drive. But it could be that with the railroads spreadin' to our part of the country, we might not be makin' many more cattle drives."

Mort agreed. "Anyway, come spring, you might be gettin' an invitation to a wedding."

"Don't be surprised if by spring me and Kio are hangin' this painting over the fireplace it was taken from back in Virginia. I know Ma would like that."

A bit later, Mort and Jeremiah were seated in Judge Storm's chambers. "The others should be along any minute now. I guess they may have been held up longer than I thought. But with Clancy doin' the interviewin', I should have known they wouldn't

—Seven Rode Together—

be back here on schedule."

"What's this all about?" Mort asked. "We were out at the Burkhalter Ranch earlier today. Tom was tellin' us about Paul and Nora comin' back to take care of business since hearin' about the Colonel."

"This is an altogether different matter, but I thought you and Mister Dundee might be interested. It's probably bad timing since Paul and Nora may be reading about it in a Boston paper before they leave for River Bend. Well, now that I've got your attention—a couple of Army officers from Washington—"

The Judge was interrupted by a knock on the door. "Come right on in," He got to his feet to greet two officers with Major's insignias on their collars.

"Gentlemen, I'd like you to meet these gentlemen. They all have an interest in what we're going to discuss. Jeremiah Dundee, here, was the Company Clerk in Colonel Burkhalter's Company during the war. At that time, I believe the Colonel was a Captain. I was about to tell them you officers had completed your assignment, here, but I'll let you tell 'em. They might know about the investigation concerning the train heist during the war, and they probably know Wade Parker's been brought in and locked up."

The officers took a seat. "The reason we were wanting to talk with you, is to tie up some loose ends. We want to talk to all those who accompanied Marshal Youngman into New Mexico, where, we understand, Colonel Burkhalter and the others held your son Joey captive for ransom. And, of course, because you were witnesses to the shooting death of Colonel Burkhalter."

"Did he muster out of the Army as a bona-fide Colonel?" Jeremiah interrupted. "I never saw him agin after the Mississippi

—John E. Cramer—

River campaign 'cause I was transferred to another command and wound up in the Army of Occupation in New Orleans after the war's end."

"Yes, he did make Colonel. I was serving in the same regiment when he got his promotion."

The smile on the Major's face disappeared as he picked up again on his explanation as to why they were seeking information on the Colonel's demise. "In all probability, you gentlemen and the others in your posse, may have cut short the Colonel's time on this earth by a few months. We believe he was facing a firing squad or a life sentence at Ft. Leavenworth. We are dead-set on recovering a quarter-million in gold or cash stolen back in 1863. It was intended for the Confederacy. Judge Storm has told us he believes the fifty-thousand taken from a Mister Keltner came from that train robbery. The money Wade Parker was carrying when Marshal Thurgold arrested him was a mere few hundred short of fifty thousand. We also know, having talked to Parker, that Jim Arkus was killed in a cattle stampede and never collected his part of the loot. Bert Pierson, whom I understand wound up as an officer in your bank, was also an officer in Burkhalter's Company. He did not take part in the train heist, but learned about it later from Arkus. It was Pierson who helped us substantiate our suspicions that Burkhalter had master-minded the whole affair."

"It appears, then," Mort said, "The rest of the quarter-million from the train robbery will have to come from the Colonel's estate. Can't the government just step in and seize the money from the Colonel's bank account?"

"That's not what we intend to do," the Major replied. "We have already learned from the bank president, Dave Shelley, that

—Seven Rode Together—

the Colonel did not trust the bank to keep all his money. We expect the money is either in the safe at the Burkhalter estate, or the sale of his property."

"You at the liberty to let us in on a secret? What'll happen to the money?" Jeremiah asked.

"It won't be a secret. The money was heading for the South, so it will still go there. We're told the Colonel's daughter and son are on their way here from Boston. We'll make time until they arrive."

"You've done one hell of a job trackin' all this down," Jeremiah said. "I kept some records for the Colonel when I was his Company Clerk. No one seemed to want 'em when I was transferred to New Orleans, so when I mustered out of the Army, I sent 'em back to Indiana to a museum on the war the folks was settin' up."

"We know. The Adjutant General now has those records."

"*My* Company records? Well how—"

"Did we get hold of them? We tracked you down a few months ago, to New Orleans. We met a mighty pretty girl there, Becky DeLaney. She said you and your Army buddy, Tom Trinity, were headed West. She also told us you'd sent some records and other things back to Indiana to lighten your load to Kansas. What you'd kept was verified by Wade Parker when he decided he had no place to run."

"Well, I'll be damned! Jeremiah mumbled. "All this time I was feelin' mighty guilty once I heard about the train heist."

"Since you're feeling guilty," the Major said, "We'll drop our charges against you for playin' fast and loose with U.S. Army property."

Jeremiah's chin dropped. He tried, but nothing came out.

Chapter 31

Mort was still thinking about all he'd learned that day in Judge Storm's chambers when he and Jeremiah returned to the Circle-K. It had been a long time since he'd last seen Nora at the Way Station at Freedom Ridge. He'd not forgotten her last words, "Take care of yourself. I need you all in one piece the day we get married." In all her letters she seemed so certain, when that day arrived, he'd be coming to Boston. He was anxious to see her again, but under different circumstances. She and Paul had left River Bend to escape the Colonel immediately following the trial. Would she ever have returned to River Bend if the Colonel hadn't been killed and Joey's kidnapping hadn't happened? Mort knew he loved Nora, and Joey, who'd never known his real mother, loved her, too. Even as he tried to make himself believe he shouldn't ask Nora to marry him, Mort knew, once he saw her, he would be thinking only about making her happy, even if it meant giving up the Circle-K and making a new beginning someplace else.

It wasn't until they'd taken care of their horses and were

—Seven Rode Together—

headed toward the house that Jeremiah noted. "You ain't much to talk when you're ridin' a horse. You ain't said a word since we rode out of town."

"I don't recall you bein' too full of talk, either." Mort said, and clapping Jeremiah on the shoulder, he added. "Come on. Let's go up to the house and I'll buy you a cup of coffee."

Jeb came out of the house with Joey a step behind. "We been wonderin' where you two been keepin' yourselves. Joey and me are headed over to our favorite fishin' hole on Kettle Creek. Thought we might snag onto some catfish for our supper. Blanche said she'd fry 'em if we cleaned 'em."

"Blanche?" Mort asked. "Pretty familiar."

"Did you find out when Nora and her brother would be gettin' in?" Joey asked. "Missus Milburn was wonderin' would they be stayin' here with us?"

Before Mort could answer, Jeb said. "I most nearly forgot, Mort. I picked up the mail in town the other day and plumb forgot, 'til I put on my jacket just now. I put the letters on your desk in the library."

Joey whistled for Sarge, and the three of them headed on out to the barn. "Hold it." Jeremiah yelled. "Would you be needin' another fisherman on this expedition?"

"Come on!" Jeb yelled back. "But you're gonna have to bait your own hook."

Jeremiah hesitated a moment and glancing at Mort, said, "I ain't been fishin' since I was a kid back in Indiana. Why don't you come along with us?"

"It's mighty tempting," Mort said. "But I got some bookkeeping I need to catch up on. After all you've been through the

—John E. Cramer—

past few weeks, you've earned a fishin' trip. Just make sure you catch a few more than Jeb or we'll never hear the last of it."

Before Mort reached the back porch, he picked up on the mouth-watering aroma of fresh-baked bread emanating from Missus Milburn's kitchen. Hanging his hat on the peg at the side of the screen door, he entered the kitchen just as she was removing another loaf from the oven. "Missus Milburn, I do believe you're the hardest working person on the Circle-K." Mort said. "Seems everyone else has taken the day off. Just talked to Jeb and Joey on the way in. They're goin' fishin,' and Jeremiah volunteered to go along."

"It's a wonder to me that Joey will be able to stop talking long enough to fish," she sighed. "He's been talking about Nora coming home ever since he came down for breakfast. He's all fired up with the idea that Nora and her brother, Paul, will be staying with us while they're here in River Bend."

"I'm afraid," Mort said, "he may be in for a big disappointment. I tried to explain they'd be staying in town or at the Double-B and they'll be busy taking care of family affairs."

"He's already asked me to bake some blueberry pie. He tells me that's Nora's favorite kind." She paused, expecting some confirmation of Joey's expectations.

"Joey's right about one thing," Mort said finally. "She really does like blueberry pie. But she's not the only one. Joey and me kinda favor blueberry, too." After a moment or two, he added, "I best be letting you get on with your baking." When he reached the entrance to the hallway leading to the library, he turned back. "Where's Amanda?"

"She's not here. She's been invited out to dinner. Marshal

—Seven Rode Together—

Youngman came by earlier today. Said his mother is coming home on the afternoon stage and he wanted Amanda to meet her. Chad says, his mother is fully recovered, and Ebert, Chad and Steve have planned a homecoming celebration for her. Chad says it's going to be just a family affair. And since Amanda would soon be a member of the family, he wanted her to join them."

"Maybe that's where Joey got the idea for a homecoming celebration for Nora and Paul." He thought a moment and then added, "You know, inviting them to have dinner with us just might be a good idea. If Joey thinks a blueberry pie is required, then, a blueberry pie it is."

Smiling, Missus Milburn returned to her baking. She knew Mort to be a quiet man who seldom displayed emotion. A blueberry pie, she thought, might be a nice touch for the evening meal. But, for Nora and Mort, she knew just being together would be all that was needed to make this homecoming an unforgettable celebration.

Mort sat down at his desk. He'd decided that when Nora got out of that stagecoach, he intended to be the first to welcome her home. He picked up the letters on his desk and began to shuffle through them. The Louisville postmark on the last letter grabbed his attention. The letter was from Lilly, Ellen's older sister. He'd not heard from her since she'd written nearly five years ago to tell him about Ellen's condition and that she was desperately in need of his help. He opened the envelope, removed the letter and began to read: "Dear Mort, My beloved husband passed away a month ago today. He had been ailing for nearly a year. I'm alone now with my thoughts of the unforgivable injustice I've been a party to all these many years. I pray you will be able to forgive me after reading what

—John E. Cramer—

I have to tell you. Somewhere in this world, Mort, you have a son who was born 24 years ago on this day in our home. A few weeks later, Milt and I went with Ellen to the Trinity Catholic Orphanage just outside Louisville and left that beautiful dark-haired baby with pretty blue eyes. He was perfectly healthy except for one small blemish. He had an almost perfect star-shaped birthmark on his right shoulder blade. When Ellen didn't want to name him, the Mother Superior, Sister Thomasina, volunteered, naming him Thomas S. Trinity. The 'S' was for the star-shaped birthmark. We've never seen or heard about him since that day.

"Ellen was desperately fearful of our father's wrath should he ever find out the real reason for her lengthy visit with us. She pleaded for both of us to swear on the family Bible that we would never tell anyone. A promise we both kept.

"Five years later you and Ellen were married. That was a year after our Father was killed when he was thrown from his horse. That very same year a fire at the orphanage destroyed the building where all the records were kept. Later, Joey was born and I came to your home, you may remember, to be with Ellen. Your Mother and Ellen were not getting along. When Ellen abandoned you and Joey, I felt Ellen lived with her guilt every day for never telling you about your first born. After Ellen passed away, and we learned all you had done to help her when she needed someone to care for her, we knew all the misery and hurt could have been avoided by simply telling the truth. And I am finally telling you what we should have 24 years ago. God only knows how much I wish I could undo all the suffering I have caused by allowing my love for my sister and her fears, overcome my better judgment. I pray every night that by some miracle, you could find the son

—Seven Rode Together—

you've never known. Although I do not deserve your forgiveness, I do hope you may find it in your heart to write me and let me know how you and Joey are getting along. I do love you both. Lilly"

Mort folded the letter and sat motionless, staring out the window in disbelief. Every date, place and name Lilly mentioned, he recalled so vividly. It was as if he had lived his whole life over in the short time taken to read her letter. The extended visit, when Ellen was gone from early spring until Thanksgiving; the year he and Ellen were married after his father had gone to war; the year Joey was born and Lilly came to be with Ellen; and later the same year she left to be on her own. The name, Thomas S. Trinity struck him like a thunderbolt and sent him mentally reeling, unrelentingly repeating itself over and over. Time seemed to stand still.

The day had gone from light to dark, and still Mort sat at his desk, thinking. Everything he knew to be true was different. Ellen. Oh, Ellen. Why hadn't she told him? Why? Had she tried, and he hadn't listened? Or had she been determined to take her secret to the grave? He wanted to write to Lilly, to thank her. At least he thought he wanted to thank her. How did he feel? What did he feel? What was he going to do?

"What's the matter, Mort? Get a bug in your ear?" Mort glanced behind him. Standing in the open doorway was Jeremiah, grinning from ear-to-ear.

"No!" Mort snapped. "I just don't cater to people sneakin' up on me when my back's turned. You got knuckles. Next time use

—John E. Cramer—

'em before you come bargin' in!"

Jeremiah froze. "Sorry Mort. I just wasn't thinkin'. We just got back from our fishin' trip. Joey landed a whopper of a catfish and he was wantin' you to see it before Jeb started cleanin' 'em."

"Where are they now?"

"On the back porch."

"I'd better have a look," Mort said as he brushed past Jeremiah.

Following the evening meal, Jeb and Joey volunteered to help Missus Milburn clean up the dishes. "If they're not doin' a good job, Missus Milburn," Mort said as he pushed back his chair and got up from the table, "give me and Jeremiah a holler. We'll be in the library."

Mort left the dining room and Jeremiah followed him into the library. "Close the door," Mort said. "And pull up a chair. I'd like to talk with you a spell about your friend, Tom Trinity."

"Sure, Mort," Jeremiah replied, relieved to see Mort in a talking mood.

"Did Tom ever talk to you about his folks, or where he was living before he joined the Army?"

"Tom isn't much to talk about hisself. He did tell me he never knew his real folks. Said he was raised in an orphanage run by Catholic Nuns." He paused, rubbed his chin and then added, "It was somewheres in Kentucky."

"Maybe, near Louisville?"

"Yeah," Jeremiah replied quickly. "Come to think of it, that's it." He eyed Mort for a moment and then asked. "Why you

—Seven Rode Together—

wantin' to know about Tom for? You thinkin' that when the Colonel's offspring gits here, Tom won't have a job at the Double-B? I heard you tell him if things don't work out, he could come to work at the Circle-K. If that's what you're gettin' at, I can tell you right off you'd never regret it if Tom was to come to work for you. And if Tom's lady friend, Becky, is causin' you to have second thoughts about them gettin' married and all, I can tell you, that little girl is used to pullin' her own weight. She'd be a big help. And I got a hunch Amanda might just up and get married to Marshal Youngman any day now. Yessir, Becky could be a big help."

"Let's just say I've takin' a likin' to that young man. I'd just like to know more about him. Did he ever tell you where he got the name?"

"I do recollect him sayin' he had a middle initial and that he never did know what the 'S' stood for. Never did bother him. He just figured one name was plenty. He figures he was named by them that raised him. You know he did run off from the orphanage when he was sixteen."

"Did he ever say anything about wanting to find his folks?"

Jeremiah shook his head. "Not that I recollect. But I don't doubt for a minute he's given it some thought. When we was doin' Army duty together, mail call wasn't somethin' Tom looked forward to, but he never showed it. Meetin' Becky has to be the best thing ever happened to him. He's lookin' forward to havin' a family of his own. It's a damn shame to spend 24 years of your life and never knowin' who you are or where you came from. Becky's had a life a little like Tom's. 'Course she does remember her parents. Her Pa was killed in the war and her mother passed away not long after. She's been raised by her uncle. You're gonna like Becky.

—John E. Cramer—

She's a lot like Tom. But, at least she knows who her folks were. Got pictures of them, and her uncle's told her about 'em. I never could figure out how anybody could just dump a baby at an orphanage and never look back. 'Course you and me both know, the world's full of all kinds of people. There's them that care and them that don't. Ain't that right?"

Before Mort could reply, Missus Milburn tapped on the door. "Mort, Seth Longlittle is here to see you. He's having a cup of coffee in the kitchen. I thought it best to let you know he was here."

"Thanks. Tell him I'll be with him in just a few minutes."

"No hurry," Missus Milburn replied. "He's also having a piece of that blueberry pie with his coffee."

Mort, who was still thinking of Jeremiah's final question, paused in the doorway. "I really appreciate you takin' the time to let me know more about Tom, and I'm looking forward to meeting Becky."

Jeremiah sat for a moment staring at the doorway. As he got up from his chair, he saw the letter Mort had received from Lilly lying face up on the desk. Although his conscience was telling him not to read someone else's mail, his eyes quickly reached the sentence that allowed him to forget he had a conscience. "Somewhere in this world, Mort, you have a son who was born 24 years ago on this day in our home—" His eyes darted quickly to "...I went with Ellen to the Trinity Catholic orphanage just outside Louisville—" Now there was no turning back, Jeremiah finished the letter. He placed it back on the desk and joined the others in the kitchen. He now knew why Mort was interested in Tom and where he was from. But now that he knew, the question was, "What can I do about it?"

—Seven Rode Together—

Besides Tom, who else in this valley could he tell that could share the burden of knowing, and knew Mort well enough to know what his reactions would be? There was one thing Jeremiah was well aware of. Mort was wrestling with his conscience, too, not knowing how best to tell Tom or whether Tom should be told at all. The one person, he thought, who knows Mort better than anyone in this valley, is Jeb. He was still mulling this over in his mind when he joined the others in the kitchen.

"Pull up a chair," Jeb said. "When Joey and me came in Mort and Seth were samplin' Missus Milburn's blueberry pie. You might as well dig in, too."

Missus Milburn, who'd already had set a place for Jeremiah, shrugged her shoulders and proceeded to set a place for herself. "Seth tells us Nora and Paul will be arriving in River Bend sometime tomorrow morning." And looking at Mort, she smiled. "Looks like the homecoming celebration we're planning got started a little early. Only one thing missing. The guests aren't here to enjoy fresh baked blueberry pie."

"Well, there's one thing for sure," Jeb chimed in. "The oven ain't broke and we got plenty of blueberries."

Although Mort and Jeremiah joined in the gaiety of the moment, both were burdened with a 24-year-old secret. Each, wondering that once revealed, what the consequences might be.

Following dessert, Mort excused himself, saying he had some paper work in the library that needed his attention. Jeb allowed that before he turned in, he'd go out on the portico and sit a spell. Actually, he was wanting to smoke his pipe, and Missus

—John E. Cramer—

Milburn didn't take too kindly to having him light up in the house. "Mind if I join you?" Jeremiah asked.

"Last time I looked," Jeb replied, "there was more than one chair out there." He glanced at Missus Milburn and added. "That is, of course, if you can stand the smell of a stinkin' old pipe."

Before Missus Milburn could respond, Jeb had already disappeared out the back door with Jeremiah following him. When they got seated on the portico and Jeb had lighted his pipe, Jeremiah said, "Jeb, there's something I need to talk to you about and hanged if I know just how to begin."

"Sounds like you already have," Jeb drawled. "I've heard about everything in my time, so let 'er rip."

"You think there's anything botherin' Mort?"

"I don't know what you're gettin' at. But I've known Mort a good many years in good times and bad, and there have been times when he had somethin' playin' heavy on his mind, I learned not to ask any dang-fool questions. When he's ready to talk to me, he lets me know."

"What would you say if I was to ask for your advice on what I should do with the information I got just today. And I ain't too proud how I came by it, but what's done is done—"

"Well, you got my attention. Let's hear it. You're beginnin' to sound like some kid tryin' to tell his Pa he's got his girl in the family way."

"You ain't too far from the truth," Jeremiah replied. "What would you say if I told you that Mort's the father of a 24-year-old son—livin' right here in this valley?"

Jeb sat quietly for quite a spell, his mouth agape. Finally, he began to speak slowly and deliberately. "I'd say you've been sittin'

—Seven Rode Together—

downwind of this tobacky smoke too long or you been eatin' loco weed. You wouldn't be knowin' the name of this feller who's claimin' Mort's his Pa?"

"That I do," Jeremiah said. "His name is Thomas S. Trinity, but he's not the one doin' the claimin'. It's Mort's sister-in-law. She lives in Louisville." Jeremiah continued his explanation of how he'd read Lilly's letter to Mort. "I know I had no business readin' that letter. But now that I have, I've been thinkin' of some way I might help in gettin' them together. I think Mort wants Tom to know. But it seems to me he's wrestlin' with his conscience. Maybe afraid of Tom's reaction after all these years. I got a feelin' he's goin' to tell Tom. Since I've been the only family Tom's ever known, I wanted to get your opinion, knowin' Mort like you do, if I was to talk to Tom about it. Maybe I could get him used to the idea before Mort dropped it on him. You got any ideas? Think if I talked to Tom it might make it easier for the both of 'em?"

"Knowin' Mort," Jeb began, "he's not gonna keep it a secret. He's got Nora and Joey to think about, too. But it seems to me that tellin' Tom, greasin' the slide, so-to-speak, might do more good than it would harm. I've heard Mort say on many occasions he wished Joey could have had a brother. I'll say one thing, Jeremiah, you sure do know how to split a can o' worms with a feller. But I figure with Nora and Paul comin' in tomorrow, we're gonna find out a few things. They'll be the new owners of the Double-B. Tom might just wind up here at the Circle-K."

Chapter 32

The following morning Mort awoke on the leather couch in the library where he'd spent the night. Across the room on the roll-top desk, he spotted Lilly's letter reminding him it was not a dream. The questions he'd been trying to sort out until the wee hours of the morning were still without answers. He knew he wasn't going to allow the circumstances as an excuse for not telling Tom Trinity he had a family. The questions still to be decided were when and how. One thing was certain, there were three people in his life who were going to be the first to know. If they could accept Lilly's letter and go on with their lives, he could make sure they never would live to regret it. If any of them could not, he'd have to live with that. He could never live peacefully with his conscience trying to justify his silence. Nora would be coming home today. If he could convince Paul and her to accept his invitation for dinner at the Circle-K, he could let both Nora and Joey learn the truth; Tom, he thought, will find out tomorrow.

Suddenly aware that Missus Milburn was preparing break-

—Seven Rode Together—

fast, and satisfied with his decision to do what had to be done, he pulled on his boots and headed for the kitchen.

"Good morning," Mort said, the moment he entered her kitchen.

"And good morning to you, Mister Kane."

"Blanche,"

Blanche? She was surprised at Mort's informality.

"I'd like to ask you to do my a favor. I know you and Doc were good friends with the Burkhalters long before I ever inherited this ranch from my Uncle Steve. And as I recall, you and Emily Burkhalter were the best of friends. I'd like to ask Paul and Nora to have dinner with us tonight. I really think they'd accept my invitation, but, under the circumstances, they may feel they should stay at the hotel. I was hoping you might help, if it becomes necessary, to persuade them otherwise.

"They'll accept your invitation alright. Why do you think I'd stay up 'til past midnight baking more of those blueberry pies Nora's so fond of? We'll have guests for dinner tonight, you can bet on that."

Jeb's prediction as to the time the stagecoach from Wichita would arrive in River Bend was correct. It was an hour late, arriving in front of the Frontier Hotel a few minutes past eleven o'clock. Mort and the entire Circle-K household, who'd been waiting in the hotel dining room, were nursing their third round of coffee when the stage arrived.

With Joey leading the way and Jeb and Mort bringing up the rear, they walked out onto the boardwalk. As Mort reached the steps leading down to the dusty street, his eyes were fixed on the stage door about to be opened by the driver. Other curious onlookers had paused on the walk in front of the hotel to see if they might recognize any of the passengers. Making his way through the group of curious spectators, was a young man bent on reaching a spot in front of the others before the first passenger emerged. Mort immediately recognized the six-foot, broad shouldered young man as Tom Trinity. Stepping from the stagecoach was a young, raven-haired, strikingly attractive lady, who paused momentarily, and seeing Tom, stepped quickly to the street and into his arms.

"Let's stand back folks," the driver said, "Give the passengers room to collect their luggage."

Mort spotted Nora as she was about to step down to the street. In two quick strides, past the driver, Mort reached up and with both hands on either side of her tiny waist lifted her gently to the ground. As she slipped her arms around him, she whispered, "I prayed you'd be here, Mort."

"I'm happier when you're arrivin' than when you're leavin'," Mort replied, adding another gentle hug.

Within seconds, they were surrounded by the entire greeting committee from the Circle-K. The driver, looking first at those surrounding Mort and Nora and then up toward Paul, the final passenger, standing in the door waiting for room to step down to the street, threw up his hands. "Is there no one in River Bend here today to greet the town's new family physician?" Paul's unexpected announcement not only caught the attention of everyone present from the Circle-K, but also the several spectators still standing on the boardwalk who'd lingered to watch the reception given the two pretty young ladies. All eyes turned toward him. Then, as if on cue, the quiet was broken by a spontaneous applause and whistles from those within earshot of Paul's announcement. Others passing

—Seven Rode Together—

by and several now making their way from across the street were asking one another "What did he say?" "Who's that fellow?" "What's all the excitement about?"

Mort, moments before, had asked Nora, "I'm hopin' you're here to stay?" He saw her lips moving but he couldn't hear her. In a much louder voice to compete with the applause for Paul's announcement, he asked again, "Are you here to stay?"

The timing was perfect. His personal question was heard by everyone. Nora, for the first time saw Mort show signs of embarrassment. Her green eyes aglow and a smile in her voice, equally loud, she replied, "Does this answer your question?" And she gave him a big kiss. This time the clapping and cheers and whistles drowned out further conversation.

Blanche, who had been watching with great interest all the unexpected welcome in Nora and Paul's arrival in River Bend, nudged Jeb. "And Mort was worried they might not accept his invitation to dinner at the Circle-K."

With Mort leading, the folks from the Circle-K turned back to the hotel, except Paul who, Mort noticed, was now being questioned by Clancy O'Riley and several of the towns leading citizens. "Looks like Paul's announcement got the attention of River Bend's finest."

"I'll see Paul joins us for lunch, Mort," Jeb said. "Jeremiah will see to it that Tom and his lady joins us too," he added.

Once everyone was seated in the hotel dining room, Mort picked up his spoon and tapped it gently on his glass, getting the attention of everyone. Still feeling a bit uneasy from the unsolicited attention he'd had moments earlier, Mort began, "I've never seen so much attention by so many people when three passengers

—John E. Cramer—

arrived here in a stagecoach." Uncertain as to exactly what he wanted to say, he looked around the table. "I suspect a good place to begin would be to make sure everybody knows everybody." He paused and looking at Tom, he added, "Tom, why don't you introduce Becky to the rest of us?"

"I'd be proud to do that," Tom replied, as he got slowly to his feet. "I'd like to introduce you to my fiancee, Miss Becky DeLaney from New Orleans. She arrived here a couple weeks earlier than we were planning. She tells me she and Miss Burkhalter and her brother, Paul, had quite an enjoyable visit on their way here from Wichita, and, we're hoping we're gonna be neighbors to all you folks from the Circle-K."

Mort had a sudden urge to let all hear about his latest discovery that Tom and Becky weren't going to be neighbors to the folks at the Circle-K—but that the folks at the Circle-K were his folks! But, knowing this was not the time or place, he said. "The folks at the Circle-K would like to extend this homecoming by inviting Tom and Becky and Nora and Paul to the Circle-K for dinner this evening. Missus Milburn has told me not to take 'no' for an answer. All of us would be proud to have you." Just as Mort was about to sit down, he noticed Judge Storm entering the dining area, heading toward their table.

"I thought I might find you all here." the Judge said. "And if you all would excuse River Bend's newest arrivals for a moment, I'd like to speak with them in private. What I have to say won't take but a minute and it'll save 'em a trip to the courthouse. Looking at Tom, he added, "I'd like you to hear what I have to say, too."

Once the five of them were seated at a table on the far side of the room, the Judge began to explain why he felt it necessary to

—Seven Rode Together—

speak to them in private. "It's a bit of family business. I took the liberty to invite Tom's fiancee because I know she'll soon be part of his family. What I have to tell you, I'm sure will be of interest to all of you. It concerns the Colonel's latest Will and Testament. A few months ago the Colonel confided in me that he'd revised his will, witnessed by his attorney, and Ethyl, his housekeeper at that time. His will is in the safe at the ranch. I feel it's necessary to have you all there to witness not only the opening of the safe but to hear what the Colonel's last wishes were. And I'm equally certain, what you decide to do with your inheritance will have an effect on the plans Tom may have for his future. I admit this may be a bit irregular, but I feel because of the circumstances, you'd like to take care of this matter as quickly and with as little publicity as possible. Do any of you have objections to my way of handling this matter?"

When no one spoke, he added. "Well, then, shall we all meet at the Burkhalter estate, say at ten o'clock tomorrow morning?"

When no comments were made, the Judge stood up. "In that case I'll see you all tomorrow morning. I apologize for taking you away from your homecoming."

Judge Storm returned with the others to their table. "I'm sorry for having to interrupt your lunch," he said. And turning to Mort, he added, "You and I and your two partners, Jeb and Joey, will have to see how the fish are biting again one of these days before the snow flies."

Mort cut his eyes toward Tom hoping one of these days he could add Tom's name to the partner list.

Mort's earlier invitation gained acceptance from everyone seated around the table except Tom. "We thank you for the invita-

—John E. Cramer—

tion, but Becky and I have asked Jeremiah to have dinner with us tonight. It's been awhile since the three of us have been together and we've got a lot of catching up to do."

"We understand," Mort said. "Maybe another time."

Following dinner that night at the Circle-K, Nora insisted she help Missus Milburn and Amanda in the kitchen while the men retired to the living room. When they finished their work, Nora joined them. Noticing Jeb had retired and only Joey and Mort remained with Paul, she asked, "Don't you think we should be getting back to the hotel?"

"Nonsense," Mort was quick to reply. "Why not stay the night here. Tomorrow morning you can use our carriage to make your appointment with the Judge." Before they could reply, Mort added, "Then it's all settled."

"In that case," Paul said, getting up from the straight-back rocking chair across the room from Mort, "I believe I'll turn in. I'll see you in the morning."

Joey, who was secretly wanting to stay and visit with Nora and his Pa, knew he was about to hear Mort tell him, as he always did every evening at this time, "Morning comes around pretty quick, Joey, you'd better hit the hay." This evening was to be an exception when he heard, much to his surprise, Mort say, "I'd like you and Nora to come with me to the library. I've got something that concerns us all, and I need to get your opinion."

Mort closed the door, walked across the room, and removed Lilly's letter from the roll-top desk. "I have a letter here from your Aunt Lilly, Joey, that I'd like to share with you and Nora. You're

—Seven Rode Together—

two of the three people who need most to know what I discovered just two days ago when I received this letter. When you've finished reading what Lilly has to say, I can only hope you'll understand why I could not, or chose not, to ignore what I know now to be the truth." He crossed the room to where they were seated together on the couch and handed the letter to Nora. "Perhaps you can share it together." Mort walked back to his desk and sat down to await their reaction to Lilly's revelation.

After what seemed to Mort an eternity, he watched as they finished reading the letter and for a moment they sat quietly, glancing first at one another and then at Mort. Finally, Nora folded the letter, returned it to the envelope and handed it to Joey. It suddenly had become so quiet. "Does this mean Ma was really a bad person, Pa? And is Tom Trinity really my brother?"

"No, Joey. She wasn't any worse or any better than I was. And it does mean that Tom is your brother. Things happen sometimes and since you can't undo what happened, you just try to live with it. Your Ma decided it best to do what she did because she feared what her Ma and Pa might do if they knew."

"Well, after you and Ma got married and I came along, why couldn't she tell you then. Neither her ma or pa could hurt her then, not with you around."

"I guess you keep a secret penned up inside, hoping it will all go away one day, but it never does. Finally, you convince yourself it's too late to tell anybody."

"You don't hate her now, do you, Pa?"

"No, Joey, I don't hate her. She did what she felt she had to do. What's done can never be undone. That's why she did more hurt to herself than anyone."

—John E. Cramer—

"You plannin' on tellin' Tom Trinity all this?"

Mort nodded. "That's right, Joey. I don't know what he'll do when he knows. Whatever he does, I'll understand and we'll have to live with it just like Ellen did. Right now, I'm wondering what Nora's going to do."

"There's one thing I'm not going to do. I'm never going to quit loving you and Joey, and I aim to do my best to help both of you convince Tom he's a lucky person, no matter what's happened, to at last discover his family. Many orphans never do. I've found my niche and I don't plan to ever leave it, unless of course," she added with a faint smile, "You and Joey won't have me."

That same night at the Burkhalter Ranch, Jeremiah was convinced that Tom should know what he'd learned after reading Lilly's letter. Jeremiah was certain Mort fully intended to tell Tom when the situation presented itself. He was equally certain Tom would more likely accept Mort's story anchored by Lilly's letter more readily if Tom was given the opportunity to think about it. Jeremiah was prepared to tell him.

After the three of them had finished dinner, Jeremiah opened the living room conversation with a subject that would dominate the remainder of the evening. "I have stumbled upon the information that offers undeniable proof," Jeremiah began, "that you, Tom, are the son of Mort Kane." He paused for a moment never taking his eyes from Tom, expecting some immediate reaction. Instead, Tom calmly and with no visible signs of emotion, replied, "From the day I first became aware that I shared one thing in common with all the others in the Trinity Orphanage, I

—Seven Rode Together—

hoped, prayed, and dreamed for the day to come when I'd no longer share that one thing in common. I would find out who my parents were. Maybe one day they would come to the orphanage and reclaim me. That dream, that hope, those prayers were never realized. Now you're telling me you know who my parents are? You'll pardon me for not believing you have, what you've described as undeniable proof."

"It's true we did plan to talk over old times this evening, so humor me, tell me more of what you've learned about these times. Especially those that go back 24 years." Before Jeremiah could reply, Becky spoke up.

"What a terrible thing to say. Do you really believe Jeremiah would tell you this without any reason to believe that it was true? I don't for one minute believe you actually think Jeremiah would tell you something he believed was not true. It seems to me you owe him an apology."

"No apologies needed," Jeremiah said.

"But I'm sorry, Jeremiah," Tom said. "Becky's right. I guess I've kept it bottled up inside so long, and I figured I was never goin' to know. My last attempt was when we were in New Orleans. I wrote to the Mother Superior at the orphanage in an attempt to find out if there were any records kept of the kids who were there. I learned a fire had destroyed all the earlier records. I just didn't want to talk about it. But I always held out some hope that one day I'd find out who my parents were. I felt that no matter what the circumstances were, it would be the happiest day of my life. I kept telling myself there had to be a good reason. But I was ready to accept any reason, good or bad, because, at least, I would finally know I really did belong to someone. So, Jeremiah, if you will accept my apology, I'd really like to hear what you were about to tell me."

"I figured I ought not be tellin' you before Mort did, seein' as how I found out the way I did. But after hearin' your reaction to only my first mention, I'm satisfied I done the right thing. At least now you'll have the opportunity to decide what questions you want to ask. Least ways you won't be landin' on Mort like you just did me."

Jeremiah continued to tell Tom all the information contained in Lilly's letter. When he was finished, he asked, "Do you have any idea how anyone could know you got a star-shaped birth mark on your right shoulder without having seen you stripped to the waist? Or how they'd know the initial 'S' is meant for your birthmark? Or that your first name, Thomas, was used as the short version of Sister Thomasina's name? I know Mort Kane to be one of the most honest men I've ever known. He's tough but he's fair. My advice would be to hear him out, get to know him better. Say what you feel you have to. If he didn't care to find out the truth, he would have destroyed that letter. But he didn't. He's savin' it 'cause I believe he intends to let you read it."

Tom nodded. "Imagine, after all these years findin' out your father is your neighbor and you have a 15-year-old brother—and they're family."

Chapter 33

It was nearly ten o'clock the next morning when Paul and Nora turned into the Burkhalter Estate, and pulled alongside the horse and buggy that belonged to Judge Storm.

As they moved up the walk to the veranda, Tom stepped out of the house and greeted them. "Good morning. Judge Storm arrived just a few minutes ago. He and Marshal Youngman are in the dining room along with a Colonel Brigham from Washington."

Paul and Nora exchanged glances. "What are they doing here?" Paul asked. "I thought this was to be a family affair."

Tom shrugged his shoulders. "I don't know, but we'll soon find out. Right now, they're all having a cup of coffee, so, let's join 'em."

When they entered the dining room, Judge Storm arose from his chair at the head of the table. The Marshal and the Colonel arose, too. "Gentlemen, I'd like you to meet Paul and Nora Burkhalter." He motioned for them to be seated on the opposite side of the table from the two unexpected guests. "Would you like a cup of coffee?"

—John E. Cramer—

"No, thank you," Paul said. And nodding toward the Marshal the Colonel, he added, "I don't recall you mentioning yesterday we would be honored with such distinguished guests at this family affair."

"I apologize for not telling you yesterday. But what we have to settle today is a much more complicated and serious matter than just the disclosure of the contents of your father's will. And by inviting these gentlemen here this morning, I felt the matter they are most interested in could be expedited more discreetly with this one meeting. After you hear what the Colonel has to say, I'm quite certain you both will agree. Marshal Youngman's presence as a member of the U.S. law enforcement body, we felt would serve as a witness to these proceedings." He paused and seeing that his explanation had captured the undivided attention of both Paul and Nora, he added. "Colonel Brigham, perhaps you can better explain your presence here this morning."

The Colonel nodded and fixing his gaze across the table at Paul and Nora, he began. "First, I would like to offer my condolences to you both on the death of your father. And what I have to say gives me no pleasure whatsoever. I will try to be as brief as possible. If you have questions after I've finished, I will answer them." He paused and cleared his throat. "Your father died owing the United States Government a quarter of a million dollars. If he were alive today, he would no doubt be serving a sentence in Ft. Leavenworth for his part in a train holdup nearly twenty years ago during the war between the states. Only one of the four Union soldiers who took part in the robbery is alive today. From him and one other, we have recovered one hundred thousand dollars. We have good reason to believe Colonel Burkhalter has the remaining one

—Seven Rode Together—

hundred fifty thousand dollars either in gold or in cash. It is not in the bank in River Bend. That, we now know. It could very well be in the safe that will be opened this morning. If it is not, we then will begin proceedings to sell Colonel Burkhalter's holdings to recover the total amount stolen."

For several moments, no one spoke. Paul and Nora sat stunned at what they had just heard. Recalling the shoot-out at the Way Station near Freedom Ridge, Paul remembered fifty thousand dollars was taken from a man named Keltner, and Keltner worked for the Colonel. Looking across the table at Colonel Brigham, he asked, "Would a man called Keltner have been a participant in this train robbery you've told us about?"

Brigham nodded. "The fifty thousand recovered from him and the fifty thousand from another of your father's employees, Wade Parker, the only one still alive, amounts to the one hundred thousand we've recovered. It was his confession that implicated your father's part in the robbery. According to Parker, it was Colonel Burkhalter who engineered the robbery."

"In that case," Paul replied, "We may as well get on with it. But neither I nor my sister have the combination to the safe."

"I have the combination," Judge Storm said.

Brigham pushed back from the table. "It appears the moment of truth is at hand. Shall we adjourn to the library?"

As the others watched, Judge Storm removed a slip of paper from his vest pocket, checked it, and moments later, opened the door of the safe. The Colonel's will, he placed on the desk along with other legal documents. The last things from the safe were greenbacks and national bank notes totaling more than one hundred twenty thousand dollars and gold bars worth nearly ninety thousand.

—John E. Cramer—

"This should take care of the government's claim," Judge Storm observed. "Now, let's see what surprises the Colonel has for us in his Last Will and Testament. He took note of the two signatures of witnesses below the Colonel's fancy penmanship that omitted the 'Colonel' from his signature, 'Felix Buford Burkhalter'. "So that's where the Double-B comes from when the Colonel selected a brand and a name for his ranch," the Judge mused. He mumbled the opening paragraphs, his eyes darting ahead to the paragraph beginning "—I hereby bequeath my entire estate including the Double-B and the one-hundred thousand acres, all of my livestock, horses and cattle, my stock in railroads, bank,other properties, all my personal and household effects, to my most trusted friend, companion and confidant, Thomas S. Trinity, in whom I have unswerving confidence will carry on in the Burkhalter tradition that is worthy of my trust in him."

Quiet settled over all those present in the library. Finally, the Judge, after glancing around the room, asked, "Where's Tom S. Trinity?"

It was Marshal Youngman who answered. "He never came into the library with us, sir. In fact, I believe I saw him leave immediately after Nora and Paul came into the dining room."

"That's correct." Brigham added. "He mentioned he had some chores he needed to look after. I guess he felt the meeting we were going to have was purely a family affair."

"Well," Judge Storm began, "I think we had best find that young man and bring him in here. I think we have some legalities concerning the Colonel's Last Will and Testament that will require his participation, and perhaps we can come to a mutual understanding that could save the interested parties a great deal of time

—Seven Rode Together—

and money." He paused and looked around the room. "They were here a moment ago."

"They just stepped out when you finished reading the Will," Brigham said.

"Well, find them and that young man, Tom Trinity, and bring them back here. As the only living heirs, I imagine they'll want to contest this Will. I need to talk to them. Maybe, I won't have to decide this in a courtroom."

A few minutes later, Nora and Paul and a confused looking Tom Trinity came into the library. "Close the door," the Judge said. "It appears Felix Burkhalter has decided, for whatever reason or justification he may have had, to leave his entire estate to you, Tom."

"That's what I've been told. But, it's obvious I can't accept that. Paul and Nora are the rightful heirs. Whatever I need to do, sign over the deed, scratch my name off the Will, just tell me and we can settle this right now."

"There's no need for that, Judge," Nora said. "We don't have any intention of contesting the Will—"

"Now, wait a minute," Tom cut in. "I've no idea what the Colonel had in mind when he did this. But whatever his reason, I don't aim to lay any claim to their rightful inheritance. Will or no Will. Now I got along real well with the Colonel but we never discussed family matters. And I'm not ready to discuss it now. Whatever caused him to do what he did with this Will was his business. So, if you just let me know what I need to do to straighten out this whole misunderstanding, I'll be much obliged."

"It may not be quite that simple, but, I would suggest the three of you think it over, talk it out among yourselves. At least, it

—John E. Cramer—

would be a favor to me. We don't have to settle this matter today. Talk it over. You can work out something and let me know. I'll be free all day tomorrow."

When Nora and Tom began to talk at the same time, the Judge held up his hand. "Save it," he said soberly, "until I see you all in my office tomorrow." Realizing there was another equally important matter he'd not yet attended to, he added. "I'll need you all to stay awhile longer until we can get Colonel Brigham and Marshal Youngman in here to inventory what we've removed from this safe. I'll give you a copy. Tomorrow when you come in to see me, we can also take care of this matter of money the Colonel owes the U.S. Government."

When all the others had gone and Paul and Nora were alone with Tom and Becky, Nora decided that while everyone seemed to be pursuing the truth about important matters this day, she would carry it one step further. This could be Mort's opportunity to let everyone involved know about his discovery after twenty-four years. Without hesitation she extended an invitation to Tom and Becky to have dinner with them at the Circle-K. "Mort told me, before Paul and I left this morning, that he would very much like for me to invite you and Becky for dinner. He told me not to take 'no' for an answer."

"What time would they be expectin' us?" Tom asked.

Without a moment's hesitation, Nora replied. "Well, he said to tell you to come as early as you like, but we won't be having dinner until seven o'clock. He had some business in town but he said he'd be home around three."

"Why not," Tom replied. "I'd be proud for Becky and me to have a good visit with Mister Kane and his son, Joey. Matter of

—Seven Rode Together—

fact, we've got one thing in common. We all were raised in Kentucky. Except, of course, Becky. She spent most of her life in New Orleans. That's where I met her, you know."

"Yes, I know," Nora replied. "I understand you and Becky are planning to be married soon."

Tom nodded. "I was supposed to make the necessary plans for our marriage." He didn't want to mention the Colonel's plans for the wedding. "Of course, now that she's here, we'll be able to make the plans together."

"Perhaps this evening after we decide what Judge Storm has asked us to do, we'll help you and Becky with your planning. If we all pitch in," she said with a smile, "you just might be surprised what Becky and I can accomplish in two weeks."

Surprised at Nora's solution and relieved that he had escaped any mention of the Colonel and the events of the past two weeks, he said, "We're going to need all the help we can get."

"Then, we can expect you for dinner this evening?"

"You can count on it," was Tom's quick response.

Nora watched Tom for a moment as he joined Becky and Paul who'd been getting acquainted. His quick smile, she thought, and something about his walk reminded her of Mort. In fact, she mused, no one could ever deny he wasn't a Kane.

When Tom and Becky arrived at the Circle-K that afternoon, Joey came out of the barn with Sarge trailing behind him. Tom pulled the rig up to the hitching rail, hopped out and was helping Becky down from the spring-board seat when Joey walked up. "Glad you got here early. We're expectin' Pa home anytime now. If you'd like, Sarge and me would be glad to show you around the place."

—John E. Cramer—

"He's a fine looking dog," Tom observed. "How old is he?"

"Nora gave him to me when he was just a pup. He's a Shepherd. Just like Major. He's the one we brought with us when we first came here." He reached down and gave Sarge a pat on the back. "Major was killed a few years back—well, anyway, Nora gave Sarge to me." He paused, and glancing at the rig and then at Becky, he added, "I was hopin' you might be ridin' over this afternoon. I could have givin' you a grand tour of the ranch. We got a line shack up on Settler's Creek. It empties into a lake. We take some good sized fish outta there once in awhile."

"Becky's not used to riding a horse," Tom said. "But she's no amateur when it comes to fishing. She and her Uncle Stanley used to catch some mighty big Marlin out of the ocean."

"I'm afraid I did more watchin' than fishing," Becky said. "And I do ride once in awhile. Perhaps we all can take that tour around the Circle-K another time."

Joey seemed to be looking at Tom most of the time they were talking. He was bursting at the seams to tell Tom what Mort had confided in him the evening before. Strangely enough, Tom seemed to be taking the same measure of Joey. Tom had to fight back the notion to ask Joey about his mother. He was hoping, before they left this evening, Mort would show him the letter he'd received from Lilly. He surmised Joey may have been too young to know much about his mother.

It was after they'd finished dinner that Mort informed Paul about the principle reason he'd decided to make the trip into River Bend. "I'm hopin' you won't think I'm rushing you into setting up your practice," he said, "but while I was in town today, I dropped in to see Clancy O'Riley. Clancy tells me that you could have a

—Seven Rode Together—

first-class office and plenty of space above his newspaper office. At least, it would be a good location until you're able to build an office and quarters at ground level."

As Tom listened to Mort's account of his day in River Bend, he was unable to take his mind off the conversation he'd had with Jeremiah who, now like the others seated around the table, was keenly interested in what was being discussed. He was beginning to believe Jeremiah when he said, "The better you know Mort Kane, the more you're going to find out, there ain't much about him you can't like." Suddenly, he became aware of what Mort was saying at the moment. "Tom, Becky, while Jeremiah and Jeb give Missus Milburn and Amanda a hand in the kitchen, I'd like the rest of us to get together in the parlor. He looked first at Tom and then at Becky, and continued. "There's something the rest of us need to discuss that's been bearing heavy on my mind. I've already talked with Nora and Joey. They know what I'm wanting to get off my chest." The puzzled expression on Paul's face told him that Paul didn't know.

When everyone was seated, Mort, who had gone into the library, entered the parlor with an envelope in his hand. "I'd like you to read this," he said to Tom. "Then perhaps we can discuss what to do about it."

It was then that Tom considered that he was a lucky man that Jeremiah had prepared him for this event. Without having to read the content of the letter, he'd already made up his mind. Mort, indeed, was his father and Joey his brother. Asking 'bout his mother, he decided, could wait for another time.

He read the letter, folded it, and slipped it back into the envelope. After a few moments, Tom walked toward Mort. Mort

— John E. Cramer —

stood up as he came closer, took the letter, and for a moment they looked at one another. It was a moment that neither would ever forget. Struggling to hold back their tears , and in a voice barely above a whisper, Mort said, "Glad to have you home, son. It's been far too long."

The others, Nora, Paul, Joey and Becky, sat quietly. Nora, tears rolling down her face, got up and moved slowly across the room where Mort and Tom stood looking at one another. Joey and Becky joined those huddled together in the center of the room. Paul stood up but made no move to intervene with those most affected until they withdrew from one another's embrace. He stepped between Mort and Tom and clapping each on the back, announced, "This calls for a celebration like nobody's ever seen."

Unnoticed, standing in the doorway, Jeb grinned, "Is this a private shindig, or can the hired help join in?"

"Come on in," Mort said, "and meet the rest of my family."

Jeb and Jeremiah were privy to the scene they were witnessing, but to Amanda and Missus Milburn, whose eyes immediately filled with tears when she looked at Becky and Nora, this was an unexpected event. Missus Milburn was quick to respond. "We can begin the celebration by having our dessert, Nora's favorite, blueberry pie and coffee, in the dining room."

Once seated around the table, Paul stood up, coffee cup in hand, and offered a toast. "To my soon-to-be brother-in-law, so Nora has told me, Mort and his newly reunited son, Tom and his soon-to-be bride, Becky Lou, and Joey, who has always wished for a big brother and now has one, and to all of the others who are witnessing this unforgettable evening, I wish all of you a long and happy life. It's not everyday a man is reunited with his family after

—Seven Rode Together—

24 years." He paused as Jeb leaned over to whisper something in his ear, then added. "Jeb says there's some fully-aged grape wine in the cellar he's been savin' for just such an occasion as this."

When Jeb returned, everyone seated at the table watched while the wine was served. Mort, realizing they were all expecting him to offer a toast, stood up. Immediately, everyone followed his cue. His gaze swept the table beginning with Nora standing beside him and then Paul, Tom, Becky, Jeb, Jeremiah, Blanche, Amanda and finally Joey standing at his left. Choosing his words carefully, he began. "I'm not sure that what kind of drink you hold in your hand makes any difference so long as what you have to say comes from the heart. I can only add my approval to what Paul has said. Everyone here this evening I consider not only to be the best friends a man ever had, but also my family. My heart tells me that Joey, Tom and I have a whole lot of catchin' up ahead of us. I hope we'll be able to keep all the good memories of the past, and put behind all the bad experiences we've had. With that in mind, we've got a couple of weddings to plan for and I've got a feelin' that Nora and I and Tom and Becky will need all the help we can get. Now, if Missus Milburn and Amanda would help Becky and Nora do the planning, Tom and me with Joey, Paul, Jeb and Jeremiah might be able to take care of the rest."

"I'll drink to that," Jeb said.

"And then if you're not savin' it for the wedding," Jeremiah added, "Let's all eat this blueberry pie if we're all through with the speech-makin'."

After the others had retired for the night, and before Tom and Becky returned home, they went into the library with Paul and Nora to decide what they would tell Judge Storm at their meeting

— John E. Cramer —

with him the next day.

The moment they were seated, Paul was the first to speak. "After hearing what Mort had to say this evening, I can't see how this decision will take very long. As we have said, Nora and I have no intention of contesting the Colonel's last Will and Testament. He made his wishes clear. God rest his soul." He paused, looking first at Tom and then at Nora, he added. "I believe that pretty well sums it up."

"Becky and I might be able to accept your decision, but however you may feel now, you and Nora are the rightful heirs. He was your father, not ours. And whatever happened with your relationship with your father is your business, not ours. We don't need to know about it now. That's all in the past—your past—not ours. It's not that we don't appreciate your kind and most generous offer, but there's too much at stake here. Too much, in fact, for us to accept what rightfully belongs to you both."

"If it requires a reason for Nora and I to feel as we do about what you describe as too much at stake for us not to contest the Will, we will then simply have to let it be known that this is our gift to you as a wedding present."

"On one condition," Tom said. "If at any time in the future either you or Nora were to change your mind, I would give you the deed and whatever else I have accepted as your gift. And, I will put that in writing. And if we need a reason to satisfy even the most curious, we will simply explain that we decided to return your wedding gift."

"Fair enough," Paul said. "No need to put it in writing. A simple handshake will do. Since I have learned that Mort Kane is your father, I know for sure, your word is your bond."

—Seven Rode Together—

Tom, with just a faint smile as they shook hands, replied, "It's good to know you have so much faith in the offspring of Mort Kane. But, for the record, my word was my bond long before I discovered Mort Kane was my father."

"Well, then, you two should have even a greater bond in a few weeks," Nora smiled. "Although it may be a relationship that will be difficult to get used to, any future agreements you enter into, will be an uncle dealing with his nephew. I just happen to be a very close friend of the uncle and I know his word is his bond, also."

"I suppose you're right," Tom said, trying hard to keep a straight face, "In a few weeks, it would be impossible not to believe my stepmother when she vouches for my uncle."

The exchange was too much for either of them to ignore any longer and they burst out into laughter. But Tom was having more difficulty in controlling his laughter than either of them.

"It can't be that funny," Paul said finally. "That is, of course, unless we missed something."

Tom shook his head. "No. You didn't miss anything. I suddenly remembered what Jeremiah always told me when someone offered to do something for me and I was hesitant to accept."

Although Tom was still not ready to reveal Jeremiah's advice, he couldn't help remembering. "Never look a gift horse in the mouth, accept it like you was entitled."

"Well, now I know we won't take long in Judge Storm's chambers tomorrow." Paul said. "I'll simply tell him, we're not contesting the Will. Whether you inherit the Colonel's estate or we do, it makes no difference. It's all in the family!"

Chapter 34

Judge Storm sat in his chambers contemplating the scheduled ten o'clock appointment with the Colonel's heirs and the young man, Tom Trinity, who had inherited the entire Burkhalter Estate. He felt reasonably certain that Paul and Nora, once they had thought it over, would decide to contest the Colonel's Will. When they arrived the Judge wasted no time getting to the point. "I suppose that since you've all had an evening together, you have reached a mutual satisfactory solution to how you intend to settle this problem with the Colonel's Last Will and Testament."

"Actually," Nora began, "there is no problem. It's my understanding that a problem requires a solution among two or more parties where there are differences of opinions. And since neither Paul nor I have any desire to contest Father's Will, there is no problem."

"You have any idea what you and Paul are giving away to someone you've just met and hardly know?"

"We are all well aware of that." Nora replied. "But are you

—Seven Rode Together—

aware that Tom is perfectly agreeable with whatever Paul and I decide to do? And are you also aware that no matter who inherits the Burkhalter Estate, it will still remain in the family?"

"Remain in the family?" Judge Storm asked. "You mean, of course, in a manner of speaking because you are all friends?"

"No. That's not what I mean," Nora said shaking her head. "You see, we learned last night that Mort is actually Tom's father. It's a long story and we have no intention of keeping it a secret. We have undeniable proof that they are father and son. That's not all, Mort and I have already set a date for our wedding." And she added quickly, "And you're invited. Now, do you understand Father's estate, no matter what happens, still remains in the family?"

"And we're all in agreement," Paul chimed in, "to try to undo at least some of the harm that the Colonel did to others while he was accumulating some of his holdings."

For the next few moments following Paul's remarks, Judge Storm sat quietly, nodding his head, eyeing each of them separately, while he rubbed the back of his neck. "Well," he began finally, "I believe this meeting is over. Unless, of course, you would care to share with me some of these wrongs you expect to right."

"For starters," Nora said, "We can certainly see that Blanche Milburn gets back the deed to her home here in River Bend. And the same goes for Dutch Van Huss and his family who lost their ranch when Father foreclosed. Their home still stands as they left it. Tom met Dutch in Oklahoma Territory where he's trying to eke out a living running a trading post. Tom says Dutch would jump at the chance to get back to ranching if ever the opportunity arose. And there are other things we believe can be done, given time to think about it. All the things we have in mind can be

—John E. Cramer—

accomplished, leaving Tom the Double-B ranch and the money it'll require to sustain the operation."

Judge Storm broke into a broad smile. "It sounds to me like you all have this figured out. But if you run into anything when you need my help, I'm available"

"There's one thing that we could use some help with," Nora said. "There's a parcel of Double-B land that's located in the northwest section of the ranch. It covers several thousand acres. It's mostly forest-land that surrounds a clear lake. We'd like to turn this over to the Government to become a National Park in memory of our mother, Emily Burkhalter."

She paused momentarily and after glancing at Paul, she added, "We believe it would be a fitting memorial to a truly great lady."

"Well, now, that shouldn't be too difficult to accomplish," Judge Storm said. "And I will personally see to it that your wishes are carried out." Turning to Tom, he asked. "You've been listening to what Nora has been saying. And you are in agreement?"

Tom nodded. "Yes sir."

"Then, the only thing left for me to do is accept your invitation to attend your wedding, Nora. And I might add you couldn't have made a better choice. As for you, Tom, I'm happy to know you and Mort, after all these years, are together as father and son. I'm happy for both of you. And I understand you and Becky will soon be exchanging vows."

"We'd be honored to have you attend our wedding, too."

"And, when might that be?"

"Well, to be honest with you, I don't know. You see, Nora and Becky are working on that right now. It wouldn't be too much

—Seven Rode Together—

of a surprise if they decided to set a date for a double wedding ceremony."

After they'd gone, Judge Storm mused, "Well, Felix, changing your Will really didn't change a thing." For a moment he leaned back in his chair and gazed at the ceiling. "A double wedding ceremony. That'll be a first in River Bend."

His meditation was interrupted by a tapping on his office door. Before he could invite him in, Clancy O'Riley's head appeared around the door. "Care if I come in?"

"Looks like you already are." Judge Storm said.

"Just saw your visitors leave. Did they tell you that Tom Trinity is really Mort Kane's son?"

"Yes," Judge Storm said soberly. "What's so strange about a man finally being united with his son? I'll admit that it doesn't happen every day, but stranger things happen most every day somewhere in the world. We just don't hear about them."

"I know, I know," Clancy admitted. "But Tom Trinity works for Colonel Burkhalter—"

"Not anymore he doesn't."

"I *know* the Colonel's dead. But Trinity still works at the Double-B for the Colonel's kids. Why wouldn't he be working with Mort at the Circle-K?"

"O'Riley," the Judge began, "you call yourself a newspaper man, then you get a piece of information and start jumping to conclusions. Didn't you ever learn to get all the facts first and then come to some more reasonable conclusion? Why would young Tom Trinity be working for his Pa on the Circle-K when he has his own ranch to look after?"

"His *own* ranch? You mean he—?"

—John E. Cramer—

"That's exactly what I mean. Tom Trinity is the new owner of the Double-B."

Clancy cut loose with a long, low whistle. "You mean the Colonel left the ranch to him, not Paul and Nora? Won't Paul and Nora have something to say about that?"

"They've already said what they had to say. That's what our meeting was about this morning. The three of them seem satisfied with what they've worked out and Tom is the new owner of the ranch. Matter of fact, they all seem to be more interested in the upcoming weddings than they were the Colonel's Will. If they're satisfied, that's all that matters."

Clancy shrugged. "I can't argue with that. Guess I'll head back to the office. Maybe, I'll just take the rest of the day off." He got up from his chair and headed for the door. "I've been thinkin', in view of all that's happened, this might just be the right time to break out a brand new bottle of Irish whiskey I've been savin' for just such an occasion, and having a good stiff drink before lunch, but, I really don't enjoy drinking by myself."

"Now there's one thing I can't argue with. And if you can hold up for a minute, I'll get my hat and join you. Later, if you're a mind to, we can head out to Eagle Creek and wet a line."

—Seven Rode Together—

of a surprise if they decided to set a date for a double wedding ceremony."

After they'd gone, Judge Storm mused, "Well, Felix, changing your Will really didn't change a thing." For a moment he leaned back in his chair and gazed at the ceiling. "A double wedding ceremony. That'll be a first in River Bend."

His meditation was interrupted by a tapping on his office door. Before he could invite him in, Clancy O'Riley's head appeared around the door. "Care if I come in?"

"Looks like you already are." Judge Storm said.

"Just saw your visitors leave. Did they tell you that Tom Trinity is really Mort Kane's son?"

"Yes," Judge Storm said soberly. "What's so strange about a man finally being united with his son? I'll admit that it doesn't happen every day, but stranger things happen most every day somewhere in the world. We just don't hear about them."

"I know, I know," Clancy admitted. "But Tom Trinity works for Colonel Burkhalter—"

"Not anymore he doesn't."

"I *know* the Colonel's dead. But Trinity still works at the Double-B for the Colonel's kids. Why wouldn't he be working with Mort at the Circle-K?"

"O'Riley," the Judge began, "you call yourself a newspaper man, then you get a piece of information and start jumping to conclusions. Didn't you ever learn to get all the facts first and then come to some more reasonable conclusion? Why would young Tom Trinity be working for his Pa on the Circle-K when he has his own ranch to look after?"

"His *own* ranch? You mean he—?"

—John E. Cramer—

"That's exactly what I mean. Tom Trinity is the new owner of the Double-B."

Clancy cut loose with a long, low whistle. "You mean the Colonel left the ranch to him, not Paul and Nora? Won't Paul and Nora have something to say about that?"

"They've already said what they had to say. That's what our meeting was about this morning. The three of them seem satisfied with what they've worked out and Tom is the new owner of the ranch. Matter of fact, they all seem to be more interested in the upcoming weddings than they were the Colonel's Will. If they're satisfied, that's all that matters."

Clancy shrugged. "I can't argue with that. Guess I'll head back to the office. Maybe, I'll just take the rest of the day off." He got up from his chair and headed for the door. "I've been thinkin', in view of all that's happened, this might just be the right time to break out a brand new bottle of Irish whiskey I've been savin' for just such an occasion, and having a good stiff drink before lunch, but, I really don't enjoy drinking by myself."

"Now there's one thing I can't argue with. And if you can hold up for a minute, I'll get my hat and join you. Later, if you're a mind to, we can head out to Eagle Creek and wet a line."